GUITAR

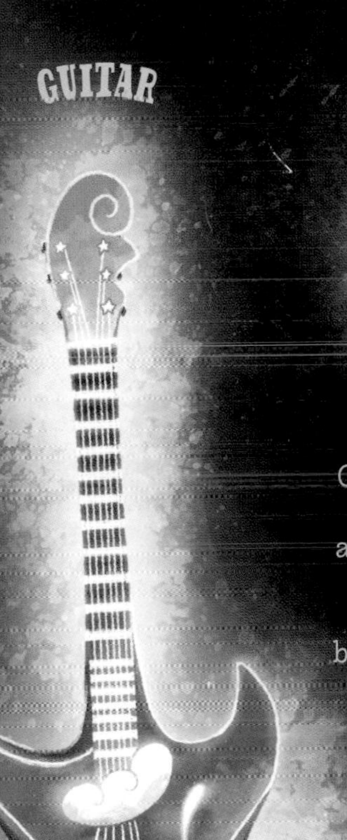

Instrument

Each girl in the Star Darlings band has a unique musical talent that helps her light up the stage.

LAVENDERITE

Power Crystal

Once a Star Darling has granted her first wish and returns to Starland, she receives a very special treasure—a beautiful Power Crystal.

NECKLACE

Wish Pendant

A Wish Pendant is a powerful accessory worn by a Star Darling. On Wishworld, it helps her identify her Wisher and store the ever-important wish energy.

Libby

Libby loves helping everyone. She's generous and gracious and wants to make things right for Starlings and Wishlings alike.

Libby can be impulsive and irresponsible at times in her efforts to make everyone happy.

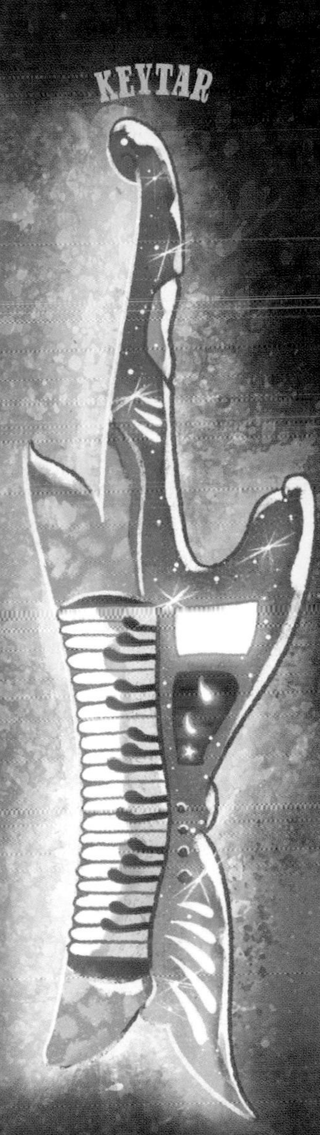

Instrument

Each girl in the Star Darlings band has a unique musical talent that helps her light up the stage.

CHARMELITE

Power Crystal

Once a Star Darling has granted her first wish and returns to Starland, she receives a very special treasure—a beautiful Power Crystal.

NECKLACE

Wish Pendant

A Wish Pendant is a powerful accessory worn by a Star Darling. On Wishworld, it helps her identify her Wisher and store the ever-important wish energy.

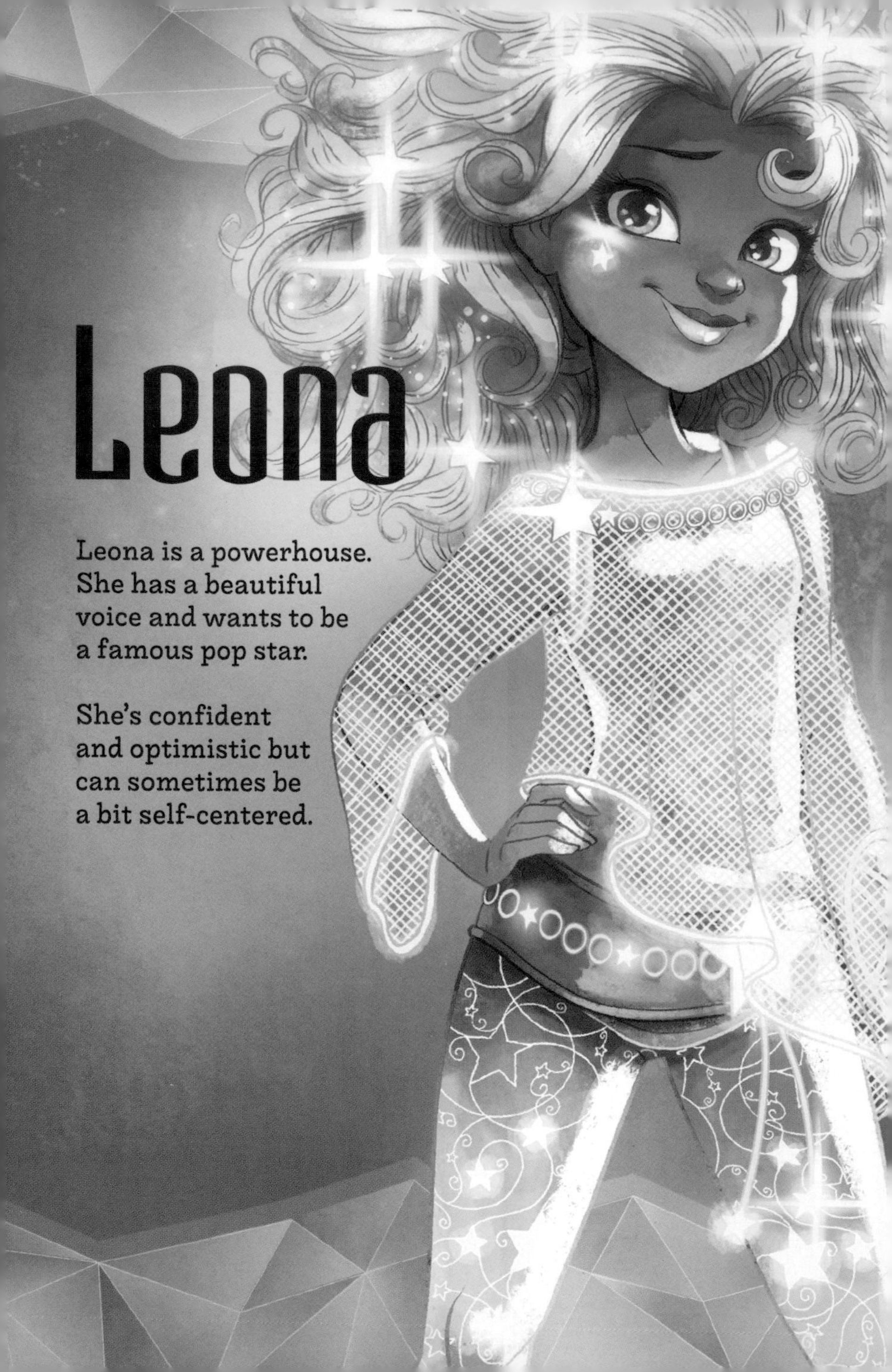

Leona

Leona is a powerhouse. She has a beautiful voice and wants to be a famous pop star.

She's confident and optimistic but can sometimes be a bit self-centered.

CUFF

Wish Pendant

A Wish Pendant is a powerful accessory worn by a Star Darling. On Wishworld, it helps her identify her Wisher and store the ever-important wish energy.

GLISTEN PAW

Power Crystal

Once a Star Darling has granted her first wish and returns to Starland, she receives a very special treasure—a beautiful Power Crystal.

MICROPHONE

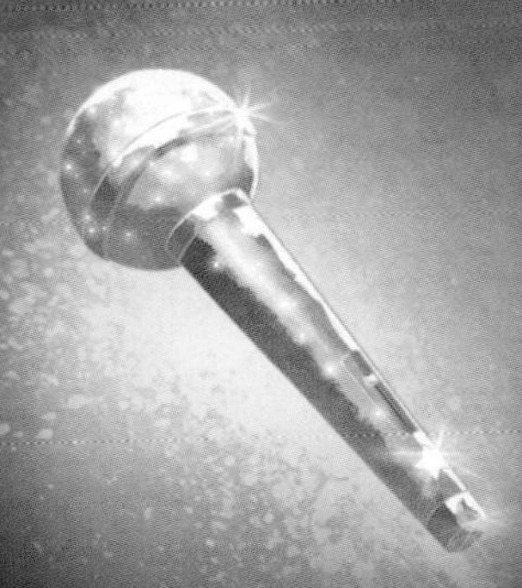

Instrument

Each girl in the Star Darlings band has a unique musical talent that helps her light up the stage.

Sage and the Journey to Wishworld

Libby and the Class Election

Leona's Unlucky Mission

Shana Muldoon Zappa and Ahmet Zappa
with Zelda Rose

Disney Press
Los Angeles • New York

For information address Disney Press,
1101 Flower Street, Glendale, California 91201.

Printed in the United States of America
Reinforced Binding
First Paperback Edition, May 2016
Sage and the Journey to Wishworld First Paperback Edition, September 2015
Libby and the Class Election First Paperback Edition, September 2015
Leona's Unlucky Mission First Paperback Edition, January 2016
1 3 5 7 9 10 8 6 4 2

FAC-025438-16106

ISBN 978-1-4847-8295-8

For more Disney Press fun, visit www.disneybooks.com

Halo Violetta Zappa. You are pure light, joy, and inspiration. We love you soooooo much.

May the Star Darlings continue to shine brightly upon you. May every step upon your path be blessed with positivity and the understanding that you have the power within you to manifest the most fulfilling life you can possibly dream of and more. May you always remember that being different and true to yourself makes your inner star shine brighter. And never ever stop making wishes.

Glow for it. . . .
Mommy and Daddy

And to everyone else here on "Wishworld":

May you realize that no matter where you are in life, no matter what you look like or where you were born, you, too, have the power within you to create the life of your dreams. Through celebrating your own uniqueness, thinking positively, and taking action, you can make your wishes come true. May you understand that you are never alone. There is always someone near who will understand you if you look hard enough. The Star Darlings are here to remind you that there is an unstoppable energy to staying positive, wishing, and believing in yourself. That inner star shines within you.

Smile. The Star Darlings have your back. We know how startastic you truly are.

Glow for it. . . .
Your friends,
Shana and Ahmet

Student Reports

NAME: Clover
BRIGHT DAY: January 5
FAVORITE COLOR: Purple
INTERESTS: Music, painting, studying
WISH: To be the best songwriter and DJ on Starland
WHY CHOSEN: Clover has great self-discipline, patience, and willpower. She is creative, responsible, dependable, and extremely loyal.
WATCH OUT FOR: Clover can be hard to read and she is reserved with those she doesn't know. She's afraid to take risks and can be a wisecracker at times.
SCHOOL YEAR: Second
POWER CRYSTAL: Panthera
WISH PENDANT: Barrette

NAME: Adora
BRIGHT DAY: February 14
FAVORITE COLOR: Sky blue
INTERESTS: Science, thinking about the future and how she can make it better
WISH: To be the top fashion designer on Starland
WHY CHOSEN: Adora is clever and popular and cares about the world around her. She's a deep thinker.
WATCH OUT FOR: Adora can have her head in the clouds and be thinking about other things.
SCHOOL YEAR: Third
POWER CRYSTAL: Azurica
WISH PENDANT: Watch

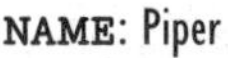

NAME: Piper
BRIGHT DAY: March 4
FAVORITE COLOR: Seafoam green
INTERESTS: Composing poetry and writing in her dream journal
WISH: To become the best version of herself she can possibly be and to share that by writing books
WHY CHOSEN: Piper is giving, kind, and sensitive. She is very intuitive and aware.
WATCH OUT FOR: Piper can be dreamy, absentminded, and wishy-washy. She can also be moody and easily swayed by the opinions of others.
SCHOOL YEAR: Second
POWER CRYSTAL: Dreamalite
WISH PENDANT: Bracelets

Starling Academy

NAME: Astra
BRIGHT DAY: April 9
FAVORITE COLOR: Red
INTERESTS: Individual sports
WISH: To be the best athlete on Starland—to win!
WHY CHOSEN: Astra is energetic, brave, clever, and confident. She has boundless energy and is always direct and to the point.
WATCH OUT FOR: Astra is sometimes cocky, self-centered, condescending, and brash.
SCHOOL YEAR: Second
POWER CRYSTAL: Quarrelite
WISH PENDANT: Wristbands

NAME: Tessa
BRIGHT DAY: May 18
FAVORITE COLOR: Emerald green
INTERESTS: Food, flowers, love
WISH: To be successful enough that she can enjoy a life of luxury
WHY CHOSEN: Tessa is warm, charming, affectionate, trustworthy, and dependable. She has incredible drive and commitment.
WATCH OUT FOR: Tessa does not like to be rushed. She can be quite stubborn and often says no. She does not deal well with change and is prone to exaggeration. She can be easily sidetracked.
SCHOOL YEAR: Third
POWER CRYSTAL: Gossamer
WISH PENDANT: Brooch

NAME: Gemma
BRIGHT DAY: June 2
FAVORITE COLOR: Orange
INTERESTS: Sharing her thoughts about almost anything
WISH: To be valued for her opinions on everything
WHY CHOSEN: Gemma is friendly, easygoing, funny, extroverted, and social. She knows a little bit about everything.
WATCH OUT FOR: Gemma talks—a lot—and can be a little too honest sometimes and offend others. She can have a short attention span and can be superficial.
SCHOOL YEAR: First
POWER CRYSTAL: Scatterite
WISH PENDANT: Earrings

Student Reports

NAME: Cassie
BRIGHT DAY: July 6
FAVORITE COLOR: White
INTERESTS: Reading, crafting
WISH: To be more independent and confident and less fearful
WHY CHOSEN: Cassie is extremely imaginative and artistic. She is a voracious reader and is loyal, caring, and a good friend. She is very intuitive.
WATCH OUT FOR: Cassie can be distrustful, jealous, moody, and brooding.
SCHOOL YEAR: First
POWER CRYSTAL: Lunalite
WISH PENDANT: Glasses

NAME: Leona
BRIGHT DAY: August 16
FAVORITE COLOR: Gold
INTERESTS: Acting, performing, dressing up
WISH: To be the most famous pop star on Starland
WHY CHOSEN: Leona is confident, hardworking, generous, open-minded, optimistic, caring, and a strong leader.
WATCH OUT FOR: Leona can be vain, opinionated, selfish, bossy, dramatic, and stubborn and is prone to losing her temper.
SCHOOL YEAR: Third
POWER CRYSTAL: Glisten paw
WISH PENDANT: Cuff

NAME: Vega
BRIGHT DAY: September 1
FAVORITE COLOR: Blue
INTERESTS: Exercising, analyzing, cleaning, solving puzzles
WISH: To be the top student at Starling Academy
WHY CHOSEN: Vega is reliable, observant, organized, and very focused.
WATCH OUT FOR: Vega can be opinionated about everything, and she can be fussy, uptight, critical, arrogant, and easily embarrassed.
SCHOOL YEAR: Second
POWER CRYSTAL: Queezle
WISH PENDANT: Belt

Starling Academy

NAME: Libby
BRIGHT DAY: October 12
FAVORITE COLOR: Pink
INTERESTS: Helping others, interior design, art, dancing
WISH: To give everyone what they need—both on Starland and through wish granting on Wishworld
WHY CHOSEN: Libby is generous, articulate, gracious, diplomatic, and kind.
WATCH OUT FOR: Libby can be indecisive and may try too hard to please everyone.
SCHOOL YEAR: First
POWER CRYSTAL: Charmelite
WISH PENDANT: Necklace

NAME: Scarlet
BRIGHT DAY: November 3
FAVORITE COLOR: Black
INTERESTS: Crystal climbing (and other extreme sports), magic, thrill seeking
WISH: To live on Wishworld
WHY CHOSEN: Scarlet is confident, intense, passionate, magnetic, curious, and very brave.
WATCH OUT FOR: Scarlet is a loner and can alienate others by being secretive, arrogant, stubborn, and jealous.
SCHOOL YEAR: Third
POWER CRYSTAL: Ravenstone
WISH PENDANT: Boots

NAME: Sage
BRIGHT DAY: December 1
FAVORITE COLOR: Lavender
INTERESTS: Travel, adventure, telling stories, nature, and philosophy
WISH: To become the best Wish-Granter Starland has ever seen
WHY CHOSEN: Sage is honest, adventurous, curious, optimistic, friendly, and relaxed.
WATCH OUT FOR: Sage has a quick temper! She can also be restless, irresponsible, and too trusting of others' opinions. She may jump to conclusions.
SCHOOL YEAR: First
POWER CRYSTAL: Lavenderite
WISH PENDANT: Necklace

Introduction

You take a deep breath, about to blow out the candles on your birthday cake. Clutching a coin in your fist, you get ready to toss it into the dancing waters of a fountain. You stare at your little brother as you each hold an end of a dried wishbone, about to pull. But what do you do first?

You make a wish, of course!

Ever wonder what happens right after you make that wish? *Not much*, you may be thinking.

Well, you'd be wrong.

Because something quite unexpected happens next. Each and every wish that is made becomes a glowing Wish Orb, invisible to the human eye. This undetectable orb zips through the air and into the heavens, on a one-way trip to the brightest star in the sky—a magnificent place called Starland. Starland is inhabited by Starlings, who look a lot like you and me, except they have a sparkly glow to their skin, and glittery hair in unique colors. And they have one more thing: magical powers. The Starlings use these powers to make good wishes come true, for when good wishes are granted, the result is positive energy. And the Starlings of Starland need this energy to keep their world running.

In case you are wondering, there are three kinds of Wish Orbs:

1) GOOD WISH ORBS. These wishes are positive and helpful and come from the heart. They are pretty and sparkly and are nurtured in climate-controlled Wish-Houses. They bloom into fantastical glowing orbs. When the time is right, they are presented to the appropriate Starling for wish fulfillment.
2) BAD WISH ORBS. These are for selfish, mean-spirited, or negative things. They don't sparkle

at all. They are immediately transported to a special containment center, as they are very dangerous and must not be granted.

3) IMPOSSIBLE WISH ORBS. These wishes are for things, like world peace and disease cures, that simply can't be granted by Starlings. These sparkle with an almost impossibly bright light and are taken to a special area of the Wish-House with tinted windows to contain the glare they produce. The hope is that one day they can be turned into good wishes the Starlings can help grant.

Starlings take their wish granting very seriously. There is a special school, called Starling Academy, that accepts only the best and brightest young Starling girls. They study hard for four years, and when they graduate, they are ready to start traveling to Wishworld to help grant wishes. For as long as anyone can remember, only graduates of wish-granting schools have ever been allowed to travel to Wishworld. But things have changed in a very big way.

Read on for the rest of the story. . . .

Sage and the Journey to Wishworld

Prologue

"Are we there yet?" Sage asked eagerly.

The only answer was a loud snore from Sage's father, Leonard. As soon as he had programmed the coordinates into their Starcar's console, he had fallen sound asleep—as usual. Sage's mom, Indirra, didn't even look up from her reading. That, too, was usual. Sage thought her mother should have been the one who was nodding off, as she was deep in a scientific holo-journal. But as one of Starland's leading research scientists, she found it engrossing. Luckily, Indirra didn't take her daughter's lack of interest in her chosen field as an insult; rather, she took it as a challenge.

Sage's seven-year-old twin brothers, Archer and Helio, paid no attention, either. They sat cross-legged on the floor, cheering on their cyber-wrestlers, which were engaged in a fierce battle. "Pin him! Pin him!" they yelled in support of their opposing fighters.

Sage stared at her family. *How can they be so blasé?* she wondered. It was no ordinary day. It was, actually, the most exciting day of her life! She leaned toward the dashboard and lifted a finger, letting it hover over the hyper-speed button. Should she press it? Suddenly, her hand was gently slapped away by her ever-watchful grandmother, a tough old lady everyone called Gran, who then uttered the words Sage had been hearing since she was a tiny Starling.

"Patience, Sage," she said.

Sage rolled her eyes. "You know I don't have any," she responded. Sage smiled sweetly at her grandmother before she added, "Just like you."

Gran shrugged and handed Sage a wrapped candy from her large purse. Sage popped the candy into her mouth and promptly spat it out. Moonberry. Dis-*gus*-ting. Sage sighed and glanced out the window. She caught a glimpse of her reflection. Slightly sparkly skin, just like all Starlings had. Long, thick glimmering lavender hair hanging in braids that nearly reached her waist. A pointy chin and large twinkling violet eyes that gave her a slightly mischevious look. Cheeks permanently flushed pink. Rosebud lips that were usually curved into a playful smile but were drawn into an irritated frown at the moment. The car was traveling so quickly that the scenery was one big blur. But to Sage, it felt like they were going in slow motion. She just wanted to get there already!

Finally, when Sage thought she might scream, they were almost there. She looked out the window and gasped. The long, straight road that led to the gates of her brand-new boarding school was lined with towering trees, their spindly branches covered in brilliant lavender blooms. The branches stretched up into a tangled canopy overhead, forming a colorful tunnel that led to the entrance.

Gran spoke, startling Sage. "Kaleidoscope trees," she told her granddaughter. "I haven't seen those since I was a young girl. They're quite rare. I forgot how beautiful they are. Keep watching—they'll change color." Sure enough, the blossoms began to turn a cheerful shade of pink before their eyes.

"Starmendous," said Sage. "I wonder how they change color like that."

"It's because they are composed of ninety-four percent iridusvapor," said Sage's mom without looking up. "Of course."

Sage and Gran exchanged grins. Indirra never missed an opportunity to share scientific information with her family. Her powers of concentration were a family legend. Once she had held a holo-conference call while the twins, convinced they needed to bathe their pet glowfur, chased it all around the house, wreaking havoc around her. She hadn't even seemed to notice. But Gran more than made up for that with her constant attention to detail and her habit of stating the obvious.

The car hovered up to the high black iron gates, which had an oddly lovely design of delicate curlicues and dangerously sharp spikes. Beyond them lay the campus of Starling Academy. Sage caught a quick glimpse of neat walkways, hedges trimmed into whimsical shapes, glittering buildings, and a lone white tower reaching high into the sky. The school, on the outskirts of Starland City, the largest metropolis on Starland, had an enviable location. The campus was near the violet-hued Luminous Lake and the stunning Crystal Mountains. The breathtaking site had inspired students for hydrongs of staryears. In the distance Sage could see the mountains in all their multicolored glory. The clouds parted and a beam of sunlight broke through, lighting up the campus with a rainbow glow while transforming the low-lying clouds into delicate spun-sugar confections. Sage shook her head. She was excited to finally be at Starling Academy, and it was almost too much to take in at once. She was superbly, stupendously, starmendously excited. That was what she had been working so hard for. Nothing was going to stop her now.

The gates rolled open slowly and the car inched forward, then came to a stop in front of a small glass booth. A Bot-Bot guard appeared and held up a hand scanner. The Starcar's window lowered, and without a moment's hesitation, Sage reached out and placed her palm on the scanner. It lit up bright blue. Accepted.

"Welcome to Starling Academy, Sage," the guard said. It handed her a holo-book.

She took it and replied, "Star salutations," the traditional Starling thank-you. She gave the Bot-Bot guard a friendly wave, which, as expected, was not returned. Her little brothers broke into peals of laughter at the clipped cybernetic voice. "Welcome. To. Starling. Academy. Sage," they echoed.

Gran looked over her shoulder. "It's the Student Manual," she whispered.

"Are you sure?" Sage replied, pointing to the on-screen title. "I thought it was the cafeteria menu."

"Fresh," said Gran, mock seriously.

Sage loved her grandmother fiercely but also liked to tease her. Fortunately, Gran liked to give as good as she could take.

Sage's mom shut off her holo-journal and looked around at everyone, blinking slowly. "Are we here already?" she asked brightly.

Sage rolled her eyes. "Yes, Mom," she said.

Sage's father startled awake with a loud snort. "What—who—where am I?" he sputtered. That sent the boys on another round of giggles.

Sage ignored them. She looked around, took a deep breath, and squinched her eyes closed as the car glided through the entrance and the gates rolled shut behind them. She could really picture herself happy there. *I wish for big, exciting things to happen to me here*, she thought.

Her wish would come true.

And then some.

CHAPTER 1

"Good afternoon, Miss Sage. Are you ready to begin your tour?"

Sage spun around.

"Up here," the voice said.

Sage craned her neck. Hovering in the air over her family members' heads was a medium-sized metallic orb. It flashed in the sunlight, forcing Sage to look away.

"What *is* that thing?" Gran asked, shielding her eyes and squinting.

"It's a floating Bot-Bot guide," explained Sage's father. "The neighbors hired one on their trip to Booshel Bay. They're supposed to be quite informative."

"Affirmative," said the Bot-Bot guide in its clipped tone. The boys giggled, but a stern look from Gran shushed them. “I am MO-J4 and I am quite informative, if I do say so myself.” He blinked when he spoke.

“So can we go to the dorm now?” Sage asked.

The Bot-Bot guide paused, apparently running the request through his program to determine its validity. “Negative,” he answered. “Before you head to your dormitory room and bid farewell to your family, you must first receive a tour to familiarize yourself with the campus.”

“Startastic,” said Archer, rolling his eyes.

Gran poked him in the shoulder. “Don’t be rude, young man,” she said.

“Sorry, Gran,” he said sheepishly.

Sage glanced around. More Bot-Bot guides had appeared and were taking other new students and their families on their tours, setting off in all directions. She turned back to her family, then did a double take. Wait—someone was missing.

“Where’s Mom?” she asked.

“She’s right he—well, she *was* right here,” said her father, looking around. “Oh, don’t worry, we’ll find her. You know how she’s always wandering off.”

Sage did know. Her mother was a very busy—and curious—woman. She was often sent on trips to distant locations to fact-find and to give talks about her specialty, interstellar positive wish energy. All Sage knew was that it took her mom away from the family frequently. That was why Gran had come to live with them when the twins were born.

"If you will follow me, we will begin our tour in the Star Quad, the heart of our state-of-the-art Starling Academy campus," announced MO-J4. He led them onto a moving walkway, which brought them to a lush green lawn. "Note the grass, perfect for relaxing or picnicking," the guide pointed out. "Here you can see the dancing fountain, the shifting hedge maze, and the band shell, where concerts are held."

"Impressive," said Sage's father, nodding.

Sage spotted a girl with an off-the-shoulder gold tunic and a halo of golden curls around her face standing on the band shell stage. She was singing and practicing some dance moves, apparently putting on her own private concert. Several students were lounging on the edge of the splashing fountain, which was tiled in a mosaic of pleasing shades of blue.

"And over here you will find the hedge maze," said MO-J4.

Sage and her family turned their attention to a tall wall of neatly trimmed greenery with an entrance cut into the side. Her little brothers' eyes lit up, and they took off toward it, disappearing into the maze without a backward glance.

"Boys!" called Gran. "We're still on the tour! Come back!"

"They'll be fine," MO-J4 assured her. "The constantly shifting paths of the hedge maze will keep them occupied for quite a while, and there are guides to help visitors find their way out if necessary." MO-J4 zoomed down to Sage's ear level and said, "Students, however, must discover the secrets of the maze all by themselves."

"No problem," said Sage in a tone more confident than she felt. She looked around. Where *was* her mother? It was just like her to disappear when Sage wanted her around. This was a big deal. Having her whole family—even her annoying little brothers—nearby would have been nice. But no, everyone seemed to want to do their own thing. Except Gran and Dad, of course.

MO-J4 next took them to the Illumination Library, a circular room crammed from floor to ceiling with thousands of tiny holo-books. Down the center of the room ran tables glowing with soft light, surrounded by lounge readers with built-in lamps. There was a padded window seat with fluffy pillows in front of each of the large windows.

Gran was impressed. "You should spend most of your time here when you're not in class," she said to her granddaughter with a nod. Sage tried not to smile as the old woman then checked out a lounge chair, which immediately adjusted to her height, weight, and preferred reading position.

Gran was less interested in the Lightning Lounge, which was housed in the same building. Sage, however, was enthralled by what she saw. It was where students went during their downtime to socialize and relax.

The lounge's main floor was split between the snack area, which was stocked with every treat and beverage the students could desire, and the sitting area, which was brightly colored and filled with floor pillows, low tables, fireplaces, fluffy rugs, soft, sumptuous chairs, and couches grouped perfectly for getting together with friends.

Downstairs was a party room big enough for dances with other schools, which were held several times a year. Next they went upstairs to cozy relaxation rooms, which sensed your mood as soon as you walked in and chose appropriate music and changed the lighting accordingly.

"Press that button on the wall to your right, Miss Sage," said MO-J4.

Sage obliged and then jumped as the ceiling high

above their heads began to roll back. "A retractable roof for stargazing," said MO-J4. "All the seats recline fully for optimal viewing comfort."

Sage smiled. They really had thought of everything to help students relax and enjoy themselves during their downtime. MO-J4 next brought them to the Celestial Café, the dining hall where students' meals were served. The view from the wall of windows was holo-card worth—the violet-hued Luminous Lake and the stunning Crystal Mountains. Sage stared at the shiny peaks. She had been dying to explore the Crystal Mountains ever since she had received a crystal for her Bright Day. Sage's dad shook his head. "Look at all this!" he said, taking in the warm lighting, the softly playing music, the table set with finery, and the Bot-Bot waiters at the students' beck and call. "When I was in school we had to bring our own lunch!"

"We must take good care of our students, sir," said MO-J4. "They need to be well fed so they can concentrate on their studies!"

They next went to Halo Hall, the largest building on campus, where all the classes were held. "Connected to this building is a tower with the famous Wishworld Surveillance Deck, accessible only to students, faculty, and graduates," MO-J4 explained.

Sage got a thrill of excitement as they peered into a neat classroom, comfortable and inviting. MO-J4 lingered in the Cybernetics Lab, a gleaming room filled with cyber-building equipment. "My home," he explained with a hint of pride in his voice.

"And then we'll go straight out these doors to the balcony, where we can get a stunning view of the fruit orchards to the north and south and of course the incomparable Crystal Mountains and Luminous Lake to the west." Everyone stepped outside and took in the view, nodding appreciatively. It was a truly breathtaking sight.

"Lovely, simply lovely," Gran murmured.

Sage's father put his hand on his daughter's shoulder. "I can't believe this is really happening," he said. "Our little Sage is about to start Starling Academy."

Sage was about to groan, "Dad, you're embarrassing me," but she held it in. Her father's eyes were shiny, and the last thing she wanted was for him to start crying. Plus he was right. This was momentous. She just didn't feel like talking about it.

"In the middle of the lake are the Serenity Gardens, accessible only by boat; and of course you can see Stellar Falls in the distance," MO-J4 noted.

"On the other side of the lake is our brother school,

Star Preparatory. Perhaps your little brothers will attend that school someday."

"Perhaps," muttered Gran before Sage could respond. The thought of her wild little brothers being studious enough to attend the prestigious school seemed like hydrongs of staryears away to Sage.

After showing them the gigantic practice Wish-House and the faculty residences—freestanding homes, each with a small backyard and garden—MO-J4 said, "Next we will move on to the Radiant Recreation Center. This is our last stop before we go to your dormitory. The recreation center is a state-of-the-art building with equipment available for every interest and sport we play on Starland. It is where our champion E-ball team, the Glowin' Glions, play every—"

Sage couldn't take the suspense any longer. "Can I go to my room now, please?" she asked. She was dying to see her room and, more important, meet her roommate.

"Sage," said Gran. "Your manners!"

MO-J4 paused again to see if the change of plan fit in with his program. "Affirmative," he concluded. Sage and her family were led past the round, gleaming rec center, along a pathway to a large white building. They stopped in front of the steps that led up to the entrance.

"There are two dormitories on campus: this is the Little Dipper Dorm, for first- and second-year students, and nearby is the Big Dipper Dorm, for third- and fourth-year students. Rooms are completely furnished for the students, with all the comforts of home, and roommates are carefully chosen to both complement and challenge each other."

Complement and *challenge*, thought Sage. *Interesting*.

Sage's father spoke up. "Sage was told not to bring anything but the clothes on her back," he said, a bit anxiously. "Are you sure she'll have everything she needs?"

"I guarantee it," said MO-J4. "Don't worry. You'll soon see what I mean."

"All right, then," said Sage's father.

"This is where I say good-bye," said MO-J4. "Once you step through the doors, hop right onto the Cosmic Transporter, which will take you directly to your room. It was a pleasure to meet you, Miss Sage. I hope we'll meet again. I will send your brothers to you. Good luck, and don't forget to count your lucky stars."

"Star salutations!" Gran and Sage's father called.

"Star salutations," Sage repeated. But MO-J4 was already gone, floating off to find her brothers.

"You should start reading it right away," Sage's

grandmother said once they had gone inside and were standing on the Cosmic Transporter, a moving sidewalk that looped throughout the entire dormitory.

"Reading what?" Sage asked.

"The Student Manual," said Gran exasperatedly.

"Oh, right," said Sage, fishing around in her pocket until she located the holo-book. She pressed a button and the manual was projected into the air in front of her. "'Welcome to Starling Academy,'" she read aloud. "'Now that you have explored the campus and are settling in, keep one extremely important thought in mind: the future of Starland depends on you.

"'As every Starling knows, the positive energy that comes from the Wishlings who live on Wishworld is our most precious natural resource. We rely on it to power our Starcars, illuminate our lights, and, in short, provide Starland with the energy it requires to function every starday.

"'You are tasked with learning how to help make Wishers' wishes come true so you can become members of the next generation of Wish-Granters. That way, the Wishers will keep making these crucial wishes, and life, for Starlings and Wishlings alike, will continue as we all know it.

"'As a student at Starling Academy, you will receive extensive, rigorous training in wish identification, wish fulfillment, wish energy capture, wishful thinking, wish probability and statistics, plus art, music, dance, and a variety of sports. . . .'"

Sage's voice trailed off. "Blah, blah, blah, blah, blah," she concluded, shutting down the holo-book with a flick of her wrist. She rolled her eyes. "No pressure or anything!" she said.

Gran laughed, but then her wrinkled face grew serious. "Sage," she scolded, "you need to pay attention. There could be some important information in that manual. It might even be on an examination!"

"What examination?" Sage asked teasingly. Her grandmother was so old-fashioned sometimes.

"An *important* examination," Gran insisted.

Sage leaned against the railing of the Cosmic Transporter. As they passed open doorways, she peeked into several of the rooms. There were girls crying as they said good-bye to their families, and others who waved merrily as their parents departed. That all made Sage even more impatient. She simply couldn't wait to see her room and meet her roommate. Finally, the transporter began to slow down. Sage straightened up as she and her family were deposited right in front of a doorway—room 261. They all stood there for a moment in silence.

They hesitated in front of the door. Suddenly, Helio and Archer came running down the Cosmic Transporter, nearly knocking into a student and her parents, who stared angrily at the boys. They jumped off the mover and dramatically rolled on the floor before coming to a stop. They bounced to their feet, not even out of breath.

"This place is pretty starmendous!" Helio shouted. "Did you see the boathouse?"

"I guess this is it," said Sage, feeling an unfamiliar fluttering in her stomach. "I . . . I think I'm a little nervous!" she admitted. Gran gave her a quizzical look. Her dad raised his eyebrows and gave her shoulder a quick squeeze.

At the same time, Archer—just as impatient as she was—reached up and slapped the hand scanner in the middle of the door.

There was a red flash and an irritating buzzing noise.

"Access denied," the Bot-Bot voice said sternly.

"Out of my way," said Sage, ruffling her brother's hair as she pushed past to show him she really wasn't mad, just pretending. She placed her hand on the scanner. "Welcome, Sage," the Bot-Bot voice said pleasantly as the scanner glowed a bright blue. They were in the right place.

The door slid open, and there stood Sage's mother.

"There you are!" she exclaimed, as though they had been the ones who had wandered off.

"How did you get in?" Sage's brother demanded.

"Oh, Sage's roommate was here," explained Indirra.

"Where is she?" Sage asked excitedly.

"She stepped out for a starmin," her mother replied.

"Where did you go, anyw . . ." Sage started. But then her eyes took in the dorm room furnishings and her voice trailed off. She stared around in disbelief. Now she understood why she had been told to come to Starling Academy empty-handed. The room was amazing. They had decorated it just the way Sage had hoped. They had asked so many questions on the school application, but this far exceeded any expectations she'd had. It reflected her personality and her love of lavender to perfection. It even had holo-powered windows so Sage could control the view!

"They've thought of everything," said her mother.

The room was circular, Sage's favorite shape, and she had a round bed and what looked like an extraordinarily comfortable round chair. Two softly glowing plants stood at either side of the bed—the perfect nightlights, in her opinion. A glimmering chandelier hung from the ceiling.

Her father blinked. "Unbelievable," he said.

Her roommate's side was pretty, too, with a star-shaped rug, a glowing staircase that led to a bed that looked a little like a very large cradle to Sage, and a single gigantic picture window with a window seat covered in sumptuous pillows.

Sage's father immediately sat on Sage's bed. "Comfy," he said.

Sage gaped at the rows of bookshelves that lined her roommate's walls. "Look at those holo-books," she marveled. "You think my roommate is a librarian or something?"

Her brothers laughed.

"Um, hello," said a small voice. Everyone turned to the open doorway, where a baby-faced girl with pale skin, big round glasses, and pinkish-white hair done up in perky little pigtail buns stood. It looked like she was trying to decide whether to step inside or run away. Despite the girl's embarrassment, Sage noticed that the girl's lashes were so thick and dark that they almost looked fake. She was wearing a light, loose shirt with spaghetti straps, shorts, swirly leggings, and pale pink ballet slippers, which laced up her legs. She was so small and neat-looking that she made Sage, who was tall and lean, feel like she was all gangly arms and legs. The girl seemed to make a decision, and she walked up to Sage uncertainly. "I'm Cassie," she said softly.

Sage gulped and smiled at her roommate. "Sorry!" she said. "It's just that you have so many books."

Gran elbowed her in the side. "And, um, I'm sure they're all very interesting!" Sage said. Impulsively, she lunged forward to hug her new roommate. Startled, the girl took a step back. She lost her balance and knocked into a pile of holo-books which sat on a table. The two girls bent down to pick them up at the same time and cracked heads. Sage rubbed her sore head and gulped again. What a way to make a first impression!

Her brothers burst out laughing. "Startastic, Sage!" Helio cried.

Sage glared at them, then turned toward her new roommate. "Sorry about that," she said. She had already apologized two times in as many starmins. That had to be some sort of new roommate record! "Um, pleased to meet you. I'm Sage and this is my family." She made a sweeping gesture. "You already met my mother. The man lying down is my father, Leonard. This is my grandmother. You can call her Gran. And the two little boys who just disappeared under your bed are my twin brothers, Helio and Archer."

Cassie looked mildly surprised at that bit of news. She stood up, adjusted her glasses, and gave Sage a tight smile—more like a grimace, actually.

"So no offense at the librarian comment?" asked Sage. "I was just trying to be funny. Just ignore it. I didn't mean any harm. The room looks great. Very homey. Actually, I love libraries. And librarians. I mean, who doesn't?" she said all in a rush.

Cassie shrugged. "No offense taken."

Sage could tell that maybe a tiny bit had been taken. But she was certain it was nothing she couldn't fix.

After taking a quick peek under her bed, Cassie began to rummage through her already jumbled drawers. Sage's father got up from her bed and stared out the window, lost in thought. Gran took one look at the slightly rumpled bed and, without warning, stripped off the linens and began remaking it. Gran certainly liked to keep busy! Sage wandered around the room, taking it all in. She stopped at the nearest closet and slid the door open.

"No!" Cassie shouted. She darted across the room,

reached past Sage, and slammed the door shut. "That's *my* closet!" She spun around, her cheeks flushed. She took a deep breath to collect herself. "I mean, um, *that* is your closet," she said more calmly, pointing across the room. Puzzled, everyone stared at her for a moment.

Note, thought Sage, *roommate is very private about her clothes.* She wouldn't be making that mistake again.

Gran fluffed Sage's pillow, then reached over to pick up a small handheld device that was sitting on Sage's desk. "What's this?" she asked.

"Got me," said Sage.

"That's a Star-Zap," Cassie explained. "We all get one. We have to keep it with us at all times, because that's how the school corresponds with us." She then gave Sage a quizzical look. "It's discussed in great detail in the Student Manual."

Gran tsk-tsked at Sage, who shrugged.

"Can we go home now?" Archer whined as he crawled out from under Cassie's bed.

Sage's mom gave a brisk nod. "Time to go home," she said. Sage's dad turned to Sage slowly. "I guess . . . it's time to leave," he said reluctantly.

"Look what I found!" cried Helio, rolling out from underneath Cassie's bed, holding a small bag of pellets.

"These look like Green Globules!" Sage gawked. They *did* look remarkably similar to the food her brothers fed their pet glowfur. (It also loved to eat flowers late at night.)

Cassie's eyes widened in alarm. "Oh, no!" she cried. "Um . . . that's actually a special snack I brought from home." And before everyone's astonished eyes, she selected a pellet and popped it into her mouth. "*Mmmm*, delicious," she mumbled. But her face told a different story.

Well, that was weird, Sage thought. Her family just stared at Cassie.

"That really did look like a Green Globule," Archer said, shaking his head. "Disgusting." He knew that quite well, Sage remembered, because he had once eaten one himself on a dare from his twin.

"Well, thanks for everything," Sage said brightly to her family. "Bye!" She hated long, drawn-out farewells. When Sage had said good-bye to her friends back home, she had made it short and sweet, too. Sure, she was sad. But there was no sense in making something painful even harder than it needed to be.

Her father squeezed her tight. "I'm so proud of you, Toodles," he whispered into her ear, using her embarrassing family nickname. He opened his mouth as if he was going to say something else, then just settled for another hug.

That gave Sage an uncomfortable lump in her throat. She squirmed out of his grasp. "Good-bye, Dad," she said.

Gran hated good-byes, too. "See ya around, kid," she said with a wink.

At their father's urging, the twins each gave Sage a hug, as well, but each one was so brief that it was as if she had a contagious illness they were afraid of contracting. Still, Sage knew they would miss her, if only because she helped them with their homework and would, if asked nicely, eat all their garble greens for them so they could get dessert.

Sage's mom put her hands on Sage's shoulders and gave her a quick, firm embrace. She stepped back and looked deep into Sage's violet eyes. "Make me proud, my dear," she said. Then she leaned forward and whispered in her ear, "You're startacular, and don't you forget it."

Sage snapped back her head to stare at her mother. "Th-thanks, Mom," she stammered. Her mom's compliments were rare, so when she gave one, you knew she meant it. When Sage was younger, she used to be jealous of kids whose mothers smothered them with accolades. "You're the brightest star in the galaxy" or "You glimmer like a supernova." But as she got older, she grew to appreciate her mother's measured but heartfelt words of praise. It felt like Sage had earned them.

Studies had never been easy for her, and she sometimes felt like she was disappointing her mom. Sage had had to work hard for every I (which stood for Illuminated, the top grade a student could receive) she was awarded. So her mother's words really meant a lot.

Indirra touched her daughter's cheek, then joined the rest of the family in the hallway. After a moment, Sage slid the door closed behind them.

The two girls stared at each other for a moment.

Sage flopped down on the bed Gran had remade so neatly, and clutched her pillow to her chest. "So, tell me everything about you," she said to Cassie. "Don't leave anything out!"

Cassie looked around the room wildly, positively panicked. "Um . . . I . . ."

Just then their Star-Zaps beeped. They both looked down at their display screens: REPORT TO THE STAR QUAD IN TWENTY STARMINS FOR THE START OF THE WELCOME PROCESSION.

"Welcome procession?" said Sage.

Cassie gave her a look.

"It's in the Student Manual?" Sage guessed.

"It's in the Student Manual," Cassie answered.

Sage considered that. "Want to fill me in?" she asked.

"Well, it's a Starling Academy tradition going back hydrongs of staryears. New students parade around the campus as the faculty and upperclassmen welcome them. Everyone wears fancy clothes and it's said to be really special. Supposedly, we're about to receive the most amazing outfits we've ever seen," said Cassie.

As if on command, there was a knock at the door. When they opened it, a Bot-Bot deliverer was hovering in the hallway, holding aloft two remarkable outfits—one lavender, one white.

"Wow," said Sage, grabbing the dresses. "Star salutations." She brought them inside and handed the white one to Cassie.

"It's startacular," said Cassie softly, touching the shiny material.

Sage nodded. "It's like they took the best parts of all my favorite dresses and made one perfect outfit."

"Once we're dressed, we'll head to the quad. Lady Stella will greet us and the procession will begin," Cassie said.

Sage looked at her beautiful dress, her eyes shining. She grinned. Things were finally starting to happen. It was about time!

CHAPTER 2

"How do I look?" Cassie asked shyly. Sage took one last look in the mirror and turned to face her roommate.

"Beautiful," she told her. Cassie was wearing a sheer white dress embroidered with a sprinkling of silvery stardust. The waist was cinched with a wide silver sash tied in the back in a big bow. Underneath she wore a simple glimmering silver slip. On her head was a wide headband of glowing moons and stars. Glitter slippers completed the ensemble.

"You look lovely, too," Cassie told Sage.

"Star salutations," replied Sage. She felt magical. Although her usual style of dress was simple and comfortable, she absolutely loved the floor-length dress and its layers upon ruffled layers of the softest lavender fabric. She admired the sheer bell sleeves and smoothed her braids, threaded with the tiniest twinkling lights she had ever seen.

The two girls headed to the Star Quad. Before she knew it, Sage was separated from Cassie, swept away in a sea of students, all smiling and laughing. It seemed as if everyone, even the girls who had had the hardest time saying good-bye to their families, was delighted to be at Starling Academy and thrilled to be in her fancy best. There were girls in ball gowns and dresses with long trains, and others with huge ruffles that spilled down their fronts. They wore jeweled tiaras, fluffy boas, and hats of all shapes and sizes: a fascinator with flowers, a towering bright pink top hat with a face-obscuring net.

Sage felt like she was part of a big, happy, festive party as they all slowly made their way to the Star Quad. A girl with long, shiny hair the same shade of pink as cotton candy stumbled on her long train and momentarily clutched Sage's arm for support. "Isn't this exciting?" she cried, looping her pink skirt over her arm. Sage nodded. It was actually the very definition of exciting, in her opinion. Finally, everyone was gathered in the Star Quad. A tall, regal-looking woman stepped onto the stage. She had sparkling olive skin and bright red lips and wore a long, flowing midnight-blue gown with enormous sleeves that shimmered like the heavens at night. A single golden star sat in the middle of her forehead. But it was her headdress that really took Sage's breath away—a galaxy of stars clustered around her head, neck, and shoulders, spinning and glittering. A hush fell over the crowd.

"I am Lady Stella," she said, although she needed no introduction. She was so famous as headmistress of the most prestigious school in all of Starland that her name was often in the holo-papers and her face on the news. Some truly obsessed girls even dressed up like Lady Stella on Light Giving Day—the holiday celebrating the first starday of the Time of New Beginnings, when Starling children dressed up in costumes and went door-to-door distributing newly bloomed flowers.

Every student in the room had gone through the same rigorous process in the hope of attending Starling Academy: application forms, essays, testing, recommendations. Only a small percentage of those who applied were granted an interview with the headmistress. And an even smaller percentage of girls was accepted. Starling Academy had a 100 percent attendance rate: every student who was admitted chose to enroll. Every year.

Lady Stella continued. "Welcome to Starling Academy and the student procession. It is a time-honored tradition for our newest students to dress in their finest clothes and walk through the campus to be received by students and faculty. We welcome you to the Starling Academy community and congratulate you on your acceptance. We thank you for joining us in the pursuit of knowledge and positive wish energy." She raised her arms. "Let the procession begin!"

A marching band began to play, and the girls started the procession. Teachers and the second-, third-, and fourth-year students, also dressed in their finest clothes, lined up along the walkways and leaned down from windows and balconies to cheer. Sage spotted a student, dressed almost entirely in black with accents of hot pink, standing apart from the others.

Iridescent bubbles filled the air, releasing the sweet scent of glimmerberries as they popped. There was something so special, so amazing about being a part of the experience. When the new students passed the Big Dipper Dorm, girls standing on the balcony cheered, showering them with flower petals that changed color as they floated down and disappeared when they hit the ground.

WELCOME NEW STUDENTS appeared in the sky in

glittering script. Sage grinned as she took in the dizzying beauty of the scene. *I will remember this forever*, she thought.

After the procession, the students were led into the auditorium, where Sage settled into a plush seat. *Very comfy*, she thought as she softly bounced up and down.

Just then she remembered something: *Hey, where's Cassie?* Sage craned her neck and looked around the room. She spotted her roommate several rows behind her, wearing a serious expression, her arms folded tightly across her chest. Sage gave Cassie a huge wave and pointed to the empty seat next to her. But the seat was immediately filled by a girl with pale blue hair with bangs and a fringed dress of the same exact color.

"Sorry," said Sage pleasantly, "but this seat is taken."

"Yeah," said the girl, an unpleasant smile on her face. "By me."

Sage was fuming, but she decided to let it go. She turned back to Cassie and shrugged.

Everyone in the audience spoke in hushed voices and sat up very straight, well aware of the significance of that starday. Some of the girls were already whispering together as if they had been friends forever. Sage felt a stab of excitement. It was possible that somewhere in that room was her future best friend. But then she thought her future biggest enemy could be there, too.

The crowd burst into thunderous applause as Lady Stella stepped onto the stage. "Welcome to Starling Academy," Lady Stella began. "I hope you enjoyed the welcome procession. You are an extremely exceptional group of students. Almost every girl on our star who has reached the Age of Fulfillment applies for a spot in Starling Academy. You've all worked very hard to get here and we are happy to have you."

Sage felt a flush of pride. Simply sitting there in the auditorium was already an accomplishment. "And now, you are about to begin the most important work of your lives." Lady Stella paused.

"As we all know, you are all here to begin your training to become Wish-Granters. Once your education is complete, you will be on your way to collecting the precious wish energy that keeps Starland operating." She paused and nodded. "And as you also know, Wishlings make many wishes," she continued. "As they are about to blow out their birthday candles." Sage sniffed appreciatively as the smell of chocolate cake filled the room. "On a shooting star streaking across the sky," Lady Stella added. The lights went out and the ceiling twinkled with starlight, a bright flash splitting the sky. She continued. "As they blow on a dandelion gone to seed." Sage reached up to touch one of the small white tufts that appeared and danced around the room. "As they toss a coin into a fountain." Students squealed as they were sprinkled with cool water droplets. "And I don't need to tell you that the wishes of Wishling children, in particular, are the purest and produce the greatest amount of energy."

The headmistress nodded and continued. "As everyone knows, when a wish is made, it turns into a glowing Wish Orb, invisible to the Wisher's eyes. The wish rapidly flies through the heavens to Starland. When the Wish Orb arrives, it is collected by a Wish Catcher, who determines whether it is a good wish, a bad wish, or an impossible wish.

"The Good Wish Orbs sprout pretty sparkly stems and are brought to the Wish-House where they are tended to and observed by trained Wish-Watchers. It can take anywhere from a few starmins to a few staryears for a wish to be ready to be granted. That is when it emits the most wonderful, magical glow. It is the most amazing sight to see, even if a Starling has seen it a thousand times.

"Then the Wish Orb is presented to the appropriate Starling for wish fulfillment. Once a good wish is granted and the wish energy collected, the Wish Orb transforms into a unique and beautiful Wish Blossom.

"Bad Wish Orbs are another story. They sprout stems that don't sparkle and are immediately transported to a special containment center, as they are very dangerous and must not be granted.

"Impossible Wish Orbs sprouts stems that sparkle with an unbearably bright light. They are taken to a special area of the Wish-House with tinted windows to cut down on the glare they produce. They are monitored in the hopes that one day they can be turned into good wishes that are within our powers to help grant. Here at Starling Academy we have a state-of-the-art practice Wish-House where you will learn to do exactly that."

Sage rolled her eyes. Every Starling toddler knew that stuff—boring! She sighed and turned around to look at Cassie. Surely she was feeling restless, too. But Cassie was completely focused on the headmistress, with the same very serious expression on her face. Unable to catch her roommate's eye, Sage looked around the room. She spotted a girl whispering to her seatmate. Her orange hair was done in a beautiful upswept style. The girl must have sensed someone's eyes on her, because she turned around, caught Sage staring, and stuck out her tongue at Sage. Sage didn't know whether to laugh or be mad. She quickly looked away. What a saucy Starling! Sage turned her attention back to the headmistress, who was still talking.

". . . and so I am happy to report that this year's class is our most talented yet. Be prepared to study hard, learn a lot, and accomplish great things, and soon you will be on your way to graduating and becoming Wish-Granters," Lady Stella concluded. "Are there any questions?"

Sage raised her hand. The headmistress shaded her eyes. "Yes?" she said.

"When do we get started?" Sage asked.

Heads swiveled around and there were a couple of giggles. Sage barely noticed.

"And what is your name, my dear?" Lady Stella asked.

"Sage," she replied.

The headmistress smiled and nodded as if she had known that all along. "Before you know it, Sage," she said. "Before you know it."

Lady Stella clapped her hands together. "So, now, everyone take out your Star-Zaps. You will be meeting in small groups for your formal orientation. You will receive a message telling you where you need to go."

Sage placed her communicator on her lap and stared at the blank screen expectantly.

"I'm group one!" shouted a girl.

"Me too!" said another.

Sage looked over the shoulder of the girl sitting in front of her. The girl's screen lit up. GROUP 3, it said. Then: REPORT TO CONSTELLATION CLASSROOM 313.

Sage watched in dismay as girl after girl received her assignment and headed to her classroom, some joining up with fellow classmates and chattering excitedly. Still, her screen remained maddeningly blank.

Finally, it lit up: SD. She stared at the letters, her brow furrowed. That made no sense.

What does that mean? she wondered. The next message read REPORT TO HEADMISTRESS'S OFFICE.

Sage nodded. Headmistress's office? Now things were getting interesting!

The girl sitting next to Sage peered down at Sage's communicator from beneath her long, pale blue bangs. "'SD'?" she said. "What does *that* stand for?" She turned to the girl next to her and elbowed her in the side before adding snidely, "I know—Super Dorky!"

Sage thought fast. "Actually, it means . . . Superbly Delightful," she countered.

The girl paused for a moment. "So Doubtful," she finally crowed, obviously pleased with herself.

Well, you are most definitely *not going to be my new best friend*, thought Sage as she stood, pushed her way past the girl, and headed down the aisle.

Sage jumped as a cold hand reached out and grabbed her elbow. She spun around, ready for another confrontation. But it was Cassie, biting her lip and looking worried. "Sage?" she said. "I just got a weird message, and I'm not sure what to think."

"SD?" asked Sage.

Cassie's face brightened. "Yes, you too?" she asked.

"Me too," replied Sage with a nod.

"Superstar!" Cassie said, looking very relieved.

"I think it must be something good," mused Sage.

Cassie blinked. "I . . . I hope so," she said. "But I'm a little worried. What if we're in trouble or something?"

Sage laughed. How funny. That had never even crossed her mind. "Only time will tell!" she said. She leaned down slightly to link arms with her roommate, and the two walked to the headmistress's office together. It was nice to face the unknown with someone familiar by your side. Even if you had just met her for the first time a short while earlier. Even if she ate strange snacks. And had weird closet issues. Even then.

CHAPTER 3

Sage counted again. Twelve. Including herself, there were twelve girls seated at the round silver table in the headmistress's enormous office. Each seat had a holo-place card in front of it. Sage was sitting between Tessa, a girl with bright green curls who seemed really kind, and Adora, whose eyes were an amazing shade of light blue. Everyone was dressed in their finery, and it looked like they were all sitting down to a fancy dinner party—minus the place settings and the food, of course. Sage was across from a girl in a black mask with pink sequins. Sage frowned as she took in the girl's magenta eyes and fuchsia hair. She wore a puffy layered skirt and a short-sleeved rhinestone-trimmed jacket with an enormous ruffled collar over a hot-pink-and-black-striped blouse. She also had on black lace gloves. She was very striking. Wasn't she the same girl Sage had spotted standing on the balcony during the procession? And didn't that mean she was an upperclassman? What was she doing at new student orientation? It was all very confusing.

Sage then looked curiously at the others around the table, matching each face with the name on the place card. Adora, Tessa, Gemma (who was chatting away; Sage recognized her as the girl who had stuck out her tongue in the auditorium), Vega, Leona (who had been singing and dancing on the quad), Clover, Libby (the girl in pink who had tripped on her train during the procession), Piper, Astra, Cassie, and Scarlet (the masked upperclassman). Sage noticed that Vega looked a bit worried and Piper seemed lost in thought, twirling a piece of her seafoam-green hair around her finger. Libby was studying everyone intently.

Astra, who somehow managed to make her bright red gown look sporty, was attempting to have a friendly chat with Cassie, who was shooting glances around the room, apparently unable to concentrate on small talk. Sage herself felt like she was going to jump out of her skin if she didn't find out what was going on. Immediately.

Then the office door slid open and Lady Stella glided inside. She looked at the girls assembled around the table, carefully studying each one. Sage gazed right back at her. Lady Stella was even lovelier up close. Her sparkling olive skin was smooth and flawless, and her eyes danced in the light from her glimmering headpiece.

Sage watched as the headmistress closed her eyes for a moment, as if to collect her thoughts. Then she said something truly incredible.

"You twelve girls are about to make Starling history," she pronounced solemnly.

There were several gasps. "Moons and stars!" Cassie cried, looking apprehensive. Sage, on the other hand, felt elated. This was good. Very good.

"What in the stars are you talking about?" cried Gemma.

"Gemma!" scolded Tessa. "Don't be rude!"

Sage stared at the two girls. Did they know each other?

"But I really want to know!" Gemma exclaimed. "I mean, you can't just say something like that and leave us hanging! I mean, I'm really . . ."

Tessa leaned forward and placed her hand over Gemma's mouth.

Everyone stared. *That* seemed pretty inappropriate.

Lady Stella laughed at their shocked faces. "Gemma and Tessa are sisters," she told everyone.

"Okay, back to business. Let me explain what I mean. We have always known that the greatest amount of positive energy is generated by granting the wishes of young Wishlings. Traditionally, this has been done only by Starling adults who have graduated from a wish-granting academy. But I have a theory that if the wishes of young Wishlings were to be granted by young Starlings, this special combination would produce an even greater amount of positive wish energy. My plan is for Starling Academy students to go down to Wishworld for the first time in history and test this theory."

A stunned silence filled the room.

"It makes perfect sense," she said. "Young Starlings could attend school, join teams and clubs, and blend in seamlessly with young Wishlings."

Sage looked down at the table, barely holding back a small smile. Starling Academy students traveling to Wishworld and granting wishes? Amazing! She was pretty sure she knew what was coming next, and she held her breath in anticipation.

"And who are these lucky students? All of you, of course! Twelve talented girls who are as unique as those they are going to help. Four third years—Scarlet, Leona, Tessa, and Adora. Four second years—Piper, Vega, Clover, and Astra. And four first years—Sage, Cassie, Libby, and Gemma."

The twelve girls stared at Lady Stella in silence as the weight of her words sank in.

Cassie was the first to speak. She looked stricken. "I don't get it!" she cried. "Why me? Why us?"

Lady Stella smiled a secret smile. "It will all be revealed in due time," she said.

The room began to buzz with excited chatter. Sage could see why Cassie might be apprehensive—Starlings had to train for four years before they were allowed to travel down to Wishworld to grant wishes! But to Sage, this was nothing but a thrilling, unexpected gift.

Lady Stella held up a hand for silence, and everyone immediately stopped talking.

"If our calculations are correct, the amount of positive energy you collect could be up to a thousand times greater than usual."

The headmistress had a serious look on her face. "There is just one thing you must know: this is highly controversial and must remain a secret. To the rest of the school, you are students, just like them. You will attend classes with your fellow classmates. You will join teams and participate in clubs. To the rest of Starling Academy, you will be no different from any other student."

She smiled. "Except for one small thing: during the last period of each starday, you will report to a specially built soundproof classroom for a class only for you. In order to divert attention away from our secret plans, the rest of the school will think you are part of a monitored study group."

"You can't possibly mean us, too!" exclaimed Leona, indicating herself and the other seven older girls.

"I mean every one of you," Lady Stella answered.

"Wait a starmin," said Vega, clearly dismayed. "You mean no one will know that we're on this special mission? That they will think we need extra help?"

"This is not about personal glory," Lady Stella said sternly. "If you don't want to be a part of Starling history, you can turn down your spot. Another student will certainly jump at the opportunity."

Lady Stella extended her arms dramatically. "So," she said. "Are you all in?"

"Yes!" shouted Sage right away.

Astra gave her a dirty look. Clearly she had wanted to be the first to speak. "Yes," she said.

All around the table, the girls accepted the challenge. Some were more emphatic in their response than others.

When it was finally Cassie's turn, she paused for what felt like an eternity before stealing a glance at Sage, who nodded at her encouragingly. "Yes," she whispered.

"Starmendous!" said Lady Stella. She then pointed to the middle of the table, where a large pile of glittery golden boxes in all shapes and sizes sat. Sage blinked. She was fairly certain the center of the table had been empty just a moment ago. From the looks on the other girls' faces, they thought the same thing.

The headmistress picked up a small square box. "Clover," she announced. "Please stand up." She opened the box to reveal a jeweled purple barrette. She clipped it into Clover's hair, where it winked in the light.

"This is your Wish Pendant," Lady Stella explained to Clover. She looked around the room. "You will each receive your own. As you all know, students usually receive these upon graduating, but you are getting them now. You may take it off at night, but you should wear it every day. Wish Pendants are of utmost importance on Wish Missions. They will glow when you make initial contact with your Wisher. They will collect the wish energy when the wish is granted. And, since you are Star Darlings, your Wish Pendants will hold extra special powers," she explained mysteriously. "This will be revealed as your education progresses."

Lady Stella continued to hand out the boxes. A watch for Adora. Bracelets for Piper. Sporty Astra looked quite pleased with her wristband. Tessa admired her brooch. Gemma was presented with earrings. Libby got a necklace of tiny clustered stars, and Scarlet received star-shaped buckles for her boots. Leona fastened a thick cuff on her arm. Cassie received a pair of very cool-looking star-shaped glasses, which she seemed delighted with, despite herself. Vega accepted her belt buckle solemnly.

Lady Stella slipped a sparkling gold star pendant around Sage's neck. It hung from a long lavender rope accented with tiny stars. It was beautiful to look at, and she could somehow sense that it had great powers. She found herself trembling as she admired it.

There was a rap at the door. Lady Stella inclined her head and the door slid open. A short, stocky woman with purple hair stood uncomfortably in the doorway. "Allow me to introduce Lady Cordial, our head of admissions," Lady Stella said.

"Hello, s-s-s-students," Lady Cordial said in a low voice.

"Lady Cordial is our admissions director and is instrumental in helping select each incoming class. I have decided to share your secret mission with her. She, a Wish-Watcher who will notify us when our wishes are ready to be granted, and a few of your professors will be the only Starling Academy members who know of your mission. Please introduce yourselves to her." So one by one, the girls stood up and said their names, doing the traditional Starling bow. Lady Cordial clasped her hands together after each bow, the Starling way.

"S-s-s-star s-s-s-salutations, girls," she said when they were done.

"Star salutations, Lady Cordial," the girls chorused.

"Now go to the Celestial Café, have a nice dinner, and get a good night's sleep. Your classes begin first thing tomorrow morning. Your schedules have already been sent to your communicators," Lady Stella told them.

Sage felt a shiver of excitement run down her spine as she stood up from the table. Cassie, her eyes large behind her glasses and her face even paler than usual, made a beeline for Sage. "I don't know about this, Sage. What have we gotten ourselves into?"

Sage patted her roommate's arm reassuringly. *What have we gotten ourselves into?* she thought. *Just the most amazingly startastic thing ever!* Cassie turned and headed out the door. Sage followed her and paused to tap her elbows together three times as inconspicuously as she could.

"Three times for good luck," someone said.

Startled, Sage turned around to find the headmistress smiling down at her. "You are eager to begin," Lady Stella said. "I like that!" She turned to walk away.

"Lady Stella!" Sage called.

"Yes?" said the headmistress.

"What does SD stand for, anyway?" Sage asked.

Lady Stella nodded. "I was wondering when someone was going to ask. You will be known—in private only, of course—as the Star Darlings."

Sage smiled. "Star Darlings," she whispered to herself. It was a good name. She liked it. A lot.

CHAPTER 4

"Let me see your schedule," said Sage that evening, standing in the middle of the room in a lavender nightgown. She had cleaned her teeth with her brand-new toothlight and taken a sparkle shower to keep her skin shiny and glittery, and she was almost ready for bed. Cassie accessed her holo-schedule, and Sage synced hers up with a flick of her wrist. Their one class in common—Lighterature, fifth period—lit up.

As first years, they had all introductory classes. Sage had Wishers 101 first period, Intro to Wish Identification second, and Intro to Wishful Thinking third. After lunch she had Astral Accounting, Lighterature, Intro to Wish Fulfillment, and The Golden Days. On Shinedays she had P.E.—Physical Energy—and every Lunaday she had Aspirational Art. And, as Lady Stella had told them, the last-period class of each starday was labeled Study Group.

"Well, we'll have Lighterature and our SD classes together—better than nothing," said Cassie as she crawled into bed and pulled up her patchwork quilt to her chin. "So do you think it's going to be hard to be in classes with everyone else? We have this huge secret we have to keep from basically everybody."

Sage fluffed her pillow. "It's not going to be easy," she agreed. But she couldn't help grinning. "But it's just so exciting! I don't even know how I am going to sleep tonight!"

"Speak for yourself," said Cassie, yawning. "Are you ready for me to shut off the lights?"

"Sure," said Sage. She watched with amusement as Cassie squinched up her face, concentrating on dimming the lights. The girl was having so much trouble that Sage secretly gave her a little help.

"There," said Cassie. "I'm getting much better at my energy manipulation!"

Sage smiled and pulled the covers over her head. She anticipated tossing and turning, but she was out in moments. It had been a draining starday.

Sage was in the Illumination Library, doing some research. She wasn't making a peep. But for some reason, the librarian was telling her to be quiet. "*Shhhhhhh!*" she hissed.

Confused, Sage looked up from her Star-Zap and gave her a "Who, me?" look.

"*Shhhhh!*" said the librarian, more loudly this time.

Sage shook her head. "But I'm not talking," she said in a loud whisper.

"*Shhhhhhh!*" the librarian said again, suddenly morphing into the tall, rude girl with the pale blue bangs from the auditorium. "Didn't you hear me say *shhhhh*?" Her eyes grew mean. "Oh, that's right, you're an SD—Sad Disappointment!"

"That's not what it stands for!" Sage yelled. "I'm a Star Darling! I'm going to travel to Wishworld right now! I'm going to collect one thousand times the wish energy of anyone else."

Everyone in the library spun around and goggled at her, their mouths open in surprise. All too late, Sage realized what she had done.

"Oops," she said, her heart sinking.

Her adversary laughed cruelly. "You told the secret. Now you can't be a Star Darling anymore," she screeched. "Too bad for you!" She put her finger to her lips: "*Shhhhhhhhhhhhhhhhhhhhhhhhhhhhhhhhhh!*"

Sage woke with a start. The room was still dark. It was the middle of the night and she had been dreaming. But then she heard that strange shushing noise again—and it was coming from right across the room. Sage rubbed her eyes. Cassie, whispering and giggling, was bathed in a golden glow. Was it Sage's imagination, or did she hear a funny little musical buzzing sound? It was quite lovely, actually.

I must still be dreaming, Sage thought. And she promptly fell back asleep.

When she woke up the next morning, Cassie was sliding her closet door closed. "Hey, Cassie," said Sage, sitting up in bed. "I had the weirdest dream last night. You were giggling and there was this weird, beautiful sound. . . ."

Cassie's eyes widened behind her glasses. "Dreams can be so strange," she said quickly.

Sage frowned. It had all seemed so real. She got out of bed, opened her closet door, and pulled on a long sleeveless lavender dress, lavender tights, and gladiator sandals that laced up her legs. She looked at her reflection in the mirror. Nice: flowing and comfortable, her favorite combination.

"Ready for breakfast?" asked Cassie.

Sage's stomach rumbled. "Sounds good to me!" she said. She picked up her communicator from the desk and put it in her pocket. As she took one quick glance back over her shoulder, she thought she saw a faint glow coming from Cassie's closet. She was about to say something, but Cassie practically pushed her out of the room. By the time the door slid shut behind them with a *whoosh*, it had completely slipped Sage's mind.

They hopped on the Cosmic Transporter and joined other students as they made their way to the Celestial Café. Adora was waving to them from across the room, where she sat with her roommate, Tessa, as well as Libby and Gemma. "Nice table," said Sage, pulling out a chair and sitting down. The view of the Crystal Mountains was starmendous.

As the rest of the Star Darlings arrived for breakfast, Adora waved them over.

"I have an idea," said Astra, looking around. "Let's make this our table. A bunch of girls who graduated last year used to sit here, so now it could be ours."

Scarlet rolled her eyes, but everyone else seemed to think that was a good idea.

When Sage's breakfast arrived, she discovered that she didn't have much of an appetite. Too excited to eat, she picked at her starcakes. She was amused that the usually anxious Cassie polished off her bowl of Sparkle-O's (a glimmering cereal that Sage's mom would never buy, despite her little brothers' begging and pleading) and even asked the Bot-Bot waiter for seconds.

"Certainly, Cassie," it said, zipping off to the kitchen. Sage sipped at her steaming mug of Zing and moved her food around on her plate.

"So tell me where you're from, Cassie," she said to her roommate.

"Old Prism," Cassie told her. Sage nodded. Old Prism was a medium-sized city about an hour from campus. It was one of Starland's original settlements and was a popular tourist destination. Sage had gone there once on a class trip.

"Do you have any starkin?" Sage asked.

Cassie shook her head.

"Lucky!" said Sage. "So it's just you and your mom and dad, huh?"

Cassie paused a moment, then nodded.

"What do your parents do?" Sage asked. "My mom is a scientist and my dad works for the government. Gran stays with us while my parents are at work."

Cassie thought for a moment. "My mom works at

the Old Prism museum and my dad is a doctor," she said softly.

"Well, I'm sorry I missed them at drop-off," Sage said. "I guess I'll meet them at Parents' Weekend. We could all go out for lunch or something. If you don't mind my crazy little brothers, that is."

Cassie stared at her bowl. "Maybe," she said.

Their Star-Zaps began to vibrate and flash. It was time for first period. The girls all stood and gave each other encouraging smiles.

"I'm off to Wishers 101," said Sage.

"Well, that sounds way better than Astral Accounting," said Cassie. "Bo-ring."

"I'll have that soon enough," said Sage. "Have fun, Cassie." The two girls left the cafeteria and headed in opposite directions, Sage walking to Constellation Classroom 113. She stepped inside the room and immediately felt the nervous excitement of all the students. The first class of the first starday at the top wish-granting school on Starland. Pretty starmendous. Sage settled into a seat, which immediately adjusted itself to her body. Ahhhh . . . comfort.

She listened carefully as the teacher began to speak. Her Star-Zap was recording everything, and when she went to bed that night, she would put on her headphones and play back the lectures from the starday so she would absorb the information as she slept. It was the most efficient way to study.

"Welcome to Wishers 101," the teacher said. An older woman with piercing blue eyes and fading purple hair, she was draped in colorful star-covered clothing and clutched a blue staff. She was hunched over and very wrinkly. "My name is Professor Elara Ursa and I am a former Wish-Granter, with the greatest number of wish missions of any Wish-Granter in Starland history," she said in a raspy voice. She was quite intimidating.

"Wishlings and Starlings look remarkably alike," the professor began. "Wishlings have a range of different skin, eye, and hair colors, just as we do. But their natural tones are not as vivid as ours. And their skin does not have our sparkling glow. But never fear. Once you have graduated and are on your way to your first Wish Mission, this will be easily adjusted by putting your hand on your Wish Pendant and repeating these words: "Star light, star bright, the first star I see tonight: I wish I may, I wish I might, have the wish I wish tonight."

Sage repeated the words to herself. Just for practice.

"There are many other differences that you must be aware of to be able to blend in seamlessly on Wishworld," the teacher cautioned. "Clothing is one. Each Star-Zap comes with an outfit changer so you can select Wishling clothing. Their clothing is made from materials found only on their planet, and they do not have access to the stain-free fibers that grow in abundance on Starland."

A girl with short bright orange hair raised her hand.

Professor Elara Ursa pointed to her. "Yes, what is your name?"

"Tweela," said the girl.

"What is your question, Tweela?"

"Does that mean Wishlings actually have to wash their clothing?" Tweela asked incredulously.

Professor Elara Ursa nodded. "They do. Also, their clothing eventually wears out and often needs to be replaced."

The room buzzed. That was so very strange!

"Wishlings also have to clean their homes," Professor Elara Ursa continued. "They do not have self-cleaning houses like we do. Wishlings may spend many hours a week keeping their surroundings dirt free."

Another student raised her hand. "So does that mean they don't have vanishing garbage?"

"Sadly for them, they do not," said the professor, trying unsuccessfully to hide her disgusted expression. "None of their trash disappears. People driving giant loud trucks ride around, grab cans full of garbage, and dump it into a massive crushing machine." She closed her eyes and shook her head. "Absolutely disgusting!" she muttered under her breath, but Sage, sitting close by, heard her.

Collecting garbage? What a strange thing to do! Sage was surprised. Life on Wishworld sounded a lot more primitive than she had imagined!

A girl in red raised her hand. "What is the weather like on Wishworld? How will we know how to dress to blend in?"

"An excellent question," said Professor Elara Ursa. "Wishlings have four seasons, as we do. But they have different names. They call the Time of New Beginnings spring. The Time of Lumiere is called summer on Wishworld. They call the Time of Letting Go fall, and the Time of Shadows is known as winter. The temperatures vary widely depending on where you are, and your outfit changer will only access weather-appropriate outfits."

Interesting, thought Sage. She'd never be able to keep all that straight!

"Do they celebrate the same holidays we do?" a serious-looking girl with purple pigtails asked.

"They do not," answered Professor Elara Ursa.

"Wishlings celebrate the new year in the middle of the Time of Shadows. This is followed by a holiday celebrating love and affection, called Valentine's Day. They give each other paper cards expressing their admiration for each other and gifts shaped like the heart organ. Some of these heart shapes contain a delicacy called chocolate—and Wishlings think it's delicious, but it's really dreadful. If you ever are offered a chocolate, I highly recommend turning it down. This is followed by a holiday when many Wishlings wear green and march in parades and men in skirts play noisy instruments. There are also holidays celebrating eggs and rabbits, and one when they eat a lot and say thank you. Wishlings place large fir trees in their homes, which bloom with attractive ornaments. Then they place colorful wrapped boxes underneath."

The girls laughed. How bizarre!

"Yes, Wishlings and their holidays can be quite strange!" the professor concluded.

Sage thought that Wishling holidays sounded interesting, but she felt sorry that they didn't know anything about Starland holidays. Imagine not celebrating the Festival of Illumination, when family and friends got together to eat cocomoon fritters and set off light rockets at night. Or Starshine Day, held on the warmest starday of Lumiere, with hiking, rock climbing, games, and sing-alongs of traditional songs. Or going door-to-door with her brothers on Light Giving Day, then returning home for zoomberry cake. She couldn't imagine life without any of those special days.

Sage's head was spinning. There was so much information to take in. Life on Wishworld certainly was different! She hoped it would all be absorbed by her brain overnight, because she was having trouble concentrating at the moment.

"There is so much for you to learn about Wishling culture," said Professor Elara Ursa. "Wishworld is a complicated, very odd place." She smiled. "But don't take my word for it. As part of this class, we will routinely go to the Wishworld Surveillance Deck and do some Wishworld Wishling watching! Come, let's go right now!"

"Wishworld Wishling watching!" the girl named Tweela repeated with a laugh. "Try to say that three times fast!" And then she did. Unsuccessfully.

Sage tried it herself as she stood and joined the others filing out of the classroom, but she couldn't do it, either. She followed the group down a long hallway, to a Flash Vertical Mover that was waiting for them, its glass doors open. They stepped inside and the doors whooshed shut.

Sage's ears popped as the mover gained speed, taking them up, up, up the enormously high tower. She swallowed hard as the ground below and the buildings of Starling Academy became tinier and tinier. Luckily, she wasn't afraid of heights.

Ding! They had arrived. By neatly dodging around the other students as they exited the mover, Sage was the first to push open the glass doors and step outside onto the surveillance deck. She froze. She had never seen anything more spectacular. The sky was so clear she could see for floozels.

Stars twinkled, distant planets glowed, and every so often a white-hot shooting star streaked across the sky. She wondered if someone was on the way down to Wishworld at that very moment. Sage finally understood the true meaning of the word *breathtaking*.

"Welcome to the Wishworld Surveillance Deck," said Professor Elara Ursa. "Find yourself a telescope and start observing!" On the ledge of the deck were dozens of large telescopes. Although there were more than enough for everyone, the students bumped into each other in their excitement to get to them. Sage found a free telescope and placed her hands on its cool metal surface. She put her eye to the eyepiece and peered through.

Then she jumped back in surprise—everything was so close—before leaning forward for another look.

The telescope was so incredibly powerful that it was as if she was right there on Wishworld, not on a distant star mooniums of floozels away. She could not believe her eyes. It was so shockingly magnificent that for a starsec she thought it might be a dream.

She saw a female Wishling walking with a small furry animal in a park. She had a sudden start as she realized just how similar Starlings and Wishlings actually looked.

"I see a Wishling animal!" she cried. The other students rushed over to take a look and marvel at how adorable it was. Sage thought it was almost as cute as her brother's pet glowfur.

"That's called a dog," said Professor Elara Ursa. "Many Wishlings keep them as pets and take them on walks several times a day." She went on to explain that many Wishworld animals did not live together as harmoniously as the plant-eating creatures of Starland, which was a lush place with an abundance of plants for the animals to eat. But there were still some similarities. Flutterfocuses were akin to Wishworld butterflies, and globerbeems a lot like Wishworld lightning bugs. Wishworld horses were the closest animal to galliopes.

And the glion was a gentle and distant cousin to the Wishworld lion.

Sage moved the telescope a tiny bit and next spotted a young male Wishling tossing an oddly shaped brown ball. She paused for a moment to watch the ball arc through the air before a second young male Wishling caught it in his hands. *They really do look a lot like Starling boys,* she thought. *Just not as sparkly, but still cute.* She next noticed a group of small Wishlings in a circle holding hands as they sang. To her surprise, they suddenly collapsed on the ground. Was something wrong? But they almost immediately jumped to their feet, laughing out loud. It was a game! It didn't look like such a fun one to her, but it certainly seemed as if they were enjoying it.

As she moved the telescope this way and that, watching Wishlings at rest, work, and play, she listened to Professor Elara Ursa's lecture. She learned that Wishlings were hopelessly behind in technology; their computers and communications devices were shockingly old-fashioned. In addition, their modes of transportation were slow and cumbersome, plus they actually had to be operated by Wishlings themselves! Oh, how the girls laughed when they saw the funny vehicles Wishlings used to travel. Life on Wishworld was very interesting indeed.

"Sage! Sage!" said a voice. Sage tore her gaze from her view of Wishworld and turned around reluctantly. Professor Elara Ursa was shaking her head. "I've been calling your name for five starmins!" she said. "Class is over!" Sage looked around, blinking. The Wishworld Observation Deck was deserted. She muttered her apologies and took off hurriedly for her next class. She slipped into the last remaining seat right before the teacher closed the door and turned around with a scowl. "My name is Professor Lucretia Delphinus and above all I value timeliness!" she announced. Her eyes flashed behind her large black glasses. She was small and intense and immediately began pacing the room.

Sage gulped. *Way to make a good first impression,* she thought.

"This is Wish Identification class," said the professor. "Once you arrive on Wishworld, blend in, and find your Wisher by using your Wish Pendant, the most difficult part of your Wish Mission begins—making sure you identify the correct wish. This is obviously quite critical to your mission and will be the difference between collecting wish energy and returning home empty-handed."

A student with long, straight midnight-blue hair and eyes the color of the sky at night raised her hand.

"Yes?" said Professor Lucretia Delphinus. She attempted to hop up to sit on the corner of her desk. As she was tiny, she didn't make it at first and had to try a couple of times. Finally, she dragged over a chair and used it to climb onto the desk. She settled herself, then stared at the girls as if daring them to giggle at her. The students, completely intimidated, did not.

"You had a question?" she asked the blue-haired girl.

The girl, nonplussed by her professor's odd behavior, stared for a moment. "Um, won't the wish be obvious?" she finally asked.

"Not necessarily," replied Professor Lucretia Delphinus. "Here's what happens: When you arrive on Wishworld, your Star-Zap will give you directions to find your Wisher. When you are near your Wisher for the first time, your Wish Pendant will light up. It will be faint when you are in their vicinity and glow brightly when you make actual contact. That is when you can start trying to identify the wish. This is very tricky, because there is often nothing to indicate that you are correct. It's just a feeling you have. Some very perceptive Starlings will get a burst of energy when the wish is identified, but many will not. This coupled with the short time frame to complete the wish results in a fifty percent failure rate."

Sage was shocked. She'd had no idea the failure rate was so high.

"My goal is to teach you how to ask the right questions, become more perceptive, sharpen your senses, and be good listeners," the professor continued.

"Have you ever identified a wish on the first try?" a girl in the front row asked.

Professor Lucretia Delphinus nodded. "Sometimes it is easy. Once I introduced myself to a Wisher and she said, 'Boy, you're friendly. I wish I could be as friendly as you.' And I knew that my mission was to build her confidence and help her make friends. But most times it is not so simple."

She put her hand to her chin. "On one mission I went on, I was fully convinced that my Wisher wanted to learn how to tap-dance."

"How to what-dance?" asked Sage.

Professor Lucretia Delphinus smiled. "It's a Wishling pastime in which they do special dances with very small metal plates attached to their shoes. Very noisy."

"So what was the real wish?" Sage asked.

"Her actual wish was to get the courage to tell her parents she wanted to quit taking piano lessons. Boy, did she hate them," Professor Lucretia Delphinus said, remembering. "I'm still not quite sure how I messed that one up. But luckily I discovered it in time." The next thing the class knew, she had hopped off the desk and started doing a strange shuffling dance. "And I did become quite the tap dancer!"

The professor finished the dance by extending her arms and shaking her hands, her palms forward and fingers splayed. "Jazz hands," she explained. The students just stared. Professor Lucretia Delphinus was certainly a character!

She cleared her throat and continued her lecture. "What makes wish identification so difficult is that the Wisher may have multiple wishes at the same time. They could even have several good wishes. So you must be sure to identify the correct wish. Here is why so many Wish Missions fail: the Starling assumes that the first wish they uncover is the correct wish. You really have to take the time to get to know your Wisher to make sure you grant the wish that is their heart's desire."

The students paid close attention. Wish granting was much more complicated than they had realized!

Professor Lucretia Delphinus looked at all the confused faces in front of her and softened. "Since it is your first day, we'll go back to the basics. We'll talk about good, bad, and impossible wishes. That will be a good way to ease into wish identification.

"So tell me this," Professor Lucretia Delphinus said. "What exactly makes a wish impossible?"

The arms of nearly half the class shot up. "Yes," said the professor, pointing to a girl with magenta hair.

"Wishes that are not within the Wishling's grasp," the girl answered.

"Good. Can I have some examples?" Professor Lucretia Delphinus asked.

Girls started calling out.

"Curing diseases!"

"Reading minds!"

"Flying!"

"All good examples," the teacher said with a nod. "We all wish that things like world peace and curing diseases were not impossible wishes.

"And how about bad wishes?" the professor prompted.

"Bad wishes are selfish," Sage said.

"Yes, anything else?"

"Bad wishes harm other people and don't take their feelings into consideration," offered another student.

"Correct," Professor Lucretia Delphinus said. "And last but not least, what is a good wish?"

"Good wishes are those made for something positive with no ulterior motives," Tweela said slowly.

Professor Lucretia Delphinus rubbed her hands

together. "Excellent, girls. Now let's try this: I am going to give you three wishes to choose from. Listen carefully and pick the wish which is not only good but is also possible." The girls nodded.

"Wish number one: a Wishling wants her coworker to perform badly at an upcoming presentation so that she will look better to their boss.

"Wish number two: a Wishling wishes for the courage to try out for the neighborhood baseball team." Puzzled expressions appeared, so Professor Lucretia Delphinus described an activity that involved a large padded leather glove, bats made of wood or aluminum, and something called a "home run," leaving the girls more confused than before.

"And wish number three: a Wishling whose grandmother is very sick wishes she could do something to make her all better."

A girl scoffed. "That's easy," she said. "It's the Wisher who wants to impress her boss."

"No, no, no," said the teacher, wringing her hands. "Why would wishing for another to fail be a good wish?"

The girl shook her head. "I think this is a trick question!" she said confidently. "It's about her job, so it has to be a good wish!"

Professor Lucretia Delphinus put her hand to her

head as if she had a sharp and sudden headache. "I see we have some work to do," she said. Sage agreed. It was pretty clear that while everyone seemed to know which wish was which in theory, when it was put into practice, it was an entirely different story.

Luckily for everyone, the bell rang. It was time to head to the next class of the day.

Sage was dismayed when she entered her Wishful Thinking class and spotted the girl with the pale blue bangs sitting in the front row. It turned out her name was Vivica, and—no surprise—she was a bit of an obnoxious know-it-all. Sage decided not to let it bother her. Wishful Thinking was an important class. Up until then, none of the students had had any formal training in wish energy manipulation. It was something you practiced at home with your family. Now that they were at the Age of Fulfillment, they were ready to hone their skills.

"As you know, positive wish energy is around us at all times. Not only does it power our lights and cars, but we can use it to manipulate things around us with our minds," said the teacher, a short, stern woman named Professor Dolores Raye. She wore sensible shoes with stars on them, and her illuminated glasses were on a glowstring around her neck so she wouldn't misplace them. "We fully expect you all to be on markedly different levels. This is not a competition. By the end of the term, you will all be skilled manipulators. But first we have to assess your skills so we know where to begin."

As the class watched, the professor pointed to the classroom door, opening and closing it with ease. She stood up and, with a flick of her wrist, moved her chair across the room. She even lifted one student out of her seat and kept her floating in midair! Professor Dolores Raye was the most talented Wish Energy Manipulator Sage had ever seen. Even better than Gran. And Gran was really good.

"And now it's your turn," the teacher said. After that stunning display, no one was about to volunteer to go first. But finally, a girl with short-cropped violet hair was brave enough to try. Professor Raye placed a beautiful stone—a brilliant pink rodangular—on the desk and asked her to move it. The girl stared at the gem. Nothing. She frowned and her face began to turn red. Still nothing. She put her hands to her temples and concentrated fiercely. Then the gem began to tremble. It moved forward the tiniest bit. It was nearly imperceptible, but the girl looked happy. "Wonderful effort!" Professor Dolores Raye said. "Don't worry, it will only get easier."

Finally, it was last period. Sage spotted Cassie in the

hallway and caught up, falling into step beside her. "So how was your day?" Sage asked.

Cassie sighed. "I read my holo-schedule wrong and accidentally went to Astral Accounting class twice. It couldn't have been Aspirational Art or Lighterature, right? And now I am going to get in trouble for skipping Wish Identification class."

"With Professor Lucretia Delphinus?" Sage asked.

"Yes," replied Cassie.

Sage grimaced. Cassie probably *was* going to get in trouble.

"So how was your first day?" Cassie asked.

"It was intense," Sage said. "I kind of felt like my brain was going to explode. But otherwise it was okay."

"Where are you going, girls?" said someone behind them.

Oh, no, thought Sage. She recognized that voice and wished she didn't.

Sure enough, it was Vivica. She pushed in between the two roommates and started walking with them. "Pretty lame manipulation attempt today, wouldn't you say, Sage? Wait till it's my turn. Then you'll really see some skills."

"Sounds good," said Sage.

"So where are you two off to now?" Vivica asked, pushing her bangs out of her eyes. She smirked before adding, "Oh, that's right, you're part of the, um . . ." She searched her mind. "Superbly Dense group," she concluded with a nasty grin.

Sage stopped suddenly in the hallway, her temperature rising. Students had to step around her. Cassie and Vivica stopped, too, Vivica's expression mocking. *Why won't this girl leave me alone?* Sage wondered. She clenched her hands.

Cassie gently put her hand on Sage's arm. It had a sudden calming effect on her. She took a deep breath. "I can't put anything past you," Sage said to Vivica with forced cheerfulness. "Turns out I do need some extra help. She does, too," she added, pointing to Cassie, much to the girl's dismay. "Can't be late! Don't want to fall even more behind!" she said, taking off down the hallway, Cassie right behind her.

"Thanks a lot," muttered Cassie. "You actually had to *volunteer* that information?"

"It was going to get out sooner or later," said Sage.

"I guess you're right," said Cassie grudgingly. The two reached the classroom and stepped inside. They sat next to Vega, who was neat as a pin in her crisp blue outfit.

The girl with the fuchsia hair entered the classroom and sat in the corner by herself.

"That's Scarlet," Vega whispered to Sage. "And she's just weird. She totally keeps to herself. Super unfriendly."

The girl definitely had a look that was all her own. That day she wore a black T-shirt decorated with a star made out of silver studs, a pouffy black tutu, pink-and-black-striped tights, and big black boots. She didn't look at anyone, just gazed down at her desk.

The classroom filled up. Gemma entered, chatting away to her sister. Leona was the last student to arrive, gesturing dramatically with her hands.

Lady Stella and another teacher walked into the room. "Welcome, Star Darlings," the headmistress said. "For these special secret classes, we will have several guest lecturers, who will each present crucial information. Today we are lucky to have Professor Margaret Dumarre, who is here to teach you all we know about Wishling schools. Since we usually send older Starlings down to grant wishes, our knowledge of Wishling schools is limited. We will be relying on you to make Wishworld observations, which you can mentally record in your Cyber Journals as they happen and we will discuss in class upon your return. These will prove very beneficial to your fellow Star Darlings, as well as to the rest of Starling Academy."

"Hello, students," said Professor Margaret Dumarre with a warm smile. Sage was immediately charmed by the pretty young teacher. Her pink-and-blue-striped hair was twisted into an elegant updo, and she was wearing a sleek high-collared bright pink dress, scattered with glowing stars. "I already know some of you from my third-year course Wishworld Relations." Several of the older Star Darlings nodded.

Professor Margaret Dumarre began her lecture and reviewed for the Star Darlings that Wishling children weren't born with knowledge of basic concepts, the way Starlings were. They had to go to school to learn simple skills such as counting, spelling, and reading. The upperclassmen were familiar with that information, but the younger students, who had learned it only that day, were even more surprised to learn that Wishling children didn't absorb their lessons in their sleep.

Their mouths fell open in shock when they discovered that Wishling children actually read and studied books made of paper.

"Moons and stars!" Cassie exclaimed. "I would love to see one of those!"

When class was over, Professor Margaret Dumarre and Lady Stella stood at the door as the students filed out. "Excellent work today, girls," Lady Stella said. "And who knows? A wish could be coming through as I speak. One of you may be on your way to Wishworld before you know it!"

Sage tapped her elbows together for luck. She hoped Lady Stella was right.

CHAPTER 5

But it was not to be. Days turned into weeks and still there were no missions for the Star Darlings. Sage fell into a routine of classes, clubs, and regular calls home. She joined the holo-book club (at Cassie's request) and the explorer's club, which met every Reliquaday. She took her first hike to the Crystal Mountains, which were just as spectacular as she had imagined. And she finally read the Student Manual from start to finish, much to Cassie's and Gran's relief.

In her classes, Sage learned a lot about Wishlings and Star-Zaps and wish identification.

But Sage could never fully relax, knowing that she could be summoned for her mission to Wishworld at any moment. Some of the other Star Darlings seemed keyed up, as well. There was a wide range of emotions running through the group, as some of them just couldn't wait to get going and others were a bit more reluctant. Some pretended to be blasé even though they were nervous. But Cassie made it no secret that she was in no rush to head for Wishworld any time soon.

Lady Stella put on a brave face. "Everything is going as planned," she said often. "Your missions could start at any moment. Be ready." But Sage had spotted the Wish-Watcher who was in charge of the Star Darlings' Wish Orbs coming out of Lady Stella's office the past week looking very worried indeed.

Sage enjoyed Wishful Thinking class most of all, although she had not yet had her turn to showcase her talents. It was fascinating to see the different skill levels of the students.

One day she arrived in class early to find that she and Vivica were the only ones there. Sage quickly sat down and started fiddling with her Star-Zap. The next thing she knew, Sage looked up to discover Vivica leaning on her desk. She jumped. "So, how's everything going, Sage?" Vivica asked.

"Just fine," replied Sage guardedly.

"Glad to hear it. I'd hate to hear that you were overwhelmed or anything."

"I'm fine," said Sage. "Thanks for asking." When she had been in Wee Constellation School, there had been a boy in her class who picked on everyone smaller than him. When Sage had gone home crying because he had said she smelled like stinkberries, her mom had assured her she smelled lovely and then taught her how to deal with bullies—by simply ignoring them. It had worked with that boy, and Sage hoped it would work now. "Bullies want to get a reaction out of you," Indirra had told her. "It makes them feel powerful. Don't give him the satisfaction."

Some other girls came into the classroom, and then Vivica had an audience. She smiled a mean smile. "So how is your study group going?" she asked in a loud voice for the other girls' benefit. "Did you all know that Sage and her roommate are in an extra class?" The other girls didn't say anything, but a couple looked intrigued. Sage shifted in her seat. "Makes you wonder why she would be accepted into such a prestigious academy," Vivica continued. "Makes you wonder if she had some help getting in. Like maybe someone's well-known scientist mother pulled some strings and got her daughter into school."

"That's not true!" shouted Sage. *Starf!* She hadn't meant to let the mean girl get to her.

Professor Dolores Raye walked into the classroom at that very moment, of course. "Sage," she scolded, "no shouting in the classroom, please!"

Sage scowled and sunk in her seat till her head was barely at desk level. Great, now her favorite professor was mad at her. Sage was angry. And maybe—just maybe—the reason she was so angry was that she herself feared that there was some truth to what Vivica had said. She had been pleasantly surprised when she had been accepted to Starling Academy. Could that be the real reason she had been accepted? Was she an imposter?

After SD class that day, Sage was on her way back to her room when she spotted a dapper-looking gentleman chatting with a Bot-Bot guard on the Little Dipper Dormitory's steps.

"This is Cassie's roommate, Sage," the Bot-Bot guard informed the man as she approached.

"Star salutations," the man said to the guard. He turned to Sage and bowed. "Hello, Sage. I am Andreas. I'm here to see Cassie."

"She stopped to drop off some holo-books at the library," explained Sage. She looked up and noticed he had the same soft burgundy eyes as her roommate. She smiled. "You must be her father!" she cried. "It is so nice to finally meet you. Cassie is a great roommate! She even got me to join the holo-book club." She looked around. "Hey, is her mom here? I can't wait to meet her, too!"

Andreas looked confused. "No, I am Cassie's uncle." He frowned and leaned forward. "You do know that Cassie's parents have completed their Cycle of Life, don't you?" he said in a low voice. "Back when she was six years old. She has lived with me ever since. I am her guardian, her mother's older brother."

Sage stared. "You mean they have begun their afterglow?" she said. "But Cassie . . ." Suddenly, she realized that the holo-pictures displayed in their room were of a much younger Cassie and her parents. And she recalled how Cassie often stared into the heavens before bed. She had assumed her roommate had been on the lookout for shooting stars, but now she realized she must have been staring at her parents' stars. She felt a sudden stab of sorrow. Poor Cassie!

"Oh, there she is!" her uncle said, a smile on his face. "Cassie!" He waved and began heading over to her. Cassie's mouth opened into an O of surprise. She ran to her uncle, her arms outstretched.

Sage decided the kindest thing to do was slip away without Cassie seeing her. She headed in the other direction. She'd hang out in the Lightning Lounge until dinnertime to give her roommate some space.

Sage returned to the room as Cassie was drawing the curtains shut. "Sorry I didn't make it to dinner tonight," Cassie said. "My uncle Andreas came for a visit and he took me out to eat. My, um, parents were busy, so he came instead."

"Cassie," said Sage slowly, "I . . . um . . . met your uncle. He told me that your parents were . . ."

Cassie opened a drawer and was suddenly very busy picking out a pair of pajamas. "Oh," she said. "Oh, I see. Okay."

"If you want to talk about it, we can . . ."

Cassie quickly got changed and slid into bed. "No, it's okay. Good night." She slipped her headphones onto her ears and turned to face the wall.

Sage put on her own headphones and tried to fall asleep. But she couldn't. She felt terribly sad for Cassie, and also awkward. She lay awake watching the shadows on the wall. She was sure Cassie was awake, too.

When Sage woke up the next morning, the room was empty. Cassie's bed was perfectly made. Suddenly, Sage's Star-Zap lit up. A holo-text appeared. DEAR SAGE, it read, I'M SORRY I LIED TO YOU ABOUT MY PARENTS. I'M ACTUALLY NOT EVEN SURE WHY I DID IT. I GUESS IT'S JUST THAT

WHEN YOU ASSUMED THEY WERE AROUND, AND TALKED ABOUT THEM LIKE THEY WERE ALIVE, IT FELT REALLY GOOD TO GO ALONG WITH IT. IT WAS EASY TO PRETEND THAT WE WERE APART BECAUSE I WAS AT SCHOOL, AND NOT BECAUSE THEY HAD BEGUN THEIR AFTERGLOW. I LIKED PRETENDING THAT THEY WERE STILL AT HOME WAITING FOR ME. I'M SORRY FOR LYING TO YOU AND I'M REALLY EMBARRASSED TOO. YOUR ROOMMATE, CASSIE. PS: I'D APPRECIATE IT IF WE NEVER TALKED ABOUT THIS AGAIN.

DEAR CASSIE, Sage wrote back after much thought, NO NEED TO EVER APOLOGIZE TO ME. I'M THE ONE WHO IS SORRY. I PROMISE I'LL NEVER BRING IT UP AGAIN. LOVE, SAGE.

Now that the truth was out there, Sage learned a lot more about Cassie's life. Her uncle was a best-selling author who sold mooniums of holo-books a year. Sage's dad was a big fan of his mysteries. He traveled Starland extensively on book tours, and Cassie often accompanied him on his trips. If she didn't feel like going, she stayed at home (in a large mansion) with their housekeeper, Marta, a sweet older woman who was as close to Cassie as if she were her grandmother.

"No wonder you love books so much!" Sage said. She was delighted to learn that Cassie was also a recurring character in the series, as a brilliant young sleuth who often assisted the main character on cases. Now that Cassie's secret was out in the open, the two girls fell into an easy friendship.

Then one day everything changed. It was finally Sage's turn in Wishful Thinking, and she was very excited. She stood in front of the class. This time there were a pitcher of glorange juice and an empty glass on Professor Dolores Raye's desk.

The teacher called her name and Sage walked to the front of the room. "Okay, Sage, time to show us what you've got," said Professor Dolores Raye.

"Here goes nothing," said Vivica under her breath. The meaner girls in the class giggled.

Sage smiled. Now she would show everyone who was supposed to be at Starling Academy! She stared at the glass and it slid gracefully across the table.

"Well done, Sage," said Professor Dolores Raye with a broad grin.

For her next trick, Sage decided she would levitate the pitcher and pour the teacher a glass of juice. Sage was an expert at wish energy manipulation. She had been practically since birth. As a baby she had shocked her parents by levitating a toy across the room and floating it into her chubby little hand. She had been crying for it and they hadn't been able to understand what she wanted. So she simply concentrated on it, and there it was. This energy had also come in handy while she was learning how to glimmerskate. It had kept her from falling over.

But just as she was lifting the glass, her Star-Zap vibrated. *Probably just a holo-text from Gran*, she thought. She stole a glance at it.

SD WISH ORB IDENTIFIED, she read. PROCEED TO LADY STELLA'S OFFICE IMMEDIATELY.

CRASH! The pitcher fell to the floor and shattered. There were glass shards and glowing orange juice all over the floor. Then it was instantly gone.

"That was a good try, Sage," said the professor sympathetically.

Several girls laughed, and Vivica shook her head. But Sage didn't even notice. Her heart was fairly leaping out of her chest with excitement. She grabbed her Star-Zap and asked to be excused. Sage walked down the hall quickly, her heels clicking on the marble floor. A classroom door opened and Scarlet came out. She spoke to Sage for the first time ever. "It's happening," she said, her black eyes shining. "It is really happening. Right here, right now."

The two girls grinned at each other and ran down the hall toward the headmistress's office.

Once again, the girls sat around the table in Lady

Stella's office. Cassie looked even paler than usual. "I can't believe this is actually happening so soon," she whispered to Sage.

So soon? thought Sage. It felt like it had taken forever!

The door opened and Lady Stella strode inside. She looked energized and, Sage noted, slightly nervous. She stood in front of the girls and clasped her hands together. "This is it, Star Darlings: the moment we have all been waiting for. A Star Darling's Wish Orb has been identified by our Wish-Watcher. It is time for us to head to the Star Darlings Wish Cavern to find out who the wish belongs to. Let's go underground."

Underground? The girls looked at each other in confusion.

"Deep underneath Halo Hall is a labyrinth of underground caves," Lady Stella explained. "They are secret—known only to a few members of the faculty. And now you. We decided to build your special Wish Cavern there to keep its existence secret from prying eyes."

Lady Stella walked to her desk and opened a drawer. She reached inside and a hidden door in the back wall slid open. Sage was one of the first through the doorway and found herself descending a circular stairway. There was a sudden change in temperature and the air grew musty and damp. Sage shivered. The girls walked in silence, the only sound the echoing clatter of their footsteps on the metal stairs. Suddenly, someone started to sing. She sang softly at first; then the song grew louder. It was a pretty tune about stars twinkling in the darkness, and the voice was clear and sweet. Sage thought it might be Leona.

Finally, they reached the bottom of the steps, and the singing stopped. The only light came from the glowing rocks set in the dripping walls of the cavernous room they stood in. "Welcome to the Star Caves," Lady Stella said, her voice echoing. "We will head to the Wish-House in a moment. But first I want you to experience just how complete the darkness is down here. Are you ready?"

"Yes," said several voices. Sage thought she recognized Leona's as the loudest.

Lady Stella closed her eyes and all the lights were suddenly extinguished. It was so utterly dark that Sage held up her hand and couldn't see it. Sage felt a small, cold hand grab hers and knew instantly it was Cassie's. Sage squeezed her hand, for her own comfort as much as her roommate's. Just then, the star on the middle of Lady Stella's forehead began to glow, illuminating her lovely face. After a moment the lights turned back on again, to everyone's relief.

"Follow me," Lady Stella said. "The Wish Cavern is ready for us."

Sage worked her way through the crowd so she was right behind the headmistress. She shivered in the damp air. She wished she had worn a sweater. A big cold drop of water hit her squarely on the shoulder. In the spooky half gloom, she could see rocky formations rising from the floor and dripping down from the ceiling like stone icicles. A sudden squeaking sound made her jump.

"Don't worry," said Lady Stella. "It's just a bitbat. They don't bite—unless they're hungry."

Sage nervously laughed along with the other girls. She hoped the headmistress was kidding, but she wasn't quite sure.

"Ah, here we are," said Lady Stella, stopping in front of what looked like a sheer stone wall. She concentrated and a section of the wall slid open. A secret entrance! To Sage's amazement, bright sunlight flooded out. The girls pushed inside, eager to be out of the damp gloom. "Welcome to the Star Darlings Wish Cavern," Lady Stella said. "This magical place has been created just for you and your Wish Missions." Though they were deep underneath Starling Academy, the girls found themselves in a working Wish-House, the sun streaming in through the glass roof. Golden waterfalls of pure wish energy streamed down the sides. Sage smiled as she felt the immediate effects of the positive energy. There was grass underneath their feet and a row of Wish Orbs, their sparkly forms bobbing. Sage counted them quickly. Eleven. She noticed that Astra had kicked off her shoes and was scrunching her toes in the velvety-looking grass.

The girls gravitated toward a grass-covered platform in the middle of the garden and stood around it uncertainly. Sage stood between Clover and Gemma, who both looked excited, and across from Cassie, who was much more reserved.

Lady Stella then announced, "One of twelve Wish Orbs is glowing, which means that a wish is ready to be granted. It is the perfect match for one of you. The timing is wonderful, as your studies have progressed enough that you are all ready to make the trip to Wishworld. Now the Wish Orb will choose which of you is the best match for its wish." The headmistress pointed to the platform. "Are you ready?" The girls nodded.

Lady Stella clapped her hands. The room darkened, and a beam of light appeared and focused on the middle of the round platform. As the girls watched, the center of the platform opened and up popped a single Wish Orb. It floated in the air. As the girls watched, it slowly moved to the edge of the platform and began to circle around, pausing momentarily in front of each Star Darling as if deciding which girl it belonged to.

Sage stared at it, hoping that it belonged to her. She closed her eyes. *Me, me, me . . . please be me, me . . .* When she opened her eyes, the orb was floating in front of her.

Lady Stella reached out and plucked the Wish Orb out of the air. She turned to Sage, her eyes brimming with tears. "This is a historic moment," she said. "The very first Star Darling has been chosen. The Wish Orb belongs to you, Sage." Was it Sage's imagination, or did the headmistress look relieved?

Sage could hardly breathe. "It's really me?" she finally managed to squeak out.

"It's really you," said Lady Stella. "Congratulations, Sage. Now it is time to prepare for your Wish Mission."

The headmistress clapped her hands again. "When we get upstairs, the rest of you girls are dismissed. Sage, you come with me. We have a lot to do before you leave. By tomorrow morning you will be on your way to helping Wishworld!"

CHAPTER 6

"Go back to that cute striped jacket and that skirt with the folds in it," said Cassie. She was lying on her bed watching Sage flip through the options on the Wishworld Outfit Selector on her Star-Zap. Pants, shirts, vests, skirts, dresses, leggings, hats. All kinds of shoes—sneakers, flats, platforms, tall boots, short boots, booties. The choices were endless. Sage pressed the CHOOSE button and a new Wishling outfit instantly appeared on her body.

"Now spin," said Cassie. Sage did, and the pleated skirt stood out, floating in the air. "Oh, I really like Wishworld fashion," said Cassie. "Can you find it in white?"

Sage flipped through several more outfits before finally settling on a comfortable pair of blue pants and some lavender sneakers. On top she wore a lavender shirt with a glittery flutterfocus—make that a butterfly—on it and a cute cropped jacket. She registered her choice by pressing a button on her Star-Zap, then put on a lavender nightgown, soft as a cloud, and crawled into bed.

"Good night, Sage," said Cassie. "I'm really excited for you. And I'm also really relieved that it's not me." She yawned. "I'm sure you'll do great." Sage stared at the ceiling, her mind racing. In mere hours she would be on her way to a strange new place where she would have to fit in, find the right Wisher, identify the wish, and help make it come true. She shivered with anticipation.

Sage stood on the private Star Darlings section of the Wishworld Surveillance Deck, her heart beating fast, her eyes protected by a pair of special safety starglasses. Two Star Wranglers stood nearby with lassos made of wish energy in their hands. Their job was to catch a falling star as it passed by and attach Sage to it. Then they'd let go and she'd be flung into the heavens.

Sage thought she'd be nervous, but she felt oddly calm. The rest of the Star Darlings, however, were buzzing with excitement as they hugged her and wished her well.

Lady Stella called for everyone's attention. "I have some last-starmin details to share," she said. "When you enter Wishworld's atmosphere, your Star-Zap will signal that it is time to change your appearance. You must make sure that your hair, skin, and clothing blend in with the Wishlings.

"That means no sparkly skin, no vibrant hair color, no Starland fashions," the headmistress stressed. "You must always keep your true identity a secret. To let the Wishlings know of our existence would be disastrous. We would be overwhelmed by wishes—many of them selfish ones. It is imperative that we keep the balance just as it is."

Sage nodded. "I understand."

"And a reminder—you must pay careful attention to the Countdown Clock on your Star-Zap. The wish must be granted before the orb dies. The timing is different in each case. A starsec too late and the wish energy will be lost forever. And keep a careful eye on the energy levels of your Wish Pendant. You can use it to help make the wish come true by using your special power." Sage nodded. "But of course, you have to figure out what your special power is!" Lady Stella smiled at her. "And remember, you never want to completely run out of wish energy, in case of an emergency.

"I cannot stress to you how important it is that each of you collect your wish energy. We need every drop."

"No need to worry," Sage said confidently. "I can do this."

Lady Stella continued. "Due to Wishworld's atmosphere, we will only be able to monitor your wish energy reserves in your Wish Pendant and see how much time you have left on the Countdown Clock. We will not be able to communicate with each other."

Sage nodded again.

"Now where is Lady Cordial?" asked Lady Stella. At that moment, the door opened and the purple-haired woman emerged, out of breath and holding a rectangular lavender bag with two shoulder straps and a purple stuffed star hanging from the zipper. "This is a bag we created to look like the ones all Wishworld children carry. This will help you fit in." Sage took it and slipped it over her arm.

Lady Stella looked at Sage proudly. "I have total faith that your journey will be a success," she told her. She smiled gently at Sage. "One last thing—don't forget your Mirror Mantra. It has been chosen especially for you: *I believe in you. Glow for it!* Recite it when you feel like you or your Wisher need reassurance and strength."

"I believe in you," Sage repeated. "Glow for it!"

Then there was a flurry of embraces and farewells, and before Sage knew it, the Star Wranglers had lassoed a falling star and attached her to it. Before she could tap her elbows together for luck, she was jolted back as the star was released and took off like a shot. Next stop: Wishworld.

The only way for Sage to describe the ride through the heavens was that it was like being on the most exciting, fastest star coaster in existence. There were flashes of light and glimmers of starshine. She passed through a gray cloud and shivered. *Must be negative wish energy*, she thought. And as soon as her ride began, it was almost over. Mooniums of floozels covered in mere starmins. Sage was entering Wishworld's atmosphere.

Her Star-Zap began to flash. COMMENCE APPEARANCE CHANGE, it read. Sage accessed the Wishworld Outfit Selector and was instantly dressed in the Wishling clothing she had chosen.

Next she closed her eyes and held her Wish Pendant tightly. "Star light, star bright," she began to recite, "the first star I see tonight: I wish I may, I wish I might, have the wish I wish tonight." Immediately, her pendant began to glow, and a warm, pleasant feeling settled over her.

Sage first concentrated on her hair, envisioning plain, light brown braids. She then focused on her skin, imagining it to be smooth and dull. The warmth went away and Sage opened her eyes.

Looking down, she felt a small stab of disappointment when she saw that her hair was no longer its rich lavender hue. The light brown braids looked very dull indeed. She was surprised to see that there was a layer of sparkles on her skin. She gave herself a quick shake and the glitter fell off. She felt plain and unadorned. But now she would fit right in.

PREPARE FOR LANDING, the Star-Zap read. Sage screwed her eyes shut and braced herself as she fell to Wishworld. If any Wishlings happened to look up and spot her arrival, they would think they were witnessing a falling star—a particularly lovely one, at that.

She landed with a gentle thump and opened her eyes. She was sitting on a small grassy hill in the middle of a cluster of yellow and orange trees. The star sat beside her, sputtering. She took off her safety starglasses and put them away. She'd need them for the return trip home. She'd also need the star. She reached out a finger and gently poked it. It was cool to the touch. With a smile, she began to fold it, as she had been instructed by Lady Stella, until it was the size of a small star-shaped wallet. She placed it in the zippered front pocket of her backpack, then slipped her arms through the straps. There! Now she looked just like a real Wishling!

She was all alone. The landing coordinates had been carefully chosen to avoid Wishling observation. The only sound was a strange yet lovely chirpy kind of music, which she soon discovered came from small winged creatures that sat in the branches of the surrounding trees.

"Take me to the Wisher I've come to help," she said into her communicator. It immediately gave her precise directions.

Sage walked for a bit until she found a pathway. As she walked she saw lawns, benches, and more trees and soon realized that she had landed in the middle of a park. She saw more of those winged creatures that were making the melodic sounds she liked so much, as well as some gray animals with bushy tails. They chattered at her as she passed.

Very soon after that, she started seeing Wishlings. She couldn't help staring at them, despite herself. They really did look remarkably like Starlings but with lusterless, non-sparkly skin and plain hair colors, though some of them embellished their appearances with bright clothing, accessories, or face paint. Some of the female Wishlings wore improbably high shoes. Many of the males had long strips of cloth tied around their necks. Some Wishlings rolled by on wheeled footgear. Others led furry animals of all shapes and sizes by long ropes. Sage vaguely remembered they were called dags, or something like that. Sage left the park and crossed a busy street.

She gaped at the oddly shaped wheeled vehicles and the Wishlings inside them. It was true—they were actually driving!

Several blocks later she reached her destination, a large redbrick building with a flag flying out front. Her Wisher's school. She felt her pulse quicken as she walked up the steps and pushed open the doors. The hallway was long, empty, and lined with small metal closets. She wrinkled her nose at the harsh sanitized smell in the air. WALK DOWN THE HALLWAY, TURN LEFT, AND GO UP THE STAIRS, the communicator instructed on-screen. Sage stepped forward confidently, hardly able to contain her excitement. Her adventure was about to begin.

Until a voice halted her. "Stop right there," someone said. The order echoed in the empty hallway.

Sage's heart dropped. Would her mission be over before it even began?

CHAPTER 7

Sage spun around. An adult male Wishling with dark brown hair and a green uniform was standing in the middle of the hallway, frowning at her.

"And what are you wearing? You know that jeans and sneakers aren't allowed in school. I'll have to write you up a detention slip!"

Sage looked down at her blue pants and her shoes. She pressed a button on her Star-Zap and made a mental note, which she knew would instantly be recorded in her Cyber Journal: *Mission 1, Wishworld Observation #1: Do not wear "jeans and sneakers" to school.* As the male Wishling began filling out the paper, Sage quickly pressed another button on the communicator and accessed the outfit changer. She was instantly wearing brand-new clothing, hopefully appropriate this time.

In her haste she hadn't been able to make an informed choice and hoped her outfit was a pretty one. The man looked up from his clipboard. "Like I said, no jeans or . . ." The man stopped talking when he took in her outfit. He blinked slowly. "Wait—what? I could have sworn . . ." He shook his head, flustered. "Well . . . then where is your hall pass?" he asked, bristling.

Sage bit her lip. What on Starland was a hall pass? She hadn't learned about that in school. Suddenly, the Wishling looked around, sniffing the air. "*Mmmmm*," he said, a smile creeping over his face. "Angel food cake."

That gave Sage a moment to think. And then, to her surprise, she found herself looking deep into his eyes and saying: "My name is Sage. I am the new student in school."

His reaction both surprised and delighted her. He nodded, his face solemn, almost as if he was in a trance. "Yes," he said. "Your name is Sage. You are the new student in school." He took another sniff and closed his eyes for a moment. "Reminds me of the cakes my grandma baked for me and my sister after school. She used to let us lick the beaters when she was done. Go right ahead!"

Sage allowed herself a small smile of victory as she resumed walking down the hallway and moved up the stairs, her footsteps echoing. She added observation number two: *Find out what a hall pass is. Seems important.*

ARRIVAL AT DESTINATION, the Star-Zap spelled out. Sage paused in front of the classroom door, took a deep breath, smoothed her braids, and opened it. Twenty-five students swiveled their heads in her direction. Sage suddenly felt self-conscious for the first time. It was an unfamiliar feeling, and fortunately only a momentary one.

A pretty adult female Wishling with straight blond hair pulled back into a low ponytail came to the door in a red polka-dotted dress. "May I help you?" she asked. She had a puzzled expression on her face. Then she looked down the hallway and breathed in deeply.

"They must be baking carrot cake in the lunchroom. Delicious." She smiled a faraway smile. "I can almost taste my mom's cream cheese frosting."

This time Sage knew just what to do. She looked deep into the teacher's eyes. "I am Sage," she said pleasantly. "I am the new student in your class."

The teacher nodded, just as the man in the hall had. "You are Sage. You are the new student in my class," she repeated. She pointed to a desk halfway down the row closest to the windows. "Please be seated. I am Ms. Daniels, your teacher."

Mission 1, Wishworld Observation #3: Young Star Darlings clearly have some form of mind control over adults. Sage walked down the aisle as some of the students gave her curious glances. She looked down at her outfit, and her eyes widened in surprise. In her rush to change, she hadn't noticed that the outfit changer had selected a bright green-and-blue-striped top, an orange skirt, and bright yellow leggings. She looked down again. And red-and-purple shoes. She grinned. She looked like a rainbow! *Well, at least I'm very bright and cheerful,* she thought.

A couple of the students tittered as she passed.

"Class," said the teacher. "There's no need to be rude to our new classmate."

"Nice backpack," said a boy. "But why isn't it on your back?"

Sage looked down at the bag, which she was wearing on her chest.

"Oops," she said. "I guess I thought it was a frontpack!"

The class laughed. But in a nice way, like she had made a joke on purpose. Sage grinned. She was off to a good start, completely unintentionally.

Sage stepped over a boy's outstretched legs and slid

into the plastic seat, resting her arms on the desk that was attached to it. *Jon was here* was scratched into the surface. She waited for the seat to adjust. But it stayed the same—hard, plastic, and uncomfortable. That was observation number four: *Wishling chairs do not adjust.*

She glanced around the room, wondering which student was the Wisher. Her Wish Pendant was glowing faintly, proof that her Wisher was nearby. Was it the redhead with the freckles? The pigtailed blonde staring into space? The one with jet-black shoulder-length hair who was gazing at her curiously? It could be anyone!

Ms. Daniels resumed her math lesson. She took a red writing utensil and copied numbers and symbols on the smooth white surface that ran across the front wall of the classroom. "Now, who wants to take a stab at this equation?" she asked.

Sage sat up with interest. Would a student actually stab it? Now *that* would be an interesting observation! But to her disappointment, no one did.

"Come on, guys," said Ms. Daniels. "Someone come up here and show Sage here how good we are at long division."

No volunteers.

"Two hundred and ninety-one thousand, six hundred and six divided by three hundred and seventy-one,"

Ms. Daniels said. "Remember: Dirty Monkeys Smell Completely Bad. You must Divide, Multiply, Subtract, Compare, and Bring Dow—"

"Seven hundred and eighty-six," Sage said automatically. The students stared at her with looks of awe on their faces. Sage felt a flush of pleasure at being the center of attention, this time in a good way. "Sage, we must first raise our—" Ms. Daniels's voice broke off. She looked down at her book. "That's right," she said slowly. She wrinkled her brow. "How is that possible? Are you using a calculator?"

"A what-ulator?" asked Sage. The class giggled in unison.

Ms. Daniels narrowed her eyes, then looked down at her book again. "Fifty thousand, one hundred ninety-three divided by ninety-nine?" she said.

"Five hundred and seven," said Sage, though she was getting the feeling that she should just be keeping her mouth shut. She started to feel uncomfortable as she realized that everyone was staring at her even harder. Sage sank lower in her seat. All that attention couldn't be good. She was supposed to blend in, after all.

Ms. Daniels looked puzzled. "Ninety-two thousand, five hundred and forty-five divided by four hundred and fifteen?"

And even though every fiber of her being wanted to shout out the right answer, Sage forced herself to say, "Two hundred and twenty-two?"

Ms. Daniels nodded, clearly satisfied. "No, it's two hundred and twenty-three! You must have had the same math book in your last school. That's got to be it."

"That's right," said Sage.

Mission 1, Wishworld Observation #5: If you want to remain undercover at school, keep your star talents to yourself. No showing off, tempting though it may be!

CHAPTER 8

Boy, did Sage feel sorry for Wishling students. Their lunchroom was nothing at all like the Celestial Café. It was noisy and smelled funny, kind of like stinkberries. There were no tablecloths, no plush chairs, no deep carpeting to sink your feet into. No climate control. There wasn't a cloth napkin to be seen.

Where was a Bot-Bot waiter to take your order when you needed one? It was positively primitive: you had to grab a plastic tray, point to the food you wanted, and wait while a lady with a net over her hair scooped it up and handed it to you. She would have to tell Professor Elara Ursa all about it when she returned to Starland.

And the food—well, Sage's stomach churned when

she saw it. Nevertheless, she pointed to something called mac and cheese and received a dense orange square on a plate. Everyone else was grabbing containers from a large cool box, so Sage grabbed one, too.

Sage stood in the middle of the room, wondering where to begin her search for her Wisher, when someone called out, "Hey, new girl! Over here!"

Sage headed over to the wildly waving Wishling and found herself at a lunch table with a bunch of girls from her class: the redhead, the one with the blond pigtails, and the one with jet-black hair were among them. They all introduced themselves—Maria, Hailey, Jenna, Ella, and Madison. Sage nodded and smiled at them. Now she was getting somewhere.

"You're really good at math," said the freckled redhead, whose name was Jenna. "You made it look like a piece of cake!"

"It looked like . . . cake?" Sage asked, confused. "What kind?"

The Wishling laughed, thinking Sage was making a joke.

"Yeah, you really did make it look easy," said Maria, who had shoulder-length dark hair and pretty brown eyes.

Sage nodded and smiled. *Mission 1, Wishworld Observation #6: Add "piece of cake" to the Wishling dictionary. It means "easy."*

"I like your outfit," said Hailey, the blonde with the pigtails. "Very colorful!"

"Thanks," said Sage. She picked up a box labeled CHOCOLATE MILK from her tray. "Ah, chocolate," she said, remembering her first Wishers 101 class. "It must be Valentine's Day!" She felt pleased to have made the connection. She was a little worried because Professor Ursa warned it would taste terrible.

The girls stared for a moment, then burst into laughter. "You are so funny!" cried Maria.

Sage shrugged. She turned the box upside down, studying it. She had no idea how to open it. They hadn't gotten to beverages in her Wishers 101 class.

The Wishlings started laughing again. "You can divide huge numbers in your head, but now you're acting like you're from another planet!" said Madison, a thin Wishling with super-short light brown hair.

Sage gulped. *Oh, starf!* Did Madison really know that she wasn't from Wishworld? What was she going to do? The Wishlings laughed and laughed. "Do you ever stop joking?" Madison asked. Sage suddenly realized that they were kidding. She sighed with relief.

Maria reached over and grabbed Sage's container, tore a short plastic tube off the back of it, and stabbed it into the box. "Here you go," she said, handing it back to Sage.

Still confused, Sage took it, then hesitantly put the tube into her mouth and drank. Her eyes widened. The drink was cold, sweet, rich, and improbably delicious. Professor Elara Ursa couldn't have been more wrong about chocolate. It was the best thing she'd ever tasted.

Madison laughed. "You act like you've never had chocolate milk before!" she said.

Sage grinned. Little did she know!

"Are you thinking what I'm thinking?" said Jenna. The rest of the girls nodded. They suddenly started whispering among themselves.

"So listen, new girl," said Jenna. "We think you're funny and we've decided to invite you to sit at our lunch table. Permanently."

Sage stole a glance at her Wish Pendant. It was still only faintly glowing. So none of these girls was her Wisher. But it meant she must be nearby.

"Thanks," she said.

"Here are some things you need to know to survive in Ms. Daniels's class. Joey Peterson picks his nose. So don't ever touch his hands if you can help it. Ms. Daniels gives surprise spelling quizzes every Friday, so be prepared."

"Molly Chow brings in the best birthday treats, so be nice to her and you'll always get seconds. And whatever you do, stay away from Genevieve," offered Hailey.

"Who's Genevieve?" Sage asked.

"Just the meanest girl in class," said Maria.

"The meanest girl in school," Ella said, correcting her. "She's over there in line in the pink dress."

"She's also the most spoiled girl in school," added Maria. "She's so mean I heard that she made this girl cry because she didn't like her outfit. You don't get much meaner than that!"

"That's pretty mean," agreed Sage.

"Well, you're a lot of fun," said Jenna. "Friendly." She made a face. "Not like that *other* new girl," she added.

"Who?" Sage asked.

"Jane," Hailey answered. "She's just so weird. She's like the complete opposite of you. It's like she thinks that *we* should be going out of our way to get to know *her*."

"She ignores us at school for an entire month but then expects us all to come to her birthday party. That takes a lot of nerve," added Jenna.

Sage sat up straight. *Interesting.* "So none of you are going to her party?" she asked.

"No way," said Ella. "Like, try to make friends with me first. I'm not just going to show up at your party when I don't know you."

"I bet she wishes you would all go to her party," Sage mused aloud.

"Well, she's going to keep wishing," said Hailey. Sage stood up, her heart racing with excitement. Could she have figured it out so quickly?

"The bell hasn't rung yet," said Maria. "Where are you going?"

"I'm going to say hello to Jane," she said. "Where is she?"

"Over there, by herself. As usual," said Ella, pointing to a table across the room. "Tell her we say hello!"

That sent the Wishlings into further peals of laughter.

Sage took that moment to head across the room. Jenna stopped laughing. "Wait," she said. "She's serious."

Sage stood at the head of the table where a female Wishling with long brown hair pulled back into a ponytail sat hunched over a book, eating a sandwich, her brow furrowed in concentration.

Sage studied her. Was she deeply engrossed in what she was reading or deeply engrossed in looking busy?

"Hey," Sage said. "Is this seat taken?"

Jane looked up, frowning at Sage's lame joke. "You're kidding, right? Not funny."

"Sorry," said Sage, leaning a hand on the table. "So, we're in the same class, huh? Any tips for the even newer girl?" She put her elbows on the table and rested her chin in her hands.

"You seem to be doing just fine," said Jane coldly. "Look at you, first day at school and you already have more friends than I do after a month."

Because I'm friendly, Sage thought. But she kept it to herself. She took a deep breath and plunged right in. "So, I hear you're having a birthday party."

Jane closed her book with a bang. "It's my mother's fault!" she exclaimed. "I didn't even want to have one. But she convinced me to invite almost every girl in the class. And then no one RSVP'd. Not a single person. Talk about humiliating! Now I'm the class loser and things are worse than ever."

"Well, I'd like to come," said Sage gently. "I love parties."

There was a momentary flash of excitement in Jane's eyes. But then her eyes narrowed. She turned away.

"Leave me alone," she said.

Sage blinked. "What did you say?"

"I said leave me alone," Jane repeated. She scowled. "I bet those girls just sent you over here to make fun of me, didn't they?"

"They didn't, I swear!" said Sage. She put up her hands and took a step backward while stealing a glance at her Wish Pendant. It was brightly lit. *Yes!*

"Oops," she said as she bumped into a passing student. "Pardon me."

"Ouch," said the student. "My foot!"

Sage turned around to see who it was. *Oh, great. Genevieve.*

"Sorry," said Sage.

"Whatever," said Genevieve with a shrug. She looked Sage up and down. "Hey, nice outfit."

Sage narrowed her eyes. She knew what Genevieve was up to. She was being sarcastic! Sage gave the girl a mean look. Genevieve stared back, about to say something. Then she walked away.

Mission 1, Wishworld Observation #7: There are mean kids everywhere—no matter what star you are on.

She turned back to her Wisher. "So would you say that you wish that people would come to your party?" she asked—quite cleverly, she thought.

"Didn't we cover that already?" Jane asked.

Sage pressed on. "Would you say that it is your heart's desire?"

Jane looked at Sage to see if she was serious. "Yeah, I guess it is," she admitted.

"Well, I really want to come to your party," Sage told Jane. "In fact, I want to help you throw the best party ever. A party so great that every Wish—I mean, girl in the class is going to beg to come."

"Everyone except for Genevieve," said Jane. "She's not invited." The scowl disappeared from her face and was replaced by a hopeful expression. "Do you really think people will come to my party?" she said softly.

"I really do," said Sage, nodding.

Now all I have to do is help Jane convince the rest of the female Wishlings in the class to come, she thought. *This is going to be a piece of pie.*

Sage felt very pleased with herself, already using a Wishling expression on her first day. *Hey, I'm a natural!* she thought. Everything was falling into place perfectly. The only thing left was to figure out *how* she was going to help make the wish come true. But the hard part was done. Professor Lucretia Delphinus would be proud.

CHAPTER 9

"There is no way I am going to Jane's birthday party," Jenna said, slamming her locker door and jamming the lock closed. She spun around, a scowl on her pretty face. "She's just not nice!"

Sage shook her head. "Listen, Jane actually *is* really nice. I think she just seems strange because she's too shy to talk to you guys."

Jenna shrugged. "Fine, I believe you," she said. Sage felt excited for a starsec. "But I still don't want to go to her party," she concluded.

Sage was flummoxed. Then she had an idea. She held her Wish Pendant in her hand. Maybe her special talent was young Wishling mind control. She looked deeply into Jenna's eyes. "You are going to Jane's party," she said. "You will tell all your friends to come, too."

Jenna stared back at Sage for a moment. "Whatever you say, Sage."

Sage grinned.

Jenna snorted with laughter. "You didn't think I was serious, did you? As if! Oh, Sage, you're so funny!"

So young Wishling mind control is not my special talent, thought Sage. *I wonder what it could be?*

Sage's heart sank. Jenna was the ringleader. If she didn't go, the rest of her friends wouldn't, either. "Is there something that would change your mind?" she asked pleadingly. "Anything you can think of?"

"No," said Jenna. But she had a funny look on her face. Sage had a feeling there was something that would convince Jenna. On a whim, she held her Wish Pendant and concentrated on the girl's thoughts to see if she could read them. She could! She had discovered her talent! Starmendous!

Jenna's thoughts flooded into Sage's mind: *Got to finish that math homework before volleyball practice. . . . Where's my notebook? . . . Wonder if Mom is making fried chicken tonight. . . . Sage has cool hair. . . . I would go to that party if they did something cool. So sick of those boring baby parties with piñatas and musical chairs. . . . Where is that notebook?*

Wow! It worked! Sage felt exhausted and she glanced

down at her Wish Pendant to see that the energy level had been seriously depleted. And she had no idea what Jenna meant—musical furniture? A pin-whatta? But it didn't matter. She knew how to make Jane's wish come true now.

Sage marched down the hallway, where she found Jane kneeling in front of her locker, shoving books into her backpack.

"Hey," Jane said to Sage. "I was looking for you. Want to come over and help me plan my party?"

"Great idea!" said Sage.

Jane zipped her bag and stood up. "I saw you talking to Jenna," she said eagerly. "Did she say she'll come?"

"I'm working on it," replied Sage.

They left the school together and walked down the sidewalk side by side. Fallen leaves crunched pleasantly under their feet. "Nice neighborhood," said Sage. The lawns were well manicured and the houses were large and imposing.

"This is the fancy part of town," Jane explained. "That's where Genevieve lives." She pointed to a particularly large home with a curved driveway.

"What's that little house for?" asked Sage, pointing. It had four doors but no windows.

Jane giggled. "Oh, Sage, you're so silly. You know that's the garage!"

"Uh, right," said Sage. "So, Genevieve seems pretty mean."

"That's what everyone says," replied Jane. "So I guess it must be true, right?" She shrugged. "I don't want to take any chances, so I just avoid her."

She glanced at Sage. "I love your lavender streak," she said. "I wish my mom would let me dye my hair."

Sage touched her hair. She hadn't realized she had a streak of lavender. If Jane liked the streak, imagine if she could see what Sage's real hair looked like.

"So, where are you from?" Jane asked Sage.

Sage had a moment of panic. "Oh, um . . . from far away," she answered.

Jane nodded. "Me too!" she said. "We moved all the way from Connecticut."

Sage hid a smile. "It's hard to be the new girl," she said.

"Tell me about it," said Jane.

Sage kicked a pebble as the two girls walked together in silence.

"Hey," Sage said suddenly. "Do you have any chocolate milk at your house?"

★

Jane's mom, Mrs. Newman, was positively beaming when her daughter arrived home with a friend.

"It is so lovely to meet you, Sage!" she gushed. "I'm so happy to meet one of Jane's new friends!" She turned to her daughter. "See? I told you it was only a matter of time!"

"*Moooom,*" groaned Jane, looking completely humiliated. Sage understood how Jane felt. Wishworld moms were remarkably similar to Starland moms—totally concerned about their kids while being utterly oblivious to how self-conscious their kids could be. Mrs. Newman hovered over Jane, tucking a stray piece of hair behind her daughter's ear. Jane swatted at her mother's hand good-naturedly. A wave of homesickness washed over Sage and she suddenly missed her family.

"So, let's get down to business," Sage said, more sharply than she intended.

Jane raised her eyebrows. "Okay," she said. "Where do we start?"

"We need to plan a"—Sage used a Wishworld expression she had overheard in the cafeteria line—"totally awesome party."

Jane nodded. "Okay. How about—"

"I have an idea!" interrupted Jane's mother, an

excited grin on her face. "How about an old-fashioned party, like from when I was a girl? You know, pin the tail on the donkey, musical chairs, bobbing for apples . . ."

"No!" shouted Sage, recalling Jenna's thoughts.

Jane and her mom gaped at her.

"I mean, great idea, but that's been done before," Sage explained quickly. "Let's be different. Unique!"

"How about a magician?" asked Mrs. Newman. "Or a funny clown who makes balloon animals?"

Sage stole a quick glance at Jane. The look of horror on Jane's face told her all she needed to know.

"*Mooooom*," said Jane. "We're not, like, three years old." She leaned over and whispered to Sage, "Let's go up to my room and plan in private."

Sage nodded with approval at Jane's bedroom. It was very tidy; her bed was made and her stuffed animals were neatly arranged on it. Sage spotted a shelf full of actual paper books. She carefully removed one and held it in her hands. She ran her fingers over the smooth cover. It was stark—black and red and white—with a picture of two girls in fur caps and capes standing on a snowy hill, with three snarling wolves below them. After a moment she lifted the cover and flipped through the thin pages. "Wow," she said.

Jane laughed. "You act like you've never seen a book

before!" she said. She looked over Sage's shoulder. "*The Wolves of Willoughby Chase*," Jane said. "It's so good. A fancy English manor. Two cousins. An evil governess. A terrible orphanage." She sighed. "It's one of my favorite books of all time."

"It sounds really exciting," said Sage.

Jane smiled. "Keep it. I've got another copy."

Sage carefully placed the book in her backpack. When she turned back around, she spotted something colorful lying on top of Jane's bookshelf. It was a pretty T-shirt, with a multicolored heart in vibrant pinks, purples, and blues. "What's that?" she asked curiously.

"Oh, it's just a T-shirt I made," said Jane offhandedly. But Sage was intrigued. She gazed at Jane's creation, taking in the bright colors, the artful placement of glitter.

"You made this?" Sage said. "It's beautiful."

Jane laughed. "I've got a dozen of them." At Sage's look of surprise, she shrugged. "I've had a lot of free time on my hands since we moved here!"

"Amazing," said Sage.

So Jane taught Sage how to make her very own gorgeous, glittery T-shirt. Sage tore different colors of crepe paper into small pieces, arranged them into a star shape (of course), and sprayed the pieces carefully with a water bottle filled with a pungent liquid called white vinegar. The wet paper left colorful shapes on the T-shirt. Jane then hit the shirt with a blast of glitter spray.

"You did a great job," said Jane when they were done and Sage's T-shirt lay drying on the desk. "Just wait till it dries."

"Thanks," said Sage. "You're a good teacher!" She held out her multicolored hands and wiggled her fingers, just like her professor had shown them.

"Jazz hands!" said Sage.

Jane laughed. "Oops, I forgot to give you gloves!" said Jane.

"Never mind," said Sage. "They're kind of pretty, in a weird way!"

"That was fun," said Jane. Then she sighed. "But we still don't have a plan for my birthday. Can you please stay for dinner so we can keep working on it?"

Sage touched the hem of her still-damp T-shirt and smiled. "Don't worry," she said to Jane. "I've got it all figured out. And I'd love to stay for dinner."

Jane's father sat at the head of the dining room table and sniffed the air. "Are we having pineapple upside-down cake for dessert tonight?" he asked hopefully. "It smells so good!"

"No," said Mrs. Newman. "We're having ice cream." She wrinkled her brow. "That's funny. I smell cake, too. But it smells like chocolate to me."

Sage stared at them. This was getting weird. "Please pass the . . . food," she said.

Mr. Newman chuckled. "You mean the spaghetti and marinara sauce? Sure!"

Sage finished two bowls of spaghetti. It was awkward to eat, but it was delicious!

For dessert they had something called strawberry ice cream. It was cold, sweet, and a lovely shade of pink.

After draining her third glass of chocolate milk, Sage volunteered to help clean up. As soon as she and Mrs. Newman were alone in the kitchen, Sage turned to her. "I have an idea," she said, looking deep into the woman's hazel eyes. "Why don't I sleep over at your house tonight?"

Jane walked in, holding a handful of forks, knives, and spoons, which she dumped into the sink with a clatter.

"I have an idea," Mrs. Newman said to Sage. "Why don't you sleep over at our house tonight?"

Jane's face lit up as she wiped her hands on a dish towel. "Really?" she said, giving her mom a quick hug around the middle. "That would be great." She grabbed

Sage's arm and steered her out of the kitchen and up the stairs. "My mom must really like you," she said. "She never lets me have sleepovers on a school night!"

After deciding to wear their new T-shirts to school the next day, the two girls did their homework (which Sage finished with impossible speed) and got ready for bed. Sage headed to the bathroom to slip into a nightgown she had borrowed from Jane. She turned to the mirror and stared at her transformed Wishling-looking self. Then she recalled Lady Stella's parting words to her: *Don't forget your Mirror Mantra!* She could use a jolt of positivity. But what was it?

Sage closed her eyes and searched her memory. Then she opened them, reached up, touched the mirror, and said: "I believe in you. Glow for it!"

Sage gasped as her reflection suddenly transformed. Her hair was its usual bright lavender, her skin was sparkly, and her eyes were clear violet once more. She looked down and saw that her braids were still light brown, then looked up again to admire her true self. She felt both rejuvenated and at peace.

There was a knock on the door. "Sage, are you almost done in there?" Jane called out. Sage jumped, grateful she had locked the door behind her. Imagine if Jane could see Sage's true self. That would be so dangerous!

"Just a star— I mean, a minute," Sage called. She quickly got changed, then headed to the door and shut off the light, giving her reflection one final glance.

She climbed into the low bed that pulled out from under Jane's bigger one and drew the covers up to her chin.

"Hey, Sage?" Jane whispered in the dark. "Do you really think people are going to come to my party?"

"I do," said Sage. "I really do."

Jane sighed. "I'm just not sure. Things were so much easier at home. I wish we'd never moved. I miss my old life."

"I know what you mean," said Sage. Now that her brain wasn't racing a moonium floozels a starmin, she realized she felt a tiny bit homesick. Sage could hear Jane shifting under the covers.

"I guess I thought it was going to be easy," Jane continued. "I had so many friends in my old school. I was really popular. Everyone always wanted to come to my birthday parties. I don't know. I just expected that people were going to want to be my friend, so I didn't even try. I'm kind of shy, you know." She sighed. "Maybe I missed my chance. Maybe it's too late."

"I don't think it's ever too late to make friends," said Sage. "I think everything is going to turn out okay. Just be yourself tomorrow—friendly and kind."

"Okay," said Jane. "I hope you're right. Good night."

"Good night, Jane." *I hope I'm right, too,* thought Sage before she drifted off to sleep. *Because if I am, everyone is going to be so proud of me.*

She rolled over. *Oh, and because I'll be helping save Starland, too, of course!*

CHAPTER 10

"Ohmigod! Where did you get that T-shirt?" Jenna squealed. "It's supercute!"

"Oh, this?" said Sage, holding back a grin. Things were going exactly as planned. She just wished she didn't feel so tired. There must be something in Wishworld's atmosphere that was sapping her strength. She was wearing her brand-new T-shirt over a turquoise long-sleeved shirt, with a lavender skirt, lavender-and-turquoise-striped tights, and lace-up boots.

It had taken a dozen tries with the outfit changer in the privacy of Jane's bathroom to pull together the perfect look. But she looked great, no doubt about it. If Jane was surprised that Sage hadn't asked to borrow clothes, she didn't mention it. Maybe young Wishlings always packed extra outfits in the backpacks they carried. Sage would have to look into that.

"Yes!" Jenna said. "It is fab-u-lous!"

The rest of the girls left their lockers ajar and gathered around Sage, admiring her outfit.

"Did you get it at the mall?" asked Maria.

The what? thought Sage. "Believe it or not, you can make one yourself," she said. "As a matter of fact, I'll be giving lessons . . ."

"Awesome!" said Hailey. "Just tell us when and where."

". . . with my friend Jane at her birthday party this Saturday," Sage finished. "She taught me how to make it. Right, Jane?"

Her eyes shyly downcast, Jane sidled across the hallway in her own colorful T-shirt. Hers was even more vibrant than Sage's. "Right," she said softly.

There was an awkward silence. The girls' eyes went back and forth as they glanced at one another.

"I totally forgot to RSVP," Jenna finally said. "Jane, can I still come?"

"Yeah," said Maria. "It's not too late, is it?"

Jane couldn't keep the smile off her face. "No, not too late at all," she said happily.

Sage noticed that Jane sat up straighter and even raised her hand a few times in class that morning. Her confidence was growing. Ms. Daniels was delighted. "Great job today, Jane," she said as the class filed out of the room. "Keep up the good work!"

Sage must have looked as tired as she felt, because the gym teacher let her sit in the bleachers for gym. She had a front-row seat for class, where she noted that Ella chose Jane to be the first one on her team. It turned out that was a wise choice: Jane was very good at the game they were playing. It was called dodgeball, and it didn't seem that fun at all to Sage. But Jane loved it: she got player after player out with her throws and caught the ball every time it was aimed at her.

When it was down to Jane and a young male Wishling with a crew cut from the other team, she threw the last ball low at her adversary with deadly accuracy. It ricocheted off his foot, winning the game for her team. She looked positively thrilled as her teammates pounded her on the back in congratulations.

At lunch, Sage and Jane grabbed trays and made their selections. Sage took two chocolate-milk boxes this time. They started to head to the other side of the lunchroom to Jane's usual table. "Hey, Jane! Sage! Over here!" cried Jenna. "Sit with us!"

Jane's eyes were shining as they made their way to Jenna and her friends. Sage felt a swell of pride for how close she was to completing her mission, and she checked the Countdown Clock on her Star-Zap. *Plenty of time*, she thought confidently.

"Sit next to me, Jane," Jenna commanded. She didn't even wait until Jane was seated before she exclaimed, "So, tell us more about your party! We can't wait!"

"I've been thinking about making a tie-dyed birthday cake!" said Jane. "What do you guys think?"

"Awesome!" several voices chorused.

Sage grinned. That was news to her. It *was* an awesome idea.

My work here is done, thought Sage. *Well, almost.* But her victorious feeling did not last long. "Uh-oh, look who's headed our way," said Ella.

Sage froze for a moment, then turned around. As she feared, it was Genevieve. Despite her apprehension, Sage couldn't help admiring the fluffy white sweaterdress the girl was wearing. It was soft and cozy-looking, with a draped collar. Genevieve's feet were clad in navy blue ankle boots; one tapped impatiently against the cafeteria floor once she came to an abrupt stop at the group's cafeteria table.

As Sage turned around to face her, she felt a sudden burst of energy. *That's odd*, she thought.

Genevieve looked from Sage to Jane and back again. "Oh, look, the two new girls are wearing matching shirts. How cute," she said.

Everyone gazed at Genevieve in silence.

Sage smiled. "Star sal—I mean, thank you," she said.

But Jenna scowled. "My mother always says if you don't have anything nice to say, don't say anything at all."

Genevieve looked pained. "But I"—she took a deep breath—"I have an idea. . . ."

Suddenly, Sage realized what was going on. Genevieve was being sarcastic again! She was making fun of Jane and messing up Sage's plan.

Sage felt her cheeks getting warm. She could hear Gran's voice saying, *Take a deep breath before you speak, Sage. You can choose a better response!* But she didn't listen. She stood up and faced the girl. "I have an idea, too," she said. "Why don't you leave us alone?"

Genevieve's face sort of crumpled. "Fine," she said. But then she suddenly glanced down and shrieked. "Look what you've done!"

Sage looked down . . . and realized she had been clenching her box of chocolate milk in her angry hands, squeezing its contents all over Genevieve's sweaterdress. It was a complete and utter mess. To her dismay, the girls at the table—everyone except Jane—erupted into laughter.

Mission 1, Wishworld Observation #8: Wishling clothing really does stain.

"You ruined my cashmere dress!" Genevieve yelled. She looked as if she was going to cry. Sage sat down, defeated and embarrassed. Her red-hot anger had disappeared as quickly as it had surfaced, replaced by an overwhelming feeling of sorrow. Genevieve spun on her heel and stormed off, her golden bracelets jangling.

"Don't worry about her," said Jenna. "She deserves it. She's so mean. Besides, her parents can just buy her a whole closetful of new dresses."

But Sage felt terrible anyway. And she felt dreadfully tired—so tired she could hardly force herself to stand when the end-of-lunch bell rang. *Oh well, at least my mission is under control,* she thought.

Jane was visiting her grandmother that night, so the two girls said good-bye after school. "Come to my house early tomorrow!" Jane called, and Sage promised she would. Sage headed back to the park where she had landed. She was excited to use the special tent that Lady Stella had told her about. When she got to the park, she reached into her backpack and pulled out her Star-Zap to project her special tent. Before her unbelieving eyes appeared a large, luxurious sleeping quarters. It was invisible to Wishlings and once inside, Sage herself was undetectable. She was pleased to realize that it contained anything she would need—food, light, holo-books, and her favorite blanket. It was warm, comfortable, and extremely cozy.

Later that night, tired as she was, Sage couldn't fall asleep. She just couldn't shake the nagging feeling that something wasn't quite right. Sage opened the tent flap and gazed up at the heavens.

Suddenly, a falling star illuminated the night sky with a flash of brilliant light. A feeling of peace swept over Sage, and she smiled. Comforted, she closed her eyes and fell into a deep and dreamless sleep.

CHAPTER 11

It had been a very busy morning, but everything was almost ready, and the backyard looked perfect. The tables were covered with brightly patterned tablecloths and jars full of eye-popping displays of wildflowers. The tree branches were twinkling with fairy lights, and paper lanterns hung between the trees.

A colorful banner, with a letter on each triangular flag, spelled out HAPPY BIRTHDAY, JANE! A fun photo booth was set up in a corner with a polka-dotted back-drop and silly paper props like hats and fake eyeglasses. Jane's mother was heating up the grill, and her father was practicing playing DJ—and he was actually pretty good. Jane bustled about, setting up the "make your own tie-dyed T-shirt" table. She looked up at Sage. "Hey, the guests are going to be here in fifteen minutes! Go get dressed!"

Sage looked down at her dusty T-shirt. "Good idea!" she said with a laugh. She headed upstairs, glancing down at her Star-Zap. Seventy-five starmins to go on the Countdown Clock. Talk about cutting things close!

Sage took a last look around Jane's bedroom as she packed up her backpack. These Wishling artifacts—her notebook and pencils from school, her math book, and the paperback that Jane had given her—would be of real interest to her Wishers 101 teacher, Professor Elara Ursa.

Sage put on her tie-dyed shirt. She used her outfit changer to select a pretty lavender skirt, turquoise leggings, and lavender flats with big flowers on them. Just as she finished brushing and braiding her hair, the doorbell rang. She bounded downstairs and opened the door with a smile.

"Welcome to Jane's . . ." She blinked in surprise. "OMS, what are *you* doing here?"

In front of her was a familiar face—Tessa! Sage blinked at her in surprise. "How . . . what . . . but you're sparkly! And your hair is still green!" Sage managed to get out. Tessa was as shimmery and vibrant as she was at home. Tessa grinned. "You look sparkly, too," she told Sage. "I think we can see each other as we actually are."

"Aren't you going to invite me in?" asked Tessa.

"Why are you here?" Sage said huffily. "Everything's fine. The party is about to start. I'm just going to collect my wish energy and come back home."

Tessa smiled. "Sage, relax. I'm sure it's no big deal, but Lady Stella thinks that something might be a little off with your mission. Your wish energy levels were getting low so she sent me down to check things out," she said. "Your vital signs were worrying her. It was pretty clear that your strength levels were falling. And that is the classic sign of a mission gone wrong."

Sage shook her head. "So I'm a little tired. So what? Look, as soon as the first guest arrives, the wish will come true. The Countdown Clock will stop. You'll see."

Just then Jane came in.

"Hey, Sage, tell me if I'm just being crazy . . ." Her voice trailed off. "Hello!" she said. "Sage, I didn't know you invited a friend!"

"Yes," Sage said quickly. "I hope that's okay. This is my friend Tessa."

"No, that's awesome!" said Jane. "Pleased to meet you, Tessa. The more the merrier. Make yourself at home. We have tons of food and extra T-shirts you can make." She pulled Sage aside. "I'm just freaking out a little," she said softly. She pointed at her T-shirt. "I wish the shirts were fancier. Doesn't it feel like something is missing?"

"Oh, don't be silly," said Sage. "They're perfect just the way they are."

"I guess you're right," Jane said with a sigh. "I just wish they were a little cooler-looking."

The doorbell rang. "The guests are here!" Jane squealed. She ran to the front door to let them in.

Sage held up her Star-Zap. "Now watch," she said. "The clock is going to stop. Her wish has been granted. The guests are here."

Tessa shook her head. "Something's wrong," she said.

"Just wait," said Sage.

"Ella! Madison!" cried Jane. The two girls looked like special party editions of themselves. Madison wore a headband with a huge flower on it, and Ella had on a pair of glittery shoes. They hugged Jane hello and handed her their gifts. They waved to Sage as Jane ushered them through the house and into the backyard.

Sage gulped as the numbers kept ticking by. She could not believe her eyes. The wish had been fulfilled—there were people at Jane's party! But the Countdown Clock had not stopped.

Tessa shook her head. "See? Something is wrong. But there's still time to fix it. We just have to figure out what happened."

Sage sat down and buried her head in her hands. What was going on? She had done everything right!

"I don't get it," she said. "My necklace lit up when I met Jane."

"Do you think that she had another wish?" Tessa asked.

"No," replied Sage. "She told me this was her heart's desire."

Tessa wrinkled her brow. "Maybe your Wish Pendant malfunctioned?"

Sage took a deep breath. Her mind began to race. The pendant had glowed when she met Jane, hadn't it? She replayed the scene in her mind. She met Jane, stepped back to look at the glowing pendant—and bumped into Genevieve.

Oh, starf. Genevieve, the girl whom she had sprayed with an entire container of chocolate milk, the girl who totally disliked her, the one girl who was not invited to the party, was her Wisher.

Sage stood up and walked to the door.

"Where are you going?" Tessa asked.

Sage shook her head. "There's not enough time to explain! But I think I know how to fix this. I'll be right back!" She raced outside to find Jane, who was grinning, her cheeks flushed pink with excitement and happiness.

Sage ran to the front gate, throwing it open and nearly knocking over one of Jane's guests in the process.

She had wasted all her wish energy on the wrong wish. She couldn't even rely on her secret talent to help make this wish come true. She was all on her own. And she literally didn't have a starmin—make that a second—to lose.

CHAPTER 12

Please be home, *please be home, please be home,* Sage thought as she rang the bell for the third time. To her great relief, the door swung open. There stood Genevieve. She did not look pleased at all to see Sage. She crossed her arms, her golden bracelets jangling.

"What do you want?" Genevieve asked crossly.

"I want you to come to Jane's party," Sage said. "And so does she." She smiled. She suddenly felt much better just standing next to Genevieve.

Genevieve's eyes lit up for a brief moment, but then she frowned. "Well, I don't," she retorted, starting to close the door.

Sage stuck out her foot to hold it open. Genevieve

looked very annoyed. "It's a little late, don't you think?" she asked.

"It was a mistake," explained Sage.

Genevieve laughed bitterly. "Don't you get it? I'm never invited to anything. For some crazy reason, everyone thinks I'm mean. And here's the funny part: I'm not even sure how that started.

"I'm not mean at all," she explained. "Maybe girls are jealous that I live in this big house or because I have fancy clothes. I don't know. But somehow the rumor got started that I'm mean. And I'm not," Genevieve repeated.

Her shoulders sagged. "I'm actually really nice."

She pointed to the shirt Sage was wearing. "Like when I came over in the cafeteria to tell you I liked your tie-dyed shirts. And everyone assumed I was just being sarcastic. And then you ruined my dress."

"I'm sorry," said Sage. "That was an accident." Then she realized something. "Hey, you really like the shirts?"

"Yeah," Genevieve said. "They're really pretty. They just need a little flash."

"That's what Jane was saying!" cried Sage. "Come on, you're the most fashionable girl in the class. What do you think the shirts need?"

"I'm the most fashionable girl in the *school*,"

Genevieve said with a smile. She studied the shirt. "I think it needs rhinestones." She reached forward and touched one of Sage's sleeves. "I also think you could decorate the sleeves. You know, gather them and tie them up with pretty satin ribbons."

Sage nodded excitedly. "Jane is going to love it," she said.

"I can lend you some ribbon and a rhinestone machine," said Genevieve.

Sage blinked in disbelief. Genevieve really *was* nice! "Actually," said Sage, "I was hoping you could bring them to the party. To show everyone how to use them." Genevieve paused for a moment. She bit her lip, sucked in her cheeks, and crossed her arms.

"You wish people would realize that you really are a nice person," guessed Sage. Oh, how she could've used her mind-reading skill just then! "Then you would be invited to birthday parties. Like Jane's." Genevieve looked embarrassed.

Sage jumped as a zap of electric current raced down her spine. It was like Professor Lucretia Delphinus had described, only much more intense.

"Are you okay?" asked Genevieve.

Sage nodded briskly. She did her best to collect

herself and said, "I can't think of anything nicer than helping someone out at their birthday party."

Genevieve still didn't look convinced.

Sage grabbed her hand. "Humor me, Genevieve," she said. "And repeat after me: I believe in you. Glow for it!"

Genevieve rolled her eyes. "What? That's crazy!"

"Please?" said Sage. She grabbed Genevieve's other hand, and together they repeated the words.

And then it happened: Sage felt a warm glow course through her, going out her right hand. She saw Genevieve smile as the surge of energy flowed through her and back to Sage's left hand. Genevieve had no idea what had just happened, but Sage had a wonderful feeling of peace and contentment. It was almost as if she was floating—though when she looked down she saw her feet firmly planted on the floor.

"Okay," said Genevieve. "Let's do this." She ran upstairs. Sage had a couple of nerve-racking moments as she watched the starmins tick by on her Countdown Clock.

But before too long, Genevieve came back downstairs wearing a pretty blue party dress and her golden bangles, a tote bag slung over her shoulder. "I've got everything we need," she said. "Let's go!"

They got back to Jane's house quickly. Genevieve suddenly grew shy as they pushed open the gate and walked to the backyard. Sage couldn't really blame her for feeling self-conscious as all eyes turned to her and the party grew quiet.

"Maybe I should just go back . . ." started Genevieve.

It didn't help when Jenna broke the silence. "Well, look who's here," she said. "Ms. Meanie herself."

But then Jane pushed forward, looking a little worried. "Hi, Genevieve," she said. "I'm glad you came to my party."

Genevieve bit her lip nervously. "Thanks for inviting me," she said. "I'm sorry I don't have a present. But I did bring these." She pulled out the rhinestone machine, containers full of sparkling stones, and thin satiny ribbons in every color of the rainbow. She grabbed an almost-dry T-shirt, and with a few lengths of ribbon and some artfully placed rhinestones, she transformed it from cute to completely dazzling.

"I want to do that!" Madison cried. Soon all the girls were clamoring for Genevieve's help. Even Jenna wanted to try it.

Jane smiled at Sage. "Wow, that's exactly what I was hoping for!"

Tessa walked over, a glass of lemonade in her hand. She had a funny grin on her face. "This stuff is goooooood," she said. She hiccupped. "But the clock is still ticking. You are almost out of time." She giggled. "Out of time!' she repeated.

Sage stared at Tessa. What was wrong with her? Then she looked at her Countdown Clock. Two starmins to go—and counting.

Her heart sank. Tessa was right. Time had run out for her.

CHAPTER 13

Just then she heard Jenna's voice. "Maybe I was wrong," she said. "Genevieve, you're actually pretty nice after all."

Genevieve grinned. "You're not so bad yourself, Jenna."

"Tessa look!" Sage cried. Tessa grabbed Sage's hand. Before Sage's amazed eyes, positive wish energy began to pour out of Genevieve, who had no idea that anything was happening. It danced through the air in a beautiful rainbow-colored arc before being absorbed into Sage's Wish Pendant.

And that's when the Countdown Clock stopped.

WISH GRANTED: MISSION COMPLETE, the Star-Zap screen read.

And then: COME HOME!

Tessa jumped up and down and hugged Sage. "I can't believe it! You did it!" she shouted. "This calls for some more lemonade."

Ella laughed. "Wow," she said. "Sage's friend *really* likes tie-dye."

Just then Mrs. Newman came up to Sage and placed a hand on her arm. "Thank you for making my daughter's birthday wish come true," she told her.

"You're very welcome," replied Sage. If Mrs. Newman only knew the half of it!

Tessa and Sage stayed until just after the birthday cake was unveiled. Because how could a Star Darling miss seeing a real live Wishling birthday cake? Everyone gasped when they saw the colorful confection—tie-dyed frosting on the outside and vibrant tie-dyed cake on the inside. Instead of candles, a profusion of sparklers rose from the center, shooting out a cascade of shimmering sparks. Everyone sang except for the Star Darlings; they didn't know the words. "I don't have to make a wish," Jane said as the cake was placed in front of her. "I got just what I wanted." She smiled at Sage. "Thank you, Sage."

"Oh, make one anyway," suggested Sage. "You can never have enough wishes. Good wishes, that is," she hastily added.

"I'll see you at home," Tessa told Sage when she had finished her third glass of lemonade. "This stuff is sooooooo good!" she said. She gave Sage a big hug, then grabbed her shoulders and looked deeply into her eyes. "Now it's time for you to say good-bye to Jane and Genevieve."

Sage gulped. How she hated good-byes! She had known this was coming, but it still was not going to be easy. Even though she hadn't really been assigned to Jane, she was still going to miss her. And Genevieve—she would never forget her first Wisher. Ever.

Sage found Jane and Genevieve together, chatting like old friends.

"I need to talk to you two," Sage told them. "In private."

The three girls walked to the front yard. Sage took a deep breath, anxiously poking at a balloon from the bunch tied to the fence. Jane's cheeks were flushed with excitement. "I can't believe it!" she gushed. "What a great party! Genevieve really made the shirts look awesome." She added, "We're going to go shopping together tomorrow; isn't that great?"

Genevieve smiled. "And we were both invited to Jenna's sleepover next weekend."

Sage smiled. Genevieve's wish was so powerful and so pure because it hadn't just involved her—it had affected everyone else at the party.

"By sharing yourself and your talents with everyone today, you made yourself happy, but you also brought joy to others, Genevieve," Sage told her. "Now you have to remember to take that happiness and hold on to it. You can close your eyes whenever you want and visualize your wish coming true. And feel that same happiness all over again."

The two girls looked at each other and nodded. "Thank you, Sage. You made both our wishes come true today," Genevieve said.

"Yeah, everyone is saying that this is the most fun party ever . . ." Jane's voice softened. "Sage, why do you look so sad?"

"I've got to go," Sage said, her voice thick. She was unable to meet Jane's gaze. "It has been great getting to know you guys and . . ."

Then her voice trailed off. But she had an idea. It went against everything she had been warned about. However, it just felt right. Summoning her energy, she held her Wish Pendant tightly in her hand and recited: "Star light, star bright, the first star I see tonight: I wish I may, I wish I might, have the wish I wish tonight."

Jane and Genevieve looked at her oddly, but their expressions quickly changed to ones of amazement.

A warm glow came over her, and Sage could feel it

coursing through her body, from the ends of her braids to the very tips of her toes. She glanced down at her now-lavender hair and admired her skin, which was glimmering once more. Jane and Genevieve just stared, their eyes wide, almost entranced. "Oh, Sage," Jane breathed. "You're so beautiful!"

Jane reached over and touched Sage's hair. "Your hair is lavender! And your skin is so sparkly!"

Genevieve shook her head. "How in the world?"

Without thinking, Sage leaned forward and gave first Jane and then Genevieve a tight squeeze. When she stepped back, she had returned to her dull Wishling appearance. The two girls stared at her blankly.

"Are you two okay?" Sage asked them.

The girls both had curious but distant looks on their faces. "Excuse me," Jane said, "but do I know you?" She smiled politely, waiting for an answer.

"Yeah," said Genevieve. "Have we met before?"

Sage blinked. It looked like her good-bye hug had completely wiped the girls' memories!

"No," she managed to say. "You don't know me at all." She took a deep breath.

"I just wanted to wish you a very happy birthday, Jane."

Epilogue

Moments after Sage had arrived back on Starland, her Star-Zap buzzed. REPORT TO WISH-HOUSE OFFICE IMMEDIATELY.

Sage knew she had come so close to failing her Wish Mission. Was she going to get into trouble? Would she be kicked off the Star Darlings team? Was it proof that Vivica was right, that she was never supposed to be at Starling Academy in the first place? Her stomach was in knots with worry, even though everything had turned out okay at the end.

Still, despite her nervousness, a feeling of peace came over Sage as she walked down the hallways of Starling Academy. Sage hadn't realized just how much she had missed Starland. She felt safe and welcome, waving to classmates who had no idea who she was. Or that she'd been gone at all. It didn't matter. She was just happy to be back, no matter what the consequences.

"Miss Sage!" said a funny voice.

Sage looked around the empty hallway. Was she hearing things?

"Up here!" said the voice.

Sage looked up. A small Bot-Bot guide hovered near the ceiling.

"It's me! MO-J4!"

"Oh, hey," said Sage, trying to remember if they had met before.

"I gave you a tour of the campus!" said MO-J4 a little peevishly. "So where have you been?"

"Oh, around," said Sage vaguely. She reached Lady Stella's door and knocked.

"Come in," said Lady Stella.

Sage concentrated and the door slid open silently.

"Nicely done," said MO-J4 admiringly. "I'll see you around, Miss Sage."

"See you," said Sage.

Pushing open the door, Sage spotted the other eleven Star Darlings seated around the table, all studying her curiously—except for Cassie, who gave her a wave and a huge grin.

"Welcome home, Sage," said the headmistress. "Congratulations on a successful mission."

And then all her fellow Star Darlings gave Sage a standing ovation.

"Really?" said Sage incredulously. "But I almost totally messed up!"

Lady Stella shook her head. "Sage, what you did was incredibly brave. You went on a mission to an unfamiliar world. Of course there were going to be glitches!" She smiled.

Sage breathed a sigh of relief. "Star salutations," she said. "But I want to thank Tessa for coming down to help me out."

"You fixed it all by yourself," said Tessa.

The headmistress held the Wish Orb and beckoned Sage to come closer, then solemnly placed it in her hands.

Sage held the Wish Orb in her hands. Its glow became more and more intense. "Look!" said Vega. "Something is happening!" To Sage's delight, the orb began to transform into a lavender boheminella, a luminous flower whose head hung like a lantern from its stem. It glowed with a soft light, and stardust drifted down from the blossom in a delicate cascade. "It's beautiful!" Sage breathed. "It is," agreed Lady Stella. "And from now on, this will be your personal Wish Blossom." Suddenly, the petals of the flower began to tremble. What was going on? Sage gasped as the flower opened to reveal a glossy dark purple stone with deep veins of shimmering starlight. It looked like a mini galaxy was locked inside its gleaming surface. Sage felt a deep sense of peace and well-being.

"Well, that is most extraordinary!" said Lady Stella, shaking her head.

"What is it?" Sage asked as the Star Darlings pressed closer to see the shimmering stone.

"All in due time," said Lady Stella. Sage thought the headmistress looked surprised—pleasantly so. "Until then, please guard this precious stone with your very life."

Sage took a deep breath and looked around the room at her fellow Star Darlings, enjoying her moment in the spotlight.

And she wondered which one of them would be next.

Sage lingered in Lady Stella's office after the room had cleared.

"Can I help you with anything, Sage?" Lady Stella asked kindly.

"I was wondering . . . I heard that maybe . . . I mean that someone told me . . ." Sage hemmed and hawed, unable to ask the headmistress the difficult question.

"The answer is no, Sage," Lady Stella answered. "You were admitted on your own strengths. No one helped you."

Sage grinned. "Star salutations, Lady Stella," was all she could say. "Star salutations."

Sage still couldn't shake the feeling that there was a look of concern on Lady Stella's face. And she hoped that she hadn't disappointed her in any way. But Sage practically skipped the whole way back to her room. She placed her hand on the scanner and it glowed bright blue. "Welcome home, Sage," the voice said. "And congratulations on a job well done!"

Sage stepped inside. Cassie was standing in front of her closet, a strange look on her face.

Sage reached into her backpack. "I brought something back for you," she said. "A Wishling book. It really is made out of paper."

Cassie gasped as Sage placed the book in her hands. "I wondered what one would look like," she said, running her fingers over the cover. She opened it and immediately started devouring the words. Then, realizing what she was doing, she laughed and closed the book, hugging it to her chest. "Wow—this is incredible. Star salutations, Sage. I'm glad you're back." Then she added shyly, "It was kind of lonely without you. I did a lot of thinking while you were away, and there's something I have to tell you." She fidgeted nervously.

"Do you want to tell me about your pet glowfur?" Sage asked with a smile.

Cassie's eyes widened. "How did you . . ."

"I had some time to think about it when I was alone on Wishworld," Sage explained. "I put it all together—the dream I had, which wasn't really a dream, was it? The Green Globule you ate, the glow from the closet, the sweet music."

Cassie opened her closet door. "Don't be afraid," she said. "You can come out." A small, furry, winged creature flew out, nuzzled Cassie's cheek, and landed on her shoulder. It began to sing the same beautiful song that Sage had heard, its belly glowing contentedly.

"I was afraid to tell you," Cassie said. "I wasn't sure if you liked pets."

"I do," said Sage. "Especially a cute one like this. What's his—or is it her—name?"

"Itty," said Cassie, blushing. "She was my mom's when she was little," she explained. Cassie lowered her eyes. "She really means a lot to me. Are you sure you're okay with this? Starling Academy has a no-pet policy, you know."

"It does?" said Sage.

"It's in the Student Manual," Cassie explained. At Sage's blank look she added, "You said you read it!"

"I must have skipped that part," said Sage.

Cassie giggled as the glowfur took off and landed on her head. "I hate to break the rules, but I'm so homesick, and Itty would be miserable without me." She smiled at her roommate. "I'm so glad you know. You can take care of her when it's time for my mission!"

"Absolutely," Sage said with a yawn. She got herself ready for bed in record time and slipped underneath the covers.

"So, tell me all about it," Cassie said, her eyes shining. "Everything that happened. What the girls were like. Exactly what the wish was. What kind of clothes did they wear? Everything!"

The glowfur began her evening song. It was sweet and gentle and calming. Sage yawned and began to speak. "It was a pretty bumpy ride down to Wishworld. I landed on a hill in the middle of a park and . . ." and then Sage fell asleep midsentence.

Her story would have to wait until tomorrow.

Libby and the Class Election

Prologue

TOP SECRET HOLO-COMMUNICATION

(Warning: This memorandum will disappear five seconds after it has been read.)

TO: The Star Darlings Guest Lecturers

Professor Margaret Dumarre

Professor Dolores Raye

Professor Illumia Wickes

Professor Elara Ursa

Professor Lucretia Delphinus

Professor Eugenia Bright

cc: Lady Cordial, Director of Admissions

FROM: Lady Stella, Headmistress

RE: Star Darlings Update

To All:

I am writing to inform you that Operation Star Darlings is up and running! My theory—that young Starlings granting the wishes of young Wishlings would result in a greater amount of wish energy—is correct.

However, I have both good and bad news. The good news is that the mission was successful and we collected a significant amount of wish energy. The bad news is there was a glitch in initial Wisher identification and the amount of wish energy that was collected was not quite as large as we had anticipated.

What have we learned from this? It is clear we must continue to diligently support and train our Star Darlings so that the remaining eleven missions go seamlessly and we will be able to collect the most wish energy possible.

When will the next mission happen and who will be chosen? Only time will tell. But I am cautiously optimistic that Operation Star Darlings will be a success.

Thank you for your help. And your continued discretion.

Starfully yours,
Lady Stella

CHAPTER 1

The first thing Libby noticed when she blinked awake was the delightful scent that permeated her dorm room. She sat up in bed and inhaled the perfumed air.

"Smells amazing, doesn't it?" asked Gemma.

Libby looked over at her roommate lying in bed across the room. Gemma's bright orange hair, messy from sleep, formed a wild halo around her head as she lay there, sniffing deeply. The two girls turned their attention to the vase of coral-colored flowers that had been waiting for them in their dorm room when they returned from dinner the evening before.

"I still can't figure out what kind of flowers they are," said Libby. "I don't recognize them, but they smell just like blushbelles." Blushbelles were her favorite flower. They were pink, released puffs of sparkling stardust, and had a sweetly spicy scent that she thought was simply the loveliest smell on all of Starland.

"Blushbelles?" Gemma snorted. "What are you talking about?" she said. "It smells like orange-and-vanilla ice pops—just like chatterbursts. I can't believe we're even having this conversation!" She gave Libby a quizzical look.

Libby liked to keep the peace. She usually carefully weighed her words before she spoke. But for some reason, she sat up in bed and heard herself say, rather forcefully, in fact, "You're crazy."

Gemma blinked in surprise. "No, *you're* crazy," she retorted. "You're as crazy as a bloombug." Libby gave her roommate an annoyed look. Bloombugs were small purple-and-pink spotted bugs that went wild every time there was a full moon during the warmer months of the Time of Lumiere, hopping up and down and squealing with delight at the warmer weather and longer daylight hours the season brought. Gemma sniffed. "Well, no matter how crazy you are, you have to admit that this is the sweetest thing you've ever . . ."

Her voice trailed off as she noticed that Libby had pulled her soft pink blanket over her head, obviously ignoring her. Gemma threw back the covers and nimbly hopped out of bed. She opened her closet and grabbed her bathrobe. "I call first stars on the sparkle shower!" she cried.

Libby sighed. Gemma had called first stars on the sparkle shower every day that week. They were supposed to take turns. She removed the covers and took a deep, calming breath. Then another for good measure. She smiled, feeling much better. There. No reason to get annoyed. She and Gemma were the perfect roommates, the envy of all the other Star Darlings. They got along well, accepting each other's idiosyncrasies, easily working through any issues that came up, and never letting resentments get in the way of their respect and affection for each other. Sure, Gemma had a mercurial personality, and Libby sometimes had difficulty making even the smallest decision without carefully weighing the pros and cons (deciding what to order for dinner sometimes required the thought process others reserved for major life decisions). But they had similar live-and-let-live personalities that served them both well. So it really confounded Libby that she was feeling irked that morning. And over something as silly as a vase of flowers that would probably be wilted by the afternoon!

Libby yawned and stretched. She slipped her feet

into a pair of fluffy pink slippers and shuffled to the mysterious bouquet of flowers, which was sitting on her pink desk, exactly where the two roommates had discovered it the night before to their delight and surprise.

She leaned over and took a deep sniff. She shook her head. The smell was actually more spicy than sweet, in her estimation. Just like blushbelles, no question about it. Maybe Gemma was teasing her. She sighed with happiness as she surveyed her half of the double room. She, like all incoming students at Starling Academy, had filled out an extensive questionnaire about her dorm room preferences. The results were spectacular. Her half of the room was pink, pink, and more pink as far as the eye could see, just as she had requested, from the round bed, with its padded fabric headboard, to the sumptuous rug, recessed wall lights, desk/vanity, and sparkling crystal chandelier. (The lovely white lacquered dresser with spindly legs that stood in the corner was the sole nonpink touch.) And the wide, low pink table was surrounded by luxurious floor cushions. It was the perfect place for friends to gather, and Libby often invited her classmates over to hang out during their free time.

Luckily, Gemma was very social and fun-loving, too. But on the occasional day that she wasn't in the mood for company, she would just draw the starry curtain that ran along the middle of the room, climb into bed, and read or listen to music. But she could usually be coaxed to join in when the conversation got too good to ignore.

Gemma stepped into the room. Her skin glimmered, covered in a fresh layer of sparkles from her shower. Star Darlings were born with glittery skin and hair, but a daily sparkle shower helped keep them as luminous as possible. Libby headed in next, and the sparkle shower, invigorating and refreshing, cleared her mind and improved her mood. She applied her toothlight, first to the top row, then to the bottom. Starlings used their toothlights twice a day, in the morning and the evening, to keep their teeth as clean, white, and sparkly as could be.

Libby put her toothlight back in the mirrored cabinet, closed it, and stared at her reflection for a moment, taking in her long pink hair, alabaster skin, rose-colored eyes, and dimpled chin. She smiled at her reflection and headed back into the other room. She found Gemma sitting on her bed, tying her yellow shoelaces. She had put on an orange mesh three-quarter-length-sleeved shirt over an orange tank top and matching capri pants and pulled her hair into two cute pigtails. She looked effortlessly hip, as always. As soon as she spotted Libby, she launched right back into the conversation, as though no time had passed. "So wouldn't you agree that they are the most delicious-smelling flowers ever? I mean, I have never smelled anything so sweet in my entire life. No lie. Have you?"

Libby had indeed smelled something sweeter. For her sixth birthday, her parents had taken her and eleven of her closest friends on a behind-the-scenes private tour of the Floffenhoofer Candy Factory. The very air in the jellyjooble processing room had nearly knocked her over with its fruity deliciousness. Just thinking about it made her mouth water. "Well, once I went on a—"

"Come to think of it, we had an orchard of goldenella trees on the farm," Gemma continued, as if she had never asked Libby her opinion. "You know, the kind that bloom nonstop for one week straight, and the flowers pop off the tree just like popcorn. When they bloomed, Tessa and I would just drop to the ground and roll around in the flowers. The smell was intoxicating! They positively carpeted the grass." She shook her head. "But even that was nothing like this delicious fragrance." She sniffed again.

"Well, I once—" Libby tried again.

"And when I call it a carpet of flowers, I am talking wall-to-wall," Gemma pressed on. "Nothing but lemon-yellow blossoms as far as the eye could see. And they didn't fade at all. It looked like a sea of sunshine. I remember one time when Tessa and I decided to . . ."

Libby, who usually listened with pleasure to Gemma's stories, found herself tuning out. Gemma's older sister, Tessa, was a third-year student and also a Star Darling. The sisters had been raised on a farm far out in the countryside, in a place called Solar Springs. There wasn't even a real town nearby, Gemma had told her, just a dusty old general store, where they did their very occasional shopping. They grew nearly everything they needed on the farm. Libby, who'd had a completely different upbringing in Starland City, had heard countless stories about their life and thoroughly enjoyed each one. It was such a different existence from hers, and she found it quite fascinating. And Gemma loved to talk about it. She liked to talk in general, actually. When she was in the mood, she could talk all day long, from the moment she woke up to when she went to bed. Libby had even been woken up in the middle of the night by Gemma talking in her sleep! But Libby had just laughed, rolled over, and gone back to bed. The truth was that Libby loved a good discussion and relished a friendly argument. But for some reason she was not enjoying it that day.

Libby finished getting dressed in a pink dress with

star-shaped pockets and white tights embroidered with pink stars. She hung her Wish Pendant, a necklace that resembled a constellation of golden stars, around her neck and fastened the clasp. Her signature look was sweetly stylish. She stood in front of the mirror in her closet, brushing her long pink hair. The exact shade of cotton candy and jellyjoobles, it rippled down her back. Her silky, flowing rosy-hued hair was her secret pride.

"So who do you think sent us the flowers?" Gemma asked. "There wasn't a holo-card. Why would anyone be so mysterious? If you're sending such a nice gift, you'd think you'd want to get credit for it. That reminds me of the time I—"

"That's a good question," interrupted Libby. She sifted through the evidence. Neither of them recognized the glittery flowers, so they must be rare (and, most likely, expensive). Receiving them had been a pleasant, unexpected surprise. And anything rare, beautiful, thoughtful, or extravagant in Libby's life always came from one place. "My parents must have sent them," she said with a smile. "They love surprises." *Especially expensive ones,* she thought.

Gemma, who was the secondary beneficiary of many a care package from Libby's parents, Erica and Miles, nodded. "Hey! I think you're right!" she exclaimed.

As if on cue, Libby's holo-phone rang and an image of her mother, drumming her fingers impatiently on the Starcar's dashboard, was projected in the air. She hesitated because she wasn't sure she felt like talking to her mom at the moment, but she accepted the call with a swipe of her hand.

"Sweetheart!" said her mother, appearing as a live hologram in front of Libby. She was sitting next to Libby's father on their way to work. Libby's parents worked hard as investment bankers at a large firm and liked to enjoy the best life had to offer, showering their daughter with pricey gifts and one-of-a-kind experiences. Of course these rare fragrant blooms had come from them!

"Hi, Mom. Hi, Dad!" said Libby.

Gemma popped her head into the frame. "Hi, there!" she shouted.

Libby's dad put down his holo-reader and smiled. "Hello, girls. How's school?" he asked.

"Fine," said Libby, not looking at Gemma. It was a weird feeling not to be able to share everything that was going on at school with her mom and dad. But the Star Darlings had to keep their new duties top secret, even from their parents. Libby changed the subject quickly. "So we got the flowers you sent. They're beautiful. Thanks a lot."

"Yeah, thank you!" Gemma called out. "We love them."

Libby's mom looked confused. "Flowers? We didn't send you any flowers," she said. She turned to her husband. "Miles, we should have sent the girls flowers! That's such a nice idea!"

"Well, how about some glimmerchips?" offered Libby's dad. "We could send you a case or two."

"Yes, please," said Gemma automatically. She had never tasted the thin, crispy, salty, and, yes, glimmery chips before she had started at Starling Academy, and she had developed quite a taste for them.

Libby shook her head. "We're fine, Daddy." She still had an unopened case under her bed. "But thank you."

"Starsweetie, the actual reason I called, besides to say hello, is to discuss your upcoming mid–Time of Shadows break," Libby's mother explained, pulling up a holo-calendar in the air in front of her. Libby could see that it was already packed with events and plans. Her parents always had a very full social calendar. "Daddy and I were thinking we'd go to Supernova Island. Or maybe Glamora-ora," she said, naming two exclusive vacation destinations. The holidays were still a ways off, but Libby's parents were so busy they had to schedule everything months in advance.

Gemma's eyes were wide. "Wow," she mouthed, stunned into uncustomary silence. Her parents didn't like to leave the farm for more than a couple of hours at a time, so the sisters always spent their holidays at home.

Libby twirled a piece of her pink hair around her finger, a grimace on her face. She hated disappointing her parents. This wasn't going to be easy.

"That's not an attractive look, my dear," said her mother. "Is something wrong?"

"I . . . uh . . . was talking to Aunt Kit about joining her on a volunteering vacation during break," Libby explained. "We're thinking of traveling from city to city, helping out at different orphanages and animal shelters. And I might even be able to get some credits for school." Aunt Kit and Libby's mom were sisters, but they couldn't have been more different. Libby adored her mother, but she had so much more in common with the young, altruistic Kit, who loved helping others even more than she enjoyed traveling—which was saying a lot.

The matching looks of dismay on her parents' faces would have been funny if they hadn't been so disconcerting to Libby. It was painful for her to disappoint anyone, particularly her generous and kind parents. But you'd think she had told them she wanted them to take her camping on the Isle of Misera, a barren, rocky, uninhabitable island off the coast of New Prism. Libby sighed. The problem was that her parents just didn't get her.

Until Libby was ten years old, she had been unaware that she lived an exceptional life. She hadn't given a second thought to any of it—the huge sprawling mansion in the fanciest neighborhood in Starland City, Starland's largest metropolis; the exclusive vacations; the closetful of expensive clothes and shoes and accessories; any toy she desired, plus many more she hadn't even realized she had wanted until she received them. All that changed one day when she was off from school. The family's housekeeper was away, so little Libby's parents took her to work with them. She was playing in the conference room with her newest toy, an exclusive child-sized doll that could have full conversations on any subject with its owner, when a little girl walked in. She was the daughter of the building's janitor and she was totally fascinated with Libby's doll. When Libby asked the girl if she had one just like it at home, she was shocked to hear that the girl didn't own a doll of any kind. Libby was dubious. Was that even possible? The girl explained that her parents didn't have money for unnecessary things. Libby felt terrible. "Take it, it's yours," she said to the girl. The look of pure joy on the girl's face staggered Libby. The feeling she got from giving was much better than the happiness she got from receiving. She went home that night and took a good look around her. Meeting the girl had really opened her eyes to her privileged existence and the joy she could bring others with her generosity.

Libby had started small, donating the toys she didn't play with to a children's hospital. Her parents were amused, calling her "our little philanthropist." But when Libby next gave away every other toy she owned, and then asked for donations to her favorite charity instead of gifts on her Bright Day, they began to object. They especially did not appreciate it when she questioned their lavish lifestyle, which they felt they deserved, as they had earned it through their hard work.

Libby's mother spoke first. "That's our Libby, always thinking about others," she said. Libby perked up. Maybe they were starting to see her point of view. . . .

"And never about us!" her parents said together.

No such luck. Libby felt her spirits deflate like a punctured floating star globe.

"The choice is yours, my love," said her father sadly. "But we were looking forward to spending some quality time relaxing together, like we always do on vacation."

Libby was careful not to smile, as she could recall many family holidays when she was left to her own devices while her parents took their daily holo-conference calls. Her parents didn't really know how to relax.

"Well, we've arrived," announced Libby's dad in the fake cheerful voice Libby knew all too well. The car would drop them off at the building's entrance, then park itself in their designated parking space.

"Bye, Mom and Dad, talk soon," said Libby, rushing off the phone. She was glad to be out of the starlight, but she still felt a lump in her throat as her parents signed off, about to begin another day of acquisitions and mergers. Or whatever it was they did all day.

She stood there for a moment. She was glad that Gemma understood that she needed a moment to collect her—

"Well," said Gemma. "That didn't go over so well. What are you going to do? Me, I guess I would just go to—"

Libby whirled around to face her roommate, about to give her a piece of her mind.

Just then, there was a knock at the door.

CHAPTER 2

Eager to work on their energy manipulation skills, both girls tried to open the door at the same time, using their powers of concentration. This resulted in a stand-off, since neither was particularly good at it yet. The door slid open an inch, then closed, then repeated the same motion several times. The visitor knocked again, louder. "Let me in!" a voice called out impatiently.

Finally, Libby backed off and allowed Gemma to do the honors. Gemma concentrated with all her might, her face turning quite red with the effort. The door slid open haltingly, and their visitor stepped inside.

It was Scarlet. "You guys might want to think about working on your energy manipulation a bit more," she said. As a third-year student, she had more practice with it and was much better than they were.

"Oh, hey, Scarlet," Gemma said casually. But Libby could tell that her roommate was a little nervous. Libby couldn't blame her: Scarlet, with her intense punk-rock look and matching attitude, was pretty intimidating. She could be standoffish, intense, and mysterious—so much so that Libby had gone out of her way to avoid her in the beginning of the school year. But then, one day, feeling blue, she had curled up in the Illumination Library to read one of her favorite holo-books from childhood and looked up to discover that both she and Scarlet were deeply engrossed in *The Starling's Surprise*. They'd had a good laugh about it, then bonded over the common bout of homesickness that had led to the book selection. (Scarlet had sworn Libby to secrecy; she had a reputation to uphold!) Libby had realized that when you got to know her, Scarlet could also be kind and fun. But Gemma was not yet convinced. "Whatever you say," Gemma had said when Libby tried to explain it to her. "But until she's kind and nice to *me*, I just won't believe it." The rest of the Star Darlings, especially Leona, Scarlet's roommate, all seemed to feel the same way.

"Hey, I thought I'd stop by to see if you wanted to walk to the Celestial Café together," Scarlet said. She looked around her. "I forgot how nice your room is," she said, nodding. "It kind of reminds me of a beautiful sunset." Gemma smiled despite herself. Libby looked at the room as if through Scarlet's eyes. The girl was right. The lighting—soft pink on Libby's side and cheerful orange on Gemma's—combined in the middle of the room to create a rosy glow that was warm and cozy. The two girls definitely had different tastes, but their furnishings fit together nicely. Libby was a bit neater, her bed always made and her belongings stowed away. Gemma had a lot of stuff for her many interests—musical instruments, holo-books on almost every subject you could think of, stuffed animals, crafting supplies, flora she had collected on nature hikes, a variety of sporting equipment—and it was all crammed onto her floor-to-ceiling shelves.

The other Star Darlings' rooms were not quite so harmonious. Sage and Cassie, also first-year students, had a room that was a study in complete opposites—one side austere and the other quite cluttered. The room that second-years Piper and Vega shared was neat as a pin, in soothing shades of blue and green, but the similarity ended there. Piper's side was soft and dreamy, with soothing curved surfaces, lots of pillows, and stacks of dream journals, while Vega's felt angular, clean, and precise. Clover and Astra's room was a jarring combination of sporty and sleek. And over in the Big Dipper Dorm, Tessa and Adora's jumbled room reflected their dueling interests in science experiments and cooking. You never wanted to pick up a glass that wasn't handed specifically to you: it could be a tasty smoothie, but there was an equal chance that it could be a putrid-tasting potion nobody in her right mind would want to ingest.

And then there were Scarlet and Leona. Their room was as discordant as their relationship. Leona was as bright, flashy, and in your face as her side of the room, with its warm golden glow, stage for impromptu shows, and desk shaped like a vanity surrounded by bright lightbulbs. Scarlet's space was designed so she could skateboard down its walls. It was certainly an interesting room. But Libby didn't feel truly comfortable there. Too much tension between the two roommates, maybe.

"Hey!" said Scarlet, spotting the bouquet. "You got those flowers, too! And so did Tessa and Adora, down the hall from me. They must be from Lady Stella, don't you think?" She took a deep sniff. "Aren't they amazing? They smell just like punkypows."

Libby and Gemma stared at each other. Now that was very odd!

Scarlet sat down on Libby's pristine pink bedding.

"So when I came out of the sparkle shower this morning, what do you think I found?"

"A hungry glion, eating your flowers," offered Gemma. Libby knew her roommate was trying to be funny, but nobody laughed.

Scarlet gave Gemma her patented disdainful look, and Gemma, embarrassed, immediately busied herself with her Star-Zap.

"Nooo . . ." Scarlet drew the word out scornfully. "I found my roommate wearing my grandfather's top hat, that's what," she said. "Again! And again I told her to keep her hands off it. I remind her all the time that it's special, not to be worn, ever, and as usual, she just ignores me." She scowled. Before Scarlet's grandfather had completed his Cycle of Life, he had been the greatest and most famous magician Starland had ever known. He had been known as Preston the Prestidigitator, and Starlings had come from near and far to watch him perform. Preston had left his granddaughter his top hat, which Scarlet kept in a glass case, as if it was in a museum. Rumor had it that the end of his life cycle had been staged and that as part of an elaborate trick, he would reappear on his next Bright Day. But Libby was too intimidated to ask Scarlet if it was true.

Scarlet shook her head. "You guys are so lucky, you get along so perfectly. What's your secret?"

Libby bristled and heard herself say, "We take turns deciding who gets to take the first sparkle shower in the morning."

Gemma narrowed her eyes at Libby. "We always listen to each other," she said.

Scarlet didn't notice the tension between the two girls. "Well, that's great," she said. "In any event, I'm hungry. Time for breakfast?"

The Star Darlings tended to sit together in the Celestial Café, at a table by the window overlooking the majestic Crystal Mountains. Libby always tried to grab a seat facing the view. Although Libby was friendly with many of the regular students, she had discovered that it was just easier to spend most of her time with her fellow Star Darlings. You could never let your guard down around the others, in case you accidentally let some top secret information slip. Libby plopped herself down on the seat next to Gemma's sister, Tessa. Scarlet sat on Libby's other side, and Gemma sat across from her, next to Tessa's roommate, Adora.

Tessa turned to them with a grin. "I just ordered the

zoomberry pancakes," she said. "You should get them, too!"

"Whatever," said Gemma dismissively. "You know they're never as good as the ones Dad makes on the farm."

"I know," Tessa told her sister sympathetically. "The zoomberries aren't as fresh. But try them—they're still pretty good."

Adora, who sat across from Tessa, rolled her eyes. "Do you think I could sit through one meal without hearing about how much better everything is on the farm?"

Tessa gave her roommate a hurt look.

Libby was surprised to hear Adora's words. She was usually so calm and collected.

The sisters looked at each other and shrugged. It was nearly impossible to ask the chatty sisters to stop talking about a subject that interested them. And farm-fresh food was one of their favorite subjects.

"May I take your order?" asked the Bot-Bot waiter, hovering by Gemma's shoulder.

"Hmmm," she mused. "I'm not sure what I'm in the mood for."

"I really think you'll like the starcakes, Sis," said Tessa. "And you know how important breakfast is."

"It's the most important meal of the day," Gemma

and Tessa said together. They laughed. "You sound like Mom!" they also said in unison.

"I was considering tinsel toast with bitterball preserves," Gemma said after a moment.

Tessa made a face. "I'm not sure if they put in enough sweetener," she said. "You know how sour it can be if it's not made correctly. I'd just go with the pancakes."

Gemma frowned. "Or how about a bowl of—"

"Enough!" said Adora. "Just order something. It's not a life-or-death decision. It's just food, for goodness' sake!"

Tessa looked puzzled. "Just food?" she said. "Who thinks that?"

Libby watched as Adora stood, walked to the other end of the table, and sat down. Libby was surprised by her unusual behavior. The two sisters didn't even seem to notice. Or maybe they just didn't care.

Scarlet nudged her with an elbow. "I don't think I've ever seen Adora act like that before," she said. "She's always so calm."

"Me neither," said Libby.

"Perhaps I could take your order now?" repeated the Bot-Bot waiter politely.

Libby decided to order since Gemma was still

deliberating. "I . . . um . . . oh . . . I guess I'll have the zoomberry starcakes," Libby said. "And a glass of Zing."

"Me too," said Scarlet.

"And I'll have the tinsel toast," Gemma said.

Tessa shook her head. "That's not going to be enough," she scolded. "Maybe you'd like a bowl of starberries and cream on the side?" she suggested.

"It's only going to remind me of Dad's starberry pie!" said Gemma.

Tessa nodded in sympathy. "You're right! Dad's starberry pie with a scoop of lolofruit ice cream," she said dreamily.

"Mmmmmmmm," said the sisters in unison.

Scarlet looked at Libby and raised her eyebrows. This was going to be one long meal. . . .

CHAPTER 3

Sage squirmed in her seat. Libby, who was sitting right behind her, felt really sorry for her classmate. This couldn't be easy. Especially since they were in their final class after a long day of school—the Star Darlings' daily private lesson. And also because that day their guest lecturer was Professor Eugenia Bright, who taught Intro to Wish Fulfillment. Professor Eugenia Bright was tall and slender, with cropped turquoise hair and matching eyes. She was the most popular teacher on campus. There was always a long line of students outside her door during her office hours, looking for extra-credit assignments, wanting to make a good impression on the brilliant teacher, or simply seeking to bask in the warm glow of her presence. Libby knew that Sage had to be completely miserable.

"So please explain to the class exactly what happened at the start of your mission," Professor Eugenia Bright said. "It will be most helpful for everyone to determine exactly when and how things took a turn."

Sage twisted the end of one of her thick purple braids between her fingers. Noticing this, the teacher added more gently, "I'm sorry to make you uncomfortable, my dear. It's just that the other students can learn from your mis—" She stopped herself. "I mean, the *challenges* you faced on your mission."

Sage took a deep breath, then began to explain that she had arrived on Wishworld and headed to the school as directed by her Star-Zap. Using her powers of suggestion, she was able to convince the faculty and teachers that she belonged there and then she employed her observational skills to get clues as to whom the Wisher could be. After receiving information about a girl in a difficult situation, Sage had realized it seemed promising. So she headed over to talk with her and, after they had chatted for a while, discovered her wish.

"And what kind of wish was it?" the teacher asked gently.

"Well, it seemed like a good wish," Sage said slowly. "She was the new girl at school, and her mother, who was trying to help her make friends, had invited her classmates to her birthday party, against her wishes. But it was a big mistake. No one RSVP'd. She was embarrassed and upset that no one was going, and she wished that someone would come to her party."

The teacher nodded. "And what did you—"

Just then, there was a knock at the door. Sage exhaled loudly, glad for a brief break from the questioning.

"Class?" said Professor Eugenia Bright, indicating that one of them should use her energy manipulation skills to open the door.

Sage brightened and took the opportunity to show off her formidable powers. The door slid open effortlessly. "Ooooooh," said the class in unison. Sage gave a smile. It was a small victory, but it was obvious it meant a lot to her at that moment.

There stood Lady Cordial, the head of admissions. The short, stocky woman, her purple hair cut in an unfortunate style that did not suit her face, had a pained expression. Leona said that she always looked like she had just broken your favorite vase and was trying to figure out how to tell you about it. Lady Cordial's eyes widened with surprise when she saw that the classroom was filled with students. "Oh, I'm s-s-s-sorry," she stuttered. "I didn't realize that class was still in s-s-s-session. I wanted to ask you a question about the admissions committee, but . . ." Her voice trailed off, and she stood in the doorway uncertainly.

"Well, hello there, Lady Cordial," Professor Eugenia Bright said kindly. She walked to the front of the room. "Always a pleasure to see you. Come right in. We can talk when class is dismissed." She thought for a moment. "Why don't you stay and observe our class until then?"

"Oh, what a st-st-startastic idea," cried Lady Cordial. She stepped inside, then somehow got her foot caught in her long purple skirt. She lunged forward, off balance, and grabbed the edge of the desk to catch herself, managing to knock over a plant sitting on it. Sparkly dirt spilled everywhere.

"Oh, my stars!" Lady Cordial said, her hands fluttering to her face in dismay.

Libby cringed. Poor Lady Cordial. She was so very clumsy.

There was a snort as one of the Star Darlings tried to hold in her laughter. Libby glanced up to see that Leona's face was bright red and her shoulders were shaking. Lady

Cordial stared at the floor in embarrassment, her cheeks flushed, as she walked past the students to the back of the room. She sat at an empty desk, fortunately without further mishap. The dirt vanished almost immediately.

"We were discussing Sage's mission and the challenges she faced," Professor Eugenia Bright explained to Lady Cordial. "By identifying where her mission took a wrong turn, the other students may be able to learn from it." Libby saw Sage's shoulders sag once more.

Professor Eugenia Bright frowned. "So, where were we, class?" she asked.

Adora raised her hand. "Sage was just telling us that she had identified a Wishling who wanted some classmates to attend her birthday party."

The professor nodded. "And that certainly does sound like a worthy wish," she said. "But something seems off to me in the order of events. Can anyone guess what it is?"

Eleven hands shot up, including Libby's. Libby caught Sage giving her roommate, Cassie, a baleful look. But the tiny pale girl in the star-shaped glasses ignored Sage, her hand held straight up in the air.

"Yes, Astra?" said the teacher.

"You always need to verify the Wisher before trying

to determine the wish," she answered. "Because if it isn't the right Wishling, it doesn't matter what the wish is."

"Correct!" said Professor Eugenia Bright. "Now, Sage, did you help make this wish come true?"

"Yes," said Sage in a low voice. Her eyes were fixed on her desk.

"And what happened when it was granted?"

"Nothing," said Sage.

"No glorious burst of light and color?" the professor asked.

"No," said Sage.

"No jolt as your Wish Pendant absorbed the wave of positive energy?"

Sage shook her head.

"Not even a tiny energy surge?" the teacher pressed.

"No," said Sage softly. She looked as if she might burst into tears.

"Exactly!" said the teacher. "No matter how worthy a wish is, if it hasn't been made by the correct Wishling, you will not be able to collect any wish energy," she said, clapping her hands together in time to her words to emphasize their importance. "In fact, you probably used a lot of your wish energy reserves in the pursuit of the wrong wish."

Sage nodded miserably.

"And the result was that you didn't collect as much wish energy as you could have."

Sage looked stricken. "I—I didn't? Lady Stella never told me that."

Professor Eugenia Bright bit her lip. "Oh," she said. She glided to the front of the room, where she walked back and forth, her hands clasped behind her back. She somehow managed to make something as commonplace as pacing look elegant and regal. "Now, did you try to confirm that you had identified the correct Wishling by looking at your Wish Pendant? Did it light up?"

Sage nodded, grimacing. "It did light up. But . . ."

Libby and the entire class leaned forward in anticipation. Professor Eugenia Bright and Lady Cordial did, too.

"But what?" the teacher prodded.

Sage sighed. "It was terrible. I didn't realize that as I was talking to the first Wishling, there was a second Wishling passing by right behind me. I stepped back and bumped into her. When I looked at my Wish Pendant for confirmation on the first Wishling . . ."

Professor Eugenia Bright held up a hand for Sage to stop talking. "Can anyone explain what happened here?" she asked. Again, eleven hands shot up in the air.

The teacher pointed to Vega.

"Sage thought that the birthday girl had made the wish she had been sent down to help grant, but it was actually the other Wishling. It's a classic case of Wisher misidentification," Vega explained. "I did some research on it in the library, and it happens more often than you would think. Historically, fifty percent of Wish Missions are failures, and the main causes are either the Wisher or the wish being misidentified."

"That is correct, Vega," said Professor Eugenia Bright. "And starkudos for your extra work."

Vega sat back in her seat, looking very satisfied with herself.

Sage cleared her throat. "That's exactly what happened. I think I was so excited when I thought I had found the Wisher so quickly that I overlooked any other options."

The teacher nodded, laying a hand on Sage's shoulder. "You were in a very confusing situation. Luckily, you were able to realize your mistake, find the correct Wishling, identify her wish, and collect energy."

Sage nodded. "Just not as much as I could have," she said with a sigh. She looked so miserable Libby felt the urge to help make her feel better. She raised her hand.

"Yes, Libby?" said Professor Eugenia Bright.

"I just wanted to say that it couldn't have been easy to go on the first mission. I think that Sage was very brave. And I think that complications are going to be unavoidable. This is all new to us. Sage taught us a lesson—that you have to make sure that no other Wishlings are around when you first verify your Wisher, just in case. And that's really helpful for all of us to know."

"Excellent point, Libby," said Professor Eugenia Bright. "I appreciate your ability to see both sides of the situation." She smiled at everyone. "Great work today, Starlings. Class dismissed."

Before Libby could stand up, Sage turned around and grabbed her hand. "Star salutations for what you said," Sage said to her. "It isn't easy being in the starlight."

Libby nodded. "I know," she said, patting Sage's shoulder. "And you're welcome." She stood up and straightened the skirt of her pink dress.

"Hold it, hold it!" cried a familiar voice. Libby turned around to see Leona climbing up onto a chair, her arms in the air. "I have an announcement to make. I'm starting a Star Darlings band, and I want you all to try out! I just ask one thing—please keep it quiet so everyone in school doesn't show up!"

Scarlet laughed. "As if!" she said.

Leona stuck out her tongue at her roommate. "We just want to keep it small so it will be laid-back and fun, just like me! Let's meet in Star Quad at the band shell. Bring your instruments and come ready to rock out!"

"What about singers?" Gemma asked.

Leona threw back her head and laughed. "We've already got a lead singer—me! Every other instrument is up for grabs."

Scarlet rolled her eyes. But Libby started thinking.

As the Star Darlings filed out of the classroom and joined the throngs of students in the hallway eager to enjoy the precious few hours before dinnertime, Libby noticed a few girls staring at them and whispering. So did Leona. "Take a holo-picture," she told them huffily. "It lasts longer."

The girls gave her scornful looks but hurried away. Libby hid a smile. In order to keep their Star Darlings status secret from the rest of the school, they all had to pretend that they were in a special study group during last period. That bothered some Star Darlings more than others. Libby felt a little strange about being singled out, but she knew that the work they were doing was just too important for them to worry about what other people thought. Others (like Leona) felt humiliated by it and couldn't seem to get past it. Of course, Libby was hopeful that someday maybe the truth would come out. But if it didn't, well, that was okay, too. Mostly because it had to be.

CHAPTER 4

Libby hurried back to the Little Dipper Dorm alone. She had her one free afternoon each week on Lunaday, and she usually waited for Gemma to finish whatever conversation she was having after class so that the two could head back together. But not that day. She pushed open the door and stepped onto the Cosmic Transporter, which deposited her right in front of room 333. She placed her palm on the hand scanner in the middle of the door. Her handprint was accepted, and the door slid open. "Welcome, Libby," the Bot-Bot voice said.

Entering the bedroom, Libby noticed that the flowers smelled twice as strong as they had that morning.

She placed her Star-Zap on her dresser and walked right over to them. It was as if they were beckoning to her. She sniffed deeply. *Ahhhhhhhh.* They were just so irresistible. She shook her head. Gemma and Scarlet were so wrong. They smelled just like blushbelles, no doubt about it.

Libby walked over to her side of the room and knelt next to her bed, the pink rug soft and fluffy under her knees. She fished around under the bed for a bit, pushed aside the unopened case of glimmerchips, then found what she was looking for. She hooked her fingers around the handle and pulled out a bright pink case. She stared at it for a brief moment, then undid the clasps and lifted the lid.

The door to the room whooshed open, startling Libby. "What's the deal? You left after class without me," Gemma said, pouting. Then she noticed the open case. "Hey, what's that?" she asked, walking over and dropping to her knees next to Libby. "I mean, I know it's an instrument of some sort, but what kind is it? It's bizarre!"

Libby bristled, running her hands over the keyboard.

"I mean, I think I've played almost every instrument there is," Gemma continued. "But I've never seen this one before in my life."

"It's a keytar," Libby said. "A portable keyboard that you play like a guitar." She lifted it out of the case and hung it around her neck by the pink strap. "See?"

"Ohhhhhh," said Gemma. "So does this mean you're trying out for the band?"

"Maybe," said Libby. "I can't make up my mind."

"Well, *I* am," said Gemma. "I just have to figure out which instrument to bring. I play so many, you know." She walked over to her shelf and began studying her choices: guitar, starflooty, star shakers, pluckalong, clarinet.

Better to play one well than many not so well, Libby thought. She blushed, immediately embarrassed by her unkind thought. *My stars*. What was getting into her these days? She carefully lifted the keytar from around her neck and placed it back in the case. Maybe she wouldn't try out. She wasn't feeling quite right. It was entirely possible that she was coming down with something and could use some rest.

"So are you sure you want to try out with that keyfar thing?" Gemma asked Libby. "It just seems kind of weird." She pointed to her shelf of instruments. "Maybe borrow one of mine instead?" She had a funny look on her face, as if she was a bit surprised at the words that had come out of her mouth.

"Key*tar*," said Libby between gritted teeth. "It's called a keytar," she repeated.

"Do what you like," Gemma said with a shrug. She stared at the jumble of instruments, considering them. Finally, she grabbed the pair of star shakers. "See you," she said.

That was just the motivation Libby needed. She snapped the case closed and, after a brief pause to give Gemma a head start, headed to Star Quad herself.

★

Libby's mood improved as soon as she stepped outside. It was a pleasant, sunny Time of Letting Go afternoon with a slight breeze, and she was looking forward to sitting in the grass near the splashing fountain and playing music with her fellow Star Darlings. Plus, she could show Gemma just how amazing and versatile a keytar could be. Her roommate had no idea that the instrument could sound like an organ, an accordion, *or* an electric guitar!

Libby stopped in her tracks as she approached the band shell. She had been expecting to see a couple of the Star Darlings—Leona, of course; Sage with her guitar; Vega and her bass; Gemma; maybe even Scarlet with her drum kit; and possibly one or two others. But there were literally dozens of Starling Academy students milling about in Star Quad, singing scales and toting guitars, violins, and other instruments. They couldn't possibly all be there to try out for Leona's band, could they? How had they even found out about it?

She spotted Orchid, a girl from her Intro to Wishful Thinking class, practicing her starflooty.

"Hey, Orchid, what's going on?" Libby asked her.

Orchid blew a few more notes, then lowered her starflooty. "Hey, Libby," she said in a friendly tone. "Everyone's here to try out for the band!" She glanced down at the pink case in Libby's hand. "Aren't you?"

Could there be tryouts for two bands? Libby wondered. "Who's in charge?" she asked.

"Oh, a third-year named Leona," the girl replied. She pointed to the band shell, where Leona stood, her hands on her hips. She was surveying the crowd, looking confused. "You know, the one with the cool golden hair."

"I know her," said Libby. *What on Starland is going on?* she wondered. Leona had apparently decided to invite the whole school to try out. But why? Libby pushed her way through the crowd to the band shell.

"Hey, Leona," she said. "What's happening?"

Leona spun around. Her hair looked even wilder than usual. "What's going on? I wish I knew!" Her eyes swept the crowd. "*Starf!* How did all these people find out about my tryouts? I didn't want the whole school to show up! This is going to take forever!" She stopped a girl walking by with a trumpet. "How did you hear about this?" she asked her.

The girl looked at Leona like she was crazy. "Is this a joke?" she asked. "From the holo-flyer you sent out to the school, of course." The girl lowered her voice and leaned forward conspiratorially. "So is it true that whoever joins the band gets class credit and can drop music class?" she asked. "That's the rumor."

Leona narrowed her eyes. "I bet you anything Scarlet had something to do with this. This sounds exactly like something she would do to annoy me."

There was a laugh behind them. Leona and Libby spun around to find Scarlet standing there, grinning. "I wouldn't mind taking credit for this madhouse," she said. "But it wasn't me. I'm here to try out!" She pointed a drumstick at her drum kit, which was sitting on the stage. "You think I want all this competition?"

Leona groaned. "I'm going to be the most hated girl in Starling Academy when I have to turn most of these girls down," she said, fretting. Libby nodded in sympathy. It would be awful to have to hurt the feelings of so many of her fellow students. Leona had a sudden realization. "And then no one will come to see the band. That would be terrible!"

Libby pulled her Star-Zap out of her pocket and quickly checked her messages. Oddly enough, she had not received Leona's holo-flyer. A quick poll revealed that neither had Vega, Scarlet, or any of the other Star Darlings.

Leona grabbed the arm of a girl who stood nearby, a guitar slung around her neck. "Hey, can you show me the holo-flyer?" she asked. The girl nodded, pulled her Star-Zap from her pocket, and projected the message into the air. Leona read it out loud:

CALLING ALL ROCKERS!

Have you always wanted to play in a band?

Desperately seeking vocalists, drummers, guitarists, melodeon players, bass players, keyboard players—and more!

Meet at the band shell in Star Quad after school today.

Contact Leona for more details.

"That's so bizarre. I totally hate melodeons! I so clearly didn't send that," she said, shaking her head. "But who did?"

The crowd began to shift. Someone was trying to push through. "Excuse me, pardon me," said a loud adult voice. The crowd parted as a teacher made her way to the bandstand. She was of average height with a round, pretty face, long silver hair parted in the middle, and a sweeping red dress with huge pockets. She was a fourth-year professor, and until then, Libby had only seen her from a distance.

"Leona?" she said. "Professor Leticia Langtree here. You're just the person I've been looking for. Once an invitation for any type of tryout on school property goes out to the entire school, Starling Academy rules require that it must be overseen by a school official. It's in the Student Manual," she added seriously. "So I'm here to make sure everything goes smoothly and fairly." She fished around in her pocket and pulled out a small silver box. "That's why we always use the Ranker in situations like this. You may have seen it used before in public speaking class. It's the only truly fair way to be able to pick a winner without showing favoritism."

Leona stared at the Ranker. Things were not going the way she had planned, and Libby could see how frustrated that was making her. "When I find out who sent out that holo-flyer, I am going to go supernova on them," she said through gritted teeth. "Not. Funny. At. All."

Professor Leticia Langtree ignored her comment. "So if we're all settled, I'm going to make an announcement explaining how we're going to proceed, and then we'll start the tryouts so we can get out of here before breakfast tomorrow," she told Leona.

"Fine," sputtered Leona. She looked both furious and confused. But it was perfectly clear that she really had no choice.

The teacher stepped onto the band shell stage. "Hello, I am Professor Leticia Langtree, and I will be overseeing the band tryouts today. I will be recording you with this machine, called a Ranker, for those of you not yet familiar with it. It will ensure that choosing the band is done in a fair way, showing no favoritism to any student. This machine is able to evaluate each performance and assemble the perfect group of musicians, the group that will sound the best together. The Ranker is unbiased and incorruptible. Please remember that I will have nothing at all to do with the choosing. It is entirely up to the Ranker." She held up the machine and moved it back and forth, scanning the crowd. She looked down at the machine and smiled. "The Ranker now has everyone's names and years in its database and is randomly shuffling them. I will call you to the stage to try out in the order the Ranker determines. You will each have two starmins to perform. The Ranker will indicate when your time is up. You must stop performing immediately."

Leona's shoulders sagged. Though she had accepted the unexpected turn of events, that didn't mean she was happy about it. She turned to Libby with a sigh. "This was just supposed to be a Star Darlings band!" she said. "A way for us to have fun and spend time together. I don't want to be the lead singer of a band where I don't know anyone!" She thought for a moment. "I guess this is the best thing to do now that everything got so messed up." She shook her head. "But who could have sent out that flyer? And why?"

The teacher stepped down from the stage and settled herself on a bench, the Ranker set up beside her. Leona, Libby, and Sage sat on a nearby bench to watch.

"Vivica!" she called. A girl with pale blue bangs walked onstage.

Sage groaned. "Vivica is the meanest girl in school," she whispered to Libby. Libby recognized the girl from her Astral Accounting class. Libby always thought that the permanently sour expression on Vivica's face made her look as if she had just bitten into a bitterball fruit.

Libby watched her with interest. She had no instrument. Then Vivica opened her mouth and started to sing.

Leona immediately sprang to her feet. "Hold it right there," she said, cutting her off.

The girl stopped singing, the look on her face more disagreeable than ever.

"Sorry," said Leona, her voice dripping with fake sympathy. "We already have a lead singer. There won't be any singing tryouts today."

The girl stared venomously at Leona. "Oh, yeah?" she said, placing her hands on her hips. "Then why does it say *vocalists* on the holo-flyer?" she insisted.

Leona laughed and shook her head. "I didn't send out that holo-flyer!" she answered, drawing out the words as if Vivica was a small child. "We don't need a lead singer. End of story."

This served to enrage the girl with the pale blue bangs further. "Well, I'm not leaving until I get a chance to try out!" she screeched.

"Next!" Leona shouted, her face red. The two girls stared angrily at each other, at an impasse.

Meanwhile, Professor Leticia Langtree was busily searching through the Student Manual. She flipped through pages in the air. Finally, she found what she was looking for and stood up. "Leona, it says right here in the Student Manual," she said, stabbing the air for emphasis, "that if the tryouts are held on school grounds, every student has the right to audition for every position. That means that every position is up for grabs. The Ranker will decide who will be the lead singer of this band. You simply can't choose yourself."

Leona looked stunned. "Wait a starsec. Are you telling me I have to try out for my own band?" she asked incredulously.

The teacher shrugged. "I am," she said. She smiled at Leona. "Good luck!"

Leona's mouth opened and closed, but no sound came out. It looked as though when she regained her power of speech, there was a very good chance she could say something she might regret. Libby grabbed Leona's hand and pulled her down to sit on the bench. "Don't worry," Libby told her. "You'll win this one fair and square." She only hoped she was right.

Vivica smirked at Leona, then began to sing. Libby was grudgingly impressed. The girl's voice was clear and strong. Leona tried to be nonchalant, but Libby noticed that she sat on her hands, quite possibly so she wouldn't start biting her nails from sheer nervousness.

After two starmins, the Ranker let out a loud beep, signaling that her time was up. The tryouts began in earnest: another singer (not as good, and she forgot some words), and a guitar player and a drummer, neither of which was particularly outstanding.

"Leona!" called the teacher.

Libby glanced at Leona, certain she would be too worked up to perform. But she had underestimated Leona's showmanship. The girl stood, smoothed her golden skirt, and made her way to the stage. She really had a great voice, though Libby recognized that her range was limited. She more than made up for that with sheer enthusiasm. The crowd began to clap along, which Leona clearly loved. She had such presence on the stage that it was almost impossible to look away. When she was done, a couple of girls in the audience gave loud whistles of approval. Libby noted with a chuckle that Leona was the only performer who took a bow—a deep one—when she was finished.

Leona walked back to the bench, a grin on her face. "And that's how it's done," she said cockily, still keyed up from her brief performance. She looked around. "Well, I guess I'll just go," she said. "Clearly I'm not needed at my own tryouts."

"Arista!" Professor Leticia Langtree called out. A girl staggered onto the stage, carrying a huge tuba. She could barely stand upright.

"Oh," said Leona, clearly intrigued. "Well, maybe just one more . . ." She plopped down next to Libby on the bench. And there she sat for the rest of the afternoon.

As their names were called, one by one, each girl got

up on the band shell stage and played her instrument or sang. Some were full of confidence but not quite so full of talent. Some were shy but good. And a couple were pretty bad, truth be told. Finally, it was Libby's turn. She slung her keytar over her shoulder and walked to the middle of the stage. She had been intending to play a current popular song when she had a sudden flash of inspiration. She laughed out loud at her idea. Flipping the keytar switch to make her instrument sound like an old-timey organ, she began to play a simple but snappy jingle that had played on holo-billboards everywhere when she was a kid.

If you like to smile

And really hate to frown,

Then get yourself a Sparklebrush.

It's the best toothlight in town! she sang, then launched into the chorus.

Oh, Sparklebrush! Sparklebrush!

How I love you so.

You leave my teeth so clean and white

With that special sparkle glow!

Libby grinned as everyone instantly laughed with recognition and started singing along. The audience cheered as Libby left the stage.

Leona stood up and punched her in the arm excitedly.

"Hey, that was pretty cool," she said. "A blast from the past!"

"Scarlet!" called the teacher. Scarlet made her way to the band shell and pushed her drum kit to the middle of the stage. She sat down, twirled her drumsticks in the air, and started playing. Even Leona had to admit—begrudgingly—that the Starling had talent. A lot of it, actually.

Then there were some novelty acts. A first-year held up a triangle and hit it—*Ding! Ding-ding-ding! Ding!*—over and over again until her two starmins was up. A third-year stepped onto the band shell stage, supporting a huge silver instrument that snaked around her body and had three large horns sprouting from it. "Is that a . . . google-horn?" Leona asked Libby incredulously.

"I do believe it is!" said Libby.

The girl began to play the instrument proudly. Its deep bass blare was actually pretty impressive, but Libby was doubtful that there was any way to incorporate that sound into a cohesive rock band.

Another girl was the proud owner of an ancient timpanpipe, which some of the girls had never even heard of before. The last person Libby had heard expressing admiration for the instrument was her dear departed great-grandmother. Its scratchy-whistly sound made everyone realize why the instrument had fallen out of favor. It was haunting. And not in a good way.

Then a couple of Star Darlings tried out in a row. Sage played the guitar very well. Vega played the bass, and she was quite good, too. Gemma got up and shook her star shakers enthusiastically. Libby caught Leona wincing, though she tried to pass it off as having something in her eye. Libby wasn't fooled.

"Well, that's it!" said Professor Leticia Langtree. She stood, turned off the Ranker, and slipped it into her voluminous pocket. "So I'll take this back and determine the results. I'll post them on the holo-announcement board by Halo Hall as soon as I can."

Leona slumped on the bench. "I'm exhausted," she said. She pointed to the Celestial Café, where a large star above the door flashed, indicating that it was dinnertime. "Let's go eat."

"Okay," said Libby. She and Leona walked over to the moving sidewalk. They stepped on and stood in silence for a moment.

"I'm still wondering who sent that holo-flyer out with my name on it," mused Leona. "I'm not fully convinced it wasn't Scarlet."

"It wasn't me, I told you," someone behind them said wearily.

Leona jumped. "Why are you always lurking behind me?" she complained. "It's kind of creepy, you know."

Gemma ran up to join them. "That was so much fun! I hope I make it," she said, rattling her star shakers for emphasis. "It would be so awesome to be in a band." She spotted Tessa on the moving sidewalk ahead and waved wildly. "Tessa, wait up!" she called as she took off after her.

Leona leaned over and whispered in Libby's ear. "I obviously have no idea who's going to make it or not," she said. "Or even if *I* will. But I think it's pretty clear that Gemma is out of the running. There were so many better musicians." She looked at Libby and shrugged. "Sorry for the bad news."

"Good," Libby heard herself say.

Leona's mouth fell open. "Good?" she repeated. "You're happy about that? I don't get it. I thought you guys were great friends."

Libby bit her lip. "I—I don't get it, either," she said. "I'll see you later." She stepped off the sidewalk and headed toward her dormitory on foot. She had lost her appetite. Why in the world was she pleased that her roommate most likely hadn't made the cut? What on Starland was wrong with her?

CHAPTER 5

Once in her peaceful room, Libby tried to distract herself, but she wasn't having an easy time of it. She refolded all of her already neatly folded clothing, then pulled holo-book after holo-book off her shelves, but nothing kept her interest. She just couldn't stop thinking about her ungracious reaction to Leona's news. She was about to call her best friend from home for a pep talk when her Star-Zap beeped. She rolled over and picked it up. The familiar message made her heartbeat quicken.

S.D. WISH BLOSSOM IDENTIFIED. PROCEED TO LADY STELLA'S OFFICE IMMEDIATELY.

Libby jumped out of bed, shoved her feet into a pair of shoes, and headed out the door.

Once outside, she discovered it was lightfall, the

magical time of day when the sun began to disappear and everyone's glow was at its brightest. Starlings got an extra burst of energy at lightfall; whether it was from being surrounded by shimmering Starlings or was a direct result of their own personal glow, Libby wasn't quite sure. Perhaps a combination of both. She breezed past groups of classmates chatting on the moving sidewalk as they returned from dinner.

"Where are you going, Libby?" someone called.

"Hey, where's the fire?" shouted another.

Libby just laughed and waved. She could never explain to them what was going on. Imagine if she told them the truth. "Oh, it's no big deal. I'm just on my way to Lady Stella's office. There's a one-in-eleven chance that I'm going to be on my way to Wishworld before you're even dressed tomorrow morning!"

By dodging around oncoming students, she soon caught up with her fellow Star Darlings, who were making their way to Halo Hall, where Lady Stella's office was located. Tessa was still eating a cocomoon. She took a big bite, the milky-white iridescent juice running down her arm.

"Where were you, roomie?" asked Gemma.

To Libby, her voice sounded accusatory. For a brief second, Libby was fearful that Gemma somehow knew she had been unkind. But as Libby's pulse began to slow down, she realized she was overreacting. "Oh, I wasn't hungry," she said.

"Well, that's just crazy talk," said Tessa with a laugh, holding up the half-eaten cocomoon.

Libby fell into step with the group, grazing shoulders with Adora. Everyone was making small talk, not mentioning where they were headed, or for what purpose, in case anyone was within earshot. But they couldn't keep still—eyes were darting, fingers were tapping, the nervous energy was palpable. They couldn't wait to find out who would be going to Wishworld next.

Sage turned around, and Libby was surprised to see that her eyes were flashing. Even she, who had been through this already and knew for certain that she would not be chosen, seemed to be filled with nervous excitement.

The moving sidewalk took the girls straight to Halo Hall, and they headed up the stairs and inside, their feet echoing in the empty hallways as they walked past silent classrooms. They filed into Lady Stella's office. The headmistress sat behind her desk, her arms folded. She looked remarkably calm. Libby sat down at the round table, placing her hands on its cool silver surface. It calmed her down—a bit. A few Star Darlings stood, fidgeting nervously. Maybe they were too anxious to sit, or perhaps they wanted a head start when Lady Stella opened the door that led down the stairs to the Wish Cavern.

Once everyone was settled, Lady Stella stood up. "Hello, my Star Darlings," she said. "As you are aware, one of you is about to be chosen for the second Wish Mission. A good Wish Orb is glowing, and it is especially suited to one particular student's strengths. Please don't be upset if you are not chosen today. You will each get your turn."

The Star Darlings all understood that. Still, Libby knew that they all must feel exactly as she did. They wanted it to be theirs. (Except, perhaps, Cassie, who looked slightly miserable. She had confessed to Libby as they sipped sparkle juice in the Lightning Lounge one evening that she wasn't in a rush to head down to Wishworld. She needed a little bit of time to get used to the idea. It was pretty clear to Libby that she had not yet.)

"When do we get to go to the caves?" Scarlet asked impatiently.

Lady Stella smiled. "Things are going to happen a little differently this time," she said. "I have been informed by our Wish-Watcher that we will not be going to the Star Darlings Wish Cavern this evening."

The girls began to murmur. Not going to the Wish

Cavern! The last time, when Sage was chosen, Lady Stella had opened a hidden door in her office wall, and a secret staircase had been revealed. The girls had headed underground into the secret caves beneath the school. Lady Stella had led them to a secret door. When it opened they found themselves in a beautiful Wish-House built just for them.

"But, Lady Stella," said Vega, "then how are we going to find out who the Wish Mission is intended for?"

"The Wish Orb will come to you this time," Lady Stella said mysteriously. "Please take a seat so we can begin." She gestured toward the large round silver table that sat in her office.

Once everyone was settled, Lady Stella continued. "Now close your eyes," she said. "When you open them, a Wish Orb will be floating in front of each of you. Everyone, that is, but Sage, since she already went on her mission." Sage nodded and smiled—a little sadly, Libby thought. Maybe she secretly hoped to be able to go back down again on another mission and do it perfectly this time.

"But only one is the true Wish Orb. The rest are just illusions and will disappear before your eyes."

Libby looked around the table. Everyone's eyes were

already closed, so she quickly squeezed hers shut, too. Her stomach was dancing with flutterfocuses. What if she was chosen? Then again, what if she wasn't? The wait seemed interminable. Finally, she heard Lady Stella say, "Open your eyes, Star Darlings!"

There was a collective gasp around the table. Eleven glowing Wish Orbs were floating in the air in front of them. Libby stared at her orb longingly. It looked quite real, pulsing with a gorgeous golden light. But was it just an illusion?

She looked at her fellow Star Darlings. Each girl was staring at her Wish Orb, wondering if it was about to disappear. One by one, Scarlet's, Gemma's, Tessa's, Leona's, and Vega's faces crumpled as their orbs disappeared. Cassie let out a gasp—perhaps of relief—as hers vanished. Libby stared at her orb, then stole a quick glance around the table. All the others were gone. She started breathing again.

"It's Libby!" cried Sage. "Good for you!"

Lady Stella walked over and placed her hands on Libby's shoulders. "The Wish Orb has chosen." She peered down at Libby, a gentle smile on her face. "And I think it has chosen wisely. I have a good feeling about this, Libby."

Libby's mouth felt dry. "Thank you," she barely managed to whisper. She pushed her seat back from the table and stood up.

Lady Stella burst into laughter, pointing to Libby's feet. "I'm guessing you were in a big rush to get here?" she asked.

Libby nodded and looked down. She was wearing her fluffy bedroom slippers!

The Star Darlings roared with laughter. Was it because it was so funny to see ladylike Libby wearing silly slippers in public, or were they mostly letting off steam after the last tense few starmins? Libby wasn't sure. But after a moment, she joined in on the laughter, too.

Long after the other girls had left to get ready for bed, Libby returned to the Little Dipper Dormitory, yawning a jaw-cracking yawn as she shuffled along in her slippers. She had stayed behind for final lessons in outfit picking and shooting-star riding and had received some last-starmin Wisher identification tips.

The campus was still and empty, and she watched as lights began to turn off in the dorm, which loomed ahead of her. Libby looked up to see a clear sky full of stars. She bent her head back and took it all in. It was so amazing that someone as small as she, in the grand scheme of the world, was about to embark on such a huge adventure. Her Star-Zap began to ring. She pulled it out of her star-shaped pocket to see that it was her parents, again.

Her parents popped up in the darkness ahead of her, wearing silk bathrobes. Her mother's hands were placed in matching anti-aging pods, as they were every night before she went to sleep.

"Hi," Libby said.

"Hi, sweetheart," they said in unison. Her mother peered at her. "What are you doing outside?" she asked. "Shouldn't you be getting ready for bed?" her father added.

"I . . . um . . . was studying late," Libby said. It was technically the truth.

"Well, it's time to get ready for bed," said her mother. "Listen, we just wanted to see if you had changed your mind about the vacation. There's still time."

Libby sighed. "I'm sorry. I haven't."

Her mother sighed, as well.

"All right, we'll figure it out somehow. So, anything exciting happen today, starsweetie?" her father asked.

Libby almost laughed. Anything exciting? Only the most thrilling thing in the history of Starland was all.

She scoured her mind for some bit of information to share. "Well, I, um, tried out for a rock band," she said. "I played the keytar."

"Oh, that's fun," said her father. "Good luck."

"I hope you make it," her mother added. "All those years of classical piano lessons will finally pay off."

"Thanks," Libby said. She was suddenly seized with an odd feeling—a mixture of longing, excitement, and a little bit of fear. Part of her wanted to hop into a Starcar, head to Radiant Hills, and have her parents tuck her into bed. The other was thrilled to be setting off on an unknown, mysterious, top secret adventure. "Mommy and Daddy?" she said.

"Yes," her parents perked up. Libby never called them Mommy and Daddy anymore.

"I miss you," she said. She had a sudden idea. "I know—I'm going to try to find out a way to combine the vacations. Maybe I can do some volunteering on Glamora-ora. And maybe Aunt Kit could come, too?"

Her parents smiled widely, looking both relieved and happy. "That would be lovely, Libby," her mother said gently. "Really lovely," her father added.

Libby stopped under a lamppost outside the Little Dipper Dormitory door. "Good night," she said softly.

"Good night, starsweetie," her parents said together.

It had been really difficult to talk to her parents and not share the exciting, world-changing thing she was about to do. But she still felt better just seeing them and hearing their voices.

The Cosmic Transporter dropped her off at her door, and she gently placed her hand on the scanner. "Good evening, Libby," the voice said in hushed tones reserved for after-dark hours. She walked into the unlit room. Gemma was already asleep, and the starry curtain that divided the room was drawn. Libby got undressed and rooted around in her drawers to find her favorite old pair of pajamas. They were a little snug, and her ankles and wrists stuck out. But they were warm and cozy and reminded her of home. Vaguely comforted, she nestled between the covers and drifted off to sleep.

CHAPTER 6

Libby stepped off the Flash Vertical Mover and walked toward the hidden door that opened onto the private Star Darlings section of the Wishworld Surveillance Deck. She pushed down her safety starglasses, then walked onto the deck. She was pleased to notice that her fellow Star Darlings were bathed in a pretty rosy glow through her pink lenses.

"Hey, Libby!"

"Over here!"

"Way to go, Libby!"

Libby was immediately mobbed by her fellow Star Darlings, all wearing different-colored safety starglasses that matched their outfits. Apparently, being chosen for the next mission had turned her into a momentary celebrity. She grinned at everyone, pleased that they had come to see her off.

Astra pushed to the front of the crowd. "How can you stand it?" she practically shouted. "You're about to set off on the biggest adventure of your life, and you're as cool as a calaka!"

"Are calakas really cool?" wondered Vega. "I've always wondered where that expression came from."

Libby shrugged. While she might have looked calm on the outside, she certainly didn't feel that way. It felt like a bunch of flutterfocuses were having a dance party in her stomach. She glanced at the far end of the deck and saw the Star Wranglers trying to spot a shooting star heading their way. They would use their lassos to grab it; then they would attach Libby to it, and she would be on her way to Wishworld to start her adventure. *Gulp.*

Leona walked up to her, a grin on her face. "Any last words?" she joked. She threw an arm around Libby's neck. "Hopefully by the time you get back, they'll have posted the results from the band tryouts." She let go of Libby and tapped her elbows together three times for luck.

The what? thought Libby. *Oh, that's right, the band tryouts.* That seemed so long ago and so inconsequential to Libby at the moment. "Yes, I hope so," she said. "Good luck."

"Star salutations," said Leona. She patted Libby on the back.

One by one, Libby's fellow Star Darlings hugged her, tapped their elbows, and offered unsolicited last-starmin advice. Libby smiled and thanked them all politely, but her mind was elsewhere. She had a moment of panic when she thought she had forgotten her Wish Pendant, but there it was, around her neck, where she had carefully put it that morning. Wait, where was her—Oh, there, her Star-Zap was in her pocket. *Relax,* she told herself. *Everything is going to be okay.*

Finally, she made it to the end of the platform, where Lady Stella was waiting.

The headmistress gave Libby a warm smile and embrace, and Libby could feel her tension begin to ebb. Lady Cordial pushed through the crowd to hand Libby a pink backpack with a stuffed glittery pink star attached to the zipper so she would blend in on Wishworld. Libby put her arms through the straps. She made a face. It felt kind of uncomfortable.

Sage pushed forward. "No, silly, you wear it on your back," she said kindly. She removed the backpack and helped Libby put it on correctly. That was much better.

"Star salutations, Sage," said Libby gratefully.

"Everything is going to be fine," said Sage, putting a comforting hand on Libby's arm.

"Now, Libby," Lady Stella said, "you are going to do a great job." She pointed to Libby's necklace. "Just remember to keep an eye on your Wish Pendant. It has enough wish energy inside for you to use your secret power. Use it wisely."

"I will," Libby said.

"You also need to watch the Countdown Clock on your Star-Zap. If the wish is not granted before the clock runs out of time, the orb will fade and the mission will fail. And no wish energy will be collected."

Libby nodded. "I understand."

"We'll be monitoring your levels from here. If we think you may be in trouble, we'll send down backup."

"Okay," said Libby. She was hoping she wouldn't have to rely on anyone's help, but it was nice to know it was there if she did need it.

"The ride down will be fast. Don't forget to change your appearance before you touch down on Wishworld," Lady Stella reminded her.

"I won't," said Libby solemnly.

"Shooting star spotted!" called the Star Wrangler.

Libby felt numb as she watched the wrangler toss out

a silver lasso of wish energy and expertly nab a shooting star. Luckily, everyone had on their safety starglasses, because it was so bright it was almost blinding, throwing off a shower of sparks. "You're on!" the wrangler called, struggling to hold the star in place. Her heart nearly thumping out of her chest, Libby stepped forward to the edge of the Surveillance Deck, where she was attached to the star.

"Ready for takeoff?" asked the wrangler.

"Ready!" said Libby.

"Libby! Libby!" Libby turned her head and saw Sage fighting her way to the edge of the balcony. "I just remembered something! When my mission started going wrong, I started feeling really—"

Whoosh! The wrangler released the powerful star, and Libby's head was thrown back as it took off. She was on her way as quick as she could say Jack Starling (an old expression of her great-grandmother's, which oddly came to mind at that moment).

What had Sage been about to say? She had felt really hungry? Angry? Sad? Hopefully, Libby wouldn't find out.

Whoa! She hadn't realized what a bumpy ride it would be down to Wishworld! Her long pink hair whipped back as she sped down, down, down. She stared out at the swirling air around her, almost hypnotized by the shifting colors, the intense glow and flashes of light.

Just then she remembered her Star-Zap. She fished it out of her pocket and realized that it was blinking. Libby snapped back to reality. COMMENCE APPEARANCE CHANGE, the screen read. APPROACHING WISHWORLD ATMOSPHERE. *Oh, starf.* How long had the Star-Zap been trying to remind her? It was flashing really intently, surely an indicator that she had been ignoring it for a while.

Quickly, she accessed the Wishworld Outfit Selector, and she was instantly dressed. She looked down at the outfit Lady Stella had helped her choose the night before. Pink denim skirt, pink-and-white-striped leggings, pink flats, and a pink shirt with white polka dots. A white jean jacket completed her Wishling ensemble. She smiled. *Adorable!*

Next step: skin and hair. She placed her hand on her star necklace and recited the words that would start the transformation: "Star light, star bright, the first star I see tonight: I wish I may, I wish I might, have the wish I wish tonight." A wonderful, warm, comforting feeling began to flow through her, and she focused first on her body. She visualized her smooth pale skin devoid of any glitter. Next she pictured plain brown hair instead of her beautiful sparkling pink tresses. (That was a tough one for her, and she was happy to notice that a streak of pink remained.) The star sped up for a moment as it swerved around a meteorite, and she watched in dismay as the sparkles were swept right off her skin. She felt very dull indeed. But now she was ready.

PREPARE FOR LANDING, read her Star-Zap. Libby shot through the clouds and began hurtling toward Wishworld. She closed her eyes as the ground rushed up to meet her. Nobody had told her how scary that would be! But to her relief, she touched down gently. When she opened her eyes, she was pleased to discover that the star had brought her to a secluded spot. She picked up the star and folded it neatly, then stowed it in her backpack. It would come in handy to help her get back home; that was for sure! She scooped up her Star-Zap, which lay on the ground beside her, and stuck it in her pocket. It was only then that she took a closer look at her surroundings. Everything was so lovely, bathed in pink light! Then she laughed as she realized she had forgotten to take off her safety starglasses. Things weren't quite so rosy anymore. Instead of the beautiful park that Sage had described landing in, Libby discovered that she was in a dreary alley, and there was a large green metal container that really stank. She could hardly breathe! She held her nose and peeked inside, morbidly curious to discover what on Wishworld could make such a terrible smell. It was filled with garbage! Papers and wrappers and leftover food scraps and used drink containers, as well as other unidentifiable items in various degrees of decay. She looked away. What a mess! Then she remembered learning in class that Wishlings did not have disappearing garbage as they did on Starland, and she felt very sorry for them. She caught another whiff and realized that at the moment, she felt sorry for herself. She held her breath and scurried out of the alley.

Libby pulled out her Star-Zap and said, "Take me to the Wisher I've come to help." Directions appeared and Libby quickly fell into step behind an adult female Wishling. After a couple of turns, she found herself on a busy city street. She stood still for a moment and tried to take it all in. It was loud, crowded, overwhelming, and totally wonderful all at the same time. Then someone bumped right into her, nearly knocking her over onto the sidewalk.

"Out of the way, kid," said a gruff voice. "You can't just stop in the middle of the sidewalk! What's wrong with you?"

Libby looked up to see an adult male Wishling in a matching jacket and pants, a thin strip of material tied around his neck. He was holding a brown satchel in one hand and what looked like a very early prototype of a Star-Zap to his ear with the other. He scowled at her. "Oh, just some dumb kid," he said into the phone before he took off, weaving through the crowd.

Libby stuck out her tongue at his departing back. *How rude!*

"Oh, don't mind him," said a voice. Libby looked over to see an adult female Wishling with a kind face pushing a large wheeled contraption with a tiny baby sleeping inside. "Some people have no manners."

Libby smiled at her. "Thank you!" she said. She decided to make her first mental note. By pressing a button on her Star-Zap, she could record in her Cyber Journal an observation made in her head. It could then be studied by the other Star Darlings for use on their missions.

Mission 2, Wishworld Observation #1: Some Wishlings are rude. And some are quite nice.

Hmmm . . . Maybe that wasn't such a mind-blowing observation. It was actually a lot like life on Starland. She knew she should probably get to the school as soon as possible, but she needed a starmin to take it all in. She moved out of the way and watched. Pedestrians rushed by, and people were spilling out of underground stairwells and onto the street. *Where did they come from?* she wondered. *Do some Wishlings live underground?* There were tons of those funny-looking Wishling vehicles—some long and boxlike, filled with many people, and some small and carrying only a few. Many of them were yellow and had signs and lights on the top. The streets were lined with large buildings with glass fronts. There were a lot of stores selling clothes, shoes, and food. There were many places called banks and others called pharmacies. And it was noisy: vehicles were honking, revving, and screeching. People were yelling, chatting, whistling, and constantly moving, moving, moving. She thought she could stand there all day watching the people walk by—wearing their Wishling clothes, their Wishling shoes, talking in their Wishling voices.

Mission 2, Wishworld Observation #2: Wishlings seem to always be in a big rush to get someplace else.

An official-looking Wishling, wearing a blue uniform with a badge and a matching blue hat on his head, stopped in front of Libby. "Shouldn't you be in school, young lady?" he asked.

Libby snapped out of her reverie. "That's right!" she said. "Thank you!"

She flipped open her Star-Zap (which looked enough like the devices everyone else was using that she wasn't afraid of standing out) and accessed the directions. She began to walk to the school. She quickly figured out the flashing signs on the street corners. The red-lighted hand meant stop and the little white-lighted person walking meant it was okay to cross the street.

The rest of her walk was uneventful (though she did start to wonder why Wishlings needed quite so many banks and those mysterious pharmacy places), and she soon stood across the street from her destination, waiting for the little walking man to tell her it was okay to cross. It was a white brick building with a flagpole in front, the starred and striped flag fluttering in the breeze. It looked a little shabby, but in a nice way, like it was well used. WELCOM TO OUR SCHOOL read big cutout letters that hung in the large windows facing the street. That puzzled Libby. *Maybe they spell words differently on Wishworld*, she thought.

"Hurry up," someone called. Libby looked up to see an adult female Wishling in a bright yellow vest and a white hat and gloves beckoning for her to cross the street. "You're late for school!" she said.

Libby did as she was told and hurried to the school entrance. She pushed open the front door and stepped inside. A large letter E was lying on the floor by the windows. Curious, Libby picked it up. Actual paper! It was very light. She tried to stick it back in the window after the *M*, but as soon as she turned, it fluttered back to the ground.

"Don't worry about that. I'll fix it later. Don't want anyone to think we don't know how to spell here!" someone said in a jolly voice. It was an adult female Wishling in a blue uniform that looked just like the one worn by the Wishling who had asked Libby if she should be in school. She held open a door that led to the school lobby. "I'm sorry to say that you're going to need a late pass."

"A late pass, of course," replied Libby. *What on Starland is a late pass?* she wondered.

Libby walked inside, and the Wishling followed her and took a seat behind a desk. She pushed some papers to the side, pulled out a binder, and flipped it open. She picked up a pen and looked up at Libby expectantly.

"Name?" she said. She peered at Libby closely. "Actually, come to think of it, you don't look familiar to me," she said with a frown. Then she smiled despite herself. "Mmmmm, chocolate cake," she said. "My grandpa used to make one every Saturday, with vanilla frosting and sprinkles. And then, after dinner, he would light a candle and sing 'Happy Birthday' to me, because I liked birthdays so much. And we'd each eat a big piece with a tall glass of milk."

Libby didn't smell anything, so she just smiled.

Oh, that's right! Whenever Starlings were around, adult Wishlings smelled the scent of their favorite bakery treat from their childhood. That was a little weird, but mostly kind of nice, she thought. Libby glanced at the name on the woman's badge. Then she leaned forward and looked into the woman's brown eyes, just as Sage had taught her. "Lady Jones," she began. "I am—"

"Lady Jones!" the adult female Wishling said with a cackle. "Do you think I'm royalty? That's Officer Jones to you, young lady!"

Oops. Libby started over. "Officer Jones, I am Libby, the new student," she said. She felt a rush of relief when the Wishling repeated, "You are Libby, the new student."

She smiled as Officer Jones wrote *Libby* on the late pass. Then Officer Jones looked up. "Last name?"

Libby opened her mouth, then closed it. They hadn't covered this in school. Starlings didn't have last names. "It's Libby . . . uh . . . Libby . . ."

In a panic, she glanced down at a folded piece of paper on the officer's desk and saw a list. A class list, maybe? She read aloud the first word she saw, which was not easy, as it was upside down. "Li . . . li . . . liverwurst," she said. That was when she realized that the piece of paper was not a class list. It was a menu.

She regretted her choice as soon as she said it out

loud. She wasn't quite sure what it was, but she did know one thing for certain: it was a terrible-sounding name!

"Libby . . . Liverwurst?" the officer said, frowning.

"Libby Liverwurst," Libby repeated glumly.

With a shake of her head, the officer wrote down the name on the late pass. "Libby Liverwurst." She looked like she was trying hard not to smile. "And what class are you in?"

"Room 546," she said, recalling the number she had read on the directions.

"Room 546," repeated the officer, writing down the numbers. She handed Libby the pass. "Have a good day, Miss Liverwurst."

"Thank you," said Libby politely.

Once she was out of the officer's view, Libby pulled out her Star-Zap and followed the directions it provided. *Up two flights, through the doors, make a left, past the gym, first classroom on the right.* The hallway was quiet, but she could hear the drone of teachers' voices from behind closed classroom doors and the higher-pitched voices of the kids. Then she caught the squeaking sound of rubber soles on wood. That had to be from the gym. She noted that the walls were painted a cheerful shade of yellow. By each doorway was a large rectangular board, covered in artwork—busy scenes, funny faces, drawings of odd creatures she had never seen before. There were also several colorful posters hanging on the walls. One had a simple white background with the words AVA FOR PRESIDENT on it in large letters. Nothing else. Another really caught her eye. On it was an image of a bearded adult male Wishling, in a red, white, and blue outfit and top hat, pointing directly at her. I WANT YOU TO VOTE FOR KRISTIE! it read.

Interesting. Libby had a secret desire to get involved in school politics and hoped one day to run for Light Leader, the head of the student government of Starling Academy. She glanced at the bottom of the poster and noticed that the election was to be held in two days' time. *Hmmm.* Maybe she'd learn a few tricks about elections while she was here. In addition to granting a wish and collecting a vast amount of wish energy, of course.

She glanced up and realized she had passed the classroom she was looking for, room 546. She backtracked, and then, taking a deep breath, she knocked and waited.

The door opened, and a teacher with a sweet round face and short curly brown hair looked down at her curiously. Libby remembered her line. Before the teacher could say a word, she announced, "I am Libby, your new student."

To Libby's relief, the teacher ushered her right in (after sniffing the air and exclaiming how it smelled just like red velvet cake, that is). "Class, this is Libby, our new student," she told everyone. She pointed to an empty desk in the back of the room. "You can sit right there," she said.

Libby made her way down the aisle, looking at the students curiously. The kids all had different skin colors, just like at home. And when she pictured them with brightly colored hair—reds, oranges, yellows, greens, blues, and purples—and a layer of glitter on their skin, they looked an awful lot like Starlings. Wishlings and Starlings weren't that different at all.

She settled herself into her seat, noting how uncomfortable Wishling school furniture was.

"My name is Ms. Blackstone," the teacher said. "And you are Libby . . ."

Oh, great. This again. "Liverwurst," Libby said miserably.

As she had feared, the class burst into laughter.

"Class!" said the teacher. "I am very disappointed in you. We don't laugh at people's names! That is completely unacceptable. Please apologize to Libby Liv—to Libby," she said.

"We're sorry, Libby Liverwurst," the class said in unison.

Libby wasn't quite certain, but she had a sneaking suspicion that her new teacher was trying hard not to laugh.

"That's okay," said Libby. "It *is* a pretty funny name."

Ms. Blackstone had a sympathetic look on her face. "I'm sorry, Libby, but we're about to head out for a class trip. And since you don't have a signed permission slip, you won't be able to come along with us. I'll see if I can get you a seat in Mr. Dilling—"

Libby thought fast. She couldn't be separated from her Wisher! "I already gave you the permission slip," she said, looking into the teacher's eyes. "So I *can* come."

Ms. Blackstone thought for a moment. "Oh, that's right," she said, nodding. "You already gave me the permission slip. So you can come."

The young male Wishling in the seat ahead of Libby's turned around. "Wait a minute, how did you do that?" he asked.

"Do what?" asked Libby innocently.

At the front of the bus, a small girl, her hair cut close to her head in a very cute shaggy style, stood and kneeled on her seat so she faced the rest of the bus. She began to sing:

Ninety-nine bottles of beer on the wall . . .

The class cheered and joined in.

Ninety-nine bottles of beer,
If one of those bottles should happen to fall,
How many bottles of beer on the wall?
Ninety-eight bottles of—

"Inappropriate!" Ms. Blackstone called out from her seat in the front of the school bus.

There was a short silence, then the girl grinned and started singing again.

Ninety-nine bottles of root beer on the wall, ninety-nine bottles of root beer . . .

The class laughed and sang along.

"That's better!" called Ms. Blackstone.

Libby took a furtive look at her Wish Pendant. She had taken a seat next to a young female Wishling with curly red hair and freckles who was staring out the window, a pensive look on her face. Libby was hoping that the young female Wishling's preoccupied look was due to deep thoughts about an unfulfilled wish. But when Libby sat down and introduced herself, she realized that her Wish Pendant was still dark. Not wanting to be rude, she tried to strike up a conversation.

"So what's your name?" Libby asked brightly.

"Susie," she said.

"And where are we going on our class trip?" Libby asked.

"Aquarium," Susie answered.

Libby had no idea what that was, but obviously she couldn't ask. Maybe her next question would clear things up. "Um . . . what's your favorite thing at the aquarium?"

"Fish," Susie said.

No such luck. Libby nodded, smiling to herself as she realized that she had traded the world's most talkative roommate for the world's least talkative seatmate.

The bus came to a stop at a red light. *Red for stop,* thought Libby. She was really getting familiar with the way things worked on Wishworld. A young female Wishling appeared at Libby's side. "Switch seats?" she asked.

"Sure!" said Libby gratefully. She crossed the aisle and sat in the empty seat next to a young female Wishling with long blond hair and bright blue nail polish. The Wishling grinned at Libby.

"Hi, Libby Liverspots," she said. "I'm Gabby."

Libby didn't correct her, although if there was one name that was less pleasant-sounding than Libby Liverwurst, that had to be it. "Hey, Gabby," she said. She looked down expectantly. Her Wish Pendant was still dark. *Sigh.*

Libby shifted in her seat. It was pretty uncomfortable. She realized that vehicle seats, like those in the classroom, didn't automatically adjust on Wishworld. But surely there was a button or something to push to get a little more comfortable. This was ridiculous. She started to examine her side of the seat.

The young male Wishling across the aisle from her was giving her an odd look.

"What are you looking for, new girl?" he asked. "You lose something?"

"No, I'm just looking for the seat adjuster," Libby said.

He looked blank.

"To fix the seat for my height and weight," Libby explained. "You know, so I'll be more comfortable."

He laughed. "Comfortable? On a school bus? What kind of buses have you been riding?" He elbowed his seatmate and pointed to Libby. "Hey, Aidan, the new girl is used to adjustable school bus seats!"

Aidan nodded. "I've heard about those," he said knowingly. "Private school, right?"

"Um, sure," said Libby, completely confused. She turned back to her seatmate. At least she seemed a little more talkative than the last one. Libby figured she could probably get some helpful information out of her. "So tell me about our class," she said. "Anything interesting I should know about?"

Gabby thought for a moment. "Well, we're all working on our term papers. So you're going to have to come up with a subject to write about."

Libby thought about that for a moment. Didn't seem promising. "Anything else?"

"We're learning how to square-dance in gym," she offered.

Aidan groaned. "She wants to know what's interesting, not what's the most hideous thing about school," he said. "Square dancing is the worst. We all have to hold hands and do-si-do. It is so painful."

Libby nodded sympathetically. She was getting good at pretending she wasn't completely confused by what everyone was saying to her. "So what's going on at school that *is* interesting?" she asked him.

He thought for a moment. "I guess I'd have to say it's

the election," he said finally. "Two best friends are running against each other. It's pretty weird."

A wave of electricity ran up Libby's spine. She sat up straight in her seat. Could that be the energy surge that Lady Stella had mentioned? She wasn't sure, but it was a definite possibility. Maybe she was on to something here!

"That seems tough," Libby said, her voice higher than usual in her excitement. She thought back to the posters in the hallway. "So is either Ava or . . . or . . . um, Kristie in our class?"

"Ava is," said Gabby.

"So which one is A—" Libby started. But then the bus shuddered to a stop with a loud squealing sound. The kids all immediately jumped to their feet and began pushing in a mad rush to get off the bus.

Libby struggled to keep her balance as she was swept down the aisle. "No pushing each other! No shoving!" said Ms. Blackstone, to no avail. "Do you want me to turn this bus around and go back right now?"

Once everyone was off the bus and had listened to a lecture about bus-exiting safety, Ms. Blackstone led them down a path to a low concrete building surrounded by a high wall. The air felt different there to Libby—salty, heavy, and damp. It smelled different, too—she couldn't quite put her finger on it—kind of pleasant and unpleasant at the same time. She couldn't decide.

Ms. Blackstone took a deep breath and smiled. "Ah, I love the smell of the sea," she said. "So briny and refreshing." She turned to the class. "Okay, class," she said. "I need you to stay right here while I sort out our tickets." She headed to the ticket booth while the students milled about on the walkway in front of the building.

Now's my chance to find Ava, thought Libby. Students were standing in groups, chatting. Some young male Wishlings were horsing around, pushing each other and laughing loudly. Libby scanned the crowd. Then she smiled as she spotted a short young female Wishling with a pin-straight brown bob that curved around her chin. Libby was smiling because the young female Wishling was wearing an AVA FOR PRESIDENT T-shirt.

"Hey," said Libby, stepping up to her. "I'm Libby. You must be Ava." She looked down at her Star Pendant, anticipating its golden glow.

But there was nothing.

CHAPTER 7

The young female Wishling laughed. "I'm not Ava. I'm her campaign manager, Waverly." She reached into her pocket. "Nice to meet you, Libby. How would you like a button?" Without waiting for an answer, she pressed a round flat object into Libby's hand. Libby looked down. It said VOTE FOR AVA on it.

"Hi, Waverly," Libby said. "And thanks for the button." She had no idea what to do with it, so she shoved it into her skirt pocket, to Waverly's obvious disappointment. "So what's a campaign manager?"

Waverly smiled. "I help her write speeches, make posters, make sure she's following the school's election rules, and convince people to vote for her. I keep things running and make sure she's focused." She leaned forward conspiratorially. "And trust me, sometimes she needs it! Basically anything that needs to be done to help get her elected. It's a really important job."

"Interesting," said Libby. She wondered who she would ask to be her campaign manager—if she ever ran for office, that is. Maybe Leona. She would be able to get lots of attention; she loved being in the spotlight. . . . Scratch that. Leona would probably want to run for Light Leader herself!

"So where's the candidate?" Libby asked Waverly.

"She's in the bathroom," said Waverly. "She should be out in a minute." She leaned forward again. "So can we count on your vote?"

Libby laughed. "Shouldn't I meet Ava first?" she asked.

Waverly peered at Libby, a scowl on her face. "Trust me, when you meet her, you'll see she is the perfect person for the job."

Mrs. Blackstone walked back to the group. "We're all squared away," she told them, brandishing a stack of tickets. "Now everyone walk single file through the turnstile. We'll have a couple of minutes to explore a bit before we head to the sea lion show."

Libby immediately perked up. Sea glions? She didn't

know glions could swim! She thought the big cats hated the water. This would be very interesting indeed.

The students were eager to get inside and began pushing again. "One at a time!" Ms. Blackstone warned. "Everyone take your turn!" She waggled a finger at them. "If there is any more pushing, I promise that this will be the very last field trip we take!"

Libby approached the turnstile with trepidation. It looked like that metal bar was going to hurt when she banged into it. But it moved down and out of her way easily and the next bar popped up behind her. She stood to the side to watch the other students go through. What a fun machine! She had never seen anything like it before.

When the allure of the turnstile had worn off, Libby realized she was in a room with glass walls. Behind those walls was a lot of water, and in the water were multicolored creatures in all shapes and sizes, swimming, floating, diving, bobbing. Libby pressed her forehead to the cool glass and stared, completely absorbed and forgetting about best friends and school elections. She had known that there would be some strange creatures on Wishworld, but this was incredible!

"But how do they breathe underwater?" she said aloud.

Aidan, who happened to be standing next to her, laughed. "You're kidding, right? Fish have gills, dummy."

"Of course I'm kidding!" said Libby, slapping Aidan on the back, a little too hard. So those were fish! She realized she should stop asking questions that could compromise her identity. She stared in silence at a vibrant yellow creature as it floated in the water in front of her, its mouth opening and closing, its strange little arm appendages fluttering up and down. It was weird and beautiful. Libby was so enthralled she completely forgot to make any wish observations. She probably wouldn't even have known where to start. There were no fish on Starland. Its waters did not contain life-forms of any kind. It was also odd for her to see creatures in captivity. While she understood that it was probably educational for Wishlings to see them up close, it still made her feel sad to see wild creatures on display. On Starland all living creatures roamed free. Wishworld was getting odder by the starmin.

"Come, class, the sea lion show is about to begin," said Ms. Blackstone. "Follow me."

The class obediently followed their teacher out the door. Libby noted there was no pushing or shoving; apparently the threat of no more field trips had done the trick. They went down a pathway to an entrance that led into a small open-air stadium with rows of seats surrounding a pool of water with a platform in the middle. Libby found herself in the first row, sitting next to Waverly. Even though it was the Time of Letting Go, once she was seated, she discovered that it was warm in the sunlight. Libby removed her jacket.

"Cute outfit," said Waverly appreciatively.

Libby smiled. She and Lady Stella had done a good job.

"Hey, could you scootch over?" Waverly asked. "I want to save Ava a seat."

"Good idea," said Libby. She wasn't quite sure what "scootching" was, but she moved over so there was room between them. Waverly looked satisfied, so Libby assumed she had done the correct thing.

While Libby waited, she stared at the platform, waiting for the glions to appear. Glions were sweet and gentle large creatures with multicolored shimmering manes of hair around their faces and long, tufted tails. Then she thought she saw, out of the corner of her eye, something moving quickly through the water right in front of her, and started. She peered into the water but didn't see anything. Must have been her imagination.

Waverly searched the crowd. The young female Wishling who had been singing on the school bus stood in the aisle, looking for a seat. "Ava! Ava! Over here!" Waverly shouted, waving wildly to her.

Was Libby seeing things, or did Ava seem to hesitate for a moment before she joined them? The young female Wishling shuffled past other students to squeeze in between Libby and Waverly.

"Ava, this is Libby," said Waverly, "the new girl in class today."

"Oh, yeah," said Ava. "Libby Luncheon Meat!" She elbowed Libby in the side. "Sorry, I couldn't resist."

"That's me," Libby said. She snuck a look at her Wish Pendant. *Startastic!* It was glowing.

Ava held up a fist and smiled at Libby expectantly. Libby stared at it. She vaguely remembered a Wishers 101 lesson during which they talked about the strange custom many Wishlings followed of shaking hands. So Libby grabbed Ava's fist and shook it. It felt awkward, and Ava confirmed that by laughing.

"Very formal!" she said. "Pleased to meet you, madam!"

Libby realized she had made a mistake. She made a quick note.

Mission 2, Wishworld Observation #3: Figure out mysterious Wishling greeting involving raised fists.

"So do we have your vote?" Waverly asked excitedly.

"Give her a break, Waverly," Ava said, crossing her arms tightly. "We're on a class trip, for goodness' sake."

The two girls gave each other pointed looks.

"Is something wrong?" asked Libby. Her pulse quickened. Maybe that was a clue.

"Nothing's wrong!" said Waverly quickly. "Why would you say that? The campaign is going great!" She narrowed her eyes. "Are you from the school newspaper?"

Ava laughed. She put her hands to the sides of her mouth. "Extra! Extra! Read all about it," she called. "Breaking election news!"

"Excuse me," said a classmate, and they stood to let her pass by. Libby took the opportunity to turn to Ava. "So nothing's wrong?" she asked softly.

Ava glanced quickly at Waverly, who was looking the other way. "Nothing's wrong, really," she said to Libby. "Well . . . actually . . . I mean . . ." Her voice trailed off.

"Tell me," said Libby, leaning forward eagerly.

"Well, actually, if you want to know, I was just thinking that I wish I could win . . ."

"Hello, ladies and gentlemen, boys and girls, and welcome to Applewood Aquarium!" a voice boomed.

Ava snapped to attention, her unfinished wish dangling in the air in front of Libby.

But Libby grinned. *You just wish you could win the*

class election, she thought, finishing Ava's sentence. The election was two days away. She snuck a look at her Countdown Clock. Forty-eight hours to go. That was two days exactly! That sealed the deal. Libby sat back in her seat with a smile on her face. The pendant had been glowing. She had figured out the wish. Now she just had to figure out how she was going to help make it come true.

But that would have to wait. Right now Libby was going to enjoy the sea glion show.

"Please put your hands together for Trainer Amy, and Felix and Oscar, our trained sea lions!" Libby and the rest of the students cheered and applauded.

An adult female Wishling in a monogrammed turquoise shirt, with a bucket in her hand and a whistle around her neck, ran out onto the platform. She blew the whistle and the strangest thing happened. Before Libby's astounded eyes, two sleek, dark creatures jumped out of the water and sailed through the air past each other before diving back in, hardly making a splash.

"My stars!" Libby cried. "What was that? Some kind of fish?"

Waverly gave her a look. "This is a sea lion show. What do you think they are?"

"Oh," said Libby, still confused. She sat back and took it all in. It turned out that Felix and Oscar were

California sea *lions*, a type of marine mammal related to other creatures called seals and walruses. (That seemed to make sense to everyone else, so Libby nodded along with the crowd.) They were smart, they were great swimmers, and they loved to eat fish. In fact, Trainer Amy had a bucketful for them. The sea lions could each eat thirty-five pounds of fish a day. This was a little tough for Libby to hear, as she had been introduced to fish just moments before and was quite charmed by them. Plus, all living creatures on Starland—Starlings and animals alike—were vegetarians, so she had never seen a carnivore before in her life. She looked away as the adorable sea lions wolfed down fish after fish. The audience learned that the seals were actually furry, even though they looked rubbery. They had excellent senses of hearing and smell and special reflecting eyes that helped them see better in the dark ocean. They had a layer of blubber under their skin to keep them warm in the cold water. They could dive up to six hundred feet and spend ten to twenty minutes underwater without needing to take a breath.

And the things they could do! The tricks amazed Libby. She watched as they jumped out of the water with ease and did somersaults in the air. Libby clapped with delight as Oscar balanced a large striped ball on his nose, then tossed it over to Felix, who caught it effortlessly and jumped into the water and started swimming, never dropping it. They could stand on their front flippers and bend their tails to touch their noses. They leapt through a series of hoops, then jumped out of the water, slid neatly across the platform, and climbed up to their perches. Libby cheered along with the crowd. Oscar clapped along to the music as Felix swam quickly around the pool; then Oscar dove in to join him in matching double backflips to end the show.

Splash! Everyone in the first two rows got sprayed in the face. Libby groaned along with the others and grimaced. But truthfully, she was kind of delighted.

Once they had slowly made their way out of the stadium, Ms. Blackstone led them to the next stop on their tour—the penguin house. As soon as Libby pushed open the door, she was momentarily stunned by the smell. The warm, moist, stinky air made her eyes water. "Leaping starberries," she muttered to herself. "That's nasty!" As she made her way to the front of the dark room, she found herself face-to-face with another glass wall. When she saw what was behind the glass, she forgot about the stench. For in front of her were the funniest creatures she had ever seen in her life—black and white with pointy beaks, beady eyes, and stubby wings that they held out from their sides as they moved around on the rocks above a pool of water. She watched with delight as they waddled and hopped, ungainly as could be. Waddle waddle waddle waddle. HOP. Waddle waddle waddle waddle. HOP. It made Libby laugh out loud. And then, with one movement, they suddenly transformed themselves from awkward to awesome. They dove into the water and began to zoom around with seemingly reckless speed, yet they never bumped into each other. She found herself switching her attention back and forth between the adorably ungainly penguins on the top half of the exhibit and the graceful swimmers on the bottom. She felt as if she could have stood in the dark exhibit watching those creatures all day. "Aren't they amazing?" she said to the student who had been standing next to her. No answer. He was gone. Blinking slowly, she looked around. The room was empty. The class had left the building without her.

Where did they go? Libby tried to stay calm. She ran into another building and looked around. But they weren't in the jellyfish room (another place Libby could have stayed all day, watching the creatures' slowly waving tentacles and the hypnotic movement of their glowing undulating bodies). She was momentarily distracted by a tank full of almost impossibly cute creatures (the sign said they were sea horses, but Libby thought they should be called galliope-fish), but then she began to search again in earnest. There was no time to linger. She was lost.

Finally, to Libby's immense relief, an adult female Wishling, wearing a turquoise shirt and a whistle around her neck, approached her. It was Trainer Amy. "You look lost," she told Libby. "You're part of that school tour, aren't you?"

Libby nodded.

"Your class is at the touch tank," Trainer Amy said. "I'll take you there." With a sigh of relief, Libby followed obediently behind her. But Trainer Amy stopped for a moment. "Do you smell vanilla cupcakes?" she asked, sniffing the air. Libby smiled and shrugged.

Libby was happy to find her class (and a little put off that no one seemed to have missed her), but she forgot everything as soon as she saw the touch tank. As its name said, it was a large low aquarium filled with sea creatures you could actually touch. Libby rolled up her sleeves and wiggled her way between two students until she had some space at the edge of the tank. She plunged her hands into the water. Luckily, there was a guide who explained what everything was, because it was new to Libby. There were prehistoric-looking horseshoe crabs, shy hermit crabs, slippery sea slugs, bumpy sea stars in all sizes, sand dollars, mussels, spiny sea urchins, small sharks, and flat stingrays with mouths like suction hoses that glided through the water, flapping their soft wings. Once again she wished she could stay all day.

After Mrs. Blackstone made sure that everyone cleaned their hands (by rubbing in some stinky gel, not passing their hands under a warm light as they did at home), they had a quick lunch in the cafeteria and then boarded the bus back to school. On the plus side, Libby had ordered something called a grilled cheese on rye and rather enjoyed it. On the minus side, she had just missed grabbing a seat next to Ava at lunch. She was hoping to sit next to her on the ride home, but to her dismay, Waverly beat her to it. Waverly was deep in conversation with Ava, who was listening with a slightly distracted look on her face. Libby chose a seat near the front of the bus and sat down. A cute young male Wishling sat next to her, his sandy brown hair falling into his eyes, and she smiled at him. As soon as the doors folded shut, the skies opened up and it began to pour. Libby was shocked to see rivulets of water run down the windows; apparently, Wishling vehicles did not have the same dry-surround protection that they had on Starland. She was intrigued by the window cleaners and watched them intently. Soon the *slish-slosh* of the rain and the steady *whoosh, whoosh* as the wipers went back and forth combined to make her feel very, very sleepy.

What a great first day! she thought. *I found my Wisher and figured out the wish right away. I'm pretty sure I can help make it come true. And the aquarium was amazing.*

Her last thought before she drifted off to sleep was *Mission 2, Wishworld Observation #4: Don't leave Wishworld without seeing some penguins.*

CHAPTER 8

Libby awoke with a start as the bus pulled to a stop. It took her a moment to remember where she was and what was going on (school bus, Wishworld, wish fulfillment).

"Nice nap?" said the young male Wishling as he stood up.

Libby nodded. She felt very refreshed, actually.

After she and her classmates got off the bus and headed to their classroom, they had to scramble to get their bags packed up before the final bell. It was time to go home. Libby, of course, had no place to go home to, so she was up for anything—hopefully something election related.

"Here you go," said Ms. Blackstone, walking over to

Libby's desk and handing her a thick book. "Everyone, your math homework for tonight is section three, pages fifteen through seventeen."

Libby's eyes lit up as she grasped the book in her hands. She flipped through the pages, marveling at the thinness of the paper and the way it was printed on both sides. She hugged the book to her chest.

The girl in the seat in front of her turned around. "Wow," she said. "I've never seen anyone so excited about math homework before!"

Ava leaned on Libby's desk and zipped up her silvery backpack. "Homework will be the death of me," she groaned, making a gruesome face. "I wish we didn't have any tonight."

Libby pricked up her ears when she heard the word *wish*. She really wanted her Wisher to be happy. Surely that meant helping her with any extra little wishes that came up when Libby was around. It couldn't hurt to have a happy Wisher; she was sure of it.

This was going to be easy. Libby placed the book on her desk and sidled up to Ms. Blackstone. She peered up into her eyes. "Maybe we shouldn't have any homework tonight," she said in a low voice.

"I'm sorry, Libby, did you say something?" Ms. Blackstone asked distractedly.

Libby glanced around to make sure the other students couldn't overhear. "Maybe we shouldn't have any homework tonight," she repeated, more intently this time.

Ms. Blackstone nodded. "Maybe we shouldn't have any homework tonight," she said loudly.

The class cheered and happily returned their textbooks to their desks.

"Wow," Libby heard Ava say. "Sometimes wishes do come true. Just like that!"

"Yeah," Libby said to herself with a laugh. "Just like that!"

The bell signaling the end of the day rang, and the students streamed out of the classroom, still cheering. Libby followed along as they merged with other kids in the hallway and marched down the stairs, past the auditorium, and out the door into the yard. She lost sight of Ava and wandered around the schoolyard in search of her, dodging flying balls and running kids. She finally found her and Waverly chatting in the corner of the yard. She couldn't help noticing that Waverly had a look on her face that Libby was beginning to recognize: one of irritation.

"I'm just not sure you're taking this election seriously enough," Libby heard Waverly say. "We missed a whole day of campaigning!" She shook her head. "Did you notice that while we were away, Kristie hung up some new posters? She's got a lot more posters up than us now."

"She did?" said Ava, looking interested. "I must have missed them."

Libby nodded. She had spotted one by the auditorium on her way out. It featured a huge blown-up photo of a young female Wishling with long, straight black hair on a bright green background. She was blowing a big pink bubble—only the bubble was actually a pink balloon that was glued to the poster board. The copy read DON'T BLOW IT, VOTE FOR KRISTIE. Libby joined in the conversation and described the poster to Ava.

Ava laughed out loud. "What a funny idea!" she said. "Kristie always has such—"

"Correction," said Waverly exasperatedly. "It's a lame idea. She's making a joke out of the election. I didn't like them at all. Plus, now she's handing out bubble gum to everyone." She pointed to a boy who was walking by, chomping away, his cheeks stuffed with bubble gum.

"Everyone knows you're not allowed to chew gum on school grounds." She pursed her lips. "She's not following school rules. Maybe I should report her to the—"

"Don't do that," said Ava quickly. "Hey, I have an idea. Let's make some cool posters of our own. I've got all those art supplies at home still."

Yes! That was exactly what Libby was hoping for. She was excited to see Ava working to make her own wish come true. "I'll help!" she offered.

But the two girls were staring at her expectantly.

"What?" said Libby, shrugging.

"Don't you have to ask your mom first?" Ava asked.

Libby nodded. "Of course!" she said. She opened her Star-Zap and randomly punched in some numbers. To her surprise, it began to ring. She made a hasty observation: *Mission 2, Wishworld Observation #5: Star-Zaps work as actual phones on Wishworld.*

"Hello," said a voice.

Ava and Waverly were watching, so Libby decided to wing it. "Hi, Mom," she said. "Can I go to my new friend's house after school?"

"Sorry, I think you have the wrong number," said the voice on the other end.

Libby had an idea. "Oh, you have a work dinner tonight?" she said. She paused. "Okay, I'll ask."

"Listen, kid, you have the wrong number," the person repeated.

She held her hand over the Star-Zap. "My mom's got a big work dinner tonight that's going to go late, and she was wondering if I could sleep over at your house tonight."

Ava shrugged. "Sure. My mom won't mind."

"Okay, so it's a plan," said Libby. "Thanks, Mom."

"You do realize that you have the wrong number and that I'm not your mother," said the voice. "Actually, I'm not anyone's mother. Because I'm a father!"

Libby almost burst out laughing. "I love you, too, Mom," she answered.

And so it was settled. Libby mentally patted herself on the back the whole walk to Ava's. Everything was going startastically on her mission so far. She'd be collecting wish energy in no time.

"Mom! I'm home!" Ava yelled. No answer. "She must be in her office," she said. "She can never hear me when she's in there." She slipped off her shoes and lined them up by the door. Libby and Waverly did the same. Libby wiggled her bare toes, with their bright pink polish. Obviously Wishling shoes were not made of materials that repelled dirt. And she remembered learning that their homes were not self-cleaning. Poor Wishlings.

Afternoon sunlight streamed through the windows. The three girls spread out their materials on the rough-hewn dining room table.

Ava headed to a big silver box in the kitchen and pulled open the door. The lighted interior revealed shelves filled with different foods and drinks.

"Can I get you anything?" she asked. Both Libby and Waverly asked for water.

Mission 2, Wishworld Observation #6: Wishling food apparently does not keep constant optimal temperature and needs to be stored in large cooling devices.

As soon as they were settled, Waverly produced a notebook and a pen from her backpack. "Let's come up with some new slogans," she said.

"I have an idea," Ava said softly. She looked excited to share it. "Hey, remember last Halloween when Kristie and I went as prisoners in those striped costumes? We could take that picture of me and draw bars in front of my face, and the message could be 'Wanted: Ava for President.' " She smiled at Waverly expectantly.

"No way," said Waverly. "Too gimmicky. How is anyone going to take you seriously as a candidate?"

Ava's face fell.

Libby thought fast. "Well, then, how about a picture of Ava with a caption?" she suggested. "Something fun and memorable. Like 'Vote for Ava, she's . . .' " Her voice trailed off. "What rhymes with Ava?"

"How about *favor*?" suggested Ava. " 'Do me a favor and vote for Ava'?" She pronounced it "favah."

"That's cute!" said Libby.

Waverly made a face. "That's terrible," she said.

Ava bit her lip and tried again. " 'Vote for Ava, she's got flava'?"

"Oh, that's good," said Libby. "Very catchy."

Waverly wadded up a napkin and threw it at Libby's head. "No offense, guys, but those really stink."

Ava didn't look so sure. "I think kids like fun stuff," she said. "It makes them laugh. It's memorable." She looked away. "I know I do. And so does Kristie," she muttered.

"This is no time for jokes. We need to let the students know that you are serious about the job!"

Ava looked down at the table. "Okay," she said.

Waverly stood up. "Can I go to your room to get the supplies?" she asked.

"Sure," said Ava.

Libby put her hand on Ava's arm as soon as Waverly left the room. "I thought those ideas were great," she said. "We should just tell Waverly you want to do something fun. It's your campaign."

Ava shook her head. "No, I guess she's right," she said. "Elections should be serious." She sighed. "Nothing really rhymes with Ava anyway."

"I've got it," Waverly said, returning with a stack of poster board. "No gimmicks, no rhymes, and certainly no costumes. We'll take a picture of you, looking responsible. We'll print it in black and white with the words 'Vote for Ava.' Simple. Classic. Effective. Trust me, it's the best way to go."

Ava thought for a moment. "Okay," she finally said.

"Are you sure?" Libby asked worriedly.

"You guys have to trust me," Waverly repeated. "I know what I'm doing."

Libby sighed. She hoped that Waverly was right.

After taking fifty-three photos of Ava with her phone (Libby counted), Waverly was finally convinced they had the right one. It was "the perfect combination of serious and approachable" per Waverly, although they all looked pretty much the same to Libby, save the one she liked best, in which Ava was crossing her eyes and making a goofy face. Libby had overheard Ava muttering, "I wish this was over," under her breath, so she had concentrated on making sure that the fifty-third photo was indeed perfect. They printed twenty copies in black and white ("Classic and classy," Waverly had proclaimed) and glued them onto the poster boards with the word VOTE on top of the photo and FOR AVA underneath.

Libby turned to Ava. "What do you think?" she asked.

Ava opened up her mouth as if to say something and then shrugged. "They're fine," she said.

Waverly looked down at the posters. "You know," she said. "I think I love them."

"Love what?" someone said.

"Oh, hey, Mom," said Ava. "Waverly was just saying that she loves the campaign posters we made."

Libby looked up. Ava's mom wore black-rimmed glasses and had short red hair, which she pushed behind her ears. She was wearing jeans and a faded red hoodie. She looked at the posters and smiled. "Very nice, girls. A little serious but I guess that's the point. Are you hungry?" She inhaled deeply. "Hey, anyone smell spice cake?" She sniffed again. "With . . . cream cheese frosting?"

Ava gave her mother a funny look. "This is Libby, the new girl at school. She's helping out with the campaign. She's going to sleep over tonight."

Ava's mom smiled. "Sounds good."

Then she stole a glance at the large timepiece that hung on the wall. "Yikes!" she said. "Sorry, I was busy working and didn't realize how late it was. You all want pizza for dinner?"

"Yes!" Ava and Waverly shouted.

Ava's mom picked up her phone, then turned to Libby. "Good with you, too?" she asked. "You're not gluten-free, vegan, paleo, or lactose intolerant, are you?"

Libby stared at her. What in the world was she talking about? "No," she finally answered. "Pizza sounds good."

And it was. Very good. Extremely good. "More, please!" she said after she had gobbled up her first slice. She ate four pieces in all. It was crispy, saucy, cheesy deliciousness. It was deceptively simple-looking, but it was the perfect combination of comforting flavors. *Mission 2, Wishworld Observation #7: Everyone must try pizza!*

Ava's mom was reaching for another slice when she gasped. She looked at her watch. "Oops, time to go pick up Jasper!" she cried. "Be back soon, girls!"

Libby looked at Ava.

"My annoying little brother," she explained.

The girls had finished cleaning up and Ava was turning on the dishwasher (another odd Wishling invention) when a male Wishling about a year or two younger than

Ava swaggered into the kitchen. He had red hair and a smirk on his freckled face. Libby eyed him warily. He flipped open the lid of the pizza box and grabbed a slice. "Good thing you saved me some, Ava," he said.

"Can't you say hello, Jasper?" Ava asked.

"Hello, Jasper," he said with a smirk.

Ava rolled her eyes. "Brothers," she said.

Waverly placed a sheaf of papers in front of Ava. "So," she said, "I took the liberty of jotting down some ideas for you."

Ava looked at her quizzically. "You . . . um . . . wrote my speech for me?" she asked.

"Just as a jumping-off point, of course," said Waverly, raising a hand as if to deflect criticism.

Ava picked up the papers and studied them. She looked up. "It looks like you wrote the whole thing."

"It's just some ideas," Waverly protested.

Ava cleared her throat and began. " 'Good afternoon, Principal Lefkon, Vice Principal Bergen, faculty, fellow classmates,' " she read. " 'My name is Ava Cunningham, and I am running for class president. This is a challenge that I accept both solemnly and wholeheartedly. There are some who think that the school government is a laughing matter.' " There Ava frowned. " 'Well, I assure you . . .'" She lost her place for a moment. "'I assure you,'" she repeated, "'that I am ready to accept this responsibility with the gravity that it commands. I intend to lead my fellow students in a manner becoming of a . . .'"

"It's good," interrupted Jasper.

Waverly put her hands on her hips and smiled.

"It is?" said Libby. She wasn't so sure about that.

"Yeah," answered Jasper. "It's good if you want your audience to die of boredom!"

Libby let out a strangled laugh. She had to agree.

"Jasper!" said Waverly huffily. "Mind your own business!"

"Here's what you should say," said Jasper. He climbed up on a kitchen stool, put one hand over his heart, and pointed a finger in the air. "I am Ava Cunningham," he said in a high, squeaky voice that sounded nothing at all like Ava's low, pleasant voice. "And you should vote for me for president because I am so kind and generous. In fact, I am so very generous that when I was eight years old, I once shared something very special with my amazing little brother. I gave him a terrible case of the itchiest . . ."

Ava's eyes opened wide. She obviously knew exactly

what was coming next. The look on her face was one of pure panic. "I wish you would stop talking!" she shouted, lunging at her brother.

Another wish from her Wisher! Libby immediately hopped into action. *Shut up, shut up, shut up,* she chanted in her head, staring at Jasper.

". . . scratchiest case of head li—"

All of a sudden Jasper fell silent. His mouth opened and closed but nothing came out. His eyes nearly bulged out of his head.

Ava looked relieved. "Very funny, Jasper," she said. "Now get out of here, please."

Jasper ran out of the room, panic-stricken. And Libby probably waited a little longer than she should have to reverse the wish. But she eventually did.

Libby yawned loudly. She was exhausted.

"Keeping you up, I see," said Waverly. "Now let's get back to the speech."

Ava gathered up the notes and took a deep breath. She looked at Waverly. "So I was thinking of maybe starting with a joke, to loosen up the audience. Have you ever heard this one?" She smiled. "What do you call cheese that isn't yours?"

"What?" asked Libby.

"Nacho cheese!" said Ava. "Get it?"

Libby laughed as if she understood, though she really didn't.

Ava smiled. "Then I could go into my campaign promise about improving the school lunch menu selections. What do you think?"

Waverly, looking slightly annoyed, shook her head. "Stick to your message, Ava," she said. "You are the serious candidate. Leave the jokes to bubble gum girl."

"Don't you mean *your* message?" Libby thought she heard Ava mutter. But she wasn't exactly sure, and then Ava shrugged and said, "Whatever you think is best," so Libby let it go.

Several hours and one serious election speech later, the girls were lying in Ava's room. Ava was on the floor in a sleeping bag, as she had graciously given her guests her large bed to sleep in. Ava had recited the speech several times, until Waverly was satisfied. Libby was feeling confident that everything was under control.

"Are you sure I shouldn't start with a joke?" Ava asked. "It just feels right, like it's going to get their attention."

Waverly yawned. "You're not running to be class clown," she said. "You're running to be class president."

Ava rolled over. "Fine," she said. She stared at Libby for a moment. "I love your hair, Libby. That pink streak is so cool." She smiled sleepily. "I wish I had pink hair. Well, good night."

Libby's eyes opened wide. Pink hair! How many wishes could one Wisher make! This was getting ridiculous. Still, she closed her eyes and concentrated. But she was so very tired. . . .

★

Starf! Libby sat up suddenly as a blaring ringing noise shocked her out of a deep sleep. It took a starmin to identify the obnoxious sound. Wishworld alarms were loud and annoying. Libby much preferred the gentle Starland alarm: your bed was gently vibrated until you got out of it. It was a very pleasant way to wake up. This, not so much. What a jarring way to start your day. Plus, they were getting up extra early to hang up the new posters. The election was the next day.

Ava was the first to get up. She unzipped her sleeping bag, stood up, and stumbled to the bathroom. Libby heard the click as the light was switched on. And then the scream.

Libby and Waverly ran to the bathroom. Libby threw open the door. Ava was staring at herself in the mirror. Her hair was half brown, half pink. Libby realized she must have fallen asleep in the middle of her wish. *Oops.*

Waverly shook her head. "No, no, no, no, no," she said. "No," she added for good measure.

Ava smiled at her reflection. "It's actually pretty cool," she said. "But how in the world . . ."

"We have to fix this before the election!" said Waverly frantically. "This is not the hair of a serious presidential candidate!"

Libby thought fast. "It's just temporary," she said. "Don't worry. It will come out in the shower."

"It better," said Waverly warningly.

"It will," said Libby. "I guarantee it." And she thought, *Mission 2, Wishworld Observation #8: Sometimes wishes are wishes. But then again, sometimes they aren't. Be careful out there; it's hard to tell the difference.*

Ava came out of the bathroom, towel drying her back-to-normal hair. Libby went in next, and she found that Ava had left her a change of clothes, a tube of something minty called toothpaste, and a brand-new instrument, still in its package—a toothbrush. Libby stood in the bathroom, staring at the toothbrush. She stuck it in her mouth and moved it around. She couldn't be entirely sure she was doing it correctly. Was it up and down or side to side? She missed her toothlight.

Libby had been deliberately avoiding mirrors since she had arrived, knowing she would be horrified by her dull Wishling appearance. And she was. She gasped at her plain brown hair, her flat-looking skin. What she wouldn't give for a little sparkle. She was feeling so tired, too, which made her look extra un-sparkly, in her opinion. Suddenly, she remembered her Mirror Mantra. She stared at her reflection and spoke the words: "It's all in the balance. Glimmer and shine." She grinned as her appearance was suddenly transformed and she looked as she did on Starland. Her eyes lit up and she touched the mirror. How she missed her long, flowing pink hair and glimmery skin! How did Wishlings deal with being so boring and uninspiring all the time?

Libby's Mirror Mantra had given her the burst of confidence and energy she needed. When they arrived at school, she bustled around the hallway, wanting to get the posters up before the rest of the students began trickling in. They had an election to win. And the next day she would have some wish energy (a lot of it, she hoped) to collect. She glanced down at her Wish Pendant, dangling from her neck. *Starf!* Her wish energy was getting low. Luckily, everything was falling into place. Libby was confident that she wouldn't need her special talent to make this wish come true.

CHAPTER 9

"This will all be over by tomorrow afternoon," said Ava as she and Libby climbed the stairs together on the way to class after they had hung all the posters. "Thank goodness."

Libby stopped on the landing. "You don't sound all that excited about it," she said.

Ava shrugged.

"So what made you decide to run for president, anyway?" Libby asked.

"It happened by accident," Ava said with a sigh. "No one was running, and the principal made an announcement at assembly one morning urging students to throw their hats into the ring."

Libby's eyes widened. Wishlings did some crazy

things. What did tossing your hat have to do with an election?

"That's exactly what she said," Ava continued. "And I was wearing a hat, so of course I tossed it up onto the stage as a joke, and then the next thing I knew, Sammy Decker nominated me right then and there. And then no one else wanted to run and the principal kept saying that someone else had to run against me, they couldn't just give it to me, so I talked Kristie into running, too. We figured that one of us would win and then the other person would help them out. It didn't matter who won to us. We thought it would be fun."

Libby considered this. "That's interesting. But then things changed, obviously."

"This girl named Holly volunteered to be Kristie's campaign manager. And then little by little things started getting competitive. Fancy posters. Free candy if you promised to vote for her. And then Kristie got really busy after school all the time and couldn't spend time with me. Then Waverly volunteered to help me, and then, before I knew it, Kristie and I just stopped talking. It was so weird."

Libby nodded. "That *is* weird. So what happens tomorrow?"

"Tomorrow afternoon the whole school comes to

the auditorium to hear our speeches," Ava said. "Then everyone votes. They count up the ballots, and the one of us with the most votes wins."

And then you *win*, Libby thought. *One more day and then you win.*

"I still don't know why the lunch lady freaked out," said Waverly as they headed out of the cafeteria that afternoon. "She just started yelling about chicken fingers out of the blue. It was so bizarre."

Libby shrugged tiredly. She had a pretty good idea about what had happened. She had discovered her special talent—the ability to turn one Wishling object into another. In line, as they held their trays, she had overheard Ava softly saying, "I wish that they would serve chicken fingers today." And before Libby knew it, she had transformed a tray of turkey sliders into chicken fingers. (Whatever those were, she didn't want to know!) Libby couldn't help herself. She hadn't realized that it would completely freak the lunch lady out. *No more little wishes!* Libby thought. *Concentrate on the big wish. You're almost done.* She stole a glance at the Countdown Clock. She was right on target for the election the next day. She just needed to focus.

"Imagine mixing up sliders and chicken fingers," said Waverly. "So strange." The three girls had finished their lunches quickly and left the cafeteria early. They walked down the hall, turned a corner, and headed toward their classroom. They all gasped at the same time. The hallway was lined with the posters they had taped up that morning. But now each picture had a large curlicue mustache drawn on Ava's serious face! They looked so funny that Libby almost burst out laughing. But a glance at Ava's confused expression and Waverly's furious one forced her to clap her mouth shut.

"I can't believe it!" said Ava. "Who would have done such a thing?"

"I can believe it," said Waverly, crossing her arms tightly. "Politics is a dirty business. It's a stupid joke that has Kristie and Holly written all over it. Well, now we have no choice. We have to retaliate." She thought for a moment and nodded. "We have to break all of the balloons on their posters."

"Waverly!" said Ava. "We can't do that!" She looked down at the floor, her expression sad. "I just can't believe that Kristie would do that to me." She shook her head. "I can't believe it's come to this."

"Believe it," said Waverly. "That's politics."

Libby thought fast. "Listen," she said. "You have to

look at both sides. Sure, maybe Kristie did draw mustaches on all of Ava's posters. If so, that's not right. But if she did and Ava retaliates, she's sinking to her level. She could get caught and be disqualified. Or people could get turned off by the bad behavior and they won't know who to vote for. Or maybe they don't vote at all. Nobody wins."

Waverly opened her mouth to speak, but Libby held up her hand.

"And just suppose Kristie *didn't* do it. It's completely possible that some random kid grabbed a pen and decided to be artistic." She smiled. "The artist didn't sign his or her work, so we'll never know."

"Well, we can't leave them up," wailed Waverly. "She'll be the laughingstock of the school!" She stomped over to one of the posters. "Fine," she spat out. "We'll just take them down."

"Wait!" Libby cried. She thought for a moment, then smiled. "I have the perfect idea."

She held out her hand. "Do either of you have one of those . . ." She searched her brain for the Wishling word. "One of those thick black writing utensils?"

The girls stared at her. "Do you mean a Magic Marker?" Ava asked, looking at her oddly.

Oh, that's what it's called! "Yes, one of those," said Libby.

Ava fished around in her bag and pulled out a black-capped pen. "Here you go," she said.

Libby marched over to the first poster and fixed it. It was awkward—and enjoyable—to write on paper instead of in the air on a holo notebook. When Ava saw what she had done, she laughed and laughed. "It's perfect!" she chortled. "Just my style!"

Waverly shook her head. "I think it's silly," she said. She walked up to the poster and looked again. "Yup, I hate it," she said.

"Get over it," said Libby saucily. "Everyone is going to love it. Trust me."

Was she right? Libby watched, holding her breath, as the end-of-lunch bell rang and students started spilling out of the lunchroom. The first group stopped short in front of one of the posters. After a moment they all began pointing and laughing.

"That's awesome!"

"So funny!"

"Hysterical!"

Libby and Ava had gone up and down the hallway drawing speech balloons next to Ava's mustachioed face. Then they had carefully lettered the words I MUSTACHE YOU TO VOTE FOR ME! in the balloons.

Ava's eyes were shining. "Everyone's laughing. They think it's funny. It's exactly what I wanted in the first place!" she said. "Thank you, Libby!"

"You're welcome," said Libby.

CHAPTER 10

Libby had one more trick up her sleeve to make sure that Ava's wish came true. She wanted to surprise Ava and Waverly. Ava because she knew she'd be delighted and Waverly because she would try to stop her. Luckily, she had a bit of wish energy left, and hopefully there was enough. "Meet me on the front steps tomorrow morning for a cool surprise," Libby told Ava. She didn't ask to sleep over that night, because she was planning to sleep on the school roof in her special Star Darlings tent. She could work her Starling magic in the privacy of her own invisible tent. And she could also sleep in. A Star Darling, especially an overtired one, needed her rest.

★

The next morning Libby stored her energy tent back in her Star-Zap, packed up her surprise, and waited for Ava on the steps. She made sure her back was turned as Ava approached her.

"Hey, Libby," said Ava, tapping her shoulder.

Libby turned around, and Ava shrieked with laughter. Libby twirled the end of her large fake mustache and waggled her eyebrows. "I mustache you to wear one of these!" she said. The night before, she had used her special talent of transformation to change hundreds of twigs she had collected after school into stick-on mustaches. She was quite exhausted. Her Wish Pendant was spent. She placed a mustache under Ava's nose. "Here," she said, handing Ava a full shopping bag. "Mustaches for everyone!"

Ava grinned, though it was hard to see under the mustache. "This is the most awesome thing ever. Thank you!" She smiled ruefully. "Waverly is going to hate this, you know."

"Don't I know it," said Libby.

Libby stood backstage, observing from a distance. She stole a glance at her Countdown Clock. It was only a matter of starmins now. Ava and Kristie would give their speeches, and the students would fill out their ballots and drop them into ballot boxes on their way out of the auditorium. It didn't have to be a landslide. If Ava got just one vote more than Kristie, her wish would come true. And Libby was sure that was going to happen.

Suddenly, Libby felt so exhausted she had to sit down, sinking onto a cardboard box that stood nearby. The top collapsed and she sat there uncomfortably, her feet dangling above the floor and her bottom firmly wedged inside. Now that was awkward.

Waverly bustled by, then grabbed Libby's hand and pulled her to her feet. "This is no time to relax," she scolded. "We have an election to win!" She clapped her hands together. "Now where's Ava?" she asked. Libby pointed Ava out and Waverly headed in her direction.

Libby walked to the edge of the stage and peeked out from behind the heavy red stage curtain. Kristie was in the middle of her speech. She was making a lot of jokes and the audience was laughing at most of them. That was worrisome. But almost everyone in the audience was sporting a fake mustache. That was a good sign. Things were looking great. Really great.

A familiar voice came from behind her. "Excuse me."

Libby had a sinking feeling in her stomach as she turned around. As she had feared, it was Sage—a Wishling version of her, with light brown hair and Wishling clothing.

"Wh-wh-what are you doing here?" Libby asked, bewildered. "I really don't think I need any help. It's all falling into place."

"Hey, what's that on your face?"

Libby reached up. "Oh, it's a mustache. Want one?" She pulled one out of her pocket, peeled off its backing, and put it under Sage's nose.

"Um, thanks," said Sage, making a funny face. "So back to business. Lady Stella seems to think that something's not quite right with your mission. Look at your pendant, it's totally empty!" She looked closely at Libby. "Plus, are you tired?"

"Very," Libby admitted. "But I think that's because I was granting these silly little wishes my Wisher was making. It took a lot out of me. The main wish is totally under control." She pointed out to the audience. "And it's just about to come true."

"I wouldn't be so sure about that," said Sage. "There's got to be something else going on. Let's think. Are you absolutely certain that you identified the correct Wisher?"

"Absolutely," said Libby firmly. "My Wish Pendant was glowing, no question about it."

"Then it must be the wish that's wrong," Sage said.

"Impossible," said Libby. Her eyes swept the backstage area. Ava stood in the wings with Waverly. It looked like she was getting a pep talk. But then Libby took a closer look. She suddenly realized that Ava was not paying attention. She was staring at Kristie. And she didn't look nervous, or competitive, or even particularly interested in what Kristie was saying. She was smiling, but there was a look of sadness in her eyes. And suddenly everything made perfect sense.

"You're right," she told Sage. "I messed up." But how was she going to fix this? She looked at Sage, panic stricken. "I'm not sure what to do," she told her. Should she stop the election? Try to get the two girls to talk to each other? Grab the microphone and talk to both of them? Sage held out her hands. "Let's say your Mirror Mantra together," she said. "It will help you decide." The two girls held hands. "It's all in the balance. Glimmer and shine," they said together. A feeling of pure peace flowed through Libby. Her jumbled thoughts were gone. And suddenly she knew exactly what she had to do.

"Good luck!" said Sage.

Libby walked over to Ava and Waverly.

Waverly looked at Libby. "I don't know what to do," she said. "She needs to get out there and give the speech of her life. And it's like she could care less. Will you see what you can do?"

"I will," said Libby. "Just give us a minute." She stared at Waverly, who was lingering to eavesdrop. "A little privacy?" she asked.

Waverly looked uncertain, but she did as she was asked.

Ava looked at Libby. "There's nothing to say. I don't need a pep talk. I'll be fine." She sighed deeply.

Libby put her hand on Ava's shoulder. "I got it wrong," she said. "When we first met, you said you wished for something. I assumed you wished that you would win the election. But what you wished for was that you could win your best friend back. Is that right?"

Ava nodded, looking at the floor. "That's right."

"Why didn't you say anything?" asked Libby sadly.

"It just seemed pointless," Ava said. "And Waverly was working so hard, and then you joined in. You guys had done so much, and I just felt bad. I felt like I had to see it through. But I don't care about this stupid election. I just want my best friend back."

Libby's heart sank. How in the world was she going to fix this?

"There's no time," she said. "You have this speech to make and . . ." Suddenly, Libby was inspired. "Hand me your speech," she said. "And make it snappy." She glanced at her Countdown Clock. "We're almost out of time."

Ava handed it over. "What are you doing?" she asked.

"Turn around," Libby instructed. Using Ava's back as a makeshift desk, she scribbled some words on the paper. "Hope you can read my handwriting," she said.

She handed the paper back to Ava, who looked panicked.

Kristie finished her speech to applause and cheers.

The principal walked over to the microphone. "And now please put your hands together for presidential candidate Ava Cunningham!" she said.

"You can do it," said Libby. "You can make your wish come true. It's a wish from the heart. Your heart."

Ava stumbled onto the stage. The audience was silent. She slowly made her way to the podium. Libby held her breath as Ava blinked for a moment at the large audience.

"Speech!" someone called out. A couple of students laughed.

Ava looked down and scanned the paper. And then she began to speak. "Hi, everyone, my name is Ava Cunningham. You've probably seen my posters around school, asking you to vote for me. I've shaken many of your hands in the hallway, telling you that I am the best candidate for this job. And here"—she held up the paper—"I have a carefully written speech about all the things I'll do as class president, and how you should vote for me instead of Kristie. But I'm not going to read it."

Waverly stomped over to Libby. "Are you kidding me?" she said furiously. "What kind of pep talk did you give her?"

Libby held up a hand. Waverly crossed her arms tightly, her mouth set in a grim line.

"I'm here to talk about something else," Ava continued. "I'm here today to tell you about someone who has a great sense of humor and really cares about this school. Someone who will be the best president you guys could want. I used to call her my very best friend. And her name is Kristie Chang."

Waverly shook her head at Libby. "What a disaster!" she said.

The crowd began to murmur. "That's right," said Ava. "I am dropping out of the race. It cost me the thing that was most important to me. So please vote for my very best friend, Kristie Chang, for class president!"

There was a stunned silence.

Libby stepped onstage. And then she began to clap. At first she was the only one. But then, one by one, the students started to applaud, until the whole school, faculty included, were on their feet, cheering for Ava.

A hush fell over the crowd. Kristie was making her way onstage. She stepped up to the microphone. "In the campaign I also lost sight of what's most important. I miss you, Ava. If it's okay with the student council, I propose that we be copresidents. No election needed!"

Ava looked shocked. Then her face broke into a huge smile, and she hugged Kristie. The audience erupted into cheers.

Libby rushed onstage and handed the young female Wishlings matching mustaches. They put them on and waved at the audience, who burst into laughter.

"I mustache you to be my best friend again," Libby heard Ava say to Kristie.

Kristie nodded. "Of course," she said. "I really missed you." The crowd cheered.

"Now watch," said Sage, appearing at Libby's side. Rainbow light energy began to flow from Ava, dancing across the stage in a joyful stream as it was absorbed into Libby's Wish Pendant. It was amazingly breathtaking. Libby felt sorry that she and Sage were the only two who could see it.

"I'm sorry, Libby, but it's time to say good-bye," Sage said.

Libby's shoulders sagged. She had really grown to like Ava. She was proud that she had helped bring two friends back together, and she wanted to enjoy the moment for a bit longer. But the mission was a success, her identity was still a secret, and the wish energy had been collected. It was time to go home.

Libby found Ava in the auditorium happily accepting congratulations from students and teachers alike. Ava threw her arms around Libby. "Thanks so much for helping me," she said. "Nice mustache."

"Thanks," said Libby, twirling the end. "I think it suits me. It was my pleasure." She took a deep breath. "I don't know how to tell you this, but I've got to go."

"I wish . . ." said Ava. Libby cringed for a moment. "I wish you didn't have to go. But something is telling me that it's important."

Libby reached forward and hugged her tightly. "You're right," she whispered. When the two broke from their embrace, Ava gave Libby a polite smile, as if Libby was just another supporter wishing her well. "Thank you," she said. "I promise to be a good copresident."

"I'm sure you'll be the best," said Libby.

Epilogue

"Star salutations," Libby told Sage as they made their way across campus back on Starland. "I couldn't have done it without you."

"No problem," said Sage. "I'm glad I could help."

As the moving sidewalk traveled past Halo Hall, the two girls noticed a crowd of students outside, grouped around the holo-announcement board. Sage looked at Libby. "Do you think it could be the band results?" she asked.

"Could be," said Libby. "Let's go see." They stepped off the moving sidewalk and headed over to see what was going on.

They joined the crowd and waited patiently so they could take a peek. A student, an exasperated look on her face, shoved her way back through the crowd. "Whatever," she said scornfully. "It's all those Star Dippers. They should just call it Stupidrock."

Libby and Sage looked at each other. Could it be true? When they got to the front of the line, they saw the list:

THE STAR DARLINGS

LEAD SINGER: LEONA

GUITAR: SAGE

BASS: VEGA

DRUMS: SCARLET

KEYTAR: LIBBY

"Can you believe it?" someone asked behind them. Libby turned around. It was Leona. She had a big grin on her face. "An all–Star Darling band. Chosen by the Ranker as the best possible combination of musicians. Who would have thought?"

Then she frowned. "I'm not sure about the name, though. I was thinking of something snappier."

"Like what?" asked Sage.

"Like Leona and the Luminaries," suggested Leona.

Libby laughed. "It's fine just as it is," she told Leona.

She grinned. This was exciting news on top of her successful mission. It was a good group. Leona, well, she could be a handful. But Libby was sure the other girls, especially Scarlet, would help balance out Leona's extra-large personality. Libby practically skipped all the way to her room.

The door slid open, and the first thing Libby saw was the flowers. Oddly enough, they hadn't faded. They were actually just as fresh-looking as the day the girls had gotten them. The smell, if anything, had gotten even stronger.

"You're back!" cried Gemma, looking up from her holo-book. "Was your mission a success?"

"It was," said Libby. "But it had its setbacks. I suppose I'll be in the starlight tomorrow in class."

"Probably," agreed Gemma, perhaps a little too quickly. "So the band results are in," she told Libby.

"I just saw them," Libby replied. "I'm sorry."

Gemma cocked her head at Libby. "Are you?"

Libby surprised herself by answering truthfully. "I—I don't know."

Gemma shook her head. "I thought so. You know, we haven't been getting along at all, and it makes me so sad. But lately I just find you so . . . so . . ."

"Annoying?" offered Libby.

"Yes, that's exactly it. Annoying!"

"Me too!" cried Libby. The girls looked at each other, momentarily glad to have something in common again. But as the reality of what it was sank in, their faces fell.

Just then their Star-Zaps went off. Libby felt relieved. It wasn't easy to tell the person you lived with that her very presence irritated you. Or to hear it, come to think of it. She frowned. She knew why Gemma was annoying, but why in the world was Gemma annoyed by her?

Everyone rose to their feet as Libby entered Lady Stella's office. "Libby!" the headmistress cried. "Congratulations on a job well done!"

Libby grinned as everyone burst into applause.

"Star salutations," she said as the girls hugged her and clapped her on the back. She basked in the admiration of her fellow Star Darlings. "It wasn't easy. But it's over!"

"I have something for you," said Lady Stella, reaching toward her desk drawer. But then her Star-Zap buzzed. She reached into the pocket of her midnight blue tunic and pulled it out. Libby watched as she read a message. A look of shock, followed by severe dismay, crossed the headmistress's face. Libby felt panicked.

"Excuse me," Lady Stella said, looking flustered. She left the room abruptly, leaving the door ajar.

Everyone stopped talking. They could hear Lady Stella speaking in low tones outside the door. Leona silently crept to the door and started listening. Even though they knew it was wrong, no one stopped her.

Leona listened intently, then turned to the group. "She said, 'How on Starland could this happen?'" she reported in a whisper.

Libby bit her lip. Tessa and Gemma put their arms around each other. Cassie wrung her hands.

"I can't hear what the other person is saying. Wait. Lady Stella is talking again." Leona paused. "She said, 'What a terrible mistake.'"

Libby felt her heart sink. There must have been a problem with her mission. She looked down at her Wish Pendant. It looked like it was full. What could be wrong?

Leona listened again. "She said, 'How can we fix this?'"

Some of the Star Darlings began to whisper among themselves. "Shhhhhhh!" commanded Leona. She strained to hear. "Oh, no," she said.

"What is it? What is it?" Gemma cried.

Leona turned to the girls, her eyes glassy with tears. She could hardly get the words out. "She said . . . she said . . ."

"Spit it out, Leona," said Astra. "You're killing us!"

"She said, 'How in the world am I going to tell her that she isn't really a Star Darling?'"

There was a collective gasp. Libby couldn't even look at the other girls. Did this mean one of them was an imposter? Libby didn't want to see the furtive looks in her classmates' eyes as they glanced at one another, each hoping it wasn't herself, wishing that someone else would receive the terrible news. It was an awful, selfish, difficult-to-deal-with feeling.

The door slid open. Leona jumped back. Everyone stared at the floor. Lady Stella stepped into the room, her face ashen. She walked to the middle of the room and simply stood there, her head bowed.

Finally, she spoke. "Girls, I just received some terrible, shocking news." Her eyes were wet and she wrung her hands. "Something very unexpected has come up. I don't even know how to begin. . . ." She sighed. "I'm going to have to ask you all to leave. Libby, I'm sorry. We will have to postpone your Wish Blossom presentation."

The girls began to file out of the room. Libby fell

into place at the end of the line. The only sound was their feet shuffling across the carpet.

Lady Stella spoke up. "Everyone except for . . . Scarlet."

Scarlet stopped in her tracks, her expression frozen. Libby didn't think she would forget that sad, resigned, fearful look for as long as she lived.

"Scarlet, we need to talk," Lady Stella said gently. "I'm afraid I have some bad news."

And then Libby didn't hear any more, because the door slid shut behind her with a loud click.

Leona's Unlucky Mission

Prologue

Dear Mom and Dad,

First, star salutations for the care package! How did you know I needed a new toothlight? (Why are they so easy to lose?) And, Mom, your gamma-chip clusters are out of this world! I've already eaten half the box. They're soooooo starlicious I just can't stop! I know you said to share them with my roommate, Scarlet, and I would have, but guess what? She had to move out. Long story. (Don't worry, it wasn't my fault.) The good news is—you remember how she used to skateboard down the walls?

Well, she won't be doing that anymore, at least in my room! So for now I've got the whole room to myself—and it looks soooo much better without all that black! I'm hoping to get a new roommate soon, though, and I'll let you know when I do. Stars crossed she's into a color that goes a little bit better with gold—and that she's a lot more relaxed and not so hard to talk to.

Oh, and guess what! More big news! I formed a new band!!!!! It's called Star Darlings! And I'm the lead singer (of course)! We haven't played a gig yet, but I know we will, and I'll send you a holo-vid as soon as we do. We even have a manager, so it's the real deal! Remember Clover? Her color is purple and she wears the hat? Anyway, her family is the Flying Molensas—as in the circus we used to go to every year! So she knows all about show business and she writes great songs. I know you keep saying that becoming a pop star is a moon shot, and that chances are a hydrong to one, but I have a starmendous feeling about us! And I might as well shoot for the stars, right? Isn't that what they're for?

Speaking of stars, I was looking at Grandpa's the other day, and I swear it winked at me!

Tell Felix congratulations on his promotion to assistant manager of the shoe shop. (I won't mention that Dad is his boss.) And tell Garfield I'll believe he has a girlfriend when he sends me a holo-pic. I'm waiting . . . ! (Ha-ha!)

Finally, tell Duchess and Francesca I'll holo-call them tonight if I have the chance. There's a first-year student here named Cassie who reminds me so much of Duchess, by the way. She has the same thick black lashes and soft rosy eyes. She's like a little doll you just want to pick up and hug!

I miss you and I love you.

Your superstar,

Leona

P.S. Send more clusters when you can!

Leona read over her holo-letter quickly, trying to think of what else to say. She tried to send one to her parents weekly, though sometimes she forgot. Sometimes, too, it was nearly impossible to write anything without giving her Star Darlings identity away. For instance, how could she explain Scarlet's moving out without mentioning that Scarlet had been dismissed from the group? She mailed her letter with a flick of her wrist. Hopefully, one day they'd all be able to share their secret with their families, but who knew when that would be?

CHAPTER 1

Twinkle, twinkle. *Twinkle twinkle. TWINKLE TWINKLE.*

That was the sound of a Star-Zap that had been trying to get its owner's attention for quite some time. Leona, who was getting ready for bed in the blissful peace of a roommate-less dorm room, had stopped singing into her hairbrush for a moment to actually run it through her hair, and she finally heard the insistent sound. She grabbed her Star-Zap eagerly, willing it to be news of another Wish Mission, hopefully hers. But her brow wrinkled in confusion as she read the message: PLEASE COME TO MY OFFICE IMMEDIATELY. I HAVE A MATTER OF GREAT URGENCY TO DISCUSS WITH YOU. LADY STELLA. Leona, already dressed in gold brocade pajama bottoms and a golden tank top, threw on a dressing jacket made of the softest glimmerworm silk, shoved her feet into a pair of golden flats, and raced out the door, feeling a heady mix of excitement, anticipation, and dread. As she hurried along on the Cosmic Transporter, she thought of what it could be. Would Scarlet be reinstated as a Star Darling (and be her roommate once more)? Maybe it would be Libby's Wish Blossom presentation (which had been postponed due to the Scarlet situation). Or what if someone had caught wind of their secret trips to Wishworld? She shook her head, clearing it. No, she decided, it was none of those. Then she had another thought, which made her heart beat double time: maybe she was going to be awarded some honor. Possibly Most Popular Starling Academy Student or Most Likely to Be a Shining Star. Leona arrived at Lady Stella's office door with a big smile on her face, in case any holo-pictures were to be taken. She chided herself for not changing her outfit into something a little less slumberrific.

The door to Lady Stella's office was ajar. That was odd. Leona walked inside the grand space she had come to know quite well. In the very center stood the round table where they had first met together as a team. There sat three of her fellow Star Darlings. They looked at her nervously. "Where is everyone?" Leona asked. Sage, Vega, and Libby looked up at her and shrugged silently.

"I was kind of hoping this was going to be my Wish Blossom presentation," Libby said, twirling a strand of her pretty pink hair around her finger. "But then where's everyone else?" She looked around the office as if the other girls were hiding behind the furniture and would soon pop out to surprise her.

Lady Stella strode into the room, followed by Lady Cordial, the head of admissions. Lady Cordial was one of a handful of Starling Academy administrators who knew of the Star Darlings' and Lady Stella's plan. Smiling tightly, as she always did, she greeted the Star Darlings with clasped hands and a tidy bow. Lady Stella used her wish energy to close the door behind them—a little more forcefully than necessary, in Leona's opinion. Leona couldn't help admiring Lady Stella, so lithe and beautiful. The headmistress was as regal and confident as the head of admissions was meek and nervous. Then Leona took a closer look at Lady Stella. In her two plus years at Starling Academy, Leona had never seen the woman look so . . . so . . . irritated. It couldn't be good news. Lady Stella looked at the four girls. "Where's Scarlet?" she asked.

Leona shrugged. "I haven't seen her since she moved out of our room," she said. The other girls nodded in agreement.

"Really?" said Lady Stella. Her smooth forehead creased with concern. "That is surprising. We had a lengthy discussion after everything happened and she was very gracious. I'm surprised she didn't respond to my holo-text."

Scarlet? Gracious? thought Leona. She'd have to take the headmistress's word for it.

Libby shook her head. "It's true. We haven't seen her anywhere," she said. "Not at lunch or at band practice."

Sage spoke up. "She missed our Wish Probability class, and study group, too."

Lady Stella frowned. "I see . . . I suppose it's entirely possible that Scarlet was more upset than she let on." She inhaled sharply. "Perhaps it's no surprise that a Starling would need some time alone."

Especially Scarlet, thought Leona. *She never seemed particularly eager to be around other Starlings before anyway.*

She stood, thinking the meeting was over.

"Not so fast, Leona," said Lady Stella. "I haven't gotten to the reason I summoned you all here."

Leona sat down with a thump.

"I have two words for you girls," the headmistress said grimly. "Star Darlings."

The girls looked at her blankly. She continued. "What in the stars were you thinking, naming your band after our secret group?"

Leona gasped. She had been so excited about being named the lead singer of the band that the actual name had barely registered with her at the moment. It *was* strange, come to think if it. Quickly she explained to Lady Stella exactly what had happened, the other girls breaking in and adding their thoughts. She had always wanted to start a rock band—since her younger years, in fact, back in Flairfield—so that she could be the lead singer, of course. And as soon as Lady Stella formed the Star Darlings, Leona couldn't help thinking that it would be the perfect place to start.

Many of the Star Darlings already played instruments, Leona knew, and it would be a startastic way to get to know each other even better than they already did.

There were never supposed to be open auditions. That was something Leona had thought she'd made perfectly clear. Somehow, though—it was still a mystery—a holo-flyer was sent out to every Star-Zap in the school. Except the Star Darlings' Star-Zaps, which just made everything even weirder. Worse was that Leona couldn't even pick the band members in the end, even though it had all been her idea. Starling Academy rules—ever fair and balanced and just—stipulated that any tryout on school property be overseen by a school official using a Ranker, a judging machine designed to be completely objective and keep any contest a hydrong percent fair.

So the Ranker had chosen a group of girls and also the name of the band. And it just so happened that the five girls who were chosen were all Star Darlings, and that the name it picked was . . . the Star Darlings.

Lady Stella shook her head. "This is very odd indeed."

Lady Cordial piped up, "S-s-s-s-so very s-s-s-s-strange Lady Stella. S-s-s-s-so very s-s-s-s-strange."

Lady Stella looked at the girls and her expression softened. "So you girls had nothing to do with this?" They shook their heads.

"And who was the professor in charge?" Lady Stella asked.

Leona thought. "It was Professor . . . Professor Leticia Langtree."

Lady Cordial touched Lady Stella's arm, and the headmistress bent down so the shorter woman could whisper in her ear. Lady Stella listened, nodded, then straightened, her mouth set in a grim line. "I will make a delicate inquiry with her to determine if this was a random mistake or done deliberately." She shook her head. "But really, what are the chances of a Ranker picking the same secret name?" she mused aloud. "What are the chances?"

Her question was rhetorical, but Starlings were born with an innate knowledge of mathematics, and the answer was on the tips of their tongues in no time. "One in five hydrong mooniums," everyone chorused.

As they stood and began filing out of the room, Lady Stella was shaking her head. "The revelation of your group's secret name is very concerning to me. Very concerning."

Leona and the rest of the band walked down the hallway, nobody saying a word. They stepped out into the still night, the sky clear and filled with twinkling stars. They all paused for a moment, looking up and taking it all in. Most of their other classmates were already in bed, dreaming their Starling dreams as they absorbed their lessons for the day. Then, without a word, the four Star Darlings headed to the campus Cosmic Transporter, the moving sidewalk that whisked Starlings across the school grounds. It wasn't until they were moving toward the dorms that Leona broke the silence.

"So what?' she said. "What is the big deal that our name is out there? I mean, we're still secretly going on missions. That hasn't changed. I think Lady Stella is totally overreacting," she said firmly.

Vega shook her blue-bobbed head from side to side. "I don't know, Leona. Lady Stella seemed pretty upset. There must be more to it."

"Time will tell," said Sage wearily. "Time will tell."

And with that, the four girls went their separate ways to try to get some sleep.

CHAPTER 2

BAM!

Leona looked up. What had that been? Had it come from the hall? It was always so quiet. Intrigued, Leona jumped off the bed to see what was going on.

Leona ran to her door and pulled it open—just a crack. She peered down the hall to see Tessa, fists clenched, facing her own door. Tessa seemed about to tell the door something, but she changed her mind and turned away. Leona watched for another starmin as Tessa stomped onto the dorm's Cosmic Transporter. Bright green sparkles flew from her hair as it swung back and forth.

Tessa could be stubborn, Leona knew, but this was a side she'd never seen before. In fact, in the two plus staryears they'd been together at Starling Academy, Leona had never witnessed Tessa losing her cool, not once. Not even with Gemma, her younger sister—a first-year student and their fellow Star Darling—whose mouth was as big as Wishworld's sun. No, Tessa was always the even-tempered Starling, the peacemaker if anyone quarreled. Her roommate, Adora, must have done something pretty outrageous to get a reaction like *that* out of her.

Twinkle-twinkle.

On her desk, Leona's Star-Zap rang. A holo-call was coming in. She dashed back to answer it. "Star greetings?"

Her fellow Star Darling Cassie popped up, waving. "It's me," Cassie chirped. She was in her reading nook in her dorm room, surrounded by star-shaped quilted pillows and piles of holo-books and holo-magazines. "So, have you heard anything more from Scarlet? I'm worried about her, aren't you?"

"I guess." Leona shrugged. "Right now, though, I'm much more interested in this fight Adora and Tessa just had."

"Fight? Tessa and Adora?" Cassie's pale skin shimmered in her surprise.

Leona made an X on her chest. "Cross my stars and hope to shine."

"Moon and stars . . . What happened?"

"I don't know. All I saw was Tessa storming down the hall."

Just then, a tiny star flashed in the upper corner of her Star-Zap, indicating that lunch would soon be served.

"Lunchtime already?" exclaimed Leona. "Sunspots! Where did the morning go? I still have to take a sparkle shower! Give me ten starmins, and I'll meet you outside, between the dorms."

Freshly sparkling and dressed in her favorite gold tunic, marigold-colored leggings, and golden boots, Leona joined Cassie in the courtyard between their neighboring dorms. Cassie, who was just in her first year at Starling Academy, roomed with Sage, their fellow Star Darling, in the Little Dipper Dorm. The building was where all first- and second-year students lived. As a third year, Leona lived with all third- and fourth-year Starlings in the only slightly larger but more luxurious Big Dipper Dorm.

Arm in arm, as was the custom for Starlings whenever traveling in pairs, they strode past the Star Quad, the star-shaped heart of the Starling Academy campus, where the iconic dancing fountain cheerfully sparkled and splashed. Just past the quad rose the semi-star-shaped band shell, Leona's favorite place on campus apart from her room. Her brand-new band hadn't played there yet, but they would soon. A few more practices and they'd be ready to take the stage and rock the school!

Behind the band shell stood the academy's enormous dining hall, the Celestial Café. In case anyone missed the signal on her Star-Zap, a great glowing star above the door flashed, announcing mealtime to everyone.

Inside the vast, warmly lit dining room, which was somehow cozy and elegant at once, Leona and Cassie joined Piper and Gemma, their fellow Star Darlings who were already seated at the table the group had made their own. Ever since they'd been chosen, the girls had eaten their meals together at the table by the window with what many thought was one of the best views from the school. Gazing out, one could see both the jewel-like Crystal Mountains and the glistening, violet-hued Luminous Lake. These landmarks were the pride and joy of Starland City, and they were beautiful indeed. Still, Leona personally enjoyed the view from her own dorm room window even more: it was of the glimmering skyline of downtown Starland City, the place she'd grown up dreaming about moving to—as a superstar, of course!

Before the girls could even exchange star greetings, a Bot-Bot waiter appeared. It filled their crystal goblets with sparkling water and placed a piping-hot roll fresh from the oven for each of them on their china plates.

"Star greetings, Leona, Cassie. What is it that you desire?" asked the Bot-Bot waiter.

"Hmm . . . let's see . . ." Leona's forehead wrinkled. What would she have that day?

There was no menu for them to choose from. They could truly order anything their Starling hearts desired, and Leona prided herself on never having ordered something more than once since she had been at Starling Academy.

"A garble-green soufflé for me, please," said Cassie.

"Really? Again? You don't get tired of that?" Leona asked.

"Not really," said Cassie. "It's tasty. And it's healthy. Why mess with something that works?"

Leona cocked her head and grinned, waggling her eyebrows. "I don't know . . . because you *can*?"

"And for you, Leona?" The Bot-Bot waiter hovered politely near her shoulder, ready to transmit her request to the café's gourmet Bot-Bot chefs.

"Right . . . okay . . . for me . . . What are you having?"

Leona asked Piper, eyeing the glossy emerald tendrils piled on her plate.

"Who, me? Oh, a starweed salad."

Leona scrunched up her nose. "Hmn . . . I'll pass. What about you?" She turned to Gemma.

"Me? A druderwomp burger," said Gemma, moving in for another bite.

"Ah! Now that's a vegetable I like! I think I'll have that, a druderwomp burger—well done—with extra mooncheese. I haven't had that before, have I?"

The Bot-Bot waiter scanned its memory to check. "No," it replied decidedly. "Never with extra cheese."

"Starmendous. Star salutations." Leona thanked their server with a wave. "*Soooo?*" she went on, gazing around. "Where's everyone else?"

"Well, we know where Scarlet's *not*," said Gemma as a glob of bright-orange mustardia-blossom sauce dribbled down her chin and onto her shirt. She glanced down, not sure where to wipe, since it was the same color as her top.

"Well, *that* I knew," said Leona. "You do know she's moved out of my room?"

"Really!" said Gemma. "Already!"

Leona nodded. "Completely. Everything's gone. Not a speck of hot pink or black. It's like she was never there." She smiled.

"Ah, but she was. Don't forget that," said Piper.

"Uh, I wasn't going to. But star salutations."

Piper tossed her pale green hair over her shoulder. "You're welcome," she replied.

Cassie spoke up. "Well, Scarlet still has to eat. Even if she's not a Star Darling, she's still a student. Is she sitting with someone else?"

The dining room was so vast it was hard to identify each and every sparkling face. But Scarlet had always stood out in a crowd in her palette of hot pink and jet black. The four Star Darlings scanned the wavy rows of tables. One by one, each shook her head. If Scarlet had been in the café, they would have spotted her in the rainbow of students, without a doubt.

"It wouldn't be the first meal she ever skipped," said Leona. "You know how antisocial she can be. Honestly, I never could see how Lady Stella ever sensed Star Darling potential in her, let alone see her granting wishes."

"Well, don't tell Libby that," Gemma warned. "She's really upset about the whole thing. And her stars get out of line so easily lately. You'd think a successful mission would have helped, but *nooooo*," Gemma groaned. "Honestly, I don't know how much longer I can room with her."

"Hey, here come Clover and Astra," observed Piper, pointing with her chin.

Leona and the others turned, eager to find out what news the second-year roommates might have. If they did have any, though, it didn't look like it was very good.

"What's wrong?" Cassie asked as they reached the table.

Clover shrugged and nodded toward Astra. "Ask her."

"No, ask her." Astra slid her warm auburn eyes to Clover. "Seriously, what were we fighting about again?"

"Well . . . if I remember correctly, you were cheating."

"But I wasn't."

"But you were."

"Oh, just admit it, Astra," Gemma cut in. "Everyone knows you hate to lose."

Astra glared down her nose at the ginger-haired Starling. Her own flame-red hair flickered indignantly. "That doesn't mean I'd cheat, Gemma. Who asked you, anyway?"

"Could somebody please start from the beginning?" said Cassie.

"It's no big deal," said Clover, shrugging the whole episode away. She shook off her plum jacket and tossed it over the back of her chair. With a flick of her head, she shook her violet bangs out of her eyes and sank into her seat. "I'm not even mad . . . anymore. . . . We were playing a friendly game of holo-cards in our room, and Astra cheated. The end."

"But I didn't cheat," groaned Astra. "I mean, what kind of Starling do you think I am? Besides, Clover, I didn't even need to cheat to win. You tried to shoot the moon when you knew I'd broken hearts."

"Let's just forget about it," said Clover, bowing her head.

"You know, I was kind of missing having a roommate," said Leona, chuckling. "But not so much anymore."

"It's not funny," Piper said, leaning intently over her salad. "I don't know if you Starlings have noticed it, but lately I've been sensing a lot of tension in the air, including from my own roommate, Vega. She wasn't talking to me this morning when she left. In fact"—Piper frowned and slowly sat back—"I wonder if that's why she's not here, because she's still so mad . . ."

"Like Tessa and Adora!" exclaimed Cassie.

"What about Tessa?" Gemma's ears glistened at her sister's name.

By that time, though, a duo of Bot-Bot waiters had returned to take Clover's and Astra's orders and serve Leona's and Cassie's food.

"Mmm! Star salutations!" Leona licked her lips

and used her wish energy manipulation skills to mentally flick open her napkin, a crisp cloth square, which she then laid across her lap. "Could we worry about all that stuff later and worry about eating right now?" she begged.

CHAPTER 3

In the end, there was no discussion of Star Darlings tension, because the rest of the girls soon arrived and the talk at the lunch table shifted quickly to Scarlet and her dismissal and, most important, what it meant. Did it really matter that there were only eleven of them now?

"I don't see why it would," Leona said. "We'll just all go on more missions. We can pick up one Starling's slack. Especially a Starling like Scarlet. I never trusted her anyway."

"Oh, Leona!" Libby's eyes flashed protectively across the table. "That's a terrible thing to say."

"Star apologies," muttered Leona. "But you didn't live with her. . . . I'm just saying I wasn't surprised."

Sage, meanwhile, tugged on her lavender braids, thinking. "Remember what Lady Stella told us all when she met with us for the first time? If we didn't want to be part of this mission, she would find another Starling who did. What if she's finding another one right now to make us twelve again?"

"Maybe . . ." Vega nodded.

"Well, I'm going to miss her," Libby said, "even if she did say more with her drums than she ever did with her mouth. I mean, she used to—"

"Wait! Hold your stars! What did you say?" Leona gasped. How in the universe had she gone so long without considering what losing Scarlet really and truly might mean?

"What are you talking about?" asked Libby.

"Drums!" Leona gulped. "Maybe our mission can succeed without Scarlet. But what about my band?"

Leona had hoped against hope that Scarlet would show up for their usual band practice, but she didn't, to no one's surprise. The rest of them—Sage on guitar, Vega on bass, Libby on keytar, and Leona on vocals—waited for a few starmins in their Lightning Lounge rehearsal room, tuning up and trading riffs.

Suddenly, a scowling face framed by blue bangs appeared in the doorway, which Leona had left open—for Scarlet, she had hoped. She regretted the mistake immediately and reached out the hand that wasn't holding her microphone to wave the rehearsal room door closed.

Unfortunately, because Vivica, the nosy Starling, was standing in its way, the door politely refused to close on her, which was how doors on Starland worked.

"We're busy," Leona growled.

Her bandmates nodded.

Vivica was just about the only Starling at Starling Academy who no one liked having around.

"Busy doing what? Not making music, that's for sure," Vivica said, laughing. She closed her eyes, enjoying her joke.

"What we need is a little privacy," snapped Leona.

"We're rehearsing," Libby explained. She even flashed Vivica a generous star-salutations-for-understanding-now-please-get-out-of-here grin.

Instead of backing out of the doorway, though, Vivica glided in.

"Oh . . . is this your little band?" She fired a look at each of them: Libby, Vega, Sage, and Leona. "I thought you had a drummer, too."

"She's late." "She quit." "She's missing." "We do."

The whole band answered Vivica at the same time with four different replies.

"Huh?"

"We don't need a drummer, if that's what you're wondering," said Leona.

Quickly, her bandmates agreed.

"We're good."

"All good."

"Thanks, though," said Libby, who could never stop trying to please.

"I know how badly you wanted to be in the band," Leona said, trying to sound sympathetic as she tossed her mic from hand to hand. "Sorry you didn't make it." She shrugged. "But there's always starchoir, I guess."

Vivica had tried out for the band, along with the hydrongs of other Starlings who had turned up.

Leona could still remember the knots that had formed in her stomach when Vivica stepped onto the band shell to audition—for lead vocals, Leona's own part, no less! Fortunately, the Ranker knew what it was doing and Leona made the band. She'd had to wait stardays for the results, though—the longest stardays of her life.

She could only imagine how disappointed Vivica

had been. *She seems to be taking it pretty well now, though,* Leona thought, studying her.

"So, um, this practicing you're doing . . . when will it be over?" Vivica asked. "I'm wondering because my band needs the practice room today, too."

"Your what?" Leona gasped.

"My band. What?" Vivica's sky-blue lashes fluttered innocently. The ice-blue eyes behind them were less naive. "You think you're the only Starling who can start one? I asked Professor Langtree if the Ranker could rank a second band from the auditions, and she said, 'Sure, why not?'" Vivica's thin blue-lipped smile spread like a stain across her face until it almost reached her ears. "I decided to call it Vivica and the Visionaries. I'm the lead singer, of course, so it makes sense."

Leona didn't turn to see the rest of the band's reaction to this. Her own shock and rage were too strong. "Vivica? And the Visionaries?"

"It's a little more catchy than Star Darlings, don't you think?"

No. What Leona thought was that it was startlingly similar to the name she'd planned to give her own band before the Ranker had named them: Leona and the Luminaries. She'd even started a fan page for them on StarBook before she knew it wouldn't be used. She'd still had hope the band could change names at some point, but how could they now, when Vivica's band's name was almost the same?

She probably saw the page! Leona thought suddenly. *She probably picked that name out of blue-hearted spite!*

"*Anyway*," said Vivica, still smiling. "You know, right, that you can only have the rehearsal room for a starhour, max?"

Leona didn't.

"I knew that," Vega said.

"And since it sounds like you can use all the practice time you can get, I guess we'll just come back in a starhour, then."

And with that Vivica turned, her long pale blue hair swinging behind her back. Leona closed the door with a swipe of her arm, leaving sparks where her hand sliced the air.

"*Starf!*" said Vega. "Two bands. After all these years with none."

"*Grrr!* Can we just play some music," Leona roared, grabbing the mic, "and not talk about other bands!"

Vega gave her bass a halfhearted twirl and started to pluck it, then looked around. "Who's going to count us in?" she asked.

"Oh, for heaven's sake," Leona huffed, "I will. We'll

do 'Heart of a Glion'—on three. A-one, a-two . . ." She clapped, once, then twice. . . .

On "three," they began.

"Stop!" Leona yelled, half a verse in. "I can't sing to this. You're all over the place!"

"We need a backbeat," Sage said, sighing.

"Maybe we should call Clover," Vega said.

"Why?" Leona snapped. "So she can write us a new song that doesn't need a beat?"

Clover had been writing songs for staryears and had immediately offered to share them with Leona's brand-new band. She'd even volunteered to be their manager. Anything, really, she was happy to do, except join them on the stage. Even though she had grown up in a huge family of famous circus performers and was very comfortable onstage, she now wished to stay as far from the starlight as possible.

"We need a drummer! Now!" Leona roared. "Or wait . . . where's my Star-Zap? Maybe it can play a beat for us? It doesn't quite have the same 'stage presence,' but at least it won't sit there sulking like Scarlet," she muttered. "Or get all galactical at the littlest critique . . ."

"Clover plays the drums," said Vega.

Sage knit her lilac eyebrows, confused. "I thought she played the guitar."

"Correct," said Vega, "and the drums, and the keyboard, and the gammahorn . . . You name it." She paused to pluck her instrument. "Including, I'm sure, the bass."

"Are you serious?" Leona said. "Why didn't you say so?"

Had Clover really been letting them play her songs and never once showed off all the musical talent she herself had? *Huh* . . . There were so many things about so many Starlings that Leona would never understand.

"Gotcha!" At last, Leona's hand found her Star-Zap in the bottom of her bag. "Clover!" she yelled before the device was even out. "I—make that we—need you in the Lightning Lounge. Now!"

"I'll sit in *today*," said Clover stiffly when she arrived. "But that's it. I'm not performing in public. Ever. Do you understand? When you guys have an actual gig, you'll have to get someone else to play with you. Just so we're perfectly clear." She perched on the stool behind Scarlet's hot-pink drum kit, drumsticks in her hands. She played a tight lick to punctuate her point, then reached up to catch her hat before it tumbled off her head.

"Hey! That was good!" Leona said.

Clover lowered her chin warningly. "Just today," she said, pointing a stick.

"Got it. And star salutations," said Leona, who couldn't have meant it more.

With Clover there, the band's practice went much better. She didn't hit as hard as Scarlet, by any means, but her timing was spot on. Of course, they were playing songs she'd written, so that helped quite a bit.

"Zow! That was stellar!" Sage gushed as their song "White Dwarf" ended. She strummed a joyful extra chord.

"That did sound pretty good," agreed Clover, giving each drumstick a fancy twirl.

Even Libby had to nod appreciatively, though Scarlet's absence still stung her the most.

"I wish we had an audience to hear us!" said Leona.

"Oh, no you don't," Clover said. "Because then I wouldn't be here. I'm serious. Practice only. Period." *Bam!* She slapped her snare to emphasize her point.

Just then, Sage's pocket began to glow. She let go of her guitar, and while it hovered, twinkling, in front of her body, she pulled out her Star-Zap. Leona stared enviously. Sage was seriously good at wish energy manipulation. And she was only a first year.

"It's a holo-text," she said, "from Cassie."

"What's up?" Leona asked.

Sage's violet eyes grew wider as she read it.

"*What?*" said Leona, straight into the microphone this time.

Cringing, but smiling, too, Sage raised her head. "So, apparently, Cassie was walking by Lady Stella's office, on the way to get her request for a transfer to Advanced Wishworld Lighterature signed by the headmistress. Long story, but apparently, her transcript from her old school somehow, somewhere, got misplaced. Anyway—"

"Yes, *anyway*," said Leona, "get on with this story!"

"Okay, so Cassie says she saw Lady Cordial going into Lady Stella's office . . ."

"*Yes?*"

"With a *Starling*! A new *Star Darling*, she thinks!"

"Really? Just now?"

"Mm-hmm."

The bandmates looked at each other.

"Well, what are we waiting for?" Leona said.

CHAPTER 4

Outside the headmistress's office the five musicians found Cassie, propped like a silver statue against the rainbow-grained starmarble wall.

"That was fast!" said Cassie, springing toward them.

"We didn't want to miss anything," Leona said. "So? Are they still in there?"

Cassie nodded. Then, all of a sudden, she craned her neck to peer around Leona's back. "What was that?"

"What?" Leona spun around.

"Did the others come with you?"

"No." The bandmates shook their heads.

"Did you text them also?" asked Sage.

Cassie adjusted her star-shaped glasses. "No . . . I

only texted you. But I thought I saw someone . . ." She shrugged. "I'm just nervous, I guess."

"Well, I'm excited!" said Leona. "I wonder who it is. And if she'll be my new roommate, too. Do you have any idea of who it might be?"

"No." Cassie shook her head. "Lady Cordial was in the way, so I couldn't see anything."

Leona thought about who she wouldn't want it to be. "You don't think it's Vivica!" she said as the image of the lead singer of Starling Academy's *other* Starling band came to her mind.

There weren't many Starlings at the school who Leona actively tried to avoid. Truth be told, Vivica and now Scarlet were the only ones. Was it because Leona was so competitive? She was, without a doubt. Was it because she and Vivica were rivals, no matter how much the school discouraged that? No. Leona had thought about it. A lot, in fact. She, like so many Starlings, avoided Vivica for one good reason: because Vivica was no fun to be around.

"Oh, starf, I hope not," said Libby.

Just then, a soft *swoosh* made them all turn their heads toward the headmistress's door. As if blown by the wind, it slid open, and Lady Stella's tall, regal form appeared. She wore a silver pantsuit that coordinated beautifully with her perfectly coifed platinum hair. She smiled at them, and Leona was relieved to see that she didn't seem upset anymore. "Why, Sage, Libby, Vega, Leona, Cassie, Clover . . ." Her mouth curved up ever so slightly at the corners. "How surprising to find you here."

"Oh . . . we're just passing through!" said Leona casually. At least, she hoped it came off that way.

Next to her, Sage nodded. "Just hanging around!" she agreed. "We had no idea you'd be in your office on a starweekend. Is there any . . . special reason . . . if it's okay to ask?"

Lady Stella's smile warmly spread. Her eyes crinkled at the edges. "As a matter of fact, there is a special reason. A very special one."

Leona and the others waited for her to go on, but instead Lady Stella turned away. They followed her gaze down the hall, where, to their surprise, they saw all five other Star Darlings riding the Cosmic Transporter toward them anxiously.

"You called us, Lady Stella?" panted Tessa. She held up her Star-Zap and pointed to the summons on the screen.

"I did indeed." The headmistress nodded. "I have important news to share."

"Wait . . . did our Star-Zaps go off, too?" Leona pulled hers out to check. The screen was blank except for the waning moon in the corner reminding her how much startime until her Advanced Wish Theory project was due.

Sage and the others checked theirs, too. They all looked up, confused.

"I didn't see a need to call you," explained Lady Stella, "since you were already . . . 'passing through.' "

With that and a wink, she ushered the Star Darlings into her grand office. Sitting at the table was a small wide-eyed Starling with a galaxy of star-shaped freckles and springy yellow pigtails. Behind her was Lady Cordial, who stood behind the new Starling, her hands grasping the top of the chair the girl sat in.

Leona did not recognize the girl, so she assumed, correctly, that she was a first year. The girl looked like a Starling who was easy to forget—quiet and timid.

"Star Darlings, please, do take your seats," Lady Stella said. She strode to the head of the table and motioned for all to sit. Once they had, and the chairs had adjusted to each Starling's height and weight, the headmistress held her hand out gracefully toward the small Starling, sprinkling sparkles from her fingers as she did. "It is my great pleasure to introduce Ophelia, your *true* twelfth Star Darling, to the group."

A flurry of gasps and glances swept around the table. Leona's mouth fell ajar.

"*Her?*" blurted Gemma.

"*Shhh!*" Tessa hissed, and rolled her eyes.

"Lady Cordial," said the headmistress, "perhaps you could explain to them."

"Why, yes . . . of course. Ahem." The Star Darlings felt for the administrator, whose glow dimmed a humble watt. "It, er, seems, er, that there was a glitch, er, s-s-somewhere in our identification program." Lady Cordial paused to swallow her stutter, then dutifully went on. "And as you all know, there was a, er, mix-up, in the student list. The *good* news"—she forced a smile; or at least it looked like a smile that was forced—"is that I corrected all the data and was able to get the *right* name."

Lady Cordial moved her hands from the back of Ophelia's chair to Ophelia's shoulders, causing the Starling to jump in her seat. "Ahem. Allow me to introduce your new and true Star Darling, Ophelia. Ophelia . . . your Star Darlings team."

Tessa led a round of welcomes while their brand-new member looked from one girl to the next.

"Star greetings," she mumbled back so softly that Leona had to guess that was what she had said.

Lady Stella turned her gaze on her. "Lady Cordial has been making arrangements for Ophelia to be your new roommate, in Scarlet's place."

"Really." Leona's eyes shifted to Ophelia, who raised her hand in a timid wave. "Great." She wasn't exactly the roommate Leona had hoped for, but at least she looked sweet and quiet, which was more than she could say for Scarlet. Actually, she looked like she would be the anti-Scarlet.

"Still no sign of Scarlet?" Lady Stella asked. The Star Darlings shook their heads.

"Well, in any event, our Wish-Watcher is watching a Star Darling Wish Orb at this very moment, which she feels quite sure will be ready to grant soon . . . and," she added, "speaking of Wish Orbs, that brings me to the *second* reason I called you all here to my office." She let her eyes orbit the table until they met Libby's rosy ones.

Leona watched Libby's cheeks flush excitedly.

"Well, it's about time!" Libby's roommate, Gemma, declared.

"Gemma! Honestly!" Gemma's sister, Tessa, groaned. "Can you just keep that big orange mouth of yours closed and say nothing for once?"

"No, she's right," Lady Stella said with a gentle nod toward both Gemma and Tessa. "This moment is long overdue." She turned to the others. "In all the . . . *confusion* of the other day, I'm afraid, something very important—for Libby especially—was left undone."

"My Wish Blossom," said Libby softly, almost as if it was a secret.

"Indeed." Lady Stella bowed deeply, then gracefully straightened, turned to her desk, and, with a tilt of her head, slid open a drawer. Leona could see the light of the Wish Orb pour out of the drawer the moment it opened, before the orb even came into view.

Carefully, Lady Stella lifted the sparkling orb with both hands and let it rest in her cupped palms like an egg inside a nest. A shadow appeared on the wall behind her, so much light did the orb emit. Its glow lit the headmistress's face like a spotlight, especially her regal cheekbones and her long, slightly upturned nose.

"Rise, Libby, and approach," Lady Stella said slowly, her voice as smooth as polished starjade stone.

Leona watched with a pang of awe and envy as Libby eagerly obeyed. She couldn't help noticing the newest Star Darling, Ophelia, also sitting there gaping at the scene. Her mouth had fallen open and was growing wider steadily.

As soon as Libby reached Lady Stella, the headmistress held out her hands and solemnly waited for Libby to do the same.

"You earned this," said Lady Stella as she placed the glowing orb in Libby's trembling hands. "My deepest star apologies that we had to make you wait."

"Oh! It's heavy!" gasped Libby, clearly surprised, cradling the orb against her chest. "Star salutations," she went on, smiling proudly at the orb. "My aunt always says that anything worth having is worth waiting for. . . . Oh! I think it's starting to change!"

As Libby spoke, Leona saw the orb's glow getting brighter . . . so bright that instead of lighting up just Lady Stella's and Libby's faces, it lit every Star Darling face in the room. Then it happened, just as it had for Sage after her Wish Mission mere stardays before: the orb transformed before Libby's eyes and theirs from a ball of light into a flower—a delicate scallop-edged bell-shaped blossom the same pale pink as a cloud at the end of a Starland sunset, just before lightfall, when the planet seems to awaken and begins to brighten and give off light of its own.

"It's a blushbelle! My favorite!" cooed Libby, leaning in for a deep, blissful sniff. As she did, stardust drifted out from the flower's feathery center, adding extra sparkle to Libby's face. "Ooh! That tickles!" She rubbed her nose and brushed the loose stardust off her cheeks and chin. "It's so beautiful, isn't it?" Libby went on.

"Indeed, very beautiful . . ." Lady Stella agreed, staring at the flower in Libby's hands. Normally, that would have been the end of the wish granting process; Libby would have had a Wish Blossom to call her own forevermore. But Leona could tell from the way the headmistress seemed to be holding her breath as she gazed into the center of the blushbelle that she was looking for something else. . . .

"Look inside!" Sage called out. "Do you see anything, Libby? Does it have a stone, like mine did?"

Libby peered into the long cup formed by the petals. "I don't think so. . . ." She shook her head. "I just see more stardust." Then, as if to answer, the pearly pink petals opened wider, trembling teasingly as they did. "Wait. What's happening?"

The petals burst wide open and fell back completely, and where there'd been only stardust, a gleaming stone appeared. It was an angular, multifaceted electric-pink jewel that pulsed with an intense inner light. Libby held it in her hand, a quizzical look on her face. "It looks rugged, but it's as light as air," she said in wonder.

"Another stone!" exclaimed Adora.

"It's just like mine!" said Sage. "How do you feel?" she anxiously asked.

Libby thought for a moment. "I feel . . . perfectly wonderful!" She closed her eyes and sighed.

"So . . . what's with the stones?" asked Leona finally.

Around the table, the other Star Darlings nodded and murmured similar questions. Every face, including Libby's, turned to Lady Stella as they waited to hear.

"That I cannot tell you . . . *yet*," she added as eleven faces fell. (Ophelia's, the twelfth, was still stuck in its gaping, bewildered stare.) "All in due time," Lady Stella went on with a benevolent smile and a sweep of her hands.

"But that's what you said the last time," said Leona.

A few Star Darlings turned to her, surprised.

"What?" Leona said. "I mean, that was then and this is now, right? I'm just wondering how long 'due time' takes."

With an almost sad smile, Leona thought, Lady Stella reached for the star-bright stone and plucked it effortlessly from the Wish Blossom's heart. "Due time," she said slowly, "in due time, I fear, Leona. And it is in due time that you will know. Until then . . ." She held out the stone for Libby to take, and she took the Wish Blossom from Libby in exchange. "Libby, you performed your mission admirably. You mistook the wish at first, but not in the end. Your mission now is to guard this precious stone with your life. And, of course, continue keeping this secret you've been keeping so well. Now everyone watch." The Star Darlings stared as the blushbelle transformed into a Silver Blossom. Lady Stella nodded. "I will save this in our own private Hall of Granted Wishes."

As Libby took the stone and clutched it to her chest, looking rather overcome and overwhelmed, the headmistress turned her full attention to the others. "As I was saying before, a wish has been spotted, correct, Lady Cordial? And it will be ready to grant soon, we think?"

Her tiny colleague replied with an unusually natural smile and a friendly dip of her head. "Yes, Lady Stella. *Very* soon. You are absolutely right."

"So please, Star Darlings, be on high alert for a holo-text summoning you to return. Sage's and Libby's successful missions brought us a lot of positive energy. But there's more work to be done." Lady Stella paused to look around the table and meet each Starling's eyes. Hers were like kaleidoscopes, full of colors, and as soon as they locked on Leona's, Leona felt a surge of confidence and trust.

Ophelia must have felt one even stronger, thought Leona, because after her turn, her eyes shut.

Lady Stella bowed. "Star salutations, Star Darlings."

"Star salutations, Lady Stella."

The Star Darlings rose to go.

"So." Leona waited for Ophelia to circle the table. Now that she was standing next to her, Leona was reminded of how slight Ophelia was. Leona had to bend her neck to meet her eyes. "I guess we're roommates, huh?"

Ophelia nodded.

"Well, come on. Let me show you your new room. What room were you in before?"

"Two fifty-nine? That's on Cassie's floor. How come I've never seen you before?"

Ophelia sighed and shrugged, her yellow pigtails bobbing. "Maybe it's because I'm quiet. No one seems to notice me."

Leona laid her arm across Ophelia's back. There was something about this little flutterfocus of a Starling that brought out the glioness in her somehow. "I'm sorry, but there is just no excuse for not being noticed. Things are going to change."

Ophelia looked up with her wide eyes. "Because I'm a Star Darling now?"

"No," said Leona, tossing her mane. "Because you're my roommate now."

"So . . . is it okay if I ask you something?" said Ophelia in a tone that still sounded as if she expected Leona to say no.

"Of course!" said Leona. She squeezed Ophelia's shoulder. "Ask whatever you like."

"Okay . . ." Ophelia took a deep breath. Her eyes slid to Leona, then darted away. "So . . . what exactly happened back there just now?"

Leona squinted. "What happened? I don't get it. Star apologies. What do you mean?"

"I mean . . . did that first year, and that other one, did they really grant wishes?" Ophelia asked.

Leona shrugged. "Well, yeah. After all, that's what we do now. That's what this whole Star Darlings thing is. They told you about it all, right? We, *young* Starlings, go grant *young* Wishers' wishes and get, like, a hydrong times the positive wish energy. That's Lady Stella's theory, at least."

Ophelia nodded meekly. "Yes. They told me. I guess . . . I guess I still don't understand how it actually works. How are you *ready*?"

"You mean, how are *we* ready?"

"How are *we* ready . . ." Ophelia looked down, wringing her hands. "How do you know how to grant wishes when we haven't even graduated yet?"

"I don't know." Leona shrugged again, this time more loosely. "Don't worry about it. We just are. I mean, obviously, right? I could go grant a wish today if an orb chose me. I can't wait for my turn to come!"

She smiled at Ophelia but could see her enthusiasm wasn't shared. "And you know we do get extra lessons," she went on. "You know about that, don't you? Our special class, last period, each day?"

"Special class?" Ophelia looked up slowly, seeming slightly less anxious at last.

"It's a secret, too, of course," Leona added. "You can't actually tell anyone what it's for or anything about the things we learn. Which is why you might get *comments* from some Starlings . . . like *Vivica*. . . ." Leona growled the name bitterly through clenched teeth. "I'm just saying," she went on, "that 'officially' "—she made quotation marks with one hand—"as far as most Starlings know, it's a study group we go to."

"Oh, that's no problem for me," Ophelia said matter-of-factly. "I don't mind."

Leona looked at her. The little Starling appeared to be serious. "Well, that makes one of us, at least. Now, come on." She steered the freckled Starling toward the exit. "Let's go get you moved into our dorm room.

Our stuff's going to go together starmendously, I can tell. Hey, have you ever considered a makeover, by any star chance? I bet I could really do something with that hair. . . ."

CHAPTER 5

The Star Darlings left Lady Stella's office and followed Leona and Ophelia to their room. They were all eager to get to know their new teammate better and answer whatever questions about their mission she might have.

When they reached the door, however, Leona herded them back onto the Cosmic Transporter and shooed them on their way.

"I need a little time *alone* with my new roommate, if you don't mind," she said.

"Moonbeams!" gasped Ophelia as they stepped through the door to the room. "Is that—is that a *stage*?"

"It sure is!" replied Leona, stepping onto the star-shaped golden platform in the center of the room.

Instantly, the floor lit up beneath her. Lights blinked in sequence around the base. The words *You're a star!* and *Leona!* took turns flashing behind her on a massive floor-to-ceiling holo-screen. Above, a disco ball covered with tiny star-shaped mirrors dangled from a crystal-studded chain. Stars of light danced over Ophelia and across the entire dorm room as it twirled like a rotating planet overhead.

"This is kind of the performance side of the room," explained Leona. "That's the dressing room side, over there." She pointed past her bed, which was large and round and piled high with silk pillows and set on a pedestal. Around it hung a lacy curtain made of strings of twinkling lights. On the other side of the bed stood a full-length three-sided mirror. This, too, was framed by lights. An antique steamer trunk, overflowing with glamorous costumes in every possible shade of gold, stood open next to it.

"I guess they haven't had time to finish your side of the room yet," said Leona, turning to what used to be Scarlet's side, which was much more empty and much less interesting than before.

There now stood a plain solar-metal bed with a basic white moonfeather comforter and a single pillow of modest size. Each was trimmed in thin yellow ribbon, but Leona had to squint to make that out. A simple chest of drawers crouched in the corner as if it wasn't sure yet that it wanted to stay.

"No, this is everything," said Ophelia.

Leona laughed, thinking it was a joke.

"Really, I don't need very much, you know."

Leona stared at her. Ophelia was serious. It took a starmin for that fact to sink in.

"You mean you don't have a desk? Or a cozy chair?" Leona gestured to her own desk and chair.

"No." Ophelia shook her head. "I just sit . . . and work . . . on my bed."

"No holo-screen?"

"No. I use my Star-Zap."

"No *mirror*? Not even *one*?"

Ophelia shrugged apologetically.

"What about personal items?" She smiled, remembering some of Scarlet's more "interesting" things—like her rather gruesome collection of globerbeem egg cases and her old moonmoth-eaten top hat and black velvet cape.

"Well, I have the Wish Pendant Lady Cordial just gave me. . . ."

"Ooh, let me see!" Leona said.

Ophelia pulled up her plain yellow sleeve to reveal

a thick metal bracelet studded with yellow star-shaped jewels.

"No way! I have a cuff, too!" exclaimed Leona. She showed Ophelia hers. "Startacular, no?" she said. "So . . . what else?" she asked eagerly.

"What else?" Ophelia looked puzzled, so Leona explained by scooping up a cute little stuffed glion from her star-shaped beanbag chair. She tickled its chin and it purred. Then she ran her hand down its golden back. "Shine like the superstar you are!" it roared.

Leona hugged it close. "This," she said proudly, "is my Glionny. I've had him since I was a baby. He never says anything more than once."

"Ooh! May I see him?" Ophelia asked. She held her hands out and Leona passed him to her. "Hello, Glionny," she said, gingerly petting its star-studded mane.

"Glow like you mean it!" the toy purred.

"See?" Leona said. "You must have some special things from home, too . . . ?" Her voice trailed off.

"No . . . not really." Ophelia kept her head down.

"Where are you from, anyway?" Leona asked.

"I'm not exactly sure," said Ophelia. "But I've lived in Starland City for as long as I can remember."

"Okay, first lesson," said Leona. "Be proud of who you are—and that includes where you're from! That's one way to stand out. How amazing that you live in Starland City! I'm sure you've had so many incredible adventures. Unlike me—who's from little old Flairfield." She closed her eyes and pretended to snore. "Not that I'm not proud of it," she said, her eyes popping open again. "Naturally, I am. But listen to this: can you believe I never once traveled farther than Flairfield Lake until I came here, to Starling Academy? For real! I *know*!" Leona groaned. "It's my parents. Ugh." She sighed. "They're homebodies." She rolled her eyes. "What can you do?" She smiled.

"All I can say," Leona went on, "is thank the lucky stars I got into Starling Academy! Best day of my life—so far. My parents made it *very* clear that if I didn't, it would be Flairfield High for me. Even when I got accepted, they asked me to think about giving up my place and staying home. Can you *imagine*? Pass up this chance? Has any Starling ever even done that before? Never once—I asked. Not that wish granting is my one goal in life, of course. Some Starlings could settle for that, but not me. As you can probably tell, I have lots of other talents." She nodded toward her stage. "I'm kind of on my way to being a superstar, which is why Starland City is *the* place for me! Still . . ." Leona picked up a holo-picture from her bedside table and blew each member of her family a kiss. The people in the picture each blew one back. "I do miss my family a lot. Aren't they cute?" She turned the picture so Ophelia could see her two little sisters, her two older brothers, and, in the middle of them all, her mom and dad. "But enough about me, already! I want to know more about *you*!" Leona set the holo-picture down. "What do you like to do for fun?"

"I don't know. . . ."

"Like music?"

"Well, um—"

"Want me to sing for you? Startastic idea!" Leona leapt back onto her stage and stuck a hand out toward a rack of gleaming golden microphones. A large one blinked, rose, and floated to her. Leona grabbed it with both hands. "Let's turn the lights down, shall we?" she said with a nod. Immediately, the room dimmed. At the same time, two gold spotlights blinked on and converged, capturing her in their beams.

"Sit! Please!" Leona nodded toward her beanbag chair, and Ophelia obliged her by plopping down. Still cradling the stuffed glion in her arms, she tilted her chin up and smiled at Leona.

"Here. Want a gamma-chip cluster? My mom made them. They're soooo good!" Leona said, offering her one. "Just watch the flowers, if you would." She nodded toward a vase of delicate coral-colored blossoms on the crystal table by the chair.

"Oh, they're so pretty. Where did they come from?" asked Ophelia.

"You know, I'm not really sure. . . . They just showed up one day—in all our rooms. It's a Star Darlings thing, we think. Maybe I should move them. . . . I'd hate for you to applaud and knock them over," she explained. "That's better for now, don't you think?"

The rest of the starday flew by—for Leona at least—as she performed her repertoire in its entirety . . . plus a few encores for fun. She was frankly stunned when the landscape began to brighten outside her windows as the sun sank behind the Crystal Mountains and the moon began to rise. All of Starland, and Starlings, too, shone brighter in the evening, at lightfall, when the halo of energy surrounding the planet reached its most glorious peak.

Just then, Leona's Star-Zap flashed. Ophelia's did, as well.

"Dinnertime? Already?" Leona let her mic drift back to its place on the stand and nodded the spotlights away. "Star apologies, Ophelia! We hardly talked about you at all! But don't worry! We will. We have plenty of time!" she assured her with a wink.

As Leona's eye reopened, she noticed the flowers sitting in the corner of the room. She walked over and took them, pausing to smell them. It was hard not to; their fragrance was so very sweet. She sighed with pleasure, then turned to give her new roommate a chance to smell them . . . but changed her mind suddenly.

"Well? Are you ready?" She sent the flowers to her dressing table and crossed her arms over her ribs.

"Um . . . yes." Ophelia jumped up from the chair and left Leona's stuffed glion on the seat.

"Hey! Careful!" Leona snapped. "Have a little respect for my things!"

"Star apologies!" said Ophelia. She hurried over to hand Leona her toy.

"Give me an *S*! Give me a *T*! Give me an *A*! Give me an *R*!" the glion roared while Ophelia's wide eyes began to fill with liquid glitter—otherwise known as Starling tears.

Instantly, Leona wished she could take her words back or at least tame them a bit. She sounded . . . she sounded like Scarlet! *What's wrong with me?* she asked herself.

She took a deep breath, let it out, and tried to find a smile somewhere within. "It's fine," she finally growled. As she heard herself, she winced. "Let's just go to dinner."

As they left the room, Ophelia used her wrist to wipe her eye. "I was careless with your things, but I'll be more careful next time."

"And I guess I was a little hot-tempered," Leona admitted. "Star apologies. I think I was just hungry. . . ." Leona gulped. *What's wrong with me?* she wondered.

CHAPTER 6

After dinner, Leona felt much, much better. And because of that, Ophelia did, too. Oddly, though, a delicious meal did not have the same effect on the other Star Darlings, who left the café seeming more irritated than ever before.

Breakfast the next morning wasn't much different, though some arguments had changed.

Sage and Cassie were bickering about holo-books. Cassie was certain that Sage had borrowed her copy of *Once Upon a Starry Night.*

"I didn't borrow it," Sage said.

"But I saw it in your hands," Cassie argued, her eyes blazing behind her star-shaped glasses.

"I picked it up, it's true," Sage admitted. "But it seemed kind of boring, so I put it back on your shelf."

Cassie's mouth opened in disbelief. "Boring? Are you serious? *Once Upon a Starry Night* is the best book ever. What's wrong with you?"

"What's wrong with *you*?" Sage retorted.

"And what's wrong with *you*?" Libby suddenly said, staring daggers at her roommate, Gemma.

"Who, me?" asked Gemma.

They had their own squabble going, about Gemma's housekeeping skills, which Libby deemed startacularly poor.

"That's what happens from living on a farm—messy seems normal," said Libby.

"That's not true," Gemma's older sister, Tessa, said. "We had to be very neat, but Gemma could never get the hang of it."

Tessa, meanwhile, had her own issues with Adora—specifically over their shared bouquet. Tessa thought the coral flowers looked much more pleasing on her green side of the room and clashed horribly with Adora's blue. Adora found the argument frankly absurd, however, as her holo-color wheel clearly proved.

As they went on and on, Leona turned to Ophelia and rolled her eyes in a weary "Who cares?" arc.

"Oh, my stars," Leona remarked to Ophelia as they left the table together, arm in arm. "Is it me, or did everyone wake up on the dark side of the moon today?"

"So they aren't always like that?" asked Ophelia.

"Oh, no," Leona said. "Well . . ." She rethought that. "Maybe, sort of, lately. But never as bad as today." She shrugged. "Lucky us, is all I can say. I was actually having the same problem with my old roommate until you took her place." She gave Ophelia's arm a happy squeeze. "We're like the perfect roommates! It's as if we've known each other forever already, don't you think?"

Ophelia smiled and nodded. "It's a cosmic connection!" Leona continued. "For instance, I used to get mad at Scarlet for moving our flowers around, too. But with you I don't care. We're roommates. We *should* share!"

"What do you mean?" asked Ophelia. "Move what flowers? Where?"

"Our bouquet. You know." They emerged from the café and into a misty, sparkly rain. Leona closed her eyes and turned her face up, and Ophelia did the same. "Did you know they say that the rain on Wishworld doesn't even *sparkle*?" she asked Ophelia. "And that the lakes there *reflect* light but don't make any of their own?"

"Amazing," Ophelia said, nodding. "How do they get glitter into their star showers do you think?"

"Beats me." Leona shrugged, pulled out her Star-Zap, and dialed up an energy bubble umbrella for them both. "Anyway, I don't know where you put the flowers, but it's fine. I don't care," she went on.

"But I didn't move them," replied Ophelia.

"You didn't?" Leona turned to her just as the lights throughout the campus shifted spectrum, turning from warm white to rosy pink.

"Time for first period already?" exclaimed Leona. "I guess I better get going to Wish Theory."

Ophelia was on her way to Wish Energy Manipulation. They arranged to meet up before Star Darlings class.

"I always thought it was strange, you and Tessa and Adora being in that special class," Ophelia told Leona as they made their way to the soundproof classroom where the secret class was held at the end of each school day. "And the others, too, I guess. You all seemed so smart in all your other classes. I mean, doesn't Adora win the Astro Science Fair every year?"

"So now you know," said Leona. "Lady Stella just made up that story to help keep our mission confidential. None of us likes it at all." Leona groaned. "But we're helping Starland, so it's worth it, I suppose."

Their special Star Darlings lesson that day was about young-Wisher theory and was taught by Professor Illumia Wickes, who led her class by tossing ideas into space to see how far they'd travel and how bright they'd grow.

"Star greetings, Ophelia!" she exclaimed as Ophelia and Leona entered the room. "I heard there had been a Star Darlings replacement, but I had no idea it would be you!" She whipped off her enormous star-shaped rose-tinted glasses and flashed a suprised but welcoming smile.

Her wraparound dress, Leona noticed, displayed a constantly shifting pattern of stars and moons. It would certainly have hypnotized anyone who stared at it too long.

"I see we're all here," Professor Illumia Wickes said as Leona and Ophelia took their seats and let them adjust to their height and weight, "so let's go ahead and get started. Our starhour always goes so fast! This starday, I want to give you a scenario and ask you what you'd do.... Say there's a young Wisher who wishes for a moonium dollars in Wishling currency—"

Libby's glittery arm shot up. "Trick question!" She grinned. "Money wishes fall into the 'greedy' category, which means we would never be called to grant a wish like that."

"Ahem. As I was saying," Professor Illumia Wickes continued, nodding at Libby, who lowered her hand to her lap, "a young Wisher wishes for a moonium dollars in Wishling currency, not for *herself*, but to pay for a new playground for her school, which doesn't have one. Now, tell me: how do you help?"

She gazed around the room as hands rose slowly.

"Yes? Sage?"

"Conjure a treasure? And help the Wisher find it?"

"Treasure . . . Interesting . . ." The professor looked around the table again. "Any thoughts?"

Vega frowned and raised her hand.

"Yes, Vega? You don't agree?"

"It wouldn't work," Vega said.

"Oh? And why not?"

"Any currency or jewels or precious metals we conjured would glow or glitter on Wishworld and give themselves away."

"Ah, interesting point . . ." Professor Illumia Wickes said, nodding. "Libby? Yes? Now you may speak."

"I *still* think it's a trick question," said Libby.

Gemma turned and asked, "Why?"

"Because as soon as you attach a price to a wish, doesn't it take the purity—and the truly good energy—away?"

"Ah, but does it?" asked Professor Illumia Wickes.

Leona spoke up. "I don't think so. It's the basic reflective property of wishing we learned last week. If the Wisher's heart is pure, then their wish has to be, too."

"Yes, but in a way, wouldn't that Wisher's wish be selfish?" Cassie asked. "I mean, the playground would be for her, as a student at that school. . . ."

"Correct," said Tessa, "and yet it would be there long after she graduates and leaves the school. . . . Perhaps, though, you could nudge her away from the 'moonium dollar' wish toward a different one—but one that would have the same result?"

"Interesting!" Professor Illumia Wickes's smile lit up. "Such as . . ."

"Such as the whole school community coming together to raise money," suggested Tessa.

"Oh, I know!" Astra exclaimed. "She could organize one of those '-athons' they do so much on Wishworld. A walkathon, or a jumpathon, or something like that!"

"Or a cake trade!" Gemma offered. "They're always doing those down there!"

"I think you mean a bake sale," said Professor Illumia Wickes. "But yes . . . I like where this is going! Don't stop! Any more ideas?"

"How about a fashion show fund-raiser?" said Adora. "Wishling garments are so dull, we know, but still it could be fun!"

"You know what would be the *most* fun?" said Leona. "A fund-raising *concert*! And if it was my Wish Mission, I would sing—of course!" Energized, she turned to her new roommate. "What do you think, Ophelia?"

"I . . . I . . ." Ophelia stared back at Leona blankly.

"Yes, Ophelia. What *do* you think? You've been very quiet!" Professor Illumia Wickes smiled. "Don't be shy just because you're new. Feel free to jump in here and tell us what *you* would do!"

"Um . . . I . . . uh . . ."

"Go ahead," Leona urged.

"It's just . . ." Ophelia winced as if her brain hurt. "It's just . . . I'm a little confused. We didn't learn much about young Wishlings' wishes in our other Wish Theory class . . . so I don't understand. And what exactly is a 'playground'?" She paused. "Is there, um, a vocabulary list I could get, by any chance?"

A few giggles circled the table along with a rainbow of raised eyebrows.

Gemma snorted and threw back her head. "What in the stars! I feel like we really are in a remedial class!" She laughed.

"Like you know *everything*," Libby muttered across the table to her roommate, not at all under her breath.

Gemma fired back a hot orange glare. "I know this: you think you're so neat and perfect, but you're not very good at making your bed."

"That's only because you crawl over it to move those flowers! Why can't you just leave them on my nightstand, where you know they look the best?"

Zwwooosh!

A ball of light appeared in the professor's hand and she tossed it to the back of the room. It skimmed right over their heads. The girls' mouths opened in disbelief.

"That's enough!" said Professor Illumia Wickes as the Star Darlings covered their heads. "So much negative energy!" She clucked and shook her head.

The light ball slowed and returned to her outstretched hand, where it dissolved into a shimmering shower, spark by spark.

"Star apologies," said Libby.

"Yes, star apologies." Gemma looked down.

"Star apologies accepted, but all this bickering has got to stop. Now . . ." She scanned her holo-notes. "I'd like to spend the rest of the class on this idea of young wishful thinking, so if you'd all get out your Star-Zaps, please. Feel free to record my lecture so you can absorb it in your sleep. . . ."

"Ophelia! Wait up!" Leona hurried after Ophelia, who was the first Starling out the door. "Don't listen to Gemma," she said, linking her arm with Ophelia's. "Every Starling knows she has the biggest mouth in school."

"But she's right," said Ophelia as they rode the Cosmic Transporter out the front door of the school. "I'm so far behind the rest of you. I don't know where to begin to catch up! And it's not just that. I've seen some of the things the other Star Darlings—and you—can do with energy, and I'm nowhere even close. . . ."

"You'll get there!" Leona tried to reassure her. "It might take some time, but you will!"

"But how? Do you know, when Lady Cordial first called me into her office, I thought I was being expelled. Do you know I got a D on my Wishworld Relations exam last week?"

"Really?" said Leona, stunned. D, for *Dim*, was the lowest grade a Starling could get.

"And it's not only that. You're so *special*! And the

other Star Darlings, too. I don't fit in at all, and I don't see how I ever will. . . ."

"Come on." Leona took a sharp right, onto a path toward the edge of the campus.

"Where are we going?" Ophelia asked.

Leona pointed toward a thick grove of pink ozziefruit trees just past the campus border. It was her favorite place to walk and sing and think. "A few berries?" She winked at Ophelia. "They make everything better, don't you agree?"

As soon as the Cosmic Transporter reached the orchard, Leona and Ophelia stepped off and walked between rows of tall pink-leaved trees heavy with ripe indigo fruit. Leona reached out and picked a berry for Ophelia and another one for herself. Instantly, two new fruits grew in their places, just as big and juicy and blue.

"Shall we sit?" Leona asked, settling in the grass at the base of the fragrant tree. As Ophelia sank beside her, Leona took a bite out of her ozziefruit. "Mmm!" Leona said as she chewed and dabbed at a stream of blue juice dribbling down her chin.

Ophelia smiled.

"See? I knew these would make you feel better. And you haven't even eaten one yet."

"It's your mouth . . ." Ophelia said, pointing.

"What?" Leona glanced down at blue ozziefruit-juice stains on her fingers. "Oh, no!" She laughed. "Are my lips blue?" She shrugged. "Who cares? It's worth it! See? I'm not that special after all!"

Just above them, a delicate twelve-legged rainbow-orb spider was busy weaving her star-shaped web. The star-silk stretched between the branches like shiny tinsel, flashing wherever the sunlight found it.

"Did you feel this way at first?" Ophelia asked Leona. "Like you didn't know why you were picked?"

Leona almost answered, "Sure," but then she realized that wasn't true. In fact, she remembered clearly how right being chosen had felt. *Of course, I'm a Star Darling!* she'd thought when Lady Stella assembled them the first day. *And I'm going to be the best!*

"Don't worry," she told Ophelia instead. "It's going to get easier. Use your Mirror Mantra! It always helps me."

"Mirror Mantra?" said Ophelia.

"Yes, you know—the words you recite when you need strength or reassurance. You can use it with your Wisher, too."

Ophelia looked at her blankly. "Um, I don't know . . . I guess I haven't gotten one yet."

"No? That's odd. Well, I'm sure you will. This is mine: 'You are a star. Light up the world.'" Leona grinned proudly. "Nice, right? When you say it without a mirror, it makes you feel good and positive. When you say it on Wishworld in front of a mirror, you can see yourself with your Starland glow."

"Do you think I could use yours? Until I get mine?"

Leona's eyes brightened. "Sure! Knock your stars out!"

Then, suddenly, both their Star-Zaps flashed.

"Ooh! What's going on?" Ophelia looked down as hers began to vibrate wildly—much more strongly than it did for a normal alert.

Leona read the screen, already knowing what it would say. "Another Wish Orb's been identified!" she told Ophelia. "Come on! We need to get to Lady Stella's office ASAS—as soon as starpossible!"

"Not to the Wish-House?" said Ophelia, scrambling to her feet.

"The Wish-House is for *regular* wishes," said Leona. "We have a special, secret one—way under Halo Hall—for no other wishes, just ours!" She quickly grabbed a handful of berries. "For energy!" she said. "After all, who knows? The Wish Orb might belong to one of us!"

CHAPTER 7

Soon Leona, Ophelia, and the other Star Darlings stood in a circle around the grass-covered platform from which a Wish Orb would soon reveal itself.

Leona looked up and saw clouds drifting slowly across the blue sky. As usual, she had to remind herself that they were underground and not in Starland City Park.

"Are you ready, Star Darlings?" asked Lady Stella, raising her arms to begin the process of the Wish Orb Reveal.

Leona knew she was ready. She gazed around and could see that the others were, as well—everyone, that is, but poor Ophelia, who looked as if she'd eaten *way* too much zoomberry cake and was about to lose it all. Cassie didn't look very confident, either.

Lady Stella clapped once and the room fell dark, save

for one pure white beam of light shining down on the platform, which slowly opened up, revealing a brilliant orb. It hovered in the air and then did something different: it started to race around the circle, zooming up to each Star Darling for a split second and then zipping across the circle toward another. Leona's eyes lit up each time it approached her, and her smile faded each time it zipped away. She closed her eyes in frustration.

"Leona!" someone shouted.

She opened her eyes. The beautiful, tantalizing orb floated in the air in front of her.

She reached out and the orb fit in her palm perfectly. She felt a wave of pure bliss as she gazed down at it.

"Congratulations, Leona," said Lady Stella, pressing her palms together and bowing over them.

"How long till I go?" Leona asked. "Tomorrow morning? Afternoon?"

"Actually . . ." The headmistress stood over the Wish Orb and studied it. "I do believe that in the case of this wish, there isn't a starmin to lose. As you know, a Wish Orb will stay fresh and healthy as long as the Wisher keeps wishing on the wish . . . but if they begin to forget . . . or change their mind . . . their Wish Orb will lose its glow and fade away."

"Is that what's happening?"

"It certainly appears so," said Lady Stella. "The glow is already fading, I'm afraid. This wish needs granting very soon. . . ."

"Then what are we waiting for?" said Leona. "All I really need is my Wish Pendant, right? Then I can go catch a shooting star!"

From the underground Wish-House, Leona followed Lady Stella out of the Star Caves. After a brief stop in the headmistress's office for a quick refresher on the features she'd need to use on her Star-Zap when she got to Wishworld, Leona raced back to her room to be sure she had everything she needed.

Back in Halo Hall, she boarded the Flash Vertical Mover, and in mere starsecs she was whisked into the sky. Lady Stella and the rest of the Star Darlings were there to see her off all wearing their Safety Star Glasses. Leona hugged all the Star Darlings good-bye, leaving Ophelia with an extra-strong, supportive squeeze.

"Remember what I told you. This is all strange and new right now, but it's going to get easier every starday! You're going to be a great Star Darling, Ophelia! Just hang in there and believe in yourself! Promise you'll try my Mirror Mantra. Remember how it goes?"

Ophelia took a hopeful breath. "'You are a star. Light up the world.'"

"Exactly! You got it!"

Lady Stella gave Leona some last-minute advice. "Focus on your mission. Be sure you don't get caught up in the excitement of being on Wishworld," she reminded Leona. "And be sure to discover your Wisher's true wish—not the wish you think she may have made."

Lady Cordial gave Leona her backpack with the stuffed star-shaped keychain and wished her luck.

On the Special Star Darling Wishworld Surveillance Deck, Star Wranglers were already waiting with lassos made of wish energy to harness Leona to the next shooting star, which came before she even had time to think *Am I ready?* or *Should I have brought a microphone?* The next thing Leona knew, she was strapped to the star and hurtling through space like a golden meteor.

It was beautiful! The colors were endless—like a giant box of cray-osmic crayons times a hydrong. Leona had to force herself to focus on her mission like Lady Stella had said, and to use the precious starmins she had to prepare for what was to come. It was hard, though, not to simply gaze around, enjoying a view of the universe that only a few Starlings ever got.

Fortunately, she had her Star-Zap to alert her when it was time to commence her appearance change. By then, she had entered Wishworld's atmosphere and could see the shapes of the continents below. She hurried to pull up the Wishworld Outfit Selector on her Star-Zap and choose something Wishlingy to wear. Then she closed her eyes, placed her hand over her golden cuff, and recited the body-transforming lines: "Star light, star bright, the first star I see tonight: I wish I may, I wish I might, have the wish I wish tonight." A soothing warmth spread through her body, and she envisioned what she'd look like on Wishworld—hair that was light brown instead of gold, and skin that was still honey brown but shimmerless and dull. She opened her eyes slowly to see if the mantra had worked.

"Starmendous!" she said out loud, shaking the stars loose from her hair.

Her Star-Zap flashed: PREPARE FOR LANDING. And Leona did, once more closing her eyes. She braced for a jolt, but she was far from ready for the icy-cold splash she got instead.

"Ahh!" she wailed, opening her eyes to find herself in the middle of a wide blue tree-lined lake.

She grabbed the star and swam to shore as fast as she could, grateful for her water ballet lessons in Luminous Lake. Unfortunately, while all bodies of water on Starland instantly adjusted to any temperature a swimmer might desire—from hot-tub warm to refreshingly cool—the water in this Wishworld lake was most *undesirably* ice-cold.

Leona reached the bank and climbed out, shivering, only to feel colder when her wet skin met the air. Without her natural star energy glow and shimmer, she had no way to keep off the chill. But she did have a Star-Zap—fortunately—which meant a whole wardrobe of dry clothes. She quickly pulled it out and dialed up the warmest outfit she could find: a butter-soft long-sleeved gold sweater with a chenille star appliquéd on the chest, a pair of brown leggings flecked with gold, and cozy fleece-lined boots covered with tiny shiny gold sequins.

Then she took a starmin to make a mental note, which would be recorded in her Cyber Journal when she pressed a button on her Star-Zap.

Mission 3, Wishworld Observation #1: Wishworld water is cold. Recommend including a drying feature in future Star Darlings' Star-Zaps.

Leona shook the water off her star and folded it up. She checked her image in her Star-Zap and was pleased—with the outfit, at least. Her hair, on the other hand, was dripping wet. On Starland, of course, this never happened. Hair looked exactly the same dry or wet. Leona wished she knew what Wishlings did with their hair in these situations, but the subject had never come up in class. All she could do was give it a shake and hope it dried by itself.

Most important, she knew, was to find her Wisher, and she turned once more to her Star-Zap for that. "Take me to the Wisher I've come to help," she said, holding the Star-Zap out to see where it would lead. *Before my Wisher forgets her wish,* she thought, *or somehow changes her mind.*

Directions appeared on the holo-screen and Leona followed them away from the lake and through the trees. Pine trees. Leona recognized them from a holo-picture in the Wishworld Relations classroom; only in that picture, the trees were frosted with plain white Wishworld snow. On Starland they had snow, as well, but the flakes were all different colors and looked like confetti when they fell. Leona remembered thinking how much fun it would be, just once, to have one-color snow. She would, of course, have picked gold.

Before too long, the directions led her out of the woods and into the sun, onto a lush green Wishworld lawn. Leona paused to let the warm rays sink in, then continued down a lane to a tall dull-black yet impressively intricate iron gate similar to the one that ran around Starling Academy. She noticed words at the top and read them: " 'Havisham Academy—Boarding School for Girls.' Havisham Academy . . . Oh!" gasped Leona. "This must be the place!" Perhaps it was even a school for special Wishlings, like Starling Academy was for Starlings.

Much like at Starling Academy, a long driveway led through the gate and was lined with stately broad-limbed trees. Unlike along Starling Academy's Constellation Lane, though, the leaves along this Wishworld road remained a single color—green. The drive circled at the end, where it reached a wide rectangular building made of rough reddish bricks. Leafy green ropes grew up the walls, all the way to the slate roof.

Leona was checking her Star-Zap again to see if it might inform her that her Wisher was inside when all of sudden, without any warning, the doors flew open and a flood of young female Wishlings poured out. And they weren't just coming from that one building, Leona soon realized, but from similar-looking structures all around. Some kept to the paths that crisscrossed the well-trimmed lawns, and some hiked across the grass. Leona froze, fearing one of the kids might run over her if she kept moving.

"Look out!"

It almost happened anyway. A line of three girls stopped short just in front of her, forcing Leona to stumble back.

"Oh, sorry," one said.

"You probably shouldn't stand here."

"Yeah, not when classes let out, at least."

"Are you looking for someone?" the first girl asked.

"Who, me?" *If they only knew*, Leona thought. "Um, actually, I go here!"

"You *do*?" Two girls raised their eyebrows. The third eyed Leona from head to toe. "Then why aren't you wearing a uniform?"

"A what?" Leona said.

The third girl nodded toward her outfit, then gave a quick chin bob to each of her friends. That's when Leona noticed for the first time that they—and every other girl in sight—were all dressed exactly alike: black shoes, tall white socks folded just below the knee, crisp white shirts with plain white buttons in a row all down the front, red-and-blue-striped strips of fabric tied in knots around their necks, plaid skirts with a large decorative pin, and, finally, boxy storm-gray blazers with shield-shaped patches affixed to pockets on their chests.

"Right. A uniform." Leona remembered now. They had learned about those in class. Only, she thought those were clothes *adult* Wishlings wore for some of their special jobs, like putting out fires or fighting crime—things that on Starland never needed to be done. And then there were the uniforms adult Wishlings wore when they played young Wishling games in front of crowds. But to school? Leona must have somehow missed that lesson. Or laughed it off as a joke.

"So . . . this is the uniform . . . today?" Her finger jumped from girl to girl. "And tomorrow, I guess, you wear a different one? Is there, by any chance, a *gold* day?"

The girls' faces wrinkled into different patterns of confusion.

"We wear this *every* day. I thought you went here," one of them said.

"I do. . . ."

Every day? thought Leona. If she'd been on Starland, she'd surely have lost her glow.

"But I'm new. . . . I just arrived. . . ." Leona forced herself to add a smile, but it was hard to make it stay. The image of *her* in *that* made her want to cry instead.

"Oh! So you're probably looking for the headmistress," said the first girl. "She'll give you a uniform and show you to your room." She pointed to the door they'd just come out of. "In there. First door on the left."

"Star salu—oh, I mean, thanks," said Leona. She waved and watched the girls walk off. Then she turned and headed in to get her . . . *gulp* . . . school uniform.

Mission 3, Wishworld Observation #2: Warning! Be prepared: choice of Wishling wardrobe is not guaranteed.

Finding the headmistress was easy, as was convincing her that Leona was enrolled in her school. The mind-control techniques Sage and Libby had taught Leona and the others worked beautifully on her. Almost instantly, Leona was being given a room assignment, a class schedule, and, of course, a uniform while the headmistress remarked on the sudden scent of baking brownies and paused now and then to lick her lips. She told Leona her room number and handed her a key. Leona politely refused her offer to show her the way. She wanted to find her Wisher immediately.

From there, Leona slipped into a restroom and quickly changed. She was more eager than ever to get on with her mission (and back to her wardrobe on Starland) as soon as possible.

"Now, where is my Wisher?" She checked to see if her Star-Zap had any further instructions to give. "*Ahh!*" she cried as she suddenly noticed a Wishling girl standing right there.

Leona reeled back in surprise. "You scared me—" she started. Then she realized the pretty, curly-haired Wishling was saying the same thing.

"*Starf!*" she said to her reflection in the mirror above the sink. She knew she was supposed to look like a real Wishling . . . but still, it was hard to accept! She fluffed her hair, which had dried out fairly well. "You are a star," she said. "Light up the world!" Her sparkly self stared back at her. And a surge of energy boosted her confidence. And with that, she opened the bathroom door and charged into the hall.

According to the headmistress, classes were over for the day. The hall, therefore, was empty, and Leona's footsteps echoed as her stiff new loafers clip-clopped across the floor.

Leona figured she'd head back outside and hope her Star-Zap directed her from there. She paused, though, as she passed a bulletin board, and did a double take. If there were two words that could catch her eye, they were the ones at the top of the pale pink flyer pinned between a cockeyed sign about a yearbook meeting and another about a semester in someplace called Spain.

Leona read the two words at the top of the pink flyer out loud: "'Talent show.'"

A happy tingle made its way up her spine as she eagerly read on: "'Auditions today from five to nine p.m. in Hawthorne Auditorium.'"

Of course! she thought. *That's got to be where I'll find my Wisher!* She glanced up at the clock above the bulletin board. The time was four forty-five. *Here I come, whoever you are!* she thought as she turned and ran, loafers clippety-clapping, to find the auditorium.

CHAPTER 8

Hawthorne Auditorium turned out to be easy to find. The building took up most of the north end of the quad. .

Leona was less sure, though, once she skipped up the steps and slipped through the front doors. There wasn't much to see: just a narrow lobby with framed posters in rows along the walls, two pairs of doors, and one wide-eyed grown-up Wishling waving a clipboard.

"Who are you? And how did you do that?"

"Excuse me?" Leona said. She covered her Wish Pendant with her hand. What exactly had she done? Something un-Wishlingish, she guessed.

"How did you open those doors like that and walk right through?"

"Uh . . ." Leona looked back at the doors behind her. "Isn't that how all doors work?" She knew Wishworld was different . . . but weren't all doors simply doors?

"But you didn't push? And they're not automatic. Your hands were down at your sides the whole time. . . ." The woman reached out and yanked hard on the door handle to open it. "See? They don't just open. They're heavy. They stick."

Leona gulped. She understood. She'd been so focused on finding her Wisher she'd forgotten to be careful not to let her energy work for her.

Mission 3, Wishworld Observation #3: When on Wishworld, never use energy when you can use your hands. Not only will you conserve energy, you'll avoid embarrassing questions.

"Um . . . you are absolutely right," she told the woman, gazing deep into her eyes. "Those doors are very heavy. That's why I pushed them very hard—with my hands. And that's how I got in."

The woman's baffled scowl softened into a friendly, vaguely hungry grin. "You pushed them very hard with your hands," she repeated. "That's how you got in. Mmm. Warm apple pie." She sighed. "I could use a piece right now."

Leona sighed, too. *That was pretty easy. Now, back to the mission at hand.* "I'm here for the auditions. Where are they exactly?" she asked.

"You're here for the auditions. Of course." The woman nodded. "They're in the auditorium, just through there." She aimed a pen at a pair of double doors. "And your name is . . . ?" she asked.

"Um, Leona . . . I'm new. . . . I sing!" she added before she could think to stop. "Uh, but I'm really just here to watch," she went on quickly. "If that's okay, of course."

"To watch?" The woman looked up. Her face was still calm and sweet and stiff. "That's okay, of course. I was just on my way in myself. I'm Ms. Frasier, the music director. I'm in charge of the auditions." She shifted her clipboard and held out her hand.

"Really? Nice to meet you!" Leona shook it heartily. "Here!" She ran to the doors to the auditorium. "Let me get the door for you, Ms. Frasier. With my hands, of course!"

Once they were inside, it all made sense to Leona. *Now, this is more like it!* she thought.

Her gaze moved down the aisle, along the rows of seats, and up onto the empty stage. No, it wasn't star-shaped, and the curtains, unfortunately, were rust-colored, with no neon twinkle at all. Still, it was all Leona could do not to run up there, grab the mic, and belt out a rocking song.

But no, this was not the time. She had to remind herself of that twice. With luck, that would come soon enough, but Leona still had to find her Wisher. Then would come the hardest part of all: identifying the Wisher's wish.

She dragged her eyes from the stage and began to scan the auditioners. She saw Ms. Frasier doing the same.

"Okay, people! Let's do this!" the music teacher shouted as she marched down the aisle toward the first row of seats. "We have a long list of auditions to get through here, so I want you ready when I call your name!"

Leona quickly counted. There were forty-eight girls in the auditorium, most scattered among the seats. Two sat at the end of the row right next to her. She decided to start with them.

"Hi," she said.

The first girl turned. It looked like she held a small child on her lap. A strange, tiny little kid.

The friend turned also, stiffly. "Hi, hello there!" she declared.

Leona jumped back.

"Oh, my stars!" she gasped.

The first girl dissolved into laughter while her small friend stared off into space.

"What?" said Leona. "What's so funny?"

"Nothing," said the girl, laughing. She covered her mouth with her free hand. "It's just that you look really startled by Dolly. Like you thought she was a real girl."

Leona didn't know what to say. She did know that her Wish Pendant did not show this was her Wisher, so she smiled and slowly backed away.

"Excuse us, we're trying to rehearse here," said a sharp voice, which made Leona spin around.

"Oh, sorry!" She smiled at the three girls. "What's your talent?" she inquired.

They all looked at her and then at each other's matching shorts and leotards.

"Dance," one said, swinging her hip to meet her hand.

Another nodded. "Jazz."

"Wait, Talia, I thought it was modern," the third one said, frowning.

"Whatever, Adeline." The first girl, Talia, rolled her eyes back to Leona and lifted one cheek in a half grin. "What's *your* talent?" she asked. "Staring? Good one, right, Kasey?"

"Ha!" Kasey laughed.

"Can you do that as a talent?" asked Adeline.

"It was a joke," explained Talia. She was their leader, Leona guessed.

Leona wondered if maybe these girls didn't want to be mean and wished they weren't that way. She checked her Wish Pendant, but it was barely glowing. None of the girls was her Wisher. Too bad. That would have been such a great wish to grant, helping one of them change into a better person.

"First up! Make-a-Move!"

"Omigosh, Talia! We're first!" Kasey squealed.

"First?" Adeline blanched.

"First is good!" Talia declared. "Then we can get out of here and eat, and we don't have to sit through all these weirdos, like Hannah and her creepy dummy."

She nodded toward the girl with the little stiff friend as she said that. The other girls giggled behind their hands.

"Come on, let's go!" Talia went on, dragging her dance mates down the aisle.

"Good luck," Leona told them.

"Thanks," Adeline said.

Talia tossed her ponytail. "Who needs luck when you have talent? But yeah . . ." She snorted. "Thanks, lemonhead."

Leona watched them head toward the stage, wishing she could take her "good luck" back. She had no idea what a lemonhead was, but it sure didn't sound like a compliment. Still, she couldn't take things on Wishworld personally. She had to remind herself of that. She was there on a mission, and it was way too important to let silly names distract her from that.

And besides, she thought, she had more talent in her little finger than those three Make-a-Moves combined.

Anyway... Leona sighed and turned at a sound behind her. A girl stood in the back of the theater, blinking nervously, looking as if she was afraid the auditorium would swallow her. Leona walked up to the girl, and feeling her wrist tingle, she looked down at her Wish Pendant. She was nearly blinded by its glow.

"Hi. My name's Leona. What's yours?"

"Er . . . Lily," the girl said, then gulped. She stared at the floor.

"Lily!" Leona nodded. "That's a pretty name! So . . . Lily . . . are you here to try out for this thing?"

Her head still down, the girl nodded.

Awesome! Leona thought. There was only one wish this Wisher could have: to win this talent show!

"So what's your talent?" she asked the girl. "Or should I say *which* talent do you want to perform?"

The girl took a long, deep breath and held it. "Singing," she said, exhaling at last.

"Really?" Leona could hardly contain her excitement. This was going to be the best mission ever! How lucky could a Star Darling get?

Meanwhile, music had started and so had Make-a-Move's routine. Leona didn't see too much talent in their dancing, yet she couldn't tear her eyes away. They did what they did with such self-confidence—just like Leona, in a way.

Even Lily looked up and watched them as most of the audience started to clap. Their dance involved a lot of rolling hips and stomping feet and crossing arms and pumping fists, along with a good bit of running in place and making fierce faces that featured curled lips.

"Wow," said Leona as the dancers finally dropped to their knees at the end. "They know how to get your attention. You have to admit that, I guess."

Onstage, the girls hugged and high-fived. Then they linked arms and took a bow. This was followed by another bow, and another—

"Okay, thank you, Make-a-Move," Ms. Frasier shouted. "Really, thank you. But let's keep it moving. We've got a long list here. Okay . . . who's next? Let's see. . . . Lily. *Lily!*" she shouted. "It's your turn!"

"Hey, that's you!" exclaimed Leona. She turned back to cheer on her Wisher, only to find that her Wisher was gone. "Wait! Lily!" she called to the closing door. "You can't go now! It's your turn!"

She slipped through the door, too, and caught Lily in the lobby, just about to go outside. "Lily! Ms. Frasier just called your name! You're up! It's your turn to get up there and shine!"

But Lily just stood there, her head shaking back and forth, her mouth clamped firmly shut. It took Leona a starsec to finally realize that her Wisher had stage fright.

Just then, Make-a-Move burst out of the theater and into the lobby.

"Omigosh! *Lily Fisher!*" Talia covered her mouth. "Are *you* the Lily Ms. Frasier's calling? Please tell me you're not really going to try out."

"Of course she's trying out!" declared Leona. No one was talking to her Wisher that way! "You tried out," she reminded Talia, "so why shouldn't she?"

"Uh, yeah," Talia said, "and we have *talent.* And since this is a talent show, that's kind of something that you need."

She laughed, and so did Kasey. Adeline, however, shrugged.

"I don't know," she said. "Haven't you heard her sing in chorus? If I were her, I might try out. She's really pretty good."

At this, both Talia and Kasey turned to their friend and glared.

Lily, though, didn't seem to hear her. She'd already opened the door to the quad and was halfway through it.

Leona brushed past the dance group to follow her, scowling at Talia as she did. "Just so you know, your routine was fine, but you were totally off beat." She was so mad she nearly forgot to open the doors like a Wishling *again*. They were already starting to open by the time she remembered and lifted her hands.

Leona ran outside and spotted Lily heading down a brick path toward a building just beyond the quad.

"Hey!" she panted, catching up. "Don't listen to them. I'm sure you can sing! Let's go back so we—I mean *you*; of course, I mean you—so *you* can try out. Come on!"

Lily slowed down but kept walking, her eyes fixed on the ground. "I'm not trying out," she said softly.

"But . . . but I thought . . . I thought you wanted to," Leona said, confused.

Lily shook her head. "No," she said very definitely. "I was just kidding when I said that. I never really wanted to. It was a joke, signing up. I don't belong in any talent show." She looked up at last as they reached a long brick building. Solemnly, she opened the door. "After you," she told Leona, forcing a smile and waving Leona past her.

"What's this place?" asked Leona. Her nose twitched at the rush of new smells. They were heavy and strange and thick.

Lily looked at her oddly. "It's the dining hall."

"Really?" Leona looked around. *Ah, yes, of course.* She spotted the line of girls taking trays and sliding them down a silver track, past a line of older Wishlings in paper aprons and gauzy hairnets.

"So, what, are you new here?" asked Lily, gazing more closely at her.

"Um . . . yes." Leona quickly nodded. "In fact, I just got here today."

"Are you a sophomore, too?"

"Um . . . sure." Leona could be a sophomore, she guessed—whatever a sophomore was.

"Well, the food's pretty good. Except for the meat loaf," said Lily. "Here, take a tray. And there's always the salad bar, and pasta and stuff like that. And we just got a frozen yogurt machine, but it keeps breaking, I'm afraid."

"Oh? That's too bad. . . ." A thought suddenly popped into Leona's head. "I bet you wish it would get fixed."

Lily shrugged. "Yeah, I guess. . . . But I'm lactose intolerant, so I don't care that much, I guess."

She seemed to care, however, because her face suddenly went pale. She'd been looking at Leona, but her eyes had shifted to something in the distance, past Leona. Leona turned and saw an older girl approaching, shaking her head.

"So." The girl crossed her arms. "Guess what I just heard."

Lily sucked in her lips. Her ears and neck flushed.

"You bailed on the talent show tryouts. Why are you always such a wimp?"

Lily's mouth fell open, but nothing came out except a meek breath.

"Excuse me!" huffed Leona, but the older girl was already walking away. "Honestly!" said Leona. "Who does that girl think she is?"

Lily swallowed, sniffed, and found her voice. "She's my big sister," she explained.

CHAPTER 9

Leona was speechless—for a starsec. But a starsec was all it took for Lily to drop her tray back on the pile and flee the dining hall.

Leona was tempted to follow her again, but she wasn't sure that she should. She had a limited amount of time to help grant Lily's wish, yet what did Professor Eugenia Bright always say? "Haste makes waste." *Think things through before you act*, in other words.

Plus, Leona's stomach was growling. Better to see what this Wishworld cafeteria had to offer, she thought, and restore her energy. One thing was for sure, though: she'd be eating by herself. She knew there were plenty of nice Wishlings on Wishworld—or so other Starlings had said—but the girls at Havisham Academy so far seemed pretty unpleasant.

Leona pushed her tray—with her hands—through the line briskly, taking a little bit of everything. Everything, that is, but the stuff labeled "meat loaf," as Lily had warned her. When she saw it, it was easy to skip. She saw the wedges labeled PIZZA and remembered what Libby had said about it—delicious! She took two.

"Wow, you must be hungry," said someone behind her.

Leona closed her eyes and sighed. *Starf,* she thought. Just what she needed. Yet another Wishling giving her a hard time.

She glanced over her shoulder to see the smiling face of one of the girls who'd almost run into her when she'd first arrived. "But you skipped the meat loaf. Smart. I see you got a uniform."

Leona nodded.

"Cool! Welcome! My name's Calley. Want to sit with us?" She pointed to some girls already sitting at a table nearby. Two were the other girls she'd met in the courtyard. They all waved back and smiled.

"Um . . . yeah," said Leona. "Sure." It was still sinking in, the fact that the girl was being nice. Leona supposed she hadn't been so mean at first, either, now that she thought about it.

"What do you want to drink?" asked the girl as they reached the beverage station. She took two plastic tumblers and offered Leona one.

"Um . . ." Leona could have used a nice cup of Zing, but that would have to wait until her Starland return. She remembered from Wishlings 101 the icy-cold drink described as the perfect sweet-sour combination.

"Do you have something here called . . . lemanode, I think?"

Calley's smile grew even wider. "Lemonade?" she said.

"Yes!" Leona grinned. "That's it!"

Calley pointed to a machine with a shiny picture of some kind of oblong bright-yellow fruit on it.

Leona read the word splashed across the bottom. "No way! Lemonade! You *do* have it! This is super startastic!" she exclaimed.

Leona filled her cup, tasted it, and then gulped most of it down and filled her cup once again. It was just as delicious as they said. Much happier than she'd been before, she followed Calley to her friends' table.

Each girl introduced herself politely.

"What year are you?" one, named Sophia, asked.

"Um . . ." Leona tried to remember. "A starmore, I think."

"A what?" The girl wrinkled her nose and frowned.

Leona tried again. "A softstar?"

"Do you mean 'sophomore'?" asked a dark-haired girl named Maya.

"Right!" said Leona. "That's it."

"Are you an exchange student?" Calley asked.

"Why . . . yes! Yes, I am! How'd you know?"

"We can just tell." Calley smiled.

"Where are you from?" Sophia asked.

"Where am I from . . ." Leona tried to recall Wishworld places they'd learned, but her mind had become a black hole. *Wait!* She remembered the sign on the bulletin board about what looked like a beautiful place. "Spain!" she said, a little more loudly than she needed to, perhaps.

"Wow," said Maya, looking impressed. "Your English is really good!"

"Uh . . . thanks." It was time to change the subject. "Sooooo . . . are any of you trying out for the talent show?" she asked.

"No."

"No way."

They all shook their heads.

Calley even made a face as if she might get sick. "I tried out last year, but I never will again."

"Why not?" Leona asked.

"Talia and her friends. They've won the last two years. And they're not even all that good."

"No," Sophia helped her explain, "but what they are is super mean, so that girls either quit and drop out or get too nervous to do their best."

"Someone should stand up to them," said Leona.

"You're right." They all agreed.

"You're welcome to try." Calley nodded at her, but she looked doubtful of Leona's success.

Not Leona, though. Her thoughts were orbiting, working to make a plan. After all, if Lily's wish was going to come true in time, Leona might have to be the one to make it happen.

After they'd eaten, the girls had to head to the library to do homework, so Leona told them good-bye. She had her own work to do, and she knew that if she didn't find Lily and get her to those auditions before they ended at nine o'clock, making her Wisher's wish come true would be impossible.

She decided to go check out her new dorm room. She fished the key out of her pocket. Room 113. She found the building—Auburn Hall—and stepped inside. She paused in front of the door, then unlocked it.

Leona heard the sound of a tap turning on through the bathroom door. Her roommate was taking one of those water showers, she guessed. Another reason she should go.

Leona turned to enter the hall, but then something made her stop. It was another sound: a voice—her roommate's, apparently—singing a sad, sweet song.

Wow . . . Leona moved to her bed and stretched out on it to listen better. The girl was really good, and with every verse her voice grew even stronger and clearer and more sure of itself. The song was catchy and easy to follow, and Leona found herself singing along. She soon stopped, though, and sat back and listened, eyes closed, as the girl hit heavenly notes Leona knew she never would. *If only other Starlings could hear this*, she thought. *Wait!* She realized they could! She pulled out her Star-Zap, held it up, and began to record.

Then the shower stopped, and, unfortunately, so did the song. A starmin later, the bathroom door opened.

"*Lily?*" Leona gasped the moment she saw her. She recognized her Wisher at once even with her wet hair and music-note pajamas.

"*Ahh!*" Lily jumped back. "You scared me! What are you doing here?" She looked confused.

"Actually . . . I'm your new roommate," Leona told

her. "They put me here this afternoon. Some coincidence, huh? I sing, and so do you!" She grinned. "And wow! Are you ever good!"

Lily was clearly trying not to smile at Leona's compliment, but she couldn't contain her grin. "I didn't know anyone could hear me," she explained.

"Oh, don't apologize! Not for a second!" said Leona. "I believe in singing as loud as you can. I also believe that a voice like yours should be heard. Honestly, it's a gift you were born to share!"

"Thanks." Lily blushed. "But I'm not *that* good."

"Um, yeah," said Leona. "You are. And you are crazy not to enter that talent show. So hurry, come on, let's go!"

At that, Lily started shaking her head. Her smile faded and her blush disappeared.

"What's wrong?"

"I'm not trying out," said Lily.

"But why not? You're so good! You'll win!"

"That's not what those girls said. . . ."

"Yeah, and I hear they say that to everyone else, too. Honestly, it's time for someone to step up and show them they can't keep using bullying to win."

"Yeah, well, someone else will have to show them. I just can't sing in front of other people, not all by myself."

"Of course you can!" Leona insisted.

"No, I can't," said Lily, stubbornly shaking her towel-wrapped head.

"Have you tried?" asked Leona.

"No . . . not really."

"Exactly! So you have no idea! In fact, if you'd tried, you'd know that all by yourself is the best way in the universe to sing!" Leona declared.

"I don't know about that. . . ." Lily laughed, but she couldn't argue. Leona could tell that her mind was beginning to change. *And not a starmin too soon*, Leona realized as she glanced at the clock by the bed. It was already eight fifty-five. They only had five minutes left!

"So will you try out?" asked Leona. "I'll go with you—for moral support. . . ." She reached out and took Lily's hands.

"Oh!"

Leona could feel Lily shiver. "Oops. Star ap—I mean, sorry!" Leona said, dropping Lily's hands.

"That's okay. . . ." Lily rubbed her palms and wiggled her fingers. "There's a lot of static in the air, I guess." Then she smiled broadly at Leona. "I can't believe I'm saying this, but yes, I'll do it. I'll try out! Just as soon as I get dressed . . ."

"That's great!" Leona checked the clock again: 8:56.

There was barely enough time to get to the auditorium, let alone to change. . . .

She reached for Lily's hands again and held them tight in hers. "You know, it's almost nine o'clock. Why don't you just go how you are? I mean, really, what's more perfect for a singing audition than musical pj's?"

Lily shivered again and nodded. "Sure . . . Whatever you say . . ."

They burst in just as the final auditioner was coming off the stage.

"Thank you, Anya. I have to say, you've brought your yodeling routine a long way from last year."

"Thanks, Ms. Frasier," said the curly-haired girl. "So . . . you'll post the results tomorrow?"

"Correct. Outside Kettlekern Hall."

"Yoo-hoo! Ms. Frasier!" Leona called as she guided Lily down the aisle. "You have one more tryout!"

The music teacher turned and lifted her eyebrows in an expression of happy surprise.

"Lily! You're back. . . ." She checked her watch. "And look at that, just in time." She paused to sniff, her chin raised. "Mmm! Warm apple pie! I hope there's some left in the dining hall."

The girl who was holding a flugelhorn stared at Lily

as she passed her. "Are you wearing *pajamas*?" she asked.

Lily glanced down, then back at Leona, who simply waved her toward the stage.

"Just get up there and sing!" Leona told her. "What's wrong with pajamas?" she barked at the girl.

"Nothing! Nothing at all. I just wondered where she got them, that's all. Do you think maybe they make some with flugelhorns instead of notes?"

"So you're going to sing?" Ms. Frasier asked meanwhile, as Lily climbed onto the stage.

Lily nodded.

"Do you need music?"

Lily shook her head.

"Well, then please go ahead," said the teacher.

Hesitant, Lily gulped down a breath.

Leona smiled up at her from the aisle. "You can do it!" she mouthed silently. "It's your gift to share!"

Lily nodded at her, took another breath, and did.

CHAPTER 10

"You made it!" Leona dragged Lily to the bulletin board outside Kettlekern Hall.

Lily read the sheet. "I made it. . . ."

"Of course you did!" Leona said. Now all Lily had to do was win for Leona's mission to be complete! "Hey, what's wrong?" She looked at Lily. "Are you okay? Are you going to faint?"

"I don't know if I can do it."

"Do what?" Leona asked.

"Sing."

Leona was confused. "Of course you can *sing*! Your voice is amazing!"

"I mean in front of the whole school. I know what you said about it being a gift and all . . ." Lily gnawed her lip and sighed. "But just thinking about it now, it feels almost like a curse."

"Oh, no, no! It *is* a gift! Just wait until you're up there onstage, and you'll see!" Leona closed her eyes, envisioning herself in that spot exactly. "When all those eyes are on *you*! And everyone is just holding their breath, waiting to hear what you can do! *Lily?*" Leona opened her eyes to find her Wisher propped up, pale, against the wall.

"Okay, maybe I didn't say that quite right. . . . Come on." She linked arms with Lily.

"Where are we going?"

"We're going back to our room, and you're going to practice your song, and I'm going to record you and play it back so you can hear how good you are!"

Back in their room, Leona took out her Star-Zap and did exactly that.

"Ooh! Is that a new phone? What kind is it?" Lily asked as soon as she saw it.

"Um . . . this? It's newish, yes . . ." Leona said. "It's a . . . prototype. . . . My dad is in the business," she added. "You'll probably have one yourself next year. Anyway! We didn't come here to compare phones. We came here to rehearse. How about you sing that song you sang at the audition, and you can hear how you sound when you're done. I love to do that! Oh, but first . . . let's do some vocal warm-ups. Do you ever do those? No? You should!"

She led Lily in a series of hummed scales and lip rolls, all while they twisted and bent their knees to loosen up.

"It sounds like we're singing underwater!" Lily laughed. The exercises not only warmed up Lily's voice; they warmed up her mood, too.

When they were done, Leona had Lily stand in front of her mirror and handed her a brush. "Too bad you don't have a stage in here, or at least a microphone. Oh, well. That'll come at the talent show, I guess."

Lily sang her song through once, and Leona played it back.

"So . . . ?" Leona said. "How did that sound to you?"

"Pretty good," Lily answered through a proud, spreading smile.

"And how did it *feel*?" Leona asked. She nodded at Lily's hairbrush. "Into the microphone, please!" she joked.

Lily giggled and held her brush to her chin. "It felt pretty good, too."

★

For Leona, the rest of the time was a blur of classes and homework and meals. She knew it was all part of the mission, since a Star Darling's first job was to fit in. But it was all so . . . well, so *boring* . . . except for the precious time she found to help Lily rehearse. And even then, while it was great to see her Wisher grow more confident, it was hard—incredibly hard—to sit back and watch another singer "take the starlight," as they say. Leona had a whole new appreciation for teachers, like Professor Dolores Raye, who could easily do things for you but instead sat on their wish energy and let you try and try again.

In their spare time, Lily taught Leona how to play a game called tennis. It was played on a court with lines painted on it and a net going across the center. Each player stood on opposite sides of the net and used something called a racket to hit a small bouncy yellow ball back and forth. It was very difficult to do, and Leona thought, *How can Wishlings possibly think this is fun?*

The rackets each had a handle and a big oval-shaped top with very tight strings that the ball could bounce off. The goal was to keep hitting the ball—either before it bounced at all or after only one bounce—over the net and within the lines.

"So you've never played tennis before?" Lily asked, even though it was quite obvious.

"Uh, no—I never have," Leona said.

"You look a little confused," Lily said. "Even if you haven't played, I'm sure you've seen it on television."

"Oh, yes, of course. But I just didn't know it was so difficult," Leona said, trying to sound like she was telling the truth. Making a Wishworld wish come true was challenge enough, but keeping her cover was exhausting work! *I will have to teach the Star Darlings how to play this game*, she thought.

On the morning of the talent show, Leona headed with Lily to the dining hall for breakfast, which Leona had decided was the best meal of the day. She'd grown especially fond of a certain cereal full of colorful marshmallows in assorted shapes. She even filled a little plastic bag with some to take back home. Whether she would share it with the other Star Darlings, however, was still up in the stars.

"Oh! French toast again!" Leona remarked, reading the chalkboard posted at the front of the hot-food line. "I liked that! *Mmm!* Let's get some! Remind me, what's that spice they use called again?"

"Cinnamon?"

"Right! Cinnamon. So good! And the syrup is . . . ?"

"Maple?"

"Right! Maple! Yum!"

"Where is it that you come from again?"

"Who? Me? Um . . . Sp-sp-something. Let's eat!" She grabbed a tray.

They joined the line, then, all of a sudden, they heard someone behind them begin to hum a familiar tune.

"Hey, that's your song!" Leona said, nudging Lily.

They both turned to discover Talia, along with her two dance mates. Since the auditions, Leona had tried to spend as little time around those girls as possible, which hadn't been that hard, as it turned out. They shared few classes, and even in those, the girls kept mostly to themselves. She'd noticed them once—no, maybe twice—passing by the music room where Lily rehearsed. The dance studio the group used was in the same building, so it made sense, she supposed.

"You know she's singing that song, right?" said Leona. "In the talent show tonight?"

"Oh, we know. We've heard her singing it," said Talia.

Her friends nodded.

No one smiled.

"Good song, right?" Leona said brightly.

Talia made a sour face, which she shared with Kasey. Adeline still seemed like she didn't agree with them.

"Yeah. Great song." Talia snickered. "If you're, like, in kindergarten, I guess."

Leona looked at Lily, whose face had turned a painful red.

Leona bristled. "So then why are you humming it?" she said to Talia, who shrugged.

"It's just one of those songs—like all those baby songs—that gets stuck in your head, I guess. I *wish* I could stop," Talia groaned. Then she started to sing it herself—*horribly*, on purpose—and soon the whole breakfast line was laughing.

"Oh, just ignore her," Leona said, turning back to Lily. "Oh, no, please don't cry!" she said. Lily's chin was quivering dangerously. "I'm really not good around tears!"

Leona was relieved, therefore, to see Lily's older sister striding up from the end of the line. Leona sighed and stepped back, making room for the older girl to swoop in and comfort Lily.

Lily looked up, too, hopefully. She sniffed and even smiled. Her sister, though, maintained a straight, stern mouth and hard, disappointed eyes.

"Really, Lily? You're going to *cry* now? You're in high school. Act like it." She shook her head and turned away, grumbling, "When are you going to grow up?"

Lily stood there, biting her lip to hold back a fresh

reservoir of tears. But it only worked for a starmin. Then the dam broke and they started to spill. Lily was out of the line and through the door before Leona could say "bless my stars."

Leona cast a longing look at the warm platter of French toast waiting to be served. It might be the last chance she had to get some on Wishworld . . . but that was how wish granting worked.

Leona found Lily in the quad sitting huddled on a bench.

"So, as I was saying, don't listen to those girls." Leona slid in next to Lily and gently nudged her, hoping to get her to look up. "They're just jealous and trying to psych you out because they know how good you are."

"Well, it worked, 'cause I'm out," Lily said softly. She kept her head down as she spoke.

"Just wait till tonight, when they watch you win first place. I've got to take a holo-p—I mean picture—of that Talia's face! Wait. *What?*" Leona's head whipped around. "You're quitting? But you can't! It's your wish!" She didn't say, *I can't fail on my first Wish Mission.* But in her head, she was screaming it.

"I can't get up there. You heard my sister. I'm a baby," Lily said.

"She didn't say that. . . ."

"She didn't have to. That's what she meant. Just once, I wish she'd take my side, like you do. But she never will."

"So show her she's wrong!" said Leona. "Show those Fake-a-Moves, too!"

"I want to," said Lily, "but I can't. Not all by myself. I thought I could do it. . . . I mean, you've helped me so much. . . . And it's funny, I've never had a problem singing in a group, in the chorus. But it's just too . . . too scary to think of singing up onstage, in front of people, all alone."

Leona threw her head back. She didn't know how to reply. How could she change Lily's mind when what she was saying made no sense? Leona had always loved singing—*alone*. She was drawn to the starlight like . . . like one of those fluttery Wishworld insects that looked like moonmoths to the big round bulb outside the front door of their Havisham dorm. Of course, she didn't mind backup singers. They made her feel like more of a superstar, in fact. And duets could be fun . . . with the right Starling. But choruses? Ugh. They were always saying things like "Try to blend in more," and "Stop stepping out of your row!" Still, Leona had to do something to get Lily's wish back on track. The success of the mission depended on it.

And she'd been so busy she hadn't taken any time to

try to figure out what her special talent was. Maybe that was a mistake. Maybe that was just what she needed to make this wish come true. . . . Then a thought suddenly tickled the corner of Leona's mind. "Are you saying that you would do the talent show if you didn't have to sing all by yourself?"

"What do you mean?"

"I mean . . . what if I got up there and sang with you? Would you do the talent show then?"

"Uh . . . well . . . I don't know. . . ."

"You wouldn't be alone," Leona reminded her.

"No." Lily nodded. "You're right. . . . Would you?" She smiled shyly. "Would you really do that for me?"

"You bet your stars!" roared Leona. "Um, I mean . . . I guess so. If it would help *you* get up there and sing, and show all these girls how talented—and brave—you are, then yes." Leona bowed humbly. "I'd be most honored to help."

CHAPTER 11

Leona was just about to follow Lily into the arts building to practice their duet when she glimpsed (Was it? Yes!) a hot white flash across the sky. It was their free period before lunch and after a class Leona had come to like a lot: History of the Ancient World. Her mind was still reeling, in fact, from that day's lesson about a place called Greece, where they believed in many gods, including one named Helios, who drove a golden chariot across the sky each day. And this, the Greeks believed, was how the sun moved from east to west.

Leona wondered if Lady Stella or any of her teachers were familiar with this Wishling myth. She added it to her Wishworld Observations just in case they weren't. She also wondered where such a myth had come from.

Could maybe—just maybe—some ancient Starling have shared their means of Wishworld travel with some ancient Greek? And maybe, as in a game of holo-phone, a few details were changed? Leona could see how it might have happened. Stories were fickle things. She had to sit on her hands to keep from raising one and saying, "That sun chariot stuff is crazy, but you really can ride a shooting star!"

But back to the flash, which Leona would have missed if a small furry gray Wishworld creature hadn't scampered across the path in front of her and made her stop and hop back. As soon as the creature reached the grass, it sat up on its hind legs and stared at her, twitching its fluffy tail as if to wave her a Wishling hello.

"Hello, to you, little Wishworld . . ." *Hmm* . . . Leona tried to remember what the species was called. A "squid"? A "squirt"? A squ-something . . . And that was when she noticed the silvery burst.

If it had been that wonderful Wishling holiday when they lit up the sky with colorful, sparkling explosions, Leona would have thought it was one of those. But since it was not a holiday, Leona guessed the source at once.

Lily poked her head out the door of the arts building. "Are you coming?"

"Yes!" Leona waved. "I mean, I am . . . in just a second. I think . . ." What did she think? "I think I left something . . . somewhere. . . . You go on and start rehearsing, and I'll be there as soon as I can."

Lily shrugged and withdrew into the building while Leona leapt over the friendly, wide-eyed Wishworld creature and dashed around the arts building, to the edge of the school grounds.

"Well, I'll be starstruck!" she said. She was right. She was not alone!

"Vega!" She ran up to give her fellow Star Darling a hug. "What on Wishworld are you doing here?"

"Leona! Star greetings!" Her eyes widened as she took in Leona's sparkly self. "Wow are you sure no one else but us sees us sparkly?"

Leona shrugged. "That's what Sage and Libby said. Plus, no one's mentioned it!"

Vega grimaced. "And that outfit! Is that *plaid*? Oh, no! Did your Wishworld Outfit Selector break?"

"Oh, this." Leona looked down. She'd almost gotten used to the whole jacket-tie-kilt thing. "It's a 'uniform.' Everyone wears them at this school, I'm afraid."

"Oh, dear . . . Star apologies," said Vega. She took Leona's hands in hers. "At least it's just for a little while. Is that the wish you're here to grant? To get rid of them?"

"No. I wondered that, too, at first." Leona shook her head and shrugged. "But why are *you* here?" she asked Vega. "My mission's almost done!"

Vega's nose scrunched and her mouth twisted. "Yes, about that . . ." she began. "Actually, the thing is . . . your wish . . . it actually appears to be a bit off track. . . . Not that it's your fault or anything!" she added quickly. "We all know this is one of the hardest jobs in the universe! What can you expect? We're all new to wish granting, after all, and it's happened every time."

"Not this time!" declared Leona. "Sorry to disappoint you, Vega, but my wish couldn't be more sure of being granted. Everything's going startacularly well! I've identified my Wisher and her wish, and in"—she checked her Star-Zap—"approximately nine starhours, her wish will be officially granted. I don't know what kind of signals Lady Stella was receiving, but feel free to take your star home and tell her they were wrong. Or stay! That would be stellar!" She gave Vega's hands a squeeze. "Then you can be here to see me not only rock this wish, but"—she shimmied excitedly—"sing!"

Vega tilted her head. "This wish . . . are you sure about it?"

"What do you mean? Of course I'm sure!"

"I mean . . . are you sure the wish is truly your *Wisher's* wish?"

"Like I said, of course I'm sure. Who else's would it be?"

"I don't know . . ." said Vega. "All I know is that the energy levels were indicating that something was amiss. That's why I'm here. Maybe if I stay, I can help you figure it out."

Gently, Leona let Vega's hands go. "Suit yourself. But you'll have to change." She nodded at Vega's silk-smooth blue shift.

"Right . . ." Vega looked down at her pretty new dress and made a face. "But how? I don't think I have anything like your uniform in my Wishworld Outfit Selector." She checked. "Not even close."

"I know," said Leona. "We'll just say you're visiting. That you're just thinking of going to this school. But let's hurry!" She cheerfully linked her arm with Vega's. "My Wisher's waiting for me to rehearse!"

Vega followed Leona to the music building. "Nice place, this school," she remarked. "You know, it reminds me a little of Old Prism."

"Really?" Leona glanced around. "They have buildings there like this?" She had never been to Old Prism, one of the oldest settlements on Starland, although it was a popular place for tourists to go. She couldn't imagine any architecture on Starland being so rectangular, though. It simply wasn't the kind of shape Starlings naturally thought of.

"I said 'a little,'" Vega clarified. "I meant in the way Old Prism is historic. This place is old for Wishworld, too, isn't it?"

"Is it?" Leona shrugged.

Vega pointed at a plaque to the side of the door.

"'Winterbottom Hall,'" Leona read. "'Built 1792.' I don't know. . . . That's only a few hydrong staryears. That's not so very old."

"I know, but on Wishworld that's lifetimes," said Vega. "It's like a star era to us."

Inside, they found Lily already rehearsing in one of the soundproof rooms. Leona and Vega caught half a chorus before Lily noticed them and stopped.

"Oh, please go on!" said Vega, applauding. "That sounded beautiful!"

"It really did!" Leona said. "Now just wait till you hear our duet! Oh, by the way, Lily, this is Vega . . . a friend of mine from home."

"Hi," said Lily shyly. "So, are you thinking of going to school here, too?"

"Er . . . maybe . . ." Vega's slender shoulders rose slightly. "We'll see how it goes. So, you two are singing a duet . . . ?"

"Yes." Lily nodded. "For the talent show tonight."

Leona grinned and laid her arm across Lily's shoulder. "It was my idea!" she proudly explained. "It was the only way I could convince her to do the show. Crazy thing is she'd been wishing to do it but came this close to backing out!"

"Really." Vega raised a thin blue eyebrow. "How . . . generous of you."

"Oh, it was nothing!" Leona squeezed Lily's shoulder. "We should probably get started," she said then. She pointed with her other hand to a stool in the corner. "You might want to sit over there."

Vega perched on the seat and listened until a bell rang to signal the end of the period. Lily had a P.E. class to go to then. Technically, Leona did, too. But Vega begged her to give her a tour of the campus, and Leona happily said she would.

"So they take Physical Energy here on Wishworld, too?" asked Vega after Lily had gone off to her class.

"No, no. The 'E' is for 'education,' not 'energy,'" explained Leona. "It's not the same at all. Even though yesterday we did play a game a bit like star ball. They call it basketball, I think. You *have* to use your hands, though, which I kept forgetting. It was so hard! Not that I was ever that good at star ball, either." She winked. "So, what would you like to see first? Oh, I know! Let me show you the dining hall. It's rather dreary compared to Starling Academy's, but there's all the lemonade you can drink!"

"Is that the drink Professor Elara Ursa told us about?" asked Vega.

"Yes! You have to try it! It's the most delicious drink! It's sour *and* sweet, all at the same time!"

"Kind of like puckerup juice?"

"A little. But without the spice . . . and the sparkle, too. Here, I'll show you!" Leona veered to the right and dragged Vega along with her.

Vega hung back, though. "Maybe later. I didn't *really* want a tour. Your Countdown Clock is ticking, and I think we need to talk."

"About what?" Leona frowned.

Vega pointed back to the music building. "About that," she said. "This duet . . . are you sure about it?"

"Sure, I'm sure!" Leona said. "Like I said, it's the only way I could get Lily to do the show."

She explained how hard even getting Lily to sing a duet with her had been after the mean things some Wishlings had said. "And it wasn't just these jealous girls—it was her own sister, too. Do you think all Wishling starkin are like this?" Leona asked.

"Moon and stars!" said Vega. "I hope not!"

Leona couldn't help thinking of her own starkin: her two brothers, who were older and already out of school, and her two younger sisters, who were students back in Flairfield, still living at home. Leona had hoped they would follow her to Starling Academy, but neither one had even applied. Just like the rest of her family, they were perfectly content with small-town life. Still, Leona holo-called them often on her Star-Zap, and she loved hearing about life at home. In fact, since she'd been on Wishworld, it was the thing she had missed the most.

She suddenly wondered what her family thought now that stardays had passed since their last holo-call. If only Leona could have told them about her mission . . . but Lady Stella's plan was too top secret to be shared with anyone. She hoped when their mission was over, she'd be able to tell them everything. And she hoped, thanks to her, that starday was coming very soon.

"Please, Vega. Trust me. I know what I'm doing here. Now, do you want to try some lemonade or don't you? It's up to you."

CHAPTER 12

At seven o'clock sharp, the curtain went up in the auditorium and Ms. Frasier took the stage.

"Welcome to Havisham Academy's sixty-fifth annual talent show!" she announced. "I think you're all in for quite a treat! We have talent this year we've never had before!

"First, of course, I'd like to thank our distinguished panel of judges. Judges, will you please stand up?"

A line of adult Wishlings stood up in the first row and turned, waving and grinning. Leona recognized several teachers as well as the headmistress who had welcomed her to school.

"As you know, the judges will be awarding a first

prize," Ms. Frasier went on, "but really, everyone who performs is a winner tonight. I hope, therefore, that you'll show them all the respect they so deserve. Now, without any further ado, ladies, may I please present our first performers, who were last year's winners . . . and the year before that, too: Talia, Kasey, and Adeline—otherwise known as Make-a-Move."

The students in the audience applauded politely as Talia and her friends ran onstage. Leona did not miss the icy glare Talia shot at Lily. On Starland, it was known as giving someone a solar flare.

"Ignore her," Leona told Lily.

"I'm trying," she said. "I really am." Lily looked down at her glittering gold outfit: lamé leggings and a sequined tank, plus shiny gold patent-leather lace-up ankle boots. Next she smiled at Leona's ensemble, a mirror image of her own. "I still don't know where you got these awesome costumes," she said.

"Oh, you know." Leona shrugged. Naturally, she had used her Wishworld Outfit Selector, but she had to keep that to herself. "They are pretty stellar, aren't they! But hey! We're stars! What else would we wear?"

Onstage, Make-a-Move was making moves, each member at a slightly different speed. Their smiles, however, were huge, and their ponytails swung impressively.

"So they've really won the past two years?" said Leona.

Lily nodded. "Mm-hmm."

Just then, Hannah, the girl with the lifelike doll, walked up beside them. She held her partner, Dolly, in her arms. "Wow! You two look like real rock stars!" she told Leona and Lily while Dolly checked them out.

"We try," Leona told her. Lily blushed. At the same time, the music ended and the crowd broke into cheers.

"Oh, I hope they don't win again," muttered Hannah as the dancers bowed and high-fived off the stage.

No one else congratulated them. A few girls rolled their eyes. Dolly whispered something into Hannah's ear that made her eyes grow wide.

"Really, Dolly! I can't believe you would say that! That's so rude!" Hannah laughed.

If Make-a-Move cared, though, they didn't show it.

"Who wants to quit right now?" Talia said.

Fortunately for everyone, Ms. Frasier soon appeared and herded the act out the stage door. "Girls," she announced, "after you've performed, please go out and join the audience so it's not so crowded back here. Next up, Hannah and Dolly!"

"Ee're ready!" Dolly declared.

Leona surveyed the other performers backstage, all waiting their turns to go on. There were a few other dancers, including one with shiny black shoes that clicked whenever the soles tapped the floor.

Several girls with instruments had made the show, as well. Along with the girl with the flugelhorn, there were a pianist and a tall copper-haired girl who blew into a thin silver tube.

Ms. Frasier had been firm about not having non-performers backstage, so Vega sat in the audience along with the rest of the school. Leona could see her from the edge of the wings, but Vega could not see Leona. Vega looked anxious, wringing her hands in her lap. Leona wished she could run down and tell her to stop. Her mission was bound for success! But no, she was going on soon and had to save her voice. She needed to focus on her performance! Wait . . . that sounded wrong.

Leona tightly squeezed her eyes closed, trying to unscramble her tangled thoughts.

Aha. She knew what she needed.

"I'll be right back," she told Lily, dashing off to find some privacy.

"Wait! Don't leave me!" Lily said. She followed Leona to a quiet corner backstage.

Leona closed her eyes, took a deep breath, and let everything else melt away. "You are a star. Light up the world," she murmured three times purposefully.

"What did you say?" asked Lily.

Leona turned to Lily. "It's just something I say sometimes that helps me . . . you know . . . find myself."

"How does it go exactly?" asked Lily.

"Like this: 'You are a star. Light up the world.' " She touched Lily's arm. "Try it. Go on. It really works."

Lily did.

"How do you feel?"

"I feel . . . better." Lily's chin rose a little higher. Her shoulders seemed to relax. "I can do this!" she said, smiling at herself.

Leona also felt better, though not quite the way she'd planned.

"Lily! Leona!" Ms. Frasier motioned from the edge of the stage. By that time, half a dozen more acts had gone on and come off. "Places, please. Charlotte is almost done, and you two are on next."

"Ready?" said Leona. She linked her arm with Lily's in the Starling way.

"Ready!"

"Then let's get out there and sing! I—I mean we—I mean *you*, most of all, are so winning first place! Get ready for your dream to come true!"

That brought a smile from Lily. "Oh I don't care if we win. Do you? I'm just happy to be doing this at all.

When we met, I was just wishing to have the courage not to chicken out the way I did last year. I'd love to show my sister that I can do it, you know, and maybe make her a little proud of me for once."

Leona stared at Lily. Now everything made perfect sense. She knew what she had to do.

The shiny-shoed dancer *tap-a-tap*ped off, waving her top hat and cane. Ms. Frasier returned to the stage with two microphone stands.

"Thank you, Charlotte! Now, please welcome your next performers, Lily and Leona!"

Leona stepped in front of one mic while Lily took the other one. Leona drank in the round of applause like it was a tall, cold glass of lemonade.

She smiled down at Vega and even waved, hoping to get her to smile back. At the same time, she tried to ignore Talia and her friends. Unfortunately, they were working way too hard at making themselves impossible to miss. Rather than clapping, they were giggling and whispering loud enough for everyone to hear. It was all Leona could do not to use her energy and shut them up with a flick of her wrist. They were lucky she kept her hands clenched around the microphone instead.

"Thank you! Thank you, everyone! Really, you're too kind! Hey, how about a round of applause for our real star of the night, Ms. Frasier. After all, without her, none of us would even be here. Am I right?"

Leona led the crowd in another round of applause, to the teacher's delight. Then she took a deep breath and leaned back over the mic to add one more thing.

"Now, I know the program lists our next act as a duet . . . but the truth is I'm not out here to perform. I'm just here to introduce my friend Lily, who'll be singing a solo for you all."

A collective gasp rose from the crowd as Leona stepped away. The loudest gasp by far, though, came from Lily, who spun toward Leona in disbelief.

"I can't!" she mouthed.

"Yes, you can," Leona mouthed back. And she had to, Leona knew. Vega was right. For Lily's true wish to be granted, she had to prove to herself that she had the courage to get up there and sing alone. Leona had gotten much too carried away with the idea of singing along with her. But there would be plenty of time for performing back on Starland. This was the time for Lily, and Lily alone, to shine in the starlight.

Leona gazed deep into Lily's eyes. "You are a star. Light up the world," she murmured, pointing to her own heart.

Lily bit down on her lip and slowly nodded. She stepped closer to the mic. At that moment, something happened. Lily changed, like the sky when the sun breaks through the clouds. And it took place so quickly that Leona wasn't even ready for the fountain of wish energy that gushed out.

It poured out at her in a blindingly brilliant arc—blindingly brilliant, that is, to Leona and Vega. The roomful of Wishlings had no idea. All they were aware of was Lily standing in the spotlight, getting ready to sing for them.

"So sing already!" someone hollered in a shrill voice.

"We're waiting!" someone else howled.

Leona tore her eyes from the flow of wish energy to scan the audience for the source. She knew, of course, who it was before she found them: Talia and her cohorts.

Leona turned back to Lily, whose face had frozen. Her wish energy flow had all but stopped. Leona knew she should be worried about her mission's success then, but all she could think about was her Wisher and her Wisher's feelings, and how she could make those bullies stop. She was just about to raise her hands and use energy to dump water on them when someone else jumped up.

"Hey! That's my sister! And she'll sing when she's

ready. Show a little respect. You can do it, Lily!" called her sister. "Take all the time you like."

"Yeah!" others yelled, and a chorus of agreement rose around her, followed by a round of supportive applause. Lily's eyes, meanwhile, filled with clear, happy Wishling tears as she and her sister shared a smile.

ZOOWWWWWHOOOSHHHHH!

If Leona had been slow to capture the first surge of wish energy, she nearly missed the next as it burst toward her like a tidal wave in a whole new, even more spectacular rainbow. It was simply startacular.

CHAPTER 13

"Moon and stars! That was starmendous, Leona! Truly!" Vega gushed. She punctuated her compliment with a warm, impulsive hug.

"Star salutations," said Leona. "Especially for opening my eyes."

They stood in a corner of the lobby, where everyone had gathered after the show. Everyone, that is, but Make-a-Move, whose members had stormed off as soon as the judges' votes were tallied and Ms. Frasier announced the results. Talia and her friends had not won first place, which surprised nobody but them. That award had gone to Lily, whose performance had earned the sole standing ovation of the night. Nor had they won second. That had gone to the pianist. Dolly and Hannah had come away with third. Make-a-Move had earned something else, however; they had been disqualified—"for behavior unbecoming to students of Havisham Academy, or anywhere else," Ms. Frasier had announced.

"Oh, you would have figured out what to do on your own, I bet," Vega told Leona. "But I'm glad that I could help."

"I don't know if I would have." Leona sighed. "I got pretty excited about singing up there. Even when I realized what helping Lily's wish come true really meant, it was hard to step out of the starlight and let her shine, alone. It would have been so startastic to sing with her, up onstage on Wishworld. . . . It would have been the chance of a lifetime."

"Well, clearly you're meant to be a Star Darling, thinking about others and not yourself. I just hope that when it's my turn, I do half as well. Literally!" said Vega. "You captured two wishes' worth of energy!"

Leona rubbed her Wish Pendant proudly while Vega pulled her Star-Zap out. "So, should we head back?"

Leona held back. "Now?"

Her eyes skimmed past Vega to Lily, who stood at the other end of the room. She looked thrilled but overwhelmed by the throng of classmates surrounding her.

Their eyes met and Lily's hand shot up in a swift "I need you" wave.

"We *can't* go yet," Leona told Vega. "I haven't even said good-bye."

Good-bye . . . The word hung in front of Leona like a dark, unexpected cloud. Somehow, this part of a mission had never occurred to her before. She'd been too busy, she supposed. And now that the time had come, she wasn't ready. Not at all.

"Of course," Vega told her. "Star apologies. You're absolutely right. But you should hurry."

"I will!" said Leona. "Wait here. I won't be long."

Leona reached Lily and threw her arms around her. "Congratulations! You were so great!"

"Thanks! Ooh!" Lily giggled and shuddered. "Wow, there's a lot of static in the air these days."

"Oh, sorry." Leona let her go. "I knew you could do it!" she went on.

"Well, that makes one of us." Lily laughed. "When you said I was singing a solo, I honestly thought I was going to faint!"

"Yes . . . but then you did it! You found the power in yourself to make your dreams come true! And I bet you can't wait to do it again! Tell me singing up there onstage wasn't the best feeling you ever had!"

"Actually . . ." Lily started, but just then, her sister appeared.

The older girl smiled at both Lily and Leona. "You're new, aren't you?" she said.

Leona nodded.

"Well, I'm glad you're here. Thanks for being such a good friend to Lily. There aren't a lot of girls at this school who would have helped her the way you did. Honestly, I didn't think I'd ever see her get up onstage."

"Well, it won't be the last time!" said Leona. "Especially when she knows you have her back."

"I know, but I'm not always going to be there. I graduate this year. That's why I keep trying to make Lily stand up for herself. If you don't," she told Lily, "who will?"

"I know." Lily nodded. Then, suddenly, she stood straighter, as if an idea had sparked in her mind. "In fact, I'm going to stand up for myself right now. . . . You owe me a duet!" she declared, turning to Leona. "We can't let all that rehearsing go to waste. Hey, what if we formed a band!"

"A band? That's the best idea ev—" Leona started when a tug on her elbow made her stop. She looked down to see Vega staring up at her with wide "are you out of your mind?" eyes.

"What I mean is, *you* should form a band," Leona clarified. "You'd be a great lead singer! And every school needs at least one band! But . . . I don't think I can start it with you. In fact, it's impossible."

"Why?"

"Uh . . . because . . . well, because . . . I didn't want to seem like a show-off, so I didn't tell you this before . . . but I actually just signed a recording deal, and I have to go cut an album . . . tonight."

"Really?" Lily's jaw fell open. Her sister's did the same.

Leona nodded matter-of-factly. "Would I lie about something like that?"

"Tonight?"

"I'm afraid so. At least, that's what my agent tells me?" She smiled at Vega. "Right . . . agent? Isn't that really why you came?"

"Uh . . . sure," Vega said slowly.

"You're her *agent*?" Lily asked.

Vega shrugged. "I know . . . it's crazy, isn't it?"

"I think it's awesome!" said Lily. "Wow . . . Now it's really too bad we didn't sing together," she joked. "I almost sang with a real star."

Lily's sister spoke up. "I'd love to hear you. In fact, I bet everyone would."

Leona felt herself blush, Wishling style, as Vega hooked her arm.

"Too bad we have a *flight* to catch," Vega said meaningfully.

"Wait." Leona held her ground. "Okay. I'll do it." She slipped her arm from Vega's and took hold of Lily's hands. "Let's go sing that duet. You talked me into it. But let's do it out under the stars!" she said. "Have you ever sung there before? Oh, you'll love it! It's the best!"

Epilogue

Leona had realized her Wishworld good-bye would be hard, but it was even worse than she had feared. She probably would never get to see Lily again. Not in person, at least. There was always the chance, Leona supposed, of catching a glimpse of her from the Wishworld Observatory. But with seven billion Wishlings on Wishworld, the odds were atom-slim. Still, Leona swore to herself she would try and try and try until she did. Lily was sure to do something great with her talent on Wishworld, and Leona was *not* going to miss it.

She tried to keep this in mind as she bid farewell to Lily after their duet.

"Text me!" Lily told her.

"I'll try . . ." Leona said. But, of course, as soon as she

hugged her good-bye, Lily's memory and those of all the rest of the students at Havisham Academy were erased.

"Just remember what a great mission this was," Vega said to comfort her as they got ready for their trip home.

"Think how much you just accomplished toward helping Starland," Vega went on. "You're not just a Star Darling, you know. You're a true star-hero."

"Star salutations," Leona said gratefully. "I couldn't have done it without you, you know."

Vega smiled. "Okay. See you back home!"

"Why, Leona! Vega! What in the universe happened to you two?" Lady Stella said, ushering the newly arrived Star Darlings into her office and helping each into a chair.

Both were pale, for Starlings, and their glows flickered on and off. The stars in Leona's hair had burned out and needed to be charged.

"I don't know," Leona panted. "Something went wrong on the trip back. All of a sudden, my star started to stall. Then it started to drift. It was terrible! Luckily, Vega was there to pick me up. . . . Otherwise"—she caught her breath—"I don't know what I would have done. . . ."

"Well, I was there." Vega patted Leona's hand. "We just need a starmin to recover our glows."

Leona bolted up straight, suddenly energized. Her trip had been stressful, but now she was home. She placed her hand over her Wish Pendant proudly. She could only imagine how much positive energy her single Wish Pendant now contained!

Vega sat up, too. "You should have seen her, Lady Stella!" she told the headmistress. "She thought she was just going to make one wish come true and she ended up granting two!"

"Two wishes!" gasped Lady Stella. Her face lit up in thrilled surprise. "Two wishes. Heavenly stars. This was a most exceptional mission, it seems. Come. Let us summon the other Star Darlings to the Wish-House and collect your most well-earned and deserved Wish Blossom. That is, if you're up to it. Or perhaps you need a bit more time . . ."

"Oh, no!" Leona sprang out of her chair. "Let's do this! I'm ready!"

The alert went out and the Star Darlings rushed from wherever they were to the headmistress's office. Leona glowed in delight at all their attention and in anticipation of the honor to come.

Leona was happiest to see Ophelia, and Ophelia clearly felt the same.

"So how did it go?" Ophelia asked her.

"Startastic! I'll tell you all about it later! How about you?"

Ophelia shrugged. "We can talk about that later, also. . . . This moment is for you."

Lady Stella walked over, gently cradling the Wish Orb. She solemnly placed it in Leona's eager hands. It glowed in her grasp and her pulse quickened in anticipation. Everyone was holding their breath, waiting for the stunning moment of transformation. But there was nothing.

A panicky feeling started to rise in Leona's chest. It was unfamiliar and decidedly unpleasant. "What's going on?" she asked, looking at Lady Stella for reassurance.

But Lady Stella looked puzzled and confused. "I don't understand," she said, inspecting the Wish Orb. "It should have happened by now."

But it had not.

"Ew!" exclaimed Gemma suddenly. "What's wrong with your Wish Pendant, Leona? Everyone look! It's all burnt up!"

"*Gemma!*" Tessa whispered harshly, scowling at her sister. Still, what Gemma had said was true.

The thing on Leona's wrist barely resembled her Wish Pendant, although it was basically the same size and shape. Instead of gleaming gold, however, it was gnarled and as black as soot.

"Leona! What did you do?" murmured Astra.

"I don't know!" Leona wailed. "Really! It was perfectly fine when we got back to Starland. You know that. You saw it, too. I don't how or when this could have happened! I don't know what I could have done!"

"Did something go wrong on your mission?" asked Adora. She was trying to be helpful, but the question still stung.

"No!" said Leona. "It went starmendously! Unless . . . oh, no . . ." she moaned. "Unless I overloaded it . . . unless the energy from two wishes was too much for my Wish Pendant to absorb."

"Moon and stars! Are you saying you granted two wishes on your mission?" said Cassie. "Can you even do that, Lady Stella?"

The headmistress, who by now stood over Leona, stared at her Wish Pendant in wide-eyed alarm. "Indeed, you can. It's entirely possible, though exceedingly rare. When it has happened, though, the positive wish energy collected has been more than double what a typical wish brings in." Carefully, she lifted the arm bearing Leona's

Wish Pendant and examined it closely, turning it slowly right and left. "What's happened here simply makes no sense. The magic of Wish Pendants comes from their limitless capacity for positive energy. Exceeding it is impossible, as astrophysics has well proved. No, I do not believe that's what happened here. Granting two wishes would never cause this kind of Wish Pendant destruction."

"Then what did?" Leona wailed. She pulled her wrist back and shook her cuff in mortification and disgust. "Oh, wormholes! I can't believe all that wonderful energy I collected is now wasted! You all should have seen it!" she went on. "I should have come right back, as soon as I had it. I should never have stayed to sing that song. . . ."

"You stayed to sing a *song*?" said Astra.

Leona hung her head and nodded. "With my Wisher."

Astra and a few others traded "there you have it" eyes.

Sage spoke up. "I stayed for a little while, too, after I collected my wish energy. And it wasn't a problem at all. You don't know what it's like," she told Astra and the other Star Darlings. "You haven't been to Wishworld yet. Good-byes are the hardest part."

"Yes, I don't believe that affected your Wish Pendant, either, Leona," said Lady Stella. "You mustn't blame yourself. I would be shocked if there was anything a Star Darling could do to render her Wish Pendant useless like this. There's no such thing as too much positive wish energy, nor would any well-meaning action cause such harm. Perhaps," she went on, "there was a flaw in your Wish Pendant that no one noticed, or a defect that could not be detected until it was used. I assure you, this is no fault of yours, but merely a malfunction which will prove most helpful, in due course."

"But how?" growled Leona. "How can a filthy, burnt-up Wish Pendant help anyone?"

The headmistress smiled kindly, almost as if she had a plan. "If I may . . ." Leona's skin tingled as Lady Stella grasped the cuff and slid it from her wrist. "It's very simple," she explained. "I'm going to have Professor Dolores Raye examine this and determine precisely what went wrong. There's no one in the universe more knowledgeable about wish energy, after all. And, as we know, knowledge is power. Her findings will help us design corrections to prevent this from happening again. Fear not, Leona. Despite this tragedy, your mission was not in vain."

"Shall I take it to her?"

Lady Stella turned, as did the Star Darlings, to see Lady Cordial emerging from the shadows of the Wish Cavern.

"Why, star salutations, Lady Cordial," said the headmistress. She bowed and held the cuff out for her colleague to receive.

"My s-s-s-stars!" Lady Cordial winced as she regarded it. She clucked in dismay. "How dreadful . . ."

"I know," Lady Stella agreed.

"Though I suppose disasters such as this are to be expected in such a new and risky endeavor . . . with such young, inexperienced St-St-Starlings. . . ."

Lady Cordial's eyes stayed focused on the Wish Pendant, but her words hit Leona like a spear. Leona felt Vega's arm wrap around her, but she shrugged it off and stepped away. Lady Stella had made her feel better for a starmin, but Lady Cordial was right. She'd been given the chance of a lifetime and ruined everything. She didn't deserve her friend's comfort or Lady Stella's or anyone's. Maybe she didn't even deserve to be a Star Darling anymore. Just like Scarlet.

The evening was still young, and everything on Starland was just beginning to reach its maximum glow, but Leona had no interest in any of the hundreds of nightly activities the students at Starling Academy normally enjoyed. The last thing she wanted to do was stargaze or play neon energy ball or collect globerbeems in crystal jars. She didn't even feel like singing. All she wanted to do was go back to her room in the Big Dipper Dorm and be alone for as long as she could. She knew Ophelia would be there eventually. Maybe by that time she'd want to talk.

She held her hand up to the scanner in the middle of her door.

"Welcome, Leona," the Bot-Bot voice greeted her as the panel glowed a bright blue. Smoothly, the door slid open, and Leona slipped into her room.

She debated for a starsec whether to leave the lights low. Finally, with a heavy sigh, she blinked to turn them up and chase the shadows from the room.

"Scarlet!"

"Star apologies," said Scarlet, stepping out from the corner where the dark had hidden her. "I didn't mean to startle you."

"You didn't startle me. You scared my stars off! What are you doing here? How did you get in?"

"I used the hand scanner. Still works." Scarlet held up her hand. "And I really thought we needed to talk." She glanced quickly around the room. "No one else is coming, right? Are we all alone? Something really weird is going on, Leona—"

"Go!" Leona raised her arm and jabbed her finger at

the door. "I don't want to talk now, Scarlet. I don't want to do *anything*. Can't you tell I'm not in the mood?" She clenched her jaw and crossed her arms. The empty spot where her Wish Pendant had been looked pale and dull. "I've had the worst starday ever, and talking to you is not going to help. If anyone should know how I'm feeling now, it should be you, I think."

"But—"

"Please!" Leona growled. "We can talk about the band or whatever you want tomorrow. Stay in it or not. But this isn't your room anymore, so you have no right to be in here. Technically, you're trespassing. Do you want me to send a holo-signal to security? Because I will."

Scarlet blew her bangs in frustration but didn't argue any more. Instead, she tugged the collar of her star-studded jacket and stomped toward the door. As it slid open, she glanced over her shoulder. There was a dark spark in her eyes that was new. "Fine. I'll go," she said. "But just know you're making a mistake."

"Well, it won't be the first one," Leona retorted, whooshing the door closed behind Scarlet. She threw herself down on her bed. She had somehow ruined what should have been her finest moment. What was she going to do?

Glossary

Age of Fulfillment: The age at which a Starling is considered mature enough to begin studying wish granting.

Bad Wish Orbs: Orbs that are the result of bad or selfish wishes made on Wishworld. These grow dark and warped and are quickly sent to the Negative Energy Facility.

Big Dipper Dormitory: Where third- and fourth-year students live.

Blushbelle: A pink flower with a sweetly spicy scent. Libby's favorite flower.

Boheminella: A luminous lavender flower. Boheminella is Sage's Wish Blossom.

Booshel Bay: A vacation destination.

Bot-Bot: A Starland robot. There are Bot-Bot guards, waiters, deliverers, and guides on Starland.

Bright Day: The date a Starling is born, celebrated each year like a Wishling birthday.

Calaka: A round yellow vegetable often used in salads or on sandwiches.

Celestial Café: Starling Academy's outstanding cafeteria.

Chatterburst: An orange flower that smells like orange-and-vanilla ice pops. Gemma's favorite flower.

Cocomoon: A sweet and creamy fruit with an iridescent glow.

Cosmic Transporter: The moving sidewalk system that transports students through dorms and across the Starling Academy campus.

Countdown Clock: A timing device on a Starling's Star-Zap. It lets them know how much time is left on a Wish Mission, which coincides with when the Wish Orb will fade.

Crystal Mountains: The most beautiful mountains on Starland. They are located across the lake from Starling Academy.

Cyber Journal: Where the Star Darlings record their Wishworld observations.

Cybernetics Lab: Where Bot-Bots are built.

Cyber-wrestlers: Popular children's toys that battle each other.

Cycle of Life: A Starling's life span. When Starlings die, they are said to have "completed their Cycle of Life."

Druderwomp: An edible barrel-like bush capable of pulling its roots up and rolling like a tumbleweed, then planting itself again.

First stars: Starlings often call "first stars" when they want to go first at something. Akin to the Wishling expression "I call first dibs."

Flairfield: Leona's hometown. This pleasant, sleepy little town has a population of 30,000 and a charming downtown area.

Flash Vertical Mover: A mode of transportation similar to a Wishling elevator, only superfast.

Floozel: Starland equivalent of a Wishworld mile.

Flutterfocus: A Starland creature similar to a Wishworld butterfly but with illuminated wings.

Galactical: Having a negative overreaction.

Galliope: A sparkly Starland creature similar to a Wishworld horse.

Gamma chip clusters: A crunchy, sweet, and salty snack.

Garble greens: A Starland vegetable similar to spinach.

Glamera: A holographic image-recording device.

Glamora-ora: A luxury vacation destination with crystal pink waters and soft purple sands.

Glimmerworm: The larval stage of the glimmerbug. It spins a beautiful sparkly cocoon from its silk.

Glion: A gentle Starland creature similar in appearance to a Wishworld lion, but with a multicolored glowing mane.

Globerbeem: Large, friendly lightning bug–type insects.
Glorange: A glowing orange fruit. Its juice is often enjoyed at breakfast time.
Glowfur: A small, furry Starland creature with gossamer wings that eats flowers and glows.
Goldenella tree: A tree with flowers that bloom nonstop for a week and pop off the branches like popcorn.
Good Wish Orbs: Orbs that are the result of positive wishes made on Wishworld. They are planted in Wish-Houses.
Go Supernova: When a Starling is said to "go supernova," she gets really angry.
Green Globules: Green pellets that are fed to pet glowfurs. They don't taste very good to Starlings.
Halo Hall: The building where Starling Academy classes are held.
Holo-phone: A Starland game—much like the Wishworld game Telephone—in which a phrase is passed from one Starling to another and the last Starling says it out loud.
Hydrong: The equivalent of a Wishworld hundred.
Impossible Wish Orbs: Orbs that are the result of wishes made on Wishworld that are beyond the power of Starlings to grant.
Iridusvapor: A gas found on Starland. It makes Kaleidoscope trees change color.
Isle of Misera: A barren, rocky island off the coast of New Prism.
Jellyjooble: A small round pink candy that is very sweet.
Kaleidoscope tree: A rare and beautiful tree whose blossoms continuously change color.
Lightfall: The time of day when the sun begins to set and everything on Starland glows its brightest.
Light Leader: The head of student government at Starling Academy.
Lightning Lounge: A place on the Starling Academy campus where students relax and socialize.
Little Dipper Dormitory: Where first- and second-year students live.

Luminous Lake: A serene and lovely lake next to the Starling Academy campus.

Melodeon: A Starling instrument similar to a tiny accordion that produces a very high-pitched sound.

Mirror Mantra: A saying specific to each Star Darling that when recited gives her (and her Wisher) reassurance and strength. When a Starling recites her Mirror Mantra while looking in a mirror, she will see her true appearance reflected.

Moonberry: A fruit that is a lot like a blueberry, but with a more intense flavor. Sage hates them.

Moonfeather: A material commonly used for stuffing pillows, coats, and toys. It is harvested from the moonfeather bush.

Moonium: An amount similar to the Wishworld million.

Moonmoth: Large glowing creatures attracted to light.

Moon shot: A very slight possibility.

Mustardia: A plant whose bright yellow blossoms are often pureed and used in savory sauces.

New Prism: This casual and easygoing port city is Scarlet's hometown.

Old Prism: One of Starland's original settlements. Cassie's hometown.

Ozziefruit: Sweet plum-sized indigo fruit that grows on pink-leaved trees. It is usually eaten raw or cooked into pies. Starling Academy has an ozziefruit orchard.

Pluckalong: A small three-stringed instrument played with the fingers. It has a round wooden body and a short neck.

Radiant Hills: An exclusive community in Starland City, where Libby's family lives.

Radiant Recreation Center: Starling Academy's state-of-the-art fitness and sports center.

Ranker: A small machine that judges competitions and picks the winners. Its unbiased program eliminates favoritism.

Rodangular: A beautiful bright pink stone.

Safety starglasses: Worn by Starlings to protect their eyes when close to a shooting star.

Serenity Gardens: Extensive botanical gardens set on an island in Luminous Lake.

Shooting stars: Speeding stars that Starlings can latch on to and ride to Wishworld.

Solar flare: A mean look designed to intimidate.

Solar Springs: A hilly small town in the countryside where Tessa and Gemma are from.

Sparkle juice: An effervescent and refreshing beverage, often enjoyed over ice.

Sparkle shower: An energy shower Starlings take every day to get clean and refresh their sparkling glow.

Star ball: An intramural sport that shares similarities with soccer on Wishworld. But star ball players use energy manipulation to control the ball.

Starberry: Large bright-red fruits that grow in clusters.

StarBook: A cyber hangout where Starlings post pictures and opinions.

Starcake: A star-shaped Starling breakfast item similar to a Wishworld pancake.

Starcar: The primary mode of transportation for most Starlings. These ultrasafe vehicles drive themselves on cushions of wish energy.

Star Caves: The caverns underneath Starling Academy where the Star Darlings' secret Wish Cavern is located.

Star Darlings: The twelve Star-Charmed Starlings chosen by Lady Stella to go on top secret missions to Wishworld.

Starday: A period of twenty-four hours on Starland, the equivalent of a Wishworld day.

Starf!: A Starling expression of dismay.

Starflooty: A wind instrument with star-shaped holes.

Starjade: A smooth green semiprecious stone.

Starkin: The Starling word for *siblings.*

Starkudos: A Starling expression of praise.

Starland: The irregularly shaped world where Starlings live. It is veiled by a bright yellow glow that from a distance makes it look like a star.

Starland City: The largest city on Starland, also its capital. Sage, Libby, and Adora's hometown

Starlicious: Tasty, delicious.

Starlight: An expression used to mean public attention. When all eyes are on a Starling, she is said to be "in the starlight."

Starling Academy: The most prestigious all-girl four-year boarding school for wish granting on Starland.

Starlings: The glowing beings with sparkly skin who live on Starland.

Starling's Surprise, The: A classic children's book, beloved by many.

Starmin: Sixty starsecs (or seconds) on Starland; the equivalent of a Wishworld minute.

Star Preparatory: Similar to Starling Academy, this is the all-boys school located across Luminous Lake.

Star Quad: The central outdoor part of the Starling Academy campus.

Star salutations: A Starling expression of thanks.

Stars crossed: An expression meaning "hoping for a favorable outcome." Similar to the Wishworld expression "fingers crossed."

Starsec: A brief period of time, similar to a Wishworld second.

Star shakers: Clear star-shaped musical instruments with handles, filled with crystals that produce a delicate tinkling sound when shaken.

Star Wranglers: Starlings whose job is to lasso a shooting star to transport a Starling to Wishworld.

Staryear: A period of 365 days on Starland, the equivalent of a Wishworld year.

Star-Zap: The ultimate smartphone that Starlings use for all communications. It has myriad features.

Stellar Falls: The stunning waterfall that cascades into Luminous Lake.

Stinkberry: A fruit with a terrible odor.

Sunspots: A Starling expression of dismay.

Supernova Island: An exclusive vacation destination with fine restaurants, fancy shops, and stunning views from its mountainous peaks.

Timpanpipe: An ancient brass instrument. It makes a scratchy, whistly sound.

Tinsel toast: Bread heated and sprinkled with ground tinsel, a sweet, aromatic, glittery plant.

Toothlight: A high-tech gadget that Starlings use to clean their teeth.

Wee Constellation School: The Starland equivalent of preschool.

Wish Blossom: The bloom that appears from a Wish Orb after its wish is granted.

Wish energy: The positive energy that is released when a wish is granted. Wish energy powers everything on Starland.

Wish energy manipulation: The ability to mentally harness wish energy to perform physical acts, like turning off lights, closing doors, etc.

Wisher: The Wishling who has made the wish that is being granted.

Wish-Granters: Starlings whose job is to travel down to Wishworld to help make wishes come true and collect wish energy.

Wish-House: The place where Wish Orbs are planted and cared for until they sparkle.

Wishlings: The inhabitants of Wishworld.

Wish Mission: The task a Starling undertakes when she travels to Wishworld to help grant a wish.

Wish Orb: The form a wish takes on Wishworld before traveling to Starland. It will grow and sparkle when it's time to grant the wish.
Wish-Watcher: A Starling whose job is to observe the Good Wish Orbs until they glow, indicating that they are ready to be granted.
Wishworld: The planet Starland relies on for wish energy. The beings on Wishworld know it by another name—Earth.
Wishworld Outfit Selector: A program on each Star-Zap that accesses Wishworld fashions for Starlings to wear to blend in.
Wishworld Surveillance Deck: A platform located high above the campus, where Starling Academy students go to observe Wishlings through high-powered telescopes.
Zing: A traditional Starling breakfast drink. It can be enjoyed hot or iced.
Zoomberry: Small, sweetly tart berries that grow in abundance on Starland.

Acknowledgments

It is impossible to list all of our gratitude, but we will try.

Our most precious gift and greatest teacher, Halo; we love you more than there are stars in the sky . . . punashaku. To the rest of our crazy, awesome, unique tribe—thank you for teaching us to go for our dreams. Integrity. Strength. Love. Foundation. Family. Grateful. Mimi Muldoon—from your star doodling to naming our Star Darlings, your artistry, unconditional love, and inspiration is infinite. Didi Muldoon—your belief and support in us is only matched by your fierce protection and massive-hearted guidance. Gail. Queen G. Your business sense and witchy wisdom are legendary. Frank—you are missed and we know you are watching over us all. Along with Tutu, Nana, and Deda, who are always present, gently guiding us in spirit. To our colorful, totally genius, and bananas siblings: Patrick, Moon, Diva, and Dweezil—there is more creativity and humor in those four names than most people experience in a lifetime. Blessed. To our magical nieces—Mathilda, Zola, Ceylon, and Mia—the Star Darlings adore you and so do we. Our witchy cuzzie fairy godmothers—Ane and Gina. Our fairy fashion godfather, Paris. Our sweet Panay. Teeta and Freddy—we love you so much. And our four-legged fur babies—Sandwich, Luna, Figgy, and Pinky Star.

The incredible Barry Waldo. Our SD partner. Sent to us from above in perfect timing. Your expertise and friendship are beyond words. We love you and Gary to the moon and back. Long live the manifestation room!

Catherine Daly—the stars shined brightly upon us the day we aligned with you. Your talent and inspiration are otherworldly; our appreciation cannot be expressed in words. Many heartfelt hugs for you and the adorable Oonagh.

To our beloved Disney family. Thank you for believing in us. Wendy Lefkon, our master guide and friend through this entire journey. Stephanie Lurie, for being the first to believe in Star Darlings. Suzanne Murphy, who helped every step of the way. Jeanne Mosure, we fell in love with you the first time we met, and Star Darlings wouldn't be what it is without you. Andrew Sugerman, thank you so much for all your support.

Our team . . . Devon (pony pants) and our Monsterfoot crew—so grateful. Richard Scheltinga—our angel and protector. Chris Abramson—thank you! Special appreciation to Richard Thompson, John LaViolette, Swanna, Mario, and Sam.

To our friends old and new—we are so grateful to be on this rad journey that is life with you all. Fay. Jorja. Chandra. Sananda. Sandy. Kathryn. Louise. What wisdom and strength you share. Ruth, Mike, and the rest of our magical Wagon Wheel bunch—how lucky we are. How inspiring you are. We love you.

Last—we have immeasurable gratitude for every person we've met along our journey, for all the good and the bad; it is all a gift. From the bottom of our hearts we thank you for touching our lives.

Shana Muldoon Zappa is a jewelry designer and writer who was born and raised in Los Angeles. With an endless imagination, a passion to inspire positivity through her many artistic endeavors, and her background in fashion, Shana created Star Darlings. She and her husband, Ahmet Zappa, collaborated on Star Darlings especially for their magical little girl and biggest inspiration, Halo Violetta Zappa.

Ahmet Zappa is the *New York Times* best-selling author of *Because I'm Your Dad* and *The Monstrous Memoirs of a Mighty McFearless.* He writes and produces films and television shows and loves pancakes, unicorns, and making funny faces for Halo and Shana.